A LEAF IN THE WIND

Margaret Hadley was born in New South Wales and came to England as a child, only to be stranded by the war. She studied in London and worked for a printing company, while writing short stories and articles. She married, lived in Borneo for two years, and brought up a family before taking up writing once more. *The Passionflower*, a novel for young adults, was published in 1991. Margaret Hadley now lives on a farm on the Isle of Wight.

A Leaf
in the
Wind

MARGARET HADLEY

This edition published 1995 for
Parrallel Books
Units 13–17 Avonbridge Industrial Estate
Atlantic Road
Avonmouth, Bristol BS11 9QD
by Diamond Books
77–85 Fulham Palace Road
Hammersmith, London W6 8JB

First published by Fontana 1993

ISBN 0 261 66699 1

Set in Linotron Janson
Printed in Great Britain

Chapter One

The lamp threw a pool of light over the table in the centre of the ward. A weary nurse was painstakingly making entries in the Ward Journal before wakening the patients to a new day.

'Heavens alive – will I never be finished?' the nurse murmured as she turned the page; sighing, she dipped the nib in the ink, and resumed the careful copying of medical notes.

Only nine of the sixteen beds in this ward were occupied. Most of the men wounded in the futile Boer War had either succumbed to their wounds or recovered. England was at peace again; this temporary military hospital was to be closed, and Barminster Abbey returned to its owner, Sir Rupert Clayton. For the past three years it had sheltered wounded soldiers; but now the few who remained here were to be sent home, if sufficiently recovered, or moved on to other institutions.

Barminster Abbey, a stone-built mansion of grand proportions, was only ninety years old. The original abbey had been destroyed by Cromwell's army, and Sir Rupert's grandfather had built this country house for his family on the site with the proceeds from his trading in India. Since then the family fortunes had prospered, and Sir Rupert, an active and crusty character now in his seventies, was a wealthy and influential man. He and his father had both married heiresses; the Clayton estates boasted extensive land in several counties, and no less than four fine country houses besides the town house in Eaton Square; so it had been no inconvenience to loan Barminster Abbey to the nation. There were no young children in the family now, and since Lady Amelia had died no-one had wished to live here. Lady Imogen, the wife of his son Arthur, was more interested in London Society than in a country life, whilst Keenlach Lodge, several miles to the south in the Great Forest, was a more convenient centre for hunting.

Only the rooms on the ground floor were occupied by patients now. The nurses were quartered in the old nurseries, and the doctor in charge used the suite in the East Wing where Lady Amelia had lived until her death eight years ago. This ward had formerly been the ballroom; now the walls were lined with beds, and two great coke-burning stoves had been installed, raising the temperature as the two original ornate fireplaces had never succeeded in doing. The beautiful moulded ceiling had been blackened in places with soot from the stoves, one at each end of the ward, now glowing red in the darkness. The thick flues looked ugly and stark against the delicate tracery of ornamental plasterwork on the ceiling. The lower half of the tall windows had been painted green, so that those outside could not see into the ward; the patients could see only the tops of the trees and the sky.

It was early March. Outside, the wind tossed the treetops wildly back and forth; there was a light, powdery snow in the air and the park was whitened with frost. In the north of England the roads were impassable under snow; but here, near the south coast, they were spared the worst of the winter.

The silence was broken by a raucous fit of coughing from a man at the end of the ward. As if this was the cue the patient in the next bed also began to cough; a moment later a third man joined the chorus. The middle-aged nurse rose and went quietly from one bed to the next, doing what she could to settle the men and relieve their distress, which was

6

very little. She spoke to them softly in her Irish brogue, empty, comforting words. In her years of military nursing she had seen many like these. All three were soon to be transferred to the Tuberculosis Sanatorium on the Isle of Wight. Their wounds were healed, but they had contracted the deadly disease of the lungs whilst weakened. There was not much the nurse could do for them.

Before returning to her chair the nurse went to a bed by the window, directly under the flue of the heater. This man had been muttering restlessly most of the night. His body was covered with a dry, scabby rash. His bed-covers were raised over a basketwork frame, keeping the weight of the blankets off his legs – or what was left of them. One had been amputated just above the knee, and the other had a thick dressing over a suppurating gash on the ankle; both injuries obstinately refused to heal. He had been a big man once; now he was emaciated and gaunt, his frame barely more than skin and bones. It was difficult to estimate his age. His hair, cut very short to combat the irritating rash, and beginning to grow over a scar on the back of his head, was grey; but his beard showed black where the stubble had not been shaved for two days. His eyes, sunk deeply into the sockets, were dark brown, dull and apathetic most of the time, but on occasions glittering with fever.

The nurse bent over him. He was neither asleep nor awake. Much of the time he was slightly delirious. Now he muttered something unintelligible, and she spoke to him soothingly. He met her eyes and for a moment seemed to be conscious.

'Water,' he said desperately. 'O'Malley – water.'

The nurse frowned; was the man deranged? Each time she passed he begged for water, the request always accompanied by this weird, desperate utterance of his own name.

She raised him a little and held a glass of water to his lips. He drank thirstily, two or three gulps, and sank back against the pillows. The nurse put the glass back on the locker. She noticed a smell: not just the sickly smell of the dressings and the lotion on the rash, which was unpleasant enough, but something else. Acrid; sour. She went to the table and fetched the lamp.

Holding it over the bed she saw several sooty smuts on the sheets. She looked up, and detected a crack in the asbestos flue above the bed. As the wind whistled against the window, a puff of smoke escaped and a few grains of soot drifted down.

Suddenly the man retched, and the water he had just drunk was vomited explosively on to the sheets. For two minutes he coughed and retched violently, desperately gasping for breath between the convulsions. When the spasm was over the nurse was busy for some while cleaning him up and changing his sheets. The fouled linen was thrown into the laundry basket, on top of the sheets he had soiled earlier; the nurse forgot about the soot and smuts she had found on his covers.

She returned to her journal at the table; an uneasy peace settled over the ward as dawn broke.

A cold, fresh morning, and the day staff came on to the ward, cheerful and bright after a night's sleep, their starched dresses rustling under the pristine aprons. Each wore a lace-edged cap, an extraordinary affair resembling a butterfly with great open wings which quivered as they sped about the ward. The men were washed, and given their breakfast. The ward-maid, a drab skivvy, began scrubbing the length of the marble-floored corridor leading into the ward.

There were three nurses on duty now, a sharp-faced Sister, a young probationer, and another young woman in nursing uniform, the blue-striped, starched dress crackling as she moved; but she was neither a probationer nor a trained nurse. The Sister-in-Charge directed her duties, but

8

addressed her respectfully. She was the niece of the deceased Lady Amelia, Miss Harriet Grant.

Miss Grant, a tawny-haired young woman of twenty-four, her face as remarkable for its determination as for its beauty, was working at the hospital under special conditions, carrying out the duties of a nurse and experiencing first-hand the round of menial duties and study required of a nursing student. Her parents had died ten years ago of typhoid fever and she had gone to live with Lady Amelia, her mother's eldest sister, who already had grandchildren older than Harriet. Unfortunately, Lady Amelia also contracted the fever two years later, probably from the same source, a well in the village near their father's country seat, where the sisters had often visited. Harriet remained with her uncle, Sir Rupert, and became his constant companion.

Lady Imogen, his daughter-in-law, had directed Harriet's coming-out and presentation at Court, but Harriet, bored with the frivolous, aimless existence of the Season, announced to the astounded family that she intended to become a doctor. She had recently visited Barminster Abbey with Sir Rupert on one of his infrequent inspections. Sir Rupert, her guardian and trustee, was shocked that his lovely young ward should contemplate a career.

'Dammit, girl – you've got a dress allowance that would keep a family of six! Why the hell d'you want a career?'

'I want to be of some use in the world. I wasn't cut out to be a social flibbertigibbet, Uncle Rupert. God gave me some brains, and I want to use them.'

When she married, or upon reaching the age of thirty, Harriet would come into a very impressive inheritance. Being a handsome and intelligent girl, she could reasonably anticipate early marriage and a home of her own. Sir Rupert had hoped she might marry one of his grandsons, her second cousins, neither of whom had so far shown any inclination to settle down; their interests were confined to horses and gambling. He had very little time for either of them. But what could he expect, he thought bitterly; the boys had a dull, oppressive father, and a snobbish clothes-horse for a mother. Harriet would make a good wife and mother. Her influence might make a man of one of them. However, she vehemently refused to consider either Gervaise or Cecil as a possible husband, and she gave no encouragement to any of the other men who had admired her during the Season.

'I'm not interested in marriage, Uncle Rupert,' she stormed. 'I want to use my brains! I want to become a doctor!'

After several months of unsuccessful cajoling and persuasion Harriet eventually informed her uncle determinedly that if he would not consent to her medical training she would go ahead without his blessing. Sir Rupert finally agreed, provided she worked for a full year at the hospital, under the conditions of a probationer nurse. If she still wanted to become a doctor after that he would give his consent, and not only ensure that she was financially secure, but would make the necessary arrangements for her to enter one of the best teaching hospitals.

Sir Rupert, her second trustee George Steadman, the family solicitor, and the doctor in charge of the military hospital, were convinced that Harriet would abandon her dreams and quit the place before the first month was out; but they had bargained without her obstinate nature, which enabled her to cope with the hard work, the night duties, and even the nausea that constantly beset her in the early days on the ward. This was the final day of her year of bondage, and she had not only held to her purpose, but was more determined than ever to become a doctor. Now she was, for the last time, helping prepare the ward for 'Rounds', first by the formidable matron, and then by Dr Mansfield.

'Hurry up and get that bucket and mop out of sight, Liz,' she snapped to the skivvy washing the corridor. The girl straightened up and stared at Harriet dully. Her hands were red and raw from washing soda and cold. She was thin and half-starved looking, in a grey, ragged dress with a sacking apron. Her dark, lank hair was scragged back and tied with a shoelace. The only colour in her face was in the huge violet-blue eyes. Harriet remembered the girl was mute, and softened her tone. 'Now hurry, Liz, or Sister will be after you.'

As Liz took her bucket and mop away Harriet hurried into the ward again with a bowl of warm water and went to the bed by the window. O'Malley had to be shaved before the doctor examined him. She had fed him earlier with some gruel, and for once he had kept it down. He was half-asleep; a pity to waken him, but he had to be made respectable for Dr Mansfield.

Talking cheerfully, she propped up his emaciated body, swathed his chest in towels, and began lathering his chin. He accepted her ministrations apathetically. She had just begun to scrape away the lather when a particularly strong gust of wind buffeted the end of the flue protruding through the wall, and part of the pipe above their heads broke away, falling on to the raised covers of the bed, and rolling to the floor with a clatter.

Harriet gave a shriek of dismay; she, the patient, and the bed were all smothered in gritty soot. The flue had fallen on to the basket protecting the patient's legs; his face was contorted with pain from the sudden jolt. Sister Ramsbottom came racing from the other end of the ward, her sharp face set in an expression of exasperation.

'What on earth is going on here – good gracious, Nurse Grant! What's happened – oh, Lord, he's being sick again.' She grabbed the kidney basin from the locker and held it while O'Malley retched.

11

Harriet attempted to wipe some of the soot from her eyes with her damp hands and succeeded in making her face even smuttier. Her eyes stung; her dress was covered in soot. The winged cap was knocked over one eye at a raffish angle, which gave her a distinctly comical appearance. Fortunately she had not cut the patient with the razor when the pipe fell.

Sister Ramsbottom went into action, taking charge of the situation as a general might take charge of a disorganized regiment. 'Nurse Grant, go and change immediately. Send Nurse Harris and Liz in here to clean up this mess. Tell the orderly to send for the maintenance workmen.'

Harriet hurried out, sent in the two younger girls, and ran up to the nurses' quarters. It took half an hour to bath and wash the soot out of her hair. She was back on the ward within the hour, in a spotless starched uniform, her damp hair rolled into a bun under a fresh cap.

Meantime the sister had completed shaving and washing the patient, moved him to an empty bed, and organized cleaning the soot-blackened end of the ward. Liz, the skivvy, set to with hot water and a scrubbing-brush to remove the soot.

After a great deal of discussion between the maintenance foreman and the matron, who had come to inspect the damage herself, it was decided that as the ward would be disused within two weeks it was not worth repairing the damage. The stove would be allowed to go out, and as soon as the flue cooled, the broken pipe would be wrapped in canvas and left. When the workmen came to dismantle the hospital fittings they would take away the furnace, restore the original fireplaces, and redecorate the ballroom in readiness for Sir Rupert and his family to return. So until the patients were removed they would have to put up with the cold. One coke-burning stove would still be in operation, and that would prevent the temperature in the ward from falling too low.

The matron examined the broken asbestos flue.

'I wonder how long that pipe was faulty?' she mused. 'It was directly above O'Malley's bed, wasn't it?'

'Yes, Matron,' Sister Ramsbottom confirmed uneasily.

'Had anyone mentioned smuts on his bedlinen?'

'Er – not that I know of, Matron – but his linen was changed so often –'

'Sister, I suspect there was a leak of fumes from that pipe,' Matron said angrily, 'and that might explain why the man has been so constantly sick! And he complains of headaches.'

'Yes, Matron, but the head-wound –'

'The head-wound was healed before he reached us three months ago, Sister. The only wound that *has* healed! Not that the fumes would have affected the wounds, but his debilitated state could be partly due to having been constantly exposed to a noxious seepage from the broken flue. In short, Sister, the man was being poisoned!'

The matron made her usual round of the ward, finding fault with almost everything, making it clear that she did not intend to put up with anything less than her usual high standard, regardless of the circumstances. Her training under Miss Nightingale in the Crimea had taught her to accept nothing short of perfection; but the nurses nowadays did not understand the meaning of the word discipline! When she had finished Sister Ramsbottom was seething, and took her temper out on the two younger nurses for the rest of the morning. Liz was made to scrub the floor round the sooted bed three times before she was satisfied. The girl went off duty looking exhausted.

O'Malley watched all this from his bed, his eyes half-closed. When Dr Mansfield appeared at the door he seemed to shrink back in the bed. A moment later Harriet Grant approached with the equipment for his dressings, drew the curtains round the bed, and pulled back the covers. She

13

put the wickerwork frame on the floor, and spoke to him gently.

'I'm sorry, Mr O'Malley, but I've got to do your dressings now – Dr Mansfield wants to examine you.'

He stared at her from sunken eyes, dreading the ordeal.

'Why the hell can't he just leave me to die?' he said fretfully. 'What use is all this – most of one leg missing, the other leg rotting away – I'd be better off dead.'

'Now, that's enough of that!' Harriet said briskly. 'You know it's got to be done – the sooner we get on with it the better. Now hold on, here we go.'

For the next ten minutes she worked at the painful, distressing task of removing the dressings, which had hardened and stuck in several places. Underneath, the flesh was raw and angry, showing no sign of healing. By the time the doctor reached the bed the nurse was exhausted and sickened, and the patient was trembling and soaked in sweat.

Dr Mansfield gravely inspected the wounds and gave instructions for fresh dressings. He told the nurse to use more lotion on the rash; in places the skin was raw. He hardly spoke to the man, addressing his remarks to Sister Ramsbottom. He followed her into her office, formerly a little withdrawing-room ajoining the ballroom, and told her to sit while they discussed the plans for the patients' evacuation. For thirty years Dr Mansfield had been a military surgeon. Now he was to retire, and his last duty was to arrange for these men to be discharged or removed to suitable institutions.

'Three will return to their homes,' he remarked. 'Three to the Sanatorium – they'll go first. Smith and Williamson are going to the Home for the Disabled, as they haven't got families, and that just leaves O'Malley. His papers, please, Sister?'

Sister Ramsbottom handed him the file of papers. He scanned them once again.

'No family . . . I suppose that's fortunate, in a way. No dependants. From Armagh . . . Perhaps we could have him sent back to Ireland.' He looked again at the sheet of closely written details. 'Sister, there's a question mark against the name here. Is there any reason to doubt that he's Patrick O'Malley?'

Sister Ramsbottom looked startled.

'No, of course not! There's never been any question –'

'This says he's a Roman Catholic. Has he seen a priest?'

'No, Dr Mansfield. He hasn't asked for a priest. But he never speaks much, or asks for anything –'

'Doesn't talk to the other men?'

'O'Malley? No. If anyone tries to be friendly he snarls at them.'

'That doesn't sound like an Irishman!'

'In fact, he's been very difficult – he's downright rude to the staff at times – that is, when he knows what's going on. A lot of the time he's semiconscious.'

'Hmmmmm . . . What do you think of Matron's theory, that he's been breathing in carbon monoxide gas from that flue all the time he's been here?'

Sister Ramsbottom looked flustered. It was nearly midday, and she'd not had so much as a cup of tea since five-thirty this morning. One thing after another had happened, all of which she would be blamed for somehow, and now she was being harassed about the remote possibility of a leaking flue poisoning one of her patients . . . It wasn't fair. How could she have known about the fumes? Dr Mansfield saw her colour rising, and decided not to pursue the matter any further for the moment.

'I'll go and have a another word with him,' he said, rising. 'See if I can get any sense out of him.'

'I wish you luck!' Sister Ramsbottom told him. 'I've not managed to get any sense out of the man since he arrived! If he doesn't completely ignore my questions, he answers

15

by repeating his own name. I suspect the wound on his head addled his brains . . . The best place for him would be the asylum.'

Chapter Two

The man they called O'Malley lay with his eyes closed. Nurse Grant had finished dressing his legs and left him. He had seen the compassion in her eyes, but far from comforting him, her sympathy aroused his resentment. He was sick of seeing that look in the nurses' eyes. He was sick of pain, of being a useless, hopeless hulk; he was sick of life.

His headache was easier, and for the first time since he had been injured when the wagon was blown up he was able to think coherently. And his thoughts were bitter.

He wasn't clear about how he came to be in the wagon in the first place. He tried to think back, remember events in the order in which they happened.

For two years he had been with the cavalry, skirmishing with the Boers, in dry, scorching heat, in mud and dirt, sometimes marching on foot for days at a time, sometimes holed up somewhere, waiting until it was safe to move on . . . A short spell at headquarters where his education had been put to good use, and he had even been recommended to apply for a commission, had come to an abrupt end when he fell foul of a certain stiff-necked Captain Harringay, who objected strongly to his lack of spit and polish, and sent him back to the lines . . .

He remembered a night reconnaissance foray where they were ambushed in a deserted farmhouse, and a blow on the head when a shell hit the barn where he and some other troopers were sheltering, then trying to walk out the next day to find the regiment . . . The other men were all dead, and the horses gone. Horses . . . They had been left tethered under the trees, but the Boers had taken them.

Then he was in a hole under some bushes. Sparse, scrub bushes . . . Not much shade, but better than nothing under that blazing sun, because somewhere he'd lost his hat and his shirt – he was wearing riding-breeches and boots. Nothing else. Perhaps he'd left them in the barn with the other men. He remembered putting a shirt over someone's face – or what was left of it . . .

Headache – that's where the headache began, under the bushes. Heat. Thirst. It got dark, and cooler. Christ, he was thirsty! He had to find water. He crawled out, and tried to walk, but everything kept swirling about. Then he was cold; cold and thirsty.

If he could find his way back to the barn he could get water. But he couldn't see clearly, his head hurt – when he touched it his hand was red with blood. He kept falling down, his legs collapsing under him.

He heard voices, but not English voices . . .

As he remembered, painfully recalling the events minute by minute, the sweat started out on his face.

The accent was guttural, foreign, but familiar. Afrikaans – Boers! They must be one of the raiding parties. He crawled into some undergrowth and lay still. Boers took no prisoners – how could they? Small groups of men living from one raid to the next – it was all they could do to feed themselves, let alone provide for prisoners. Kitchener's scorched earth policy, herding women and children into camps to prevent them giving succour to their menfolk, had made things difficult for the Boer marauders, but equally difficult for any British troops separated from their units.

The Boers moved on, and eventually he crawled out of his hiding-place and struck out, as far as he could judge, towards the east, which he thought would lead him to his own regiment.

He found a road and stumbled on, praying for water. When he had finally fallen and been unable to get up he had given up hope. Then he heard the wagon. In the darkness the horses nearly stumbled on him. When they shied away the driver got down to investigate, and found him. He was dumped in the back of the wagon with some sacks of supplies, hay, and ammunition boxes. Someone gave him water, which made him retch. It tasted foul.

'Sorry it's a bit sour, mate, but it's all we got,' the man told him in a broad Irish brogue.

'Come on, O'Malley, we're late enough as it is!' another voice urged. 'He'll last until we reach camp – then he'll be in the quack's care, God 'elp 'im.'

Shortly afterwards there was a flash, and a loud explosion; the wagon had been attacked. There was a searing pain in his legs; the heavy ammunition boxes had fallen on them. He heard the horses thrashing about, then four shots and nothing more from the horses. Someone jumped on to the back of the wagon. He lay still, holding his breath. They took some of the ammunition boxes and the food supplies. Either they didn't see him, or mistook him for dead. He heard horses' hooves receding into the night.

The wagon had nearly reached the camp, for soon afterwards a party of British soldiers arrived, having seen the flash of the explosion. He was taken to the camp, but remembered nothing of the journey. He remembered waking up to see someone bending over him. He was unbelievably thirsty – he had to have water, if it was only the foul, brackish water he had had earlier. Was this O'Malley?

'Water,' he gasped.

'Who are you?' the man asked. 'You have no identification.'

'Water . . .'

'Name?' He tried to think, but the headache made him dizzy. He had to give them a name to get water, but he

19

couldn't remember one – he had no idea who he was.

'O'Malley!' he said desperately. 'Water . . .'

The men with the wagon had been killed and their bodies buried on the veldt. They had lost the track and travelled miles out of their way, eventually getting back on to the road at dusk, hours after they should have reached the camp. They'd filled their water canteens from a pool by the roadside. Papers in the wagon showed that a Patrick O'Malley had been with the driver. None of the men at the camp knew O'Malley, or recognized the wounded man; consequently he was identified as Patrick O'Malley. He was delirious for weeks with fever contracted from the foul water.

The head-wound healed, but the headaches continued, although whether they were caused by the wound, or the fever, the doctors could not determine. The falling ammunition box had smashed his left knee, splintering the bone into fragments. Infection set in, and the surgeon at the camp had to amputate. The gash on the right ankle refused to heal, but at least it resisted infection.

He had little memory of the next five months, during which time the camp he was in was besieged then relieved, and he was taken across country by wagon, then by train, and finally put on a ship to England just as the news of the peace treaty was received in London. He had no memory of being passed from one reception hospital to another, until he finally finished up at Barminster Abbey, in a bed under a broken flue, being slowly poisoned by carbon monoxide gas . . .

Dr Mansfield went back into the ward and sat down by the man's bed. The man watched him, his eyes half-closed.

'O'Malley?' the doctor said. The man was silent. 'Are you O'Malley?'

'That's what they told me,' the man finally replied sullenly.

'Don't you know?'

'No.'

'Don't you care?'

'No. O'Malley's as good as any other name for a man with one leg hacked off and the other going rotten.'

'D'you want a priest, O'Malley?' the doctor asked.

'Priest? No! I'm not a bloody Catholic.' There was no trace of the Irish brogue in his voice. He spoke with an educated accent – almost like a gentleman. The doctor would have expected to hear that accent from an officer, not a semi-literate trooper.

'Do you remember –'

'I remember nothing!' He looked at the doctor, a flash of anger in his eyes. His eyelids closed again, and after a moment Dr Mansfield realized he was asleep. He got up and left the ward.

But that momentary flash of anger had shown that the man was not quite finished. Dr Mansfield left a little more hopeful than he had been five minutes earlier.

The man awoke to the clatter of crockery. The red-haired, green-eyed nurse Harriet Grant was serving the afternoon tea. As she passed his bed she saw his eyes open, and brought a mug to him.

'Tea, Mr O'Malley?'

He struggled to raise himself; she helped him, slipping an extra pillow behind his back to prop him up. She had to help him hold the mug, but he drank thirstily. His eyes went to the trolley.

'Would you like some more? And a sandwich – or a cake?'

'Both,' he muttered thickly. Harriet hurried to bring them.

'Here you are, Patrick,' she smiled, putting the plate where he could reach it.

'Not Patrick; Edward,' he muttered, extending a thin, shaking hand to take the sandwich.

'Edward? Edward what?' she asked. But he couldn't remember. He stared at her blankly, then turned his attention to the food. Harriet walked across the ward to where Sister Ramsbottom was checking a temperature chart, and spoke to her for a moment.

'Sister – O'Malley says his name is Edward, not Patrick. He seems to have remembered something.'

The Sister looked at Edward, then turned back to her chart and tartly told Nurse Grant to continue with her duties. That patient had caused her enough headaches for one day.

Edward finished the sandwich and cake, and stared unseeingly at the skinny little ward-maid polishing a window. Now he recalled his Christian name, but could not drag his surname from the depths of his subconscious mind.

He remembered his father calling him Edward. His father had been a professional soldier, a Captain; a cheerful, devil-may-care man, always surrounded by friends, many of them good-looking young women. He didn't remember his mother; she had died when he was a few months old. He had spent his early years with his grandmother and grandfather, in a tiny cottage near the sea – almost on the shoreline. His earliest memories were all set against a background of waves murmuring on the sandy beach. That had been a good time, except when the old man had been sick with a fever. He hadn't called a doctor; a gypsy woman from the Romany camp had come, and he'd recovered. Grandfather had been a fisherman, a great, strong fellow, who loved his dark-skinned, sharp-tongued wife and the sea with equal passion. Their only daughter had married the dashing young soldier against their wishes, and had died only two years later, but they loved their grandson dearly and gladly accepted the task of raising him. The Captain's family had disowned him for marrying the girl, and when he ran into debt in the regiment they had paid off his creditors on the understanding that he would keep out of their lives.

Of course, young Edward did not know that at the time. He learned of it after his father was killed trying to stop a runaway team of horses. When he left the regiment (it was leave quietly, or be cashiered, Edward eventually discovered) he got a job training horses, and took the boy, then nine years old, to live with him. For four years they lived a happy, carefree life; then Captain Clayton was killed and his employer at that time – he never stayed with anyone for long – had to find the kin of young Edward.

Captain Clayton – Robert Henry Clayton. So his own name, he deduced, was Edward Clayton . . .

Supper was served and the ward settled down to the long night. Edward Clayton dozed fitfully, fidgeting restlessly to relieve the irritating rash, his mind worrying away at the lost years

After several weeks Captain Clayton's employer discovered that Edward had a wealthy grandfather, Sir Rupert Clayton, who had disowned the Captain many years earlier. As he was unable to find the boy's mother's family, for the old fisherman and his wife had died by this time, he put Edward on a train for London with a letter for his grandfather, addressed to the house in Eaton Square, and washed his hands of him. He had enough worries without the responsibility of a thirteen-year-old boy. He had paid some of the debts the dashing Captain had left; he wanted no more of the Claytons.

Edward presented himself at the house just as Sir Rupert and Lady Amelia were going out to dine. He was dressed in threadbare corduroy shorts, a torn guernsey, and thick, tattered boots. At first the butler refused to let him in, but eventually he was persuaded to take the letter to Sir Rupert, who read it incredulously and flew into a rage. He had been unaware of Edward's existence. Only Lady Amelia's tact was able to coax him to see the boy; and then he allowed him into the house on sufferance.

For several miserable days Edward remained at Eaton Square, and then was sent to a boarding-school. Not, of course, the public school where his young cousins Gervaise and Cecil were being educated; that might be too embarrassing for them, as his father's unfortunate reputation was well known; but a reasonably good and well-established school, where he worked hard and did well, his natural intelligence making study easy. Holidays were usually spent at a farm in Norfolk belonging to the family estate, and near the school. Twice Edward met Gervaise and Cecil, when they visited the farm; but he had not liked them much, and they had eyed him contemptuously, having heard various discreditable stories about his father.

When Edward finally finished school at eighteen he went to London and presented himself at Eaton Square once again. This time his grandfather was in a more amenable frame of mind, and he was received in the drawing-room where his grandparents were having afternoon tea. A green-eyed young girl of about fifteen was with them.

'Harriet, this is your second cousin Edward,' Lady Amelia said, as the tall, gangling youth stood uncertainly in the doorway.

'Oh!' The girl looked at him curiously, and then turned to her aunt. 'Is he the one – his father –?'

'Yes, dear, but we don't talk about it,' Lady Amelia said crisply. 'Come in, Edward, and have some tea.'

Edward went into the room, and sat awkwardly on a small chair with spindly legs. He had outgrown his suit, and his hands and feet appeared unnaturally large and clumsy.

Sir Rupert began to question him about his future plans. Edward had none; unlike most of his companions at school, he had not anticipated going on to University, and had little idea of what he wanted to do. He muttered that he would like to work in the open air – he had enjoyed working on the farm during his holidays.

'There's no place for you on the family estates,' Sir Rupert told him shortly. 'I'll arrange for you to go into the offices of George Steadman, our solicitor. If you work hard you should do all right. You'll have to arrange your own lodgings, but I'll make you an allowance until you're qualified. Right, that's settled.'

And settled it was. Edward found himself articled to the solicitor, where he worked steadily for several years, studying hard. But he had not enjoyed those years. The stuffy office had stifled him and he longed for a life in the fresh air. Several times his high spirits had almost led Mr Steadman to send him packing, and his inborn dislike of authority did nothing to endear him to those who considered themselves his betters; however, a natural ability to study and a particularly high degree of intelligence eventually enabled him to qualify, and he was grudgingly received into Mr Steadman's practice as a Junior. But by that time he resented the Law and everything about it. For two years he stayed at the office in London, working by day and roistering about the town by night.

'I don't think your grandson was particularly cut out to be a solicitor, Sir Rupert,' Mr Steadman remarked wryly one day when he was called to the house in Eaton Square.

'The young puppy should be grateful for the opportunity of becoming anything better than a horse-trainer,' Sir Rupert said sourly. 'I've given him his chance; now it's up to him. I don't want to hear any more about him.'

Edward became an addict of the music-halls, spending all his spare cash on the actresses he met at the stage door. One night in 1899, soon after the outbreak of the second Boer War, he and several companions answered the call to the colours in an inebriated fit of patriotism, and it was only when he found himself in uniform, being barked at by a sergeant major, that he realized what he had let himself in for.

At twenty-four he was a tall, muscular young man, despite the years spent over dusty law books. He had not seen his grandparents for several years. He wrote to inform them that he was off to the wars. They received the news with neither surprise nor dismay; they had done their duty, and he had no place in their lives.

As his mind roamed back through the years, during that long night, Edward Clayton wondered bitterly what Sir Rupert would think of him now. Had he been informed that his grandson was missing? Perhaps he didn't know – or care. Edward would not call on him for help now. When he joined up he had cut all connection with the Clayton family. There was no need for him to let them know he was still alive. They had shown little interest in the boy, or the young man. He had been fed, clothed, and educated out of duty, nothing more. He would not throw himself on their mercy now.

In the ward the new day began long before daylight appeared at the top of the obscured windows. Temperatures were taken, and pulses counted. Pills were doled out to some, purgative medicines to others. The angry rash on O'Malley's back was dabbed with camomile lotion, which eased the irritation temporarily.

Edward faced the new day with a new resolve. His headache, which had driven him to the edge of despair, was almost gone. His memory had returned. And wonder of wonders, he was looking forward to breakfast!

Chapter Three

Liz started work at six. She began by rinsing out the sluices, cleaning the bathroom, and then washed up the morning mugs. By the time this was done the patients had had their breakfast, so she washed up the breakfast dishes. Now she started at the end of the marble-tiled corridor, mopping, rinsing, and drying the cold, hard floor. When she reached the door of the ward her back ached, and her hands were raw from the soda in the gritty and now cold water.

This morning, at the door of the ward and still on her knees, she glanced back, to see that the man who had been under the soot-fall yesterday was watching her. His present bed faced the door; he must have watched her work her way, backwards, from the far end of the corridor. Embarrassed, she stood up, stretching to ease her aching back, saw his shocked expression when he caught sight of the bruises on her face, and hurriedly turned away.

The previous evening Liz's step-father had come in from the pub the worse for drink, as he frequently did, shouting at her to fetch his dinner. He was a big, uncouth brute, who resented this dumb girl his wife had borne to her first husband. Her silent, mute watchfulness constantly aggravated him. This evening, as she put the meal on the table in front of him, he imagined she looked at him insolently; and in a drunken rage he lashed out, his heavy fist catching her on the side of the face and knocking her to the floor.

Still Liz made no sound. She had not uttered a word nor a whimper for five years, since she had diphtheria at the age of fourteen. The two youngest children – girls, mere babies, and his own – had died of the disease; but Liz had survived, as had his three sons, though she had never spoken since. Joe Spragg was convinced she could talk if she tried; he felt it was a silent expression of contempt when she refused to speak or cry out when he struck her, and was goaded on to further violence. Now he struck her again and again; and still she was silent. His wife came running into the room and pulled the girl away, sending her to the room she shared with the three young boys.

'Joe, the next time you touch that girl I'll leave you,' Agnes Spragg threatened.

'Then you be here to feed me when I come in, instead of leaving it to the dummy,' Joe snarled.

'How can I, you great fool – I was upstairs getting those kids of yourn into their bed,' Agnes snapped, dropping wearily into the wooden chair opposite him. 'If you came home from work instead of going to the pub every night –'

'I'll go to the pub if I want!' he shouted, thumping his fist on the table. 'Just be thankful I come home at all, woman! With that dummy staring at me I'm tempted to stay in the bloody pub all night!'

'Leave the girl be, Joe, or – or I'll have the police on you, I will!'

'Shut up, woman, and pour the tea. When I asked you to wed me I didn't know that miserable creature would plague me for life. God knows, no man will ever have her! As thin as a rake, and miserable with it. The look of her is enough to give a man indigestion.'

'It's not her fault she can't speak –'

'She could speak if she made her mind up to it. She's touched in the head, that's what. Now pour that tea before I give you a taste of the same medicine. I'm sick of women – moaning, staring, miserable cows!'

The next morning Liz was up and out before her mother or her step-father saw her; and just as well, for her face was a livid mass of bruises, one eye swollen almost closed. Her harassed mother would not have let her leave the house in that state. But if she lost her job what would become of her? She could not face the thought of staying in the house indefinitely with Joe Spragg. There must be some way of escaping from the trap of fear and poverty, but with her affliction she could get no work but scrubbing and polishing in the hospital, and she was lucky to have that. Her future held no hope. God knew what would become of her when the hospital closed.

When Liz had looked back over her shoulder at Edward Clayton he was shocked at the evidence of the beating. It was the first time he had taken sufficient interest in his surroundings to notice the skivvy, poor little mouse of a thing that she was, and the first time in months he had given a thought to anything outside his own pain-racked existence.

Liz got to her feet and took the bucket and mop to the sluices. She was back a few minutes later to begin work on the polished floor of the ward, pushing the soft polishing-mop over the woodblocks with smooth, practised strokes. Despite the humble task and a bruised hip her movements were graceful and restful to watch. Clayton waited until she was near the bed and then spoke to her.

'What happened to your face, girl? Who beat you?'

She glanced at him and shook her head. He frowned. Was she afraid to answer the question? She looked as if she was frightened of her own shadow. He'd never heard her speak.

'Cat got your tongue?' he asked abruptly. Now Liz smiled, but shook her head again – then nodded. She put two fingers on her lips, and looked at him. Puzzled, he watched her for a moment. All at once he understood.

'You can't speak?'

Liz nodded, continuing to move the mop across the floor with broad, sweeping strokes that gathered every particle of dust without sending any of it flying back into the air.

'But you can hear?' Liz nodded. 'I'm sorry, miss. I didn't know . . . Who hit you – your husband?' Liz shook her head vehemently. 'You have no husband? Your father – no? Mother? A man?'

He got no further. Sister Ramsbottom came bearing down on them, her starched dress rustling, her eyes snapping. She wasn't going to have the patients wasting the skivvy's time in her ward.

'Now, then – no talking to Liz, if you don't mind, Mr – er – oh, O'Malley will have to do! This girl can't speak, and she hasn't got time for you to play guessing games.'

'Sister, have you seen her face?' Edward Clayton demanded. 'She looks as if she's been beaten –'

The Sister looked vexed, as if she had found dust under the bed, or the beds untidy when Matron was due for 'Rounds'.

'Not again! Liz, you'll have to find somewhere else to live – you can't let that step-father do this every couple of weeks!' Her voice softened. 'Now get on with your work like a good girl.'

She bustled away, leaving Edward Clayton to his thoughts. Poor girl! Her predicament was as bad as his own. Her step-father! Surely she could get away from him if she tried? But with her handicap she'd have difficulty finding a safe place to live – she might be jumping out of the frying pan into the fire. She was a timid creature. In her patched grey dress, she looked like a pathetic bundle of rags. In her case, he doubted if she could hope for the escape marriage might provide. She was not likely to inspire any man to passion!

Liz had moved further down the ward now. He noticed she was limping. A flash of anger flared for a moment at the thought of the bully step-father setting about her – then died, forgotten, as he inadvertently moved and the pain in his leg made him forget the ward-maid.

Nurse Grant was not on the ward this morning. He wondered where she was. Perhaps it was her day off. Even nurses had time off sometimes, he surmised vaguely. Nice girl. Bright coloured hair. Like a flame under the preposterous, starched nurses' bonnet, with its stiff, fly-away wings ... And those intriguing green eyes. He dozed again.

Liz finished the floor and put the mop away.

Matron came in and sailed round the ward, searching for dust, or wrinkles in the bed-covers. She was as buxom and self-possessed as the Sister was skinny and tense. The men lay in their beds at attention, watching her progress. If they moved, Sister Ramsbottom would give them a piece of her mind when Matron had gone. She was not above giving them an extra dose of castor oil, too! This morning Matron could find nothing with which to find fault, for a change.

She came over and spoke kindly to Edward Clayton for a few minutes. She had been told that he remembered he was not Patrick O'Malley, but Edward something. He had not admitted yet that he had recalled his surname. He had a vague idea that if he withheld this information he would retain some independence; his whereabouts would not be reported to the Clayton family. He was unaware that the temporary military hospital was quartered in Sir Rupert Clayton's country mansion.

He answered the matron's questions shortly, determined not to be tricked into revealing his identity. His rash was irritating unbearably again after the bed-bath with coarse soap. He took his bad temper out by being surly and unhelpful. Matron departed with a furious rustling of starched apron and cap.

Dr Mansfield came in and did his morning rounds. Sister

Ramsbottom herself dealt with the dressings, which were changed daily; when she had finished Edward Clayton was reduced to a sweating wreck.

Nurse Harris brought him a mug of tea and a couple of analgesic tablets. At first, when they changed his dressings, he was given strong painkillers, but now, for fear of addiction, he was reduced to simple herbal analgesics. The nurse lingered near his bed. Sister was in her office talking to the doctor, and she was not in danger of being caught idle for a few minutes. She thought this man would be an attractive fellow if he wasn't so gaunt and bad-tempered. Those dark, deep-set eyes looked interesting.

'Not long to go now before the big move,' the nurse remarked brightly, tidying his bed-covers. 'I'm getting a week's holiday before I go to my new place. In London, it is. St Thomas's. The new hospital, near the Houses of Parliament.' She smiled cheerfully at the man, who looked puzzled.

'The big move? What big move?'

'Closing this place down, next week. Everyone being sent home, or to another hospital. Didn't you know?'

'No. What hospital are they sending me to, d'you know?'

'Oh, no, they wouldn't tell a junior like me! Haven't you got any family to go to, Mr O'Malley? Someone to take care of you?'

'No, no family . . .' He was quiet for a moment. He looked over at the two men opposite, who had both had amputations like himself. They spent most of the day out of bed now, learning to walk on crutches. 'What about them? I suppose I'll go where they do.'

'They're going to a home for the disabled. No, you won't go there – no nursing, you see. Just a home for – for –' She faltered, and coloured.

'For wrecks,' Edward Clayton finished bitterly. The girl moved away.

'Must go, work to do,' she muttered, and fled to the other end of the ward.

Dr Mansfield came back, his plump face worried. He still hadn't solved the problem of where to send this man. Most of the suitable places were already over-full. He came to the bed and looked down at the ravaged face.

'Sister tells me you've remembered your Christian name.' Clayton didn't answer. 'Look here, man, we've got to find out who you are – if I'm to send you to another hospital, they'll have to have a name for you, dammit! D'you remember where you come from? London, I suspect –'

'Where are you sending me?'

The doctor wouldn't meet his eyes. He had been considering the Sister's suggestion of an asylum, for the time being. That head-wound and the amnesia could make him eligible for the Returned Soldiers' Asylum in Bedford . . .

Clayton repeated his question.

'Where are you sending me?'

'I'll let you know when I've completed the arrangements,' Dr Mansfield said hastily. Clayton watched him suspiciously; the doctor was uneasy. There was something underhand going on.

'Why not just release me and let me make my own arrangements?' he asked abruptly. He should have some money coming, several months' pay from the army and, presumably, a pension. If he could get out of this depressing hospital atmosphere into the fresh air, and get some decent food – not institution slops, but real food! – he was sure he'd have a better chance of recovery. Or he'd die – and that might be just as well . . .

'I can't do that,' Dr Mansfield said. 'You've no next-of-kin, apparently – I could discharge you into the care of a wife or a close relation, but without a responsible custodian you'll have to go where the authorities think best.'

'Damn the authorities – I want to get out of here – out

of hospitals – I'm a man, not a bloody carcase!' He moved restlessly, and winced as a twinge of pain shot through the leg. 'These damn dressings – I'm sure the flesh would heal faster without them,' he muttered. The doctor looked down at him impatiently.

'Without them the flesh would be septic in two days,' he answered. He turned and left the ward. He was convinced O'Malley had remembered who he was.

The matron had been right. He had been half-poisoned by that faulty flue; now he was clear-headed his memory had returned, but for some reason he was keeping his knowledge to himself. Perhaps he was hiding from a deserted wife, or maybe he was wanted by the authorities for some reason.

He'd pass the man on to the Bedford Asylum. There they could deal with his wounds, and the psychiatrists – those members of the new branch of medicine – could see what they could do. At least that would solve the problem of his disposal. Pass him on. Let them find an answer to the long-term problem, if he lived long enough for that question to arise.

The mid-day meal was brought round: a small lump of unidentifiable meat swimming in a grey, greasy gravy, over-cooked vegetables, and a hunk of half-stale bread. It tasted little better than it looked, but Edward Clayton finished it hungrily, and then did the same with the thick, gluey rice pudding.

One man had been coughing all night and most of the morning. The three consumptives were all at one end of the ward, as far removed from the other patients as possible. The other five men were out of bed most of the time, but they kept away from the consumptives. At first they had tried to make friends with Edward Clayton, but he had been in no condition to favour their company, and now they ignored him. They had their meal at the central table, those with amputated legs sitting in wheelchairs.

After the meal they were all ordered to bed for two hours, while the nursing staff had their food in relays. Edward Clayton lay considering his situation while the probationer and staff-nurse were at lunch. When they returned Sister Ramsbottom took her turn. Edward called Nurse Harris over as soon as the Sister left the ward.

'I want a pen, some writing paper and an envelope,' he told her quietly. 'Can you get them for me?'

'Yes, but after you've had your rest –'

'No, now! It's important.'

'Oh – all right, but have them out of sight before Ramsbottom gets back, or I'll be ticked off again!' She rustled off, but came back two minutes later with the writing materials. 'There's a pencil – you can't use a pen in bed. You're trouble enough without getting ink all over the bed-sheets!'

For twenty minutes Edward Clayton laboured over the letter. It was the first he had written for over two years. The last letter he had penned had been from Ladysmith, during the seige in 1900, just before they were relieved. He had written to the actress, Bella Pollard, who was indirectly responsible for his being in South Africa in the first place, assuring her of his undying devotion despite the desperate situation he was in. At the time he had believed it might be the last letter he would ever write. When the British reinforcements had arrived a few days later the letter had been dispatched to London with the rest of the garrison mail, but to his intense disappointment no reply had been forthcoming. Had the lovely Bella forgotten him completely?

The pencil felt clumsy to his hand, and the words had to be searched out with a conscious effort. But eventually he was satisfied, and put the note in the envelope, sealed it, and lay back.

Now – to get it delivered. The envelope was unaddressed. He did not yet know the name of the man to whom it was to be dispatched. Nurse Harris came hurrying over and straightened his bedsheets.

'Finished? Sister's due back in five minutes. Shall I take it –'

'Do you know the name of a solicitor in the town?'

'A solicitor? No, I don't know Barminster well – I come from Liverpool, myself – but I can ask the porter, if you like.'

'Perhaps he could deliver the letter to the solicitor for me – I want it to go this afternoon.'

'I'll ask. Now close your eyes before Sister gets here or I'm in trouble again!'

A little later she found an excuse to speak to him when Sister Ramsbottom was taking temperatures at the other end of the ward.

'Charles Oatis – solicitor, in the High Street,' she whispered. 'The porter's not off 'til late, but Liz – the ward-maid – she's going off in ten minutes.'

'Ask her to deliver the letter for me,' Clayton said quietly, handing it to her. 'Tell her it's very, very important that he gets it immediately. And don't let on to anybody else – not the Sister, the doctor, or anyone!'

'All right, Mr O'Malley – I hope I'm not – oh, Lord, here comes Sister!' Pocketing the letter, she departed at speed as Sister Ramsbottom bore down on the bed with the thermometer in her hand.

'You seem to be much improved, Mr O'Malley,' she remarked drily, thrusting the thermometer in his mouth. 'I've not seen you wasting the nurses' time with idle chatter before.' She took his wrist and counted his pulse, then checked the temperature. 'Ah, splendid! Pulse and temperature both normal. We'll have you up for an hour tomorrow at this rate, Mr – er – O'Malley. Not been sick today?'

'No, Sister.'

'Splendid.' She bustled off.

The men were allowed visitors on Tuesdays and Thursdays, and at the weekend. This was Tuesday. Most of the patients had been sent to this hospital because it was near their homes, and convenient for relatives and friends. Some of them, like Edward, had no visitors. Today, after tea, the doors were opened, and several people came in to sit quietly by the beds under Sister's watchful eye for an hour.

Half-way through visiting time a red-haired young man appeared in the doorway, and looked into the ward. He had not been here before, and Sister immediately hurried across to ask who he wanted.

'I've come to see a Mr O'Malley,' he said. Surprised, Sister asked if he was a relative.

'No, I'm here on a matter of business,' he replied. 'Private business.'

'He's in the bed facing the door,' Sister Ramsbottom said coldly, and returned to her office. The young man walked across to the bed she had indicated, and looked at the patient.

'O'Malley?' he queried. Edward Clayton nodded.

'I wondered if you'd come, Mr Oatis. I appreciate your visit at such short notice, but the matter's urgent, and I need your help.' The young man pulled up a chair and sat down close to the bed. 'First I need your word that what I tell you will be in the strictest confidence.'

'Understood, Mr O'Malley. I'm not Charles Oatis, incidentally, I'm his son. John Oatis. Father's the senior partner in the firm. I'm just qualified, and frankly, I've more time on my hands than I know what to do with – that's why I was able to come so promptly.'

'I see. Well, I'm not O'Malley. I'm Edward Clayton, and

37

as I said, I'm in urgent need of help. And I might as well tell you now, I'm not sure I'll be able to pay you.'

'We'll discuss that later, Mr – Clayton? I'll do what I can for you. I wasn't able to join up myself, and I think I owe you fellows something for doing my share of the fighting.'

For the next half an hour, heads close together, the two men talked in low voices. There was an exclamation of surprise when Edward Clayton discovered where the hospital was situated, and who owned the building, but apart from that the inquisitive ears of the other visitors could not hear a word of the conversation. From time to time John Oatis made notes. At one point he walked into the Sister's office and asked her a question.

'When exactly is this ward to be closed, Sister?'

'The hospital will be closed finally on Tuesday of next week, sir. Seven days from today, in fact.' She looked at him coldly. 'All the patients will be removed, at the latest, next Tuesday morning.'

'When and where do you propose to have Mr O'Malley transferred?'

'Are you a relative of Mr O'Malley, sir?'

'No, ma'am.'

'Then I'm not in a position to discuss his case with you, Mr –?'

'Mr Oatis – John Oatis. I'm Mr O'Malley's solicitor, ma'am.'

'His solicitor! Oh.' Sister Ramsbottom tried not to show her dismay. She was at a loss to know what she should do. Her instructions were quite clear – no patients could be discussed with anyone except their next-of-kin. In this particular case things could be very tricky. Would the unfortunate business of the carbon monoxide gas come out? Was O'Malley going to sue for compensation from the authorities? 'You'd better talk to the doctor,' she said hastily. 'He's not here at the moment, but I can send him a message and perhaps he'll see you when the visiting hour is over, if you wish.'

'Thank you, Sister. That will be fine.'

John Oatis returned to the ward and continued to talk quietly with his client until the bell went. When he left Edward Clayton was ashen-faced and exhausted, but for the first time for months he was taking an interest in his future.

Dr Mansfield received the solicitor warily in his own office on the first floor of the mansion.

'Did O'Malley tell you who he is?' he demanded as soon as John Oatis was seated across the desk from him.

'The matter my client and I discussed is confidential,' Oatis replied coolly. He was not a big man – of medium height, stocky, but well-muscled, a keen football player. He was not going to be brow-beaten. The plump, autocratic doctor, several stones heavier, felt that O'Malley had found himself a good champion, despite the solicitor's youth – he was, in fact, twenty-seven, but looked younger. 'I want to know what arrangements you're making for his future care.'

The doctor looked down at the blotter on his desk. He picked up a pen, and appeared to examine it closely as he replied. John Oatis was young, but not stupid; he realized that the doctor was not being open with him. He suspected that the older man was slightly uneasy about something.

'We have a problem with this man, Mr Oatis,' Dr Mansfield admitted. 'To begin with, we don't think he is the Patrick O'Malley his papers claim. He has, indeed, been suffering from amnesia, probably caused by the head-wound he received. We think he's regained his memory, but for some unknown reason is withholding his identity from us. He has not been co-operative with the authorities in any way, and we're at a loss to know just what we should do with him.

39

'Early next week he has to be transferred to some other institution, but he doesn't fit into any of the usual categories. Most of these emergency hospitals are being closed now. The convalescent homes are all full – and won't accept patients still in need of full nursing care. So we're sending him to the Returned Soldiers' Asylum in Bedford –'

'Asylum?' The question came sharply. The doctor refused to meet the young man's eyes.

'Not a regular mental asylum, sir – a hospital where we deal with particularly difficult patients – and in view of his amnesia –'

'I see. And when do you intend to transfer him to this – asylum?'

'The arrangements are tentatively made for Monday afternoon.'

'My client would prefer to be discharged.'

The doctor looked up, meeting the younger man's eyes for the first time.

'That's impossible. Unless he can produce a relative to accept responsibility I can't sign his discharge papers. And if he discharges himself, he will, in effect, become a deserter from the army. His discharge from the regiment is dependent upon his discharge by the hospital authorities; without that he'll forfeit the pension to which he is without any doubt entitled.'

'Suppose,' Mr Oatis said quietly, 'I take it upon myself to accept responsibility for him?'

'Are you related to him in any way?'

'No.'

'Then I'm afraid it won't do,' Dr Mansfield said reluctantly. This could be a solution to the problem, but he was bound to act by the rules laid down by the military authorities. 'We could take it to the authorities concerned, and possibly get a special ruling, but that will take time.'

'Ahhh . . . And time we don't have.' Mr Oatis was silent

for a moment. 'So – a wife, mother, father – any other relative would be acceptable?'

'A close relative – and one that I am satisfied will be able to cope with the problems involved.' Dr Mansfield stood up. 'I'm sorry, Mr Oatis, but I have no more time at the moment. We still have five wards here, and I have a lot to do. If I can be of any further assistance let me know, and I'll be at your service.'

John Oatis left. He had a lot to do in the next few days. And he was far from sure he would be able to complete his task in the time allotted.

Chapter Four

The next morning Edward Clayton did a strange thing. When he saw Sister Ramsbottom leave the ward for a moment he deliberately allowed his plate of porridge to slide off the tray on to the floor. Nurse Harris tut-tutted over his clumsiness, and sent the ward-maid in to clean up the mess. As soon as the nurse was out of earshot Edward thanked the dumb girl for delivering his note to the solicitor.

Liz smiled briefly, and continued to scrape up the spilled porridge. Edward frowned.

'Liz! Look at me!' She looked up, startled, and shrank back nervously. The bruises were still evident on her face, but the swelling had gone down, and the huge violet-blue eyes met his apprehensively. 'Has your step-father hit you again?' She shook her head, and went back to mopping up the mess with a rag. 'Liz – do you want to get away from him?'

The girl nodded without looking up. Edward glanced round; several of the other patients were watching them curiously, one or two with smirks on their faces. They had tried chatting up the little ward-maid before now, and got nowhere. They waited for her to follow her usual custom and walk away, ignoring anyone who spoke directly to her. But she stayed where she was, meticulously cleaning the sticky mess off the floor.

'Liz, come here, where I can talk without being overheard,' Edward said quietly. The girl looked round, undecided, then moved a few feet across the floor, still on her knees, so that she was close to his face.

'Can you cook, Liz? If I was out of here, could you cook my meals and look after me?' The girl stared at him uncomprehendingly for a moment, then a flicker of a smile crossed her face, and she nodded. 'Have you a sweetheart?' Startled, she looked at him, shaking her head vehemently. 'No young man you want to marry? Are you old enough to get married? Eighteen? Nineteen? Ah, nineteen.' He looked at her thoughtfully. For a moment she met his eyes, and then lowered her lids.

Edward made up his mind. She would do.

'Would you consider marrying me?' Edward asked quietly. 'A marriage of convenience, for both of us,' he said hastily. 'I could get out of here, and you can get away from your step-father. You'd have to help me get well again, and then you'd be free. I won't hold you to the marriage after I can manage without you, and I'll see that you're provided for.'

The girl knelt there, motionless, for so long he began to think she hadn't heard him, or hadn't understood. Then she went back to the mess on the floor, finished wiping it up, and stood up. She limped away to the sluice-room without looking back.

Edward Clayton stared after her. She had not expressed surprise, dismay, pleasure, or anything else. She had just walked away.

Presumably she thought he was such a bad bargain he wasn't worth an answer! He started to get angry.

Nurse Harris came in with another plate of porridge for him. She was annoyed; she had traipsed all the way out to the kitchens for this, and now O'Malley didn't even seem to want it! He took it without a word, and began to spoon it down automatically. It was half cold and lumpy; but if he didn't eat it he'd get nothing else, and it was a long time to mid-day.

How could a man thrive on this sort of muck? he thought

43

angrily. And where had that girl gone? Surely she could at least give him the courtesy of a reply, if it was only a shake of the head!

He lay and fumed for half an hour until the sister came in to deal with his dressings. After that, for an hour, he lay sweating and trembling, not giving the girl a thought. He closed his eyes and concentrated on quieting his jangling nerves by reciting almost-forgotten lines of Shakespeare; he had discovered that helped him to regain his composure.

He heard a quiet step by his bedside. He opened his eyes. Liz stood there, her eyes on his face. He forced a smile.

'Yes or no?' he enquired. The girl nodded. He gave a sigh of relief. 'Splendid. Now – have you a mother?' Another nod. 'Then ask her to come and see me, tomorrow afternoon at four. Official visiting hours. She's not to tell anyone she's coming or why, and neither are you. Do you understand?'

Liz nodded, and walked back to the door, where she picked up the polishing mop and began working her way across the floor.

A plateful of leathery liver, grey mashed potatoes, and greasy fried onions was served at twelve. That was followed by the usual two hours of enforced rest, and then the Sister, with the assistance of the orderly, a beefy individual who obligingly smuggled in beer and spirits to those who could afford them, got Edward Clayton out of bed and sat him in a chair for half an hour.

At first he felt great, despite the discomfort he experienced while being lifted out. It was wonderful to sit upright, and hold his head squarely on his shoulders instead of lolling helplessly on the pillows. But after ten minutes he began to feel tired, and when the half-hour was up he was glad to be lifted back into bed, close his eyes, and drift off to sleep for an hour.

The following day he was lifted out into the chair to eat his breakfast, and returned to bed only when it was time for the dressings to be changed; but he was up again for half an hour before tea. He spent some time chatting to the man who occupied the next bed, a pleasant fellow who had lost his right arm. He was returning to his family next week, but was not sanguine about his chances of employment, as one-armed teachers were not particularly sought after.

When the doors were opened for the visitors Edward was sitting up in bed in his rough calico nightshirt, watching anxiously for a figure who might be his future mother-in-law.

Mrs Agnes Spragg sidled in almost furtively, her eyes darting from one bed to another. Liz had been able to convey to her that she was to go to the hospital to visit one of the men, but had not given her any clue as to what it was about. Mrs Spragg would not have been surprised if she had been turned away by the Sister. She looked fairly respectable in her best coat (second-hand three years ago from the tally-man), but thin and tense. A life of hard work and constant childbearing had left her with a defeated expression. Now she scanned the room uncertainly; Edward Clayton caught her eye, and beckoned. She walked across to his bed, and stood there looking at him curiously.

'Liz's mother?' Edward Clayton asked her. She nodded. For a moment he wondered if she, too, was mute; that would certainly make things difficult. 'Pull up that chair, and sit down.' Still without speaking, the woman obeyed, sitting close to him so that their conversation would remain private.

'I'm Agnes Spragg, sir,' she said, calmly enough, when she was settled into the chair. 'Liz seemed to want me to come to see you – she drew me some pictures, but I'm not sure what she was trying to tell me.'

'You don't know what it's about?'

'No, sir. But she seemed to think it was a secret. Can I do something to help you?'

Edward looked at her thoughtfully. A nervous woman, but with a will of her own, or he was mistaken. And kindly.

'I've asked Liz to marry me.' Agnes Spragg gaped at him in astonishment. 'She said she will. Have you any objection?'

'Objection – no! But why – marry Liz?' She recovered her wits, and drew a deep breath. 'I've no objection, sir, but I'd like to know what's behind it. You're no young boy in love, I can see that. And you're an educated man – I can tell by your voice. The likes of you don't marry the likes of us! And a dummy, into the bargain. What do you want of our Liz? I'll be straight with you, sir. I'll be glad to get the girl away from my husband, she gets on his nerves something shocking. One day I'm afraid he'll do her a real mischief! But there's more girls about, happy, cheerful girls who can talk and sing, than there are men, and I never thought to find her a husband! So you tell me why you want to marry the girl, and I'll do my best to help you.'

'I need a wife to get me out of this place,' Edward Clayton said bluntly, 'and a wife who will help me to get well. I'll treat her decently, and if she wants to leave me when I'm on my feet again – my foot! – I'll let her go. But I must have a wife within days. Liz is the only hope I've got.'

'Within days – but getting married takes time, Mr –? I don't even know your name!'

'Edward Clayton – but here they know me as O'Malley, so you'd better call me that for the moment. Ah, here comes Mr Oatis – he'll make all the arrangements. You'll have to help him.' He shook hands with John Oatis, whose cheerful looks told him that he had been able to discharge his duties successfully. 'Mr Oatis, this is Mrs Spragg – I'm going to marry her daughter.'

John Oatis looked surprised, as well he might. Two days

ago his client had said he had a girl in mind for a wife, but had not yet spoken more than a few words with her.

'Congratulations, Mr Clayton – er – O'Malley. That was fast work!' He pulled a chair up to the side of the bed and spoke in a low voice. 'Well, I've been to London, and done the business you asked me about. I saw Mr George Steadman and I've got some news for you. When Lady Amelia died she left you a small legacy, but it's tied up in bonds, and you can't touch the capital until you're thirty-five. She doesn't seem to have placed much faith in your financial judgement! But meanwhile you have a small income from the dividends. So you're not penniless.

'Mr Steadman received notification from the War Office that you were missing, believed dead. That's been cleared up now, of course – I went to the authorities myself and sorted that out. There's a tidy sum due from the Army Pay Office – it's been accruing since you went to South Africa, so that's waiting for you. Your pension's also sorted out.'

'And were you able to arrange that without disclosing my whereabouts?'

'Your Mr Steadman was very pressing, but I told him he'd have to contact you through me for the time being. The military authorities are a different matter. They had to have full details, of course. I think Dr Mansfield will receive directions from them in the course of the next day or two.'

'It should be interesting to see what his reaction will be! There's no reason, though, why he should connect me with the family of Sir –' He glanced at Mrs Spragg; he had no intention of letting her, or her daughter, know that he had any wealthy relations. But she was watching the other visitors to the ward, and seemed to find their conversation more absorbing than his. He continued: '– with the other Clayton family. Now, did you make enquiries about the Register Office marriage?'

'Yes, I did, though it seemed a waste of time. I'll have to

go in tomorrow morning – it's too late today – and arrange the special licence. I'll ask Mrs Spragg to accompany me – she can give the details, and we'll have to have her special consent, as the girl is under twenty-one. Mrs Spragg – Mrs Spragg!' Agnes looked back with a start, and gave John Oatis her attention. 'Was the girl's father – er – your husband?'

'Liz's father and I were legally married, if that's what you want to know,' Agnes told them frankly. 'He was in the navy, and was in an accident when she was a month old. Fell into the hold and broke his neck – or that's what they told me. I suppose he was drunk. I married Joe Spragg three years later.'

'What's the girl's full name?'

'Elizabeth Mary Fuller – but o' course, she's always called Spragg nowadays. And she weren't born dumb, sir. When she was fourteen she got the diphtheria, and at the hospital they had to cut a hole in her throat – awful, it was! She lived through it, but she's never said a word since. My two youngest died that same week. I thought Joe Spragg would go crazy, he was that grieved. That's why he's so took against Liz, you see. She got better, but his little girls died.' She looked at Edward Clayton. 'And now he's took to the drink – like me first did. So I'll be glad to get Liz out of his way.'

'I think that's all settled, then, Mrs Spragg. Will you come to my office at nine in the morning, please, and we'll finish the arrangements.'

Agnes Spragg found Liz waiting for her at the gates and they walked back into the town together. It was less than a mile to the town square.

'Well, Liz, I never thought I'd see you married, girl, but it looks as if you'll be settled within days! And a real gent he is, too, even if he is sittin' up in bed in a hospital night-shirt the like of which even Joe wouldn't be seen dead in. He don't pretend to be loving, Liz, but I reckon you'll be

48

able to live with that. Well, girl – we'll have to see what we can do about some decent clothes for you. We'll call on the tallyman on the way home.'

Edward Clayton and John Oatis were still in conference.

'When we get you out of here, where do you intend to go?' John asked. 'You can't marry the girl and live on the streets.'

'I've been thinking about that,' Edward Clayton said. 'I know what I'd like to do, but I don't know if you can arrange it. When I was a boy I lived with my mother's people for a time. They're both dead now. But they had a little cottage, almost on the sea-shore, near a village – I think it was called Forestwidden, or something like that. Near the Great Forest. The cottage was on a bay called Honey Beck by the locals. A little stream ran nearby. It's at the end of a farm track, not really on a road at all. It's not much of a cottage, and it's so out of the way it's possible no-one wants to live there. D'you think you can find out if it's occupied?'

'Well, I can try,' John Oatis said doubtfully. 'I think I know the village. There can't be two Forestwiddens! A pub, a church, and a village shop, that's about all there is of it.'

'That sounds like the place. If I can rent the cottage I'll go there for a while. If not, perhaps you could find somewhere like it – somewhere quiet, mind, and near the sea.'

'I'll do my best,' John Oatis promised. 'Now, the marriage is to take place Saturday afternoon, right? I suppose you wouldn't like to tell me how you intend to get to the Register Office?' he added thoughtfully, looking round. Edward grinned.

'It's the Sister's afternoon off. I'm going to wheel my chair out to the door, where you'll be waiting, John Oatis. You can push the wheelchair into town, I'll be married, and you can push me back again before the rest period is over.'

'Whew!' exclaimed John Oatis.

'With luck I'll not be missed! Don't forget to bring a warm overcoat, a rug, and a sock and shoe – size ten. I don't want to celebrate my freedom with a case of pneumonia. Then you and Liz can come and legally claim me on Monday morning. Until I'm out of here, and get my affairs organized, could you act as my banker? I'll need some money –'

'I've already seen to that, Mr Clayton. I've given my office as your address for the moment – to the military authorities and to Steadman. I'm going to need your signature on some papers shortly, but in the meantime I'll advance you something to tide you over. If you decide to run out on me, I think I can run faster than you can!' They heard the bell announcing that visiting time was over. John got up, and shook his client's hand.

'Good luck, Edward Clayton. Oh, don't you want to know how much your grandmother left you?'

'Not much, I'll be bound!' Edward grinned.

'A thousand pounds, my friend! Not bad, eh? At least you'll be able to pay my fee!'

Chapter Five

During the night Edward Clayton could hear the wind howling, and the rain spattering against the windows. The severe cold had abated at last, but March was going out with a final wintery blast. From the end of the ward the constant coughing kept the nurse occupied and disturbed the other men.

Edward dozed fitfully, his sleep troubled by dreams. At one point he was back at the cottage by the sea with his grandmother and grandfather. He could see the old woman sitting in her rocking-chair by the fire, her hands busy at the knitting with which she augmented the family income. The black kitchen range had provided both cooking facilities and heat, warming the one big room where they lived, and the loft above where they slept. His bed had been in a lean-to room at the end of the cottage, originally added as a storeroom. The loft was reached by an open stair, little more than a ladder, against the back wall of the main room. When his grandfather was ill he used the bed in the lean-to, being unable to negotiate the ladder, and Edward had shared his grandmother's bed, revelling in the comfort of the billowing goose-feather mattress.

In his dream he saw his grandfather lying in the truckle bed, his grizzled grey beard over the bright patchwork quilt. Then he saw Old Meg, the gypsy woman, bending over him. She was muttering unintelligibly – or chanting, perhaps, a spell to cure the fever. The old man woke, and his eyes were clear, the fever gone. The gypsy, too, had gone.

Suddenly Edward was awake, but the dream remained

with him. He could almost hear Old Meg's voice. He tried to sit up but the dressings caught against the sheets made him wince with pain. He reached out for the glass of water on his locker, and took a long drink.

Presently he dozed again, and this time the dream was different; he was at the music-hall, watching the girls dancing and singing the patriotic songs so popular when the Boer War broke out. Then Bella Pollard, the singer with whom he had been infatuated for some time, came on stage and sang 'The Boers Have Stolen My Daddy', a song guaranteed to have every female in the audience in tears before the final chorus. He felt again the patriotic fever that had overcome him that fateful night, three years ago, induced partly by the song, and partly by the ale he had consumed. A raucous fit of coughing from the end of the ward woke him sweating; he had been ready to go and sign up again with the rest of the mob, signing away his leg and three years of his life.

Bella Pollard . . . He wondered what she was doing now. She had not replied to the emotional letters he had written when he was first in uniform. He remembered the boisterous evenings they had spent when he had taken her out to supper after the theatre; and the Sunday outings to Southend, walking down the pier, dining and drinking in the posh hotels near the front . . . On one memorable occasion they had taken the pleasure boat round to Brighton, and been sick most of the way, too sick to return to London that night. They stayed in a hotel, signing the register as Mr and Mrs Jones . . . When he didn't turn up for work until the Tuesday old Steadman had threatened to report his wayward conduct to Sir Rupert. He must have thought better of it, for Edward never heard any more of the matter. He continued to spend his evenings at the music-hall, and if he had not joined the colours when he did, might very well have found himself looking for employment elsewhere

– not easy for a newly qualified young solicitor with no money and a doubtful reputation.

After the visitors had left the previous afternoon Edward asked to be lifted into a wheelchair for his supper. He had practised wheeling himself about for ten minutes before the meal. At first he had difficulty controlling the direction of the chair, but soon got the hang of it. The other men watched him, commenting derisively on his performance. One of them had procured a bottle of whisky, which he offered round after they had eaten, including Edward in the party. When the orderly helped Edward back to bed he was feeling mildly inebriated. Perhaps that accounted for the dreams. But he was determined to persevere with the chair tomorrow. He was getting stronger daily now that he was able to keep his food down. He still suffered intermittently from a raised temperature, presumably a touch of the fever that he had picked up from the contaminated water, but perhaps he would soon be strong enough to try to walk on crutches.

Nurse Harris chatted with him on Friday morning while she gave him his bed-bath, carefully washing the raw, red skin covered in the irritating rash, using the coarse yellow hospital soap. It had not occurred to anyone that the soap might be aggravating the irritation. In answer to his questions, she confirmed that Sister Ramsbottom would be off duty from mid-day on Saturday. She was curious about his visitor, and finally Edward decided to take her partially into his confidence, telling her he was planning to be married on Saturday if he could escape the vigilance of the nurse in charge during the rest-period. He did not tell Nurse Harris who the bride was, but her romantic temperament delighted to be included in the conspiracy, and she promised to help him if she could.

'Ramsbottom goes off at noon, and the Staff Sister from another ward will be keeping an eye on things here, but she'll only come in if I need help during the rest-period. Oh, Mr O'Malley – what a lark!' She finished drying his back, and dabbed the rash with the foul-smelling lotion. She pulled the rough calico nightshirt down over his legs. 'But what about clothes – it's so cold out. How are you going to get dressed?'

'My friend will bring an overcoat, and I'll be wrapped in a blanket in the chair. I'll have a sock and shoe on. No-one will know I'm in a nightshirt underneath the blanket!'

'Fancy – being married in a nightshirt!' She giggled as she straightened the bedclothes. 'Is she a pretty girl, your financy?'

'Er – yes, very,' Edward said hastily, trying to play the part of the romantic lover. He hadn't given this aspect of the matter any thought previously, and couldn't remember for the life of him whether Liz was pretty or not, before her step-father had disfigured her face with bruises. However, that was beside the point. She was clean, she could cook, and she was willing to look after him; that was all she would be called on to do. Her personal appearance was irrelevant. Collecting up the bathing equipment, Nurse Harris sighed wistfully.

'It's sort of like an elopement, isn't it, Mr O'Malley . . . Now just be sure you're back here before tea-time, and we'll be all right. If you're not, you'll be caught, and I'll get the sack! Here comes Ramsbottom to do your dressings. Good luck!'

On Saturday morning Edward stayed in bed until the last minute before the mid-day meal, conserving his strength. The orderly lifted him into the chair, and pushed it to the table where the other men were already waiting to be served. Sister Ramsbottom came in to take a last look round before going off for the afternoon. Over the unappetizing stew, Edward told the other men what he was planning.

'Blimey, mate – they'll murder you if you're caught,' exclaimed the man in the next chair.

'I don't intend to get caught,' Edward told him.

'And you're coming back after the knot's tied? If yer running off, y'might as well keep running,' commented another.

'I've got to have something to live on, and that way I'd lose my pension,' Edward pointed out.

'What about the bloomin' bride? Won't she mind, being left high and dry on the wedding night?' The man looked at Edward's legs, one a mangled stump, the other bandaged from heel to calf. 'Not that you'd be much use to a bride like that, mate. I reckon she'll 'ave to wait a while before she finds out what sort of 'usband she's got!'

'She knows what she's doing,' Edward said evenly. He hoped it was true; he didn't want Liz to change her mind when it was too late.

They finished the meal and the other men went to their beds. The porter came in to help them. Nurse Harris walked briskly into the ward and dumped a red blanket and a bundle in a white pillowcase on his bed, then pushed his chair up beside it. Before he could protest, she drew the curtains round, and produced a thick tweed coat from the pillowcase.

'Quick, let's get you into this,' she whispered. She also had a thick sock, a shoe, a tie, and a warm woollen muffler. With the tie in place, the nightshirt could pass for a shirt at a quick glance. When he was dressed, she wrapped the red blanket round him hiding the coat, and drew the curtains back.

As if it was the most natural thing in the world, she pushed his chair across the ward, through the door, down the long marble-tiled corridor, and into the entrance hall. One of the other men, meanwhile, was keeping the orderly occupied; he didn't see the nurse illicitly removing one of the patients.

John Oatis waited nervously in the hall. Without a word,

but without any obvious hurry, he took charge of the chair, and wheeled it to the door. A dark travelling rug and a tweed cap had been left in the porch. With the rug concealing the red hospital blanket, and the tweed cap on his head, there was nothing remarkable about the figure wheeled out of the door, down the ramp, and out on to the drive. Neither man spoke until they were out on the road and making rapid progress in the direction of the town.

'I never thought we'd do it,' John Oatis said jubilantly, as his jaunty strides carried them along the footpath. 'When I got to the door that nurse grabbed the clothes and disappeared. I thought she had caught me red-handed stealing her patient! How did you persuade her to help us?'

'I suppose I appealed to her romantic disposition,' Edward grinned. 'Hey, John – take it a little easier, if you don't mind! This chair isn't very well sprung – I'm getting the teeth rattled out of my head!'

'Hmmm ... We'll have to get you a more comfortable one than this on Monday,' John commented. 'And you're going to need some clothes to leave in.'

'Have you done anything about that cottage?' Edward asked.

'Yes, I went to Forestwidden yesterday, after I arranged for the special licence. And you'll never guess who owns Honey Beck Bay.'

'No, I'll never guess. Tell me!'

'Your grandfather – old Sir Rupert himself.'

'Good heavens! I never thought of that!'

'He also owns the farm nearby – that's let to a chap called Henry Willoughby. The Clayton family also has a hunting lodge in the forest between here and Forestwidden, about eight miles away. There's a rumour that Sir Rupert is staying there at the moment, incidentally. His son, the Honourable Arthur, is standing for Parliament in Barminster in the next General Election, so they say. I suppose your father met your mother when he was staying at the hunting lodge. Anyway, the cottage has been empty for three years, and I've arranged to rent it. I didn't have time to go out and see it – I had to go to the vicarage to get the information I needed, and then hurry back to Barminster to see the agents, so I can't tell you what condition it's in. I didn't give your name – the agents would have been a bit curious, and might have mentioned it to Sir Rupert's bailiff. I had the rent book made out to myself, and I'll pay the agent in cash – it's a monthly agreement, by the way. That suit you?'

'That's fine – splendid!' Edward could hardly believe things were going so well. They soon reached the town, and slowed down a little; there was no point in making themselves conspicuous by racing along like an express train. The Register Office was in the Town Hall, in the square.

They had a bit of a problem getting into the Town Hall. There was a flight of steps up to the door. But a couple of hefty young men passing by saw their plight, and good-naturedly lent a hand in hoisting the chair up the steps, while Edward hung on for dear life. He was afraid he would be tipped out in their enthusiasm and then what a fool he would feel, sprawled on the steps of the Town Hall in his nightshirt!

The door of the office was open. Liz and her mother waited inside, Mrs Spragg in her best black, and Liz looking nervous and frightened in a gown of blue serge, with a short jacket in a darker blue to match her bonnet. Her face was white under the bruises. They were sitting on a wooden bench under the window. As the chair was wheeled in, they both got up, and stood looking at the two men, uncertain of what they should do.

Edward held out his hand to Mrs Spragg.

'Thank you for coming,' he said, shaking her hand. He smiled at Liz. The Registrar came hurrying in, a thin, weedy looking man in a black suit, with an almost completely bald head.

He already knew the solicitor.

'In good time, Mr Oatis,' he said breathlessly. 'I'm glad you're not late – I have another ceremony shortly. Is this Mr Clayton? Have you got the licence? The ring?'

Edward had not given the ring a thought, and nor had John Oatis. They looked at each other blankly.

'I'll run out and buy one –' John said hastily, but Mrs Spragg was drawing a worn ring off her right hand.

'Here, Mr Clayton – use this,' she said matter-of-factly. 'It's the one Liz's father gave me.'

'We can proceed, then,' the Registrar said. He went through the ceremony without further ado, and five minutes later Liz Fuller was Mrs Edward Clayton. There had been a moment's awkwardness when he had waited expectantly for Liz to make her replies.

'She's mute, sir,' Mrs Spragg said quickly. The Registrar looked up at the bride, who nodded her agreement to his question, after which he ran through the rest of the formalities at top speed.

Signing the register completed the ceremony. Edward noticed that Liz signed her name very slowly, forming each letter with exaggerated care.

'You'll have to remember to sign "Elizabeth Clayton" on Monday,' he commented as they left the office. Liz looked at him anxiously, and then at her mother. Mrs Spragg sighed.

'My daughter can't read nor write, Mr Clayton,' she confessed. 'But don't worry – we'll practise the new signature tomorrow, and I'm sure she'll be able to do it on Monday.'

'Can't write!' Edward exclaimed. 'Didn't you send the girl to school, Mrs Spragg?'

'Sometimes she went, until she was about eight,' her mother said, 'but she didn't seem to learn nothing, then I had the twins, so she stayed at home and kept an eye on them while I went to work. But none of the girls round our way go to school much – you don't have to read and write to wash floors and have babies!'

At the doors of the Town Hall they again had the problem of the steps. This time they were assisted by a young man in a bowler hat who had been drinking, and again Edward was in danger of being tipped out of the chair. But eventually he was on the pavement, and said goodbye to his bride, shaking hands with both her and her mother. John Oatis turned the chair towards the country lane that would take them back to Barminster Abbey.

Before they left the shopping district, however, John went into an off-licence, and bought a bottle of rum.

'You can share this with the other men at suppertime,' he said wryly. 'Not much of a wedding breakfast, but a token, at least.'

'D'you reckon this a suitable vintage to go with tripe and onions?' Edward chuckled. 'Because that's what we have for supper on Saturday!'

As they hurried back towards Barminster Abbey the sun came out and shone weakly through the clouds. Edward wondered if this was a good omen. At last he was beginning to feel optimistic about his future.

However, by the time they reached the hospital doors he was feeling the reaction. There was no-one about as John pushed his chair up the ramp into the hallway, where Nurse Harris was hovering anxiously. It was nearly tea-time, and the staff nurse from the other ward was likely to appear at any moment. She whipped the dark rug off the chair, and wheeled Edward quickly into the ward. Several of the other men were up, and they raised a cheer when they saw him.

Nurse Harris hurriedly divested him of the coat, shoe, sock and tie, rolled them into a bundle and raced them back to John Oatis.

'Scat!' she hissed, and ran back into the ward.

Edward was now slumped in the chair, grey-faced and exhausted. He was still clutching the bottle of rum. She thrust it into his locker.

'You look terrible,' she commented as she wrapped the red blanket round his knees. 'Well – did you get married?'

'Yes,' he said, with the ghost of a smile. 'Thanks to you, Nurse. I'll not forget it.'

'You'll have to stay up until after tea,' she said worriedly. 'I'll need help to get you back into bed. Lord – here's the staff nurse, and I've not made the tea yet! Liz didn't turn up this morning – she doesn't often let us down, and it had to be today, of all days!' She rushed off to make the tea.

Edward was glad when the orderly came to lift him back into the bed. He felt utterly exhausted now the excitement was over. His legs ached, his head ached, and he was almost too weary to think. He wondered bleakly if he would have the strength to cope with life outside the hospital.

While the visitors came and went he lay and dozed. He thought about Liz. She had looked quite presentable, he thought, except for the bruises, in the blue serge dress and the modest bonnet. He wondered where the money had come from to pay for them. Perhaps her mother had saved a few pounds against the day when the girl might get married? When he had some money he would buy her some pretty clothes. And a warm coat. And a wedding ring of her very own. She deserved them. She might not be much of a prize in the matrimonial stakes, but she had turned up trumps so far as he was concerned.

Chapter Six

On Monday morning Sister Ramsbottom and her staff began their duties, as usual, at six. When she came on the ward the men were drinking their early tea, served by the outgoing night nurses. Sister Ramsbottom was not in a good humour; she was already short of a nurse, as Miss Grant had left them, and now she found that the ward-maid had not come in this morning.

'She wasn't here on Saturday, either,' Nurse Harris reminded her.

'I suppose she's found another job, and not bothered to let us know,' Sister Ramsbottom said crossly. 'She'd be finishing tomorrow, anyway, the same as the rest of us. I just hope that step-father of hers hasn't been beating her again. Poor little creature – not much of a life! However, that won't get the floors cleaned, and we've had a message that Sir Rupert Clayton will be visiting sometime today. Apparently he's in the district, and has decided to take a last look at the hospital before it closes down. As if we hadn't enough to do without having to shine the place up for his benefit!'

At eight-thirty she was in her office filling in the temperature charts when Dr Mansfield appeared at the doorway, rather red in the face, having run down the stairs from his own office with more speed than dignity. He dropped into the spare chair and pushed a couple of letters across the desk to her.

'You'd better read those,' he puffed. Sister Ramsbottom picked up the first letter and read it through. Then she read it again.

'Well!' she commented. 'It looks as if someone has sorted out the O'Malley mystery. I wonder – this must be something to do with that young solicitor who came in the other day.'

'Yes, yes, but look there, Sister – see the name!'

'Edward Clayton – Clayton! Good heavens!'

'Yes, Sister – Clayton! The man's a private, not an officer, though, so he can't have any connection with Sir Rupert's family. Can he? Is that girl – Harriet Grant – about? She should know.'

'No, she left a few days ago. But she nursed him, and if he was a cousin or something, I expect she would have recognized him. You know Sir Rupert is coming here sometime today?'

Dr Mansfield groaned.

'I know we have a lot to thank the man for, he's been very generous in lending us Barminster Abbey, and he's paid a lot of the bills for supplies, but really – I wish he had come to be thanked sometime when we were not so frightfully busy! Now take a look at that second letter. That Mr Oatis wants to see me at ten-thirty. He says it's urgent.'

Sister Ramsbottom stood up.

'I expect he'll want to see Mr O'Mall – I mean, Mr Clayton, as well, so I'll go and get his dressings dealt with now. Do you want to see him this morning, Dr Mansfield?'

'I suppose I'd better – I've got to sign him over to the Bedford Hospital this afternoon, and I'd better make sure there's no infection there before he goes. I wish them luck in clearing up that dermatitis – I've tried everything I can think of, and if anything, the blasted rash gets worse! Well, at least we've got his correct name and number to send on the documents with him.' He stood up. 'I suggest, Sister, that you say nothing about the re-documentation until after we hear what Oatis has to say.'

While the doctor and Sister dealt with Edward's dressings

and gave him a thorough examination, they said nothing directly to him, but this was not unusual; they normally spoke only to each other over the patient's body, as if his condition was none of his business. Edward truculently demanded to be told if they had decided where he was to be transferred; but neither gave him an answer. As Dr Mansfield left the ward Edward heard the Sister tell Nurse Harris that Mr O'Mall – Clayton was to be ready to leave the premises at two o'clock.

At ten-thirty Dr Mansfield was in his office when the orderly showed Mr Oatis and a young woman in.

'Good morning,' Dr Mansfield said. 'I received your letter this morning. Also one from the Regimental Welfare Department. I gather that you – er – unravelled the mystery of Mr O'Malley's identity.'

'Yes, sir. And now I've come to collect him. He has made his own arrangements for his future, Dr Mansfield, and wishes to leave directly.'

'That's all very well, young man, but as I told you last week, it's impossible!' the doctor said testily. 'You know I can release him only to a close relative or a wife. So if that's all –'

'Dr Mansfield, this lady is his wife, and she has come to take him home.'

The doctor sighed.

'Clayton has no wife – his papers report him unmarried, without next of kin! The only person to be notified in the case of his death is a solicitor –'

'Who was very surprised last week when I was able to tell him that his client, who had been posted missing, believed dead, is alive! Here is Mrs Clayton's marriage certificate, Dr Mansfield.'

The paper was snatched from his hand, and the doctor studied it closely.

'Good heavens, man – this is dated two days ago – last Saturday! Edward Clayton was here in the hospital on Saturday –'

'For two hours he was not, Dr Mansfield. He went out and got married in the Barminster Register Office. Now, there's nothing illegal in that – he's not a prisoner! And he went willingly, so you can't accuse anyone of abducting him. Now his wife is ready to take him home, so if you please, we'll be on our way.'

For three years the doctor had been daily in and out of the ward where the little skivvy washed the floors, and did all the dirty work involved in keeping the ward spotless, but he had never actually looked at the girl; and now he did not recognize her in Mrs Clayton. The bruises on her face had faded, the thick dark hair was shining clean, and instead of being scraped back and tied with a shoestring it lay back in deep waves from her brow into a heavy chignon on the nape of her neck. She was wearing the blue dress and bonnet. Although far from elegant, she looked respectable, modest, and capable. A very suitable person, in fact, to take charge of the crippled soldier, had it not been for her extreme youth.

However, there was nothing the doctor could do about it. His instructions had been to hand the men over to their families wherever possible, and there was no doubt that this young woman was Clayton's wife. He went downstairs to tell Sister Ramsbottom that Mrs Clayton had come to collect her husband, and asked her to see that he was prepared for the journey. A suitcase containing his clothes had already been handed to the orderly.

Astonished at this turn of events, Sister Ramsbottom herself assisted the crippled man into the clothes John Oatis had provided, and settled him into the sturdy, second-hand wheelchair Liz had found for him. She pushed the chair out to the hall, where the solicitor and Liz waited, to the cheers of the other men in the ward. All the formalities had been attended to. Elizabeth Clayton had signed her name painstakingly, but legibly, on the necessary documents, and they were ready to go. John Oatis did not want to loiter; he was not sure that, given a little time to think, Dr Mansfield might not yet find reason to refuse Edward Clayton's release.

The doctor had not recognized Liz, and Nurse Harris was occupied at the far end of the ward and had not even seen her, but Sister Ramsbottom knew her the instant her astounded eyes fell on the slender figure. For a moment she could not believe it.

'Sister, I'd like you to meet my wife,' Edward Clayton said, turning in the chair to see her reaction. Sister Ramsbottom was staring incredulously, her mouth open. She snapped it shut.

'Liz!' she exclaimed.

'Elizabeth Clayton, ma'am,' Edward said quietly.

Liz had dropped her eyes, and was gazing nervously at the floor.

Sister Ramsbottom was basically a kind-hearted woman, and had been shocked when the little ward-maid had come in with the evidence of her step-father's mistreatment on her face. There was little she could do about it; she had urged the girl to leave home and find somewhere else to live, but realized that this was more easily said than done, and the mute young woman might be no more at risk in her mother's house than she would be in some dingy boarding house somewhere. Her situation had been wretched and without hope; yet here she was, in an attractive dress and bonnet, with a husband and protector (albeit a useless one), and a new life in front of her. Common sense warned Sister Ramsbottom that the girl was being used, and she would have a hard life with this maimed man, if he recovered from his wounds at all. But at least she had been taken out of that filthy slum in which she lived, and away from the violence she had no way of combating. The change could only be for the better.

Sister Ramsbottom stepped forward and gave her hand to the bride. She smiled at her, a smile of congratulation and sincere good wishes.

'I'm delighted to meet you, Mrs Clayton,' she said steadily. 'I hope you and your husband will be very happy. I'll be leaving here within the next few days,' she added, 'but if you want to get in touch with me, letters will be forwarded on. And I'll be at the Nurses' Rest Home, Barminster, for the next two weeks.'

Edward Clayton looked surprised, but appreciative. He had not expected any offer of support, lukewarm though it might be, from this quarter. The Sister further surprised him by insisting on giving Liz some items of equipment they would need, including a pair of crutches.

'Thank you, Sister,' he said. John Oatis put the warm rug over his knees, and pushed him through the door, down the ramp, and into the drive.

As they turned towards the gates a light chaise, drawn by two fine bay horses, swept into the drive and drew up in front of the mansion. John had to pull the chair to the side to let it go by. Sitting under the hood, out of the wind, was a tall, elderly man and a smartly dressed young woman.

Matron herself came out to welcome the visitors.

'Sir Rupert – so kind of you to come and see us,' Matron greeted him warmly. 'And Miss Grant. I would have thought you had seen enough of this place for the time being, my dear. Now do come in out of the cold – I have coffee waiting for us in my office.'

Miss Grant was staring down the drive after the blue-clad girl and the young man pushing the wheelchair.

'Matron – wasn't that O'Malley in the chair? Has he been discharged?'

'Well – not exactly, Miss Grant. A wife turned up and he sort of discharged himself. As she was ready to accept responsibility for him, we had no choice but to let him go. But there's no need for you to concern yourself, my dear – come in and get warm.'

Harriet Grant turned to the elderly gentleman who stood by her side. 'Come on, Uncle Rupert – I'll show you what I've been doing for the past year.' They went inside, and the people making their way down the drive were forgotten.

John Oatis pushed the chair through the gates and into the road. The wind was cold, and Edward pulled the thick muffler closer round his throat. The tweed cap protected his head, for his grey hair was hacked so short his scalp was exposed.

Elizabeth Clayton walked beside them, carrying the crutches Sister Ramsbottom had insisted on giving them, taking little skips now and then to keep up with John's longer legs. Seldom has a bride started out on her married life with more determination to be a good wife, more hope for the future, and more blind faith in her new husband's honour and integrity.

She felt like a leaf in the wind, tossed from one place to another, without any choice; but for once the wind was blowing to her advantage. Life was beginning anew for Liz, and she was determined to live up to the trust that Edward Clayton had invested in her. She knew that their life was not going to be easy, but it could not be worse than the past she had now put behind her. Despite the bitter cold and the threatening clouds, she had a warm feeling in her heart. Her only fear was that Edward might yet succumb to his wounds; as she hurried along the road she sent a heartfelt prayer winging to heaven that he would be proved right in believing that in time, fresh air and good food would put him on the road to recovery.

Chapter Seven

'This good lady of yours,' John told Edward, 'had me out and about this morning at cockcrow – long before the usual time a solicitor begins the day. She's certainly been busy since you last saw her! She's found the necessary goods to furnish your cottage and supply the larder, hired a carter, and arranged for the goods, and you, to be hauled down to Forestwidden this afternoon. I've just got to pick up the key to the cottage from the agent and pay the carter, and you can be on your way.' Having reached the outskirts of the town they were more protected from the wind by the surrounding buildings. John decreased his rapid pace, and they were able to talk as they walked.

'We've got a bit of business to see to first,' Edward reminded him. 'I'll have to give you a deed of attorney for the bank, and there's another document I want you to attend to for me.'

'Yes, that's why we're going to my office now,' John agreed. 'The bank manager's meeting us there to sort out the necessary documents. Incidentally, there won't be a lot left in the kitty when these bills are paid. I've had to pay three months' rent in advance. But there should be enough to live in reasonable comfort with your pension and the interest from your bonds.'

'I'm sure Liz will manage to keep the bills down – won't you, Mrs Clayton?' Edward smiled at the girl, who gave him a timid smile in return, and nodded. 'I'm going to need some clothes, John –'

'Oh, Mrs Clayton has already seen to that!' he was told.

'She and her mother have bought everything you are likely to need for a while, anyway. Not all new, I'm afraid – Mrs Spragg told me that would be unnecessary extravagance! The biggest expenditure was at the chemist's shop. There are enough bandages and medical supplies to equip a small hospital. I'm told there's a good doctor in the village, so we'll see how you get on. Here we are – my office.' He stopped and opened the door of a handsome building fronting on to the square, and with some difficulty manoeuvred the heavy wheelchair up one step and into the entrance hall. A middle-aged woman was sitting at a desk, typing on a very noisy machine. She looked up, and smiled.

'Ah, the young man from the Soldiers' Hospital!' she exclaimed. 'I'm glad to see you managed to abduct him, Mr John. I'll bring some tea through to your office – you'll be ready for it after that walk in the cold, I expect.'

'Thank you, Miss MacFarlane – and bring Mr Billings in as soon as he arrives, will you, please.' John pushed the chair through to an office at the back of the building, overlooking a yard. Liz followed quietly, looking about her curiously. John placed a chair by the desk for Liz, but Edward Clayton spoke before she was seated.

'John, have we enough in the kitty to get a few things for Liz?'

'Yes, indeed, as long as she doesn't want silks and velvets!'

'Can we give her some cash to get a few things for herself while we go through our business?'

'Right. Here you are, Mrs Clayton.' He pulled out his wallet and handed the girl a few notes. 'Back in three quarters of an hour, right?'

Edward looked up at the surprised girl.

'Get whatever you need to wear in the house,' he instructed her. 'I don't want to see you in those grey rags you wore at the hospital ever again, understand? I want to see you in something cheerful!'

70

Liz nodded, smiled her thanks, and hurried out. Edward turned to John Oatis.

'And I want you to draw me up a will, without delay. Just in case – well, in case this damn leg gets the better of me yet. The girl has to be taken care of.'

By the time Liz got back, a large parcel wrapped in brown paper under her arm, the business had all been taken care of. The bank manager had called, witnessed Edward's signature on several documents, and arranged an account into which his pension could be paid, and on which he could draw. John was to pay his rent, and look after his interests. After John's account had been paid, and he had been reimbursed for the expenses he had met on Edward's behalf, just over one hundred and forty pounds would remain in the bank account; little enough, but sufficient to give Edward Clayton a little security.

John treated them to a good meal at the Golden Eagle Hotel, which was unbelievable luxury to Liz; and then they were ready to make the fourteen-mile journey to Forestwidden. As arranged, waiting for them in the yard behind John Oatis's office was an open cart, loaded with furniture and household goods, and covered with a tarpaulin. At the front a wooden plank bench provided seating for the driver and two passengers. Two heavy horses were between the shafts. There was no sign of the driver.

Edward stared at the vehicle in silence. He turned to John Oatis and, making no attempt to hide his chagrin, asked bitterly if he was expected to travel fourteen miles sitting on that bench? 'You'd need a crane to hoist me up there, to begin with,' he said sourly.

Liz ran to the cart, nimbly climbed on to the seat, and turned back part of the tarpaulin. Lying across the width of the cart was a thick mattress with several pillows piled at one end. Edward was gazing at the arrangement in silence

71

when the carter appeared, followed by a second brawny fellow.

'Ready, mate?' he asked cheerfully, and climbed up on to the seat. Before Edward had time to protest, he was picked up by the second man, lifted up to the carter, and laid on the mattress. Liz quickly covered him with the rug, and looked at him anxiously, mutely asking for his approval. John Oatis, meanwhile, stood back and watched proceedings from a safe distance, grinning. Edward lay back and closed his eyes.

'I feel like a bloody fool,' he muttered. 'John, thanks for your help. I don't know how you managed to find the time to get through all the work involved in a few days. You can't know how much I appreciate your assistance.'

'Think nothing of it, old man,' John Oatis said, embarrassed. 'A young solicitor starting out has to do all he can to drum up business! Just take good care of yourself – my clients are few and far between, as yet, and I value their good health!'

Liz settled herself on the wooden seat. The chair was hoisted on to the back of the cart, and John Oatis came forward to say farewell.

'I gave you the key?' he checked with Liz. She nodded. 'Off you go, then, and I'll see you again soon. I'll come to the cottage. Goodbye – and good luck!'

The carter gave the word to the horses, and they trundled out of the yard into the road. As he waved them out of sight John Oatis wondered bleakly if he would see his client alive again.

'I'm Jack Johnson,' the carter remarked cheerfully. He already knew that Liz was a mute, and as Edward did not reply, he lapsed into silence. Presently he began to sing old folksongs, which Liz enjoyed hearing, and apparently so did the horses. Soon they were clear of the town, and bowling along country lanes. Within minutes, despite the jolting of the cart, Edward was asleep. He was extremely tired, and glad to rest. When they reached the outskirts of the Great Forest Liz gazed about her with interest; she did not remember being this far out of Barminster before. The great oak and beech trees were bare of leaves at this time of the year, but she was delighted to see a few of the forest ponies grazing in one of the clearings. Had she known it, they passed within a few hundred yards of the hunting lodge where her new husband's grandfather was staying for the remainder of the hunting season. Sir Rupert's son Arthur was planning to take up residence at Barminster Abbey when it had been refurbished and returned to its former glory. But Edward slept easy, ignorant of all this; he didn't wake up until they turned off the main road, some hours later, and trundled slowly down a rutted farm lane. It was still bitterly cold, and the track was frozen; otherwise the cart could not have got through the mud.

Fortunately, the carter knew the district. He had made deliveries to Willoughby's Farm several times, or they would never have found the cottage. They passed the farmhouse, and the lane deteriorated into a steep cart track between tall trees. Finally they made a U-turn, and ran down almost to the sea-shore. The old cottage stood back a little from the sandy beach, in a small bay, with a high cliff behind it. Rocky headlands jutted out at each end of the bay into the English Channel, and waves broke over the sand. At the eastern end a tall stand of trees grew almost to the shore, with an old boathouse nearby. There was no fence or hedge in front of the cottage; the neglected garden was edged by the beach. The stony track petered out more or less at the door of the old stone building, and a half-frozen little brook ran over the cliff into the sea just beyond.

Liz jumped down from the cart and stared wonderingly

about her. She did not remember having seen the sea before; her mother had left Portsmouth, where she was born, when she was no more than a toddler. She gazed with awe at the stormy waters. Dusk was beginning to fall, and the wind was rising. She pulled her shawl more closely about her shoulders. For a moment fear of the future touched her; this place was so different to anything she remembered. Could she turn this cottage into a home? Could she nurse this stranger, her husband, back to health? She stared out to sea, shivering in the cold wind.

Edward raised himself on one elbow, and looked at the cottage. It was as he had remembered it, perhaps a little more dilapidated; several of the roof-slates were missing, and the window of the lean-to room was broken. But he felt he had come home.

He looked out towards the sea. The tide was low, about to turn. Perhaps this too was an omen.

Now they had another problem: unloading the cart. The brawny Jack Johnson soon had the tarpaulin off, and began to lift things down.

Liz hurried to the door of the cottage and unlocked it with the key John Oatis had given her. The first thing she saw was a rat, its red eyes gleaming in the dim light. She retreated hastily, gathering up her blue serge skirts, and ran back to the cart with more speed than decorum.

She helped the carter unload the smaller items until they had unearthed the broom, a lamp, and a bundle wrapped in a coarse black shawl. She took these back to the cottage and went in, gingerly stepping through the accumulated rubbish on the floor, her eyes darting nervously about in search of vermin. In case of any further encounters, she was determined to have a head start.

By the light of the lamp she climbed the steep ladder to the loft. Apparently this had been used for storage, for a few sacks half-full of grain and a pile of dry straw lay in one corner. There was a small window high up near the apex of the ceiling, but as it faced the east, it let in little light at dusk. The walls of the loft were only three feet high at the sides under the eaves, but rose to about eight in the centre. The end letting on to the main room was not walled; a wooden partition of waist height gave the loft comparative privacy.

Liz stripped off the blue dress and jacket, and produced a coarse black calico dress from her bundle. She got into this, tied a kerchief round her head and an apron round her waist, and started work with the broom. By the time the carter had all the smaller items piled up round the door, she had swept the worst of the dirt of three years from the flagstones in the main room.

Meantime, Edward Clayton could do nothing but watch them, seething with impotent rage at his uselessness. He could not even climb down from the cart unaided. He could not see for the life of him how he was to get down into the wheelchair waiting below, even with the help of Jack Johnson.

Now another man appeared on the scene. He came down some rough steps cut into the cliff about thirty yards from the back of the cottage. At this point the cliff was not so high as further along, and a thick hedge of thornbushes ran along the top. The man, middle-aged, square-built and with the red cheeks of one who spent most of his time out of doors, was wearing rough tweeds and heavy boots. He stood watching the new arrivals for a moment in the fast-fading light.

'That you, Jack?' he called.

'Aye, Mr Willoughby,' the carter replied, a note of relief in his voice. 'I've brung new tenant to 'Oney Beck Cottage. 'E's in back o' cart.'

'In the back of the cart?' Henry Willoughby exclaimed.

He peered at Edward in the semi-darkness. 'What the dickens is he doing there?'

'Nothing, that's what,' Edward said bitterly. 'I'm a useless bloody cripple, and I can't even get myself off this damn mattress!'

'Then I'd better lend a hand, or you'll be out here all night,' the newcomer said cheerfully, and fell to with a will.

Liz turned her attention to lighting the rusty old black kitchen range. She had found a few pieces of driftwood among the debris in the big room, and there was a small heap of coke in the storeroom. As soon as she had the fire going, she lit a second oil-lamp and a hurricane lamp. The two men lifted Edward down, put him into the wheelchair, and brought him into the cottage.

The first thing he saw was the bright fire in the old range. To his dismay he felt tears of weakness and grief for his grandparents and his lost childhood coursing down his cheeks. He closed his eyes and turned his head away, retreating into the sullen silence he had lived in for so long at the hospital. He was ashamed that the two strong, healthy men might see his tears. Liz saw him turn his face away from the light, and instinctively understood his need for privacy. There was nothing she could do to help her husband, so she ignored his misery and continued with her work, keeping the other two men out of his way until he had himself in hand.

Henry Willoughby had seen the cart passing the farmhouse, and wondered where it could be going, as there was nothing down the track except the old disused cottage. As soon as he had finished the milking he made his way to Honey Beck Bay by way of the fields and the cliff path, which was considerably shorter than the track the cart had to take. Now he helped Jack finish unloading the cart, two of them making light work of lifting the scanty furniture into the main room, and saw the carter on his way, the tired horses dragging the lightened cart up the steep track. Jack had two lanterns, but they did little to light the path. He had another load to pick up nearby tomorrow, and was not returning to Barminster tonight. He had arranged to spend the night with a cousin in Forestwidden.

The farmer helped Liz bring the rest of the goods into the house. Most of the smaller items were deposited haphazardly in the storeroom; she would sort them out tomorrow. Willoughby was curious about this strange couple. The crippled grey-haired man appeared to be years older than the girl, who hadn't spoken a word, and the man sat by the fire in sullen silence. As they worked together the farmer realized the girl was mute. She replied to his questions with a nod or a shake of the head. Now and then she shot a worried, anxious glance in the direction of the man in the chair. Was she his daughter, or perhaps employed as a housekeeper?

Edward was in a sort of trance. His legs were giving him a lot of pain. Heartily sick of his uselessness, he had been embarrassed to see the two men and a girl doing the work that he felt he should be doing, and then making a fool of himself by giving way to tears, he had withdrawn into a private world of frustration and pain. The jolting of the cart had racked his debilitated body; the irritation of the rash had driven him almost insane; and the unaccustomed activity and excitement had brought back his headache. He closed his eyes and retreated into a state of oblivion.

They carried in the final teachest containing kitchen stores, and put it down near the ancient built-in dresser at one side of the stove. Liz heaved a great sigh of relief, and smiled shyly at the farmer.

'Right, then, I'll be off,' he said awkwardly. 'If you'd like milk and eggs tomorrow, miss, walk up to the farm – it's not far if you follow the path over the fields, you'll find it easily, and the wife will be able to supply you.' Liz nodded to show she understood. Henry Willoughby went to the door. 'Goodnight, then, miss – goodnight, sir.'

Edward started, and looked up.

'Thank you, Mr – Willoughby? I'm sorry – I'm not feeling too well tonight. I appreciate your help. Goodnight, sir.'

Willoughby left, closing the door firmly behind him, and made his way back up the rough steps to the top of the cliff, where there was a small paddock. A steep bank at the far side, with a thick hedge, adjoined the road, and the little brook ran through one end of the field.

The moon was not out yet, but it was not completely dark, so he could see his way fairly clearly – although he knew the path so well he could have safely traversed it had the night been pitch black. He tramped through the long grass, his heavy boots sinking into the soft boggy ground round the brook. He thought about the strange couple as he walked. He had noticed the fading bruises on the girl's face, and when she had rolled back her sleeves he had seen more bruises on her arms. She had obviously taken a beating from someone recently, and he wondered if it had been from the man in the wheelchair. Looking back from the top of the cliff Willoughby could see the light shining through the windows of the cottage.

'That wretched girl's got her work cut out with that surly beggar,' he thought. 'God knows how she'll manage. I'll look in on them again soon and make sure they're all right. Thank the good Lord I'm hale and hearty – if I was in that poor devil's place I think I'd be ready to put an end to myself.' He made his way back to the farm where his wife had a good hot supper ready for him.

Chapter Eight

Liz made up the fire and put the kettle – filled earlier from the brook – on to boil. She made up the bed for Edward to retire as soon as he was ready. Sheets of strong unbleached twill, two new white blankets, and an eiderdown – not new, but clean; that should be enough to keep him warm. The kettle came to the boil and she made tea. She put bread and cheese, a large slab of fruit cake, and a bowl of fruit on the table. The room was warm now. The lamps and the firelight cast a pleasant glow over the few pieces of cheap furniture. In this light the stained walls and flaking paint were less noticeable. An icy draught blew under the door to the lean-to storeroom; the broken pane in the window allowed the full fury of the rising wind to penetrate the room.

Edward was dozing. Liz touched him on the arm to call him to the table. Taken by surprise, he nearly jumped out of the chair.

'Christ, woman – don't startle me like that!' he exclaimed angrily. Liz shrank back, sudden fear in her eyes. As Edward saw it a pang of conscience made him squirm; there was no need to take his ill-humour out on the girl. 'Sorry, Liz, but you startled me,' he said gruffly. 'Pour the tea, and let's eat. You must be starving – you've been working like a Trojan, while I've been sitting here like a useless log. First meal in our new home! Pity we haven't got some booze to drink a toast.'

Liz darted to the teachest, and triumphantly produced a half-bottle of whisky. Edward gave a shout of laughter, and held out his hand to her.

'Is there anything you've forgotten, girl? I think I chose a very fine wife, despite the shortage of suitable applicants! Let's have our supper first, and then we'll see what we can do with that bottle.'

When she had cleared the food away, and washed the dishes, Liz got out two glasses and poured them each a small drink. Edward finished his and held out his glass for more. She refilled it, and put the bottle away in the teachest, smiling anxiously and shaking her head. In her experience men who drank became violent, and she didn't think she could cope with that. Edward stared into the fire, sipping the whisky slowly. He didn't talk; he found it difficult to speak to a companion who never answered. When his glass was empty Liz finished her own, then stood up, and wheeled his chair towards the waiting bed. Edward looked down at his legs and then at the bed.

'Liz, I think this is where the fun begins,' he said wearily. 'Now we're going to find out just how good a nurse you are.' He undid the buttons of the tweed jacket and began to struggle out of it. Clumsily, she helped him. Then she pulled the shirt over his head. He sat in his thick woollen undershirt, sweating with the effort.

'Pull this thing off me and get me some water,' he said thickly. 'I want to wash – I feel filthy.' There was a pail of water on the back of the range. Liz poured some into a basin, and put it on the table. She brought soap and a towel, and wheeled him to the table. Then she pulled off the undershirt, and saw the fiery rash on his back. She gasped in dismay; it was angry and red, and in places had broken out in weeping, moist patches, almost like mould. The undershirt was stained with the discharge. Edward looked down at his chest; it was in the same state.

'Christ almighty!' he swore. 'I look as if I'm going rotten! It must be that woollen undershirt! Where the hell did you get it?'

She stared at him wide-eyed, terrified. She'd bought it this morning in the square. Hastily she showed him the label giving the name of the shop.

'New?' She nodded. 'Hell – it must be the wool.' He began to wash himself, splashing the water carelessly all over the table and the floor round about. He gave her the flannel and told her to wash his back. The cool water relieved the burning irritation, at least. She brought one of the blue-striped cotton nightshirts and slipped it over his head.

'Now for the difficult bit,' he said bleakly. 'How the devil am I to get these trousers off?'

Liz had already given this some thought. She wheeled him back to the side of the bed; then she brought one of the sturdy wooden chairs and placed it beside his wheelchair, with the back facing him. Kneeling, she removed his shoe and sock, put his foot on the floor, and, placing his two hands on the back of the wooden chair, gestured to him to stand on his one leg.

'Stand?' He glared at her. 'I can't stand – you know I bloody can't stand! What are you trying to do, woman? Kill me?'

Liz shook her head, tears starting to her eyes. But still she urged him to stand – willed him to stand, until with an oath he finally made the effort and took his weight on his one leg, holding firmly on to the back of the chair. Hastily she unbuttoned his trousers, and slid them to the ground, with his undergarments, modestly averting her eyes as she pulled the nightshirt down over him.

'You're right – I can stand,' he said, with a wry grin. 'Now all I've got to do is get into that bed. Thank God it's not one of those high ones the hospital uses!' Liz hastily pulled back the bedclothes. Still using the chair to steady himself, Edward turned his back to the bed, and let himself down until he was sitting on it. He dropped back against

81

the pillows. Liz lifted his legs on to the mattress and stood back smiling in triumph. He grinned at her, as pleased as she was with their joint efforts.

'Liz – I think we both deserve another drink,' he said weakly, and she went to retrieve the bottle.

By the time she had cleared up the spilled water on the table, folded his clothes carefully over the chair, and set the room to rights, he was asleep and gently snoring. She blew out the lamp on the table, collected a bundle wrapped in a shabby old patchwork quilt from the storeroom, and took the other lamp up the steps to the loft.

She spread the patchwork quilt on the pile of straw heaped up in one corner of the loft, after making sure it contained no rats. Soon she was in her thick flannel nightgown; she wrapped herself in a blanket, pulled one end of the quilt over her, blew out the lamp, and fell asleep within minutes.

A shaft of weak sunlight was filtering through the tiny window in the loft when Liz awoke, that first day in the cottage in Honey Beck Bay. Her makeshift bed had been surprisingly comfortable, although she would have slept well on the bare boards after that exhausting day. Although accustomed to rising early, she had slept later than usual. She lay quietly and looked at the homely loft-room, a happy smile on her face. This was her own room – hers alone. It was the first time she ever remembered waking in a room by herself. In the terrace house in Barminster she had shared a room with her three young brothers – they lay two at one end of a bed, one at the other, and she had a mattress on the floor under the window. Now her bed was a pile of straw, but it was warm, soft – and private. Liz turned over, the straw rustling under her, yawned, and stretched. She watched the motes of dust dancing in a ray of sunlight. Then she heard Edward's light snores interrupted by a snort, and started up; the snores resumed a moment later, and she relaxed. But she could not waste the day like this; reluctantly she rose, wrapping the coarse black shawl round her shoulders, and made her way quietly down the ladder.

Edward was still asleep. Making as little noise as possible, Liz made up the fire on the red embers, and put the kettle on to boil. Shivering, she made her way out to the brook to fill the bucket, which she then left on the back of the range to heat. But now she took a basin of cold water out to the storeroom and had a good wash before going back to the loft to dress. Despite the cold water, this was a real treat for Liz; in the overfilled house in Barminster, there had been nowhere she could wash in privacy. Every drop of water had to be carried from the pump at the end of the narrow street. Cleanliness was a luxury. Tonight, she told herself, she must leave the bucket to heat on the range overnight. There was a rusty old pump over the sink under the window, but all she had been able to extract from it had been a few rusty drops of water and an ominous gurgling noise. Until it was repaired she would have to carry water from the stream.

She carried the parcel she had bought at the shops yesterday up to her loft, and debated wearing one of the two new gingham dresses; but as she intended to spend most of the day scrubbing the cottage, she decided against, and pulled on the black calico again. However, with a brightly coloured gingham apron round her slender waist, and a red kerchief tied round the thick, dark hair, she thought hopefully Edward Clayton would not find her too depressing a sight. She descended the ladder again, and made the tea.

How to wake him? She had to avoid startling him, as she had yesterday, and risk his anger. She solved the problem by rattling the cups and spoons as she poured the tea.

Edward woke slowly. He had almost finished the whisky

last night, and had slept like a baby – the first really good night's rest he had had for months. He could hear the rattle of crockery, and as he regained consciousness for a moment he thought he was back in his childhood. He looked over at the range, half-expecting to see his grandmother there, and his grandfather at the table reading the big old bible, a chapter of which always started his day; but instead he saw the slender figure of his bride, intent on pouring tea from the big brown pot.

'Good morning,' he said formally, and she turned and smiled at him. Her cheeks were delicately rose-tinted, and her eyes a deep violet-blue in the pale face; the bruises were fading, but still marred the soft cheek. A strand of dark hair had escaped the kerchief, strayed across the brow, accenting the creaminess of her skin. For the first time Edward Clayton realized that this girl he had married could become a beauty, if she were not so thin and waif-like.

Liz brought his tea in a thick white cup. She took her own to the table, and sat gazing through the window for a few minutes while she drank it, watching the morning breeze chasing a few light clouds across the sky. Edward watched her from his bed, wondering what she was thinking. Was she regretting their hasty marriage? Did she intend to keep her side of their bargain?

The weak, wintry sun glinted on the waves breaking on the shore. The cottage garden, adjoining the beach, was on an incline, and there was no danger of their being washed out to sea in a storm. Edward remembered that as a boy he had sat in this room on a stormy night listening to the waves breaking, and an occasional spattering of spray on the windows; but the old stone cottage was strongly built, with walls nearly two feet thick, and could stand fast against the elements.

Liz prepared their breakfast, giving Edward a generous plateful of eggs and bacon – a great improvement, he reflected, on the lumpy, watery porridge the hospital had served!

After breakfast, Liz went to the storeroom and brought out an odd-looking wooden chair on casters. Up to now his personal needs had been served by a bottle supplied illicitly by Sister Ramsbottom. Now Liz removed the cushion on the seat of the chair and triumphantly revealed it as – a commode!

'By Jove, Liz – you seem to have thought of everything,' Edward grinned. 'All I have to do now is sit on the damn thing – and that's not going to be easy!' However, with her help, he managed it. She collected the water-bucket and went out to fetch more water, leaving him his privacy.

She took the opportunity to look at the cottage's sur-roundings. A short distance away, almost hidden behind some bushes, she found a wooden shed; this was the water-closet. Part of the tin roof had blown away, and the wooden seat was broken, but it was serviceable, she decided thank-fully. Liz hoped it wouldn't rain before she managed to get the roof repaired! She walked back to the brook and filled the bucket. She would need a lot of water today to get the cottage scrubbed ...

Back in the cottage Liz set a basin of warm water on the table, with soap and towels, a razor and a small mirror. She left Edward in the wheelchair to deal with his ablutions while she swept the floor thoroughly and prepared to scrub it. She opened the bottom cupboards of the dresser to brush them out – and leapt back in dismay. An enormous brown rat sat in a heap of paper and straw, looking back at her with as great a shock as she looked at it, before fleeing through a hole in the side of the cupboard.

Intent on scraping the lather from his face, Edward failed to see the rat, but he heard Liz gasp, and saw her leap backwards.

85

'What's up now?' he demanded. Liz pointed to the cupboard. Edward manoeuvred his chair round to a position where he could see what she was pointing at. 'Oh – a rat's nest,' he said calmly. Some of the places he had been in South Africa had been overrun with rats, and they held no fears for him. But Liz was shaken, and she attacked the cupboard with a brush and pan, ready to leap and run if she saw another of the horrid creatures. 'We'll have to find something to stop up that hole,' Edward commented. He finished his shave, and wheeled himself back to the bed.

'Liz, go and get the dressings,' he said abruptly. 'We'll have to get these bandages dealt with before I get dressed. Go on, girl! Fetch them!'

This was the moment she had been dreading. She went to the storeroom and brought out a wooden chest, about the size of an orange box, with a solid, close-fitting lid. It was heavy for her to carry. She put it on the floor beside the bed and washed her hands thoroughly – as she had seen the nurses at the hospital do before they touched the dressings. When the nurses were dealing with the wounds they had always drawn the curtains round the beds and Liz had never actually seen the wounded limbs or the dressings; but she had watched, and taken note of, all the careful preparations. Now, she brought a rubber sheet and spread it on the bed, and helped Edward lie back on it. From the box she took a small metal basin, which she filled with water that had already boiled and been allowed to cool. Then she lifted the nightshirt and exposed his legs.

The bandages, both on the ankle and the stump of the other leg, were stained and discoloured. With trembling hands she began to unwind the yards of bandage from the ankle. After a minute Edward swore as it began to stick, sat up, and pushed her away.

'I'll do that myself,' he snapped curtly, and started pulling at the bandage, gritting his teeth. After several minutes only the lint dressing remained over the wound. This had stuck fast. As he pulled at it the colour left his face, and his hands began to tremble.

'I can't do it,' he grated finally, and fell back on to the pillows. Fighting back her fear of what she would discover, Liz put a second small metal basin under the leg and began gently to lave the dressing with warm water. After several minutes she left it to soak under a warm, dripping towel, and began to unwind the bandage on the stump. It was nearly half an hour before she had gently soaked and bathed both dressings off. Edward's nightshirt was soaked in sweat.

Both wounds were raw and angry. Liz looked at them, her face almost as white as Edward's. She had no experience of nursing, and had little idea of what to do next. Yesterday morning she and her mother had gone to a chemist, where Mrs Spragg explained their problem, and he had supplied the items he thought she might need, giving her some advice on using them; but now she was faced with the raw, suppurating flesh, she was frightened to touch it, fearful of making things worse.

'Get on with it, get on with it!' Edward snapped through clenched teeth. Liz looked at him hopelessly. 'Christ! I'll do the bloody things myself!' he swore, sitting up.

In fact he had never seen the injuries without their dressings for himself; the nurses had made sure of that. Now he struggled into a position where he could see the wounds – and fainted away like a girl, almost toppling out of bed as his senses left him. Liz grabbed him and laid him back on the pillows.

She turned back to the box, scrabbling through the supplies to find something that might give her a clue as to how to proceed. She found a bottle of strong disinfectant, poured a little into one of the bowls and bathed both wounds with that. Then she powdered them lightly with boracic powder, and left them. As she dropped the discarded bandages into the fire Edward opened his eyes and groaned.

Liz flew back to the bed, and put her hand on his chest to prevent him sitting up, shaking her head vehemently.

'I think I fainted,' he said shakily. She nodded. 'Have you finished –' He looked down and saw the wounds still uncovered. 'God Almighty, woman – you could have finished the job while I was out cold,' he said bitterly. She shook her head, pushed him back on the pillows, and mimed fanning air on to the wounds. Frowning, he watched her. He tried to sit up again; again she pushed him back, and waved her hand over the stump.

'I don't know what the hell you're trying to tell me,' he said hopelessly. 'I'm going to have to teach you to write. This is ridiculous.' He tried to pull the nightshirt over his legs; she snatched at it, and pushed it up again, wrapping it round him, but leaving the stump and the leg exposed. Suddenly his face cleared.

'Ah! You want to leave it open – to let it seal!' Edward looked at her thoughtfully. Liz beamed back at him, delighted that he had understood. 'Well, if there's no dressing, it can't stick. They've tried everything else, so let's try that. For an hour or two, anyway.' He relaxed back on the pillows. 'I suppose that puts paid to my intentions of getting dressed. What are you planning to do for my entertainment now?'

Liz mimed scrubbing, and waved at the floor. He grimaced.

'Then I might as well stay here – I'll only be in your way. How about a cup of tea first?'

Liz put the kettle on, and got out the scrubbing brush and some rags. She had scrubbed the dresser out and begun on the floor when the kettle came to the boil. She made their tea, using the last of the milk, but didn't stop working to drink her own. By the time the big tin clock on the mantelshelf said eleven the flagstoned floor was spotless. She pointed out a couple of mouse-holes in the skirting board.

'We'll have to do something about those right away,' Edward said gloomily. 'They should be stopped up with cement, but I can't do it, and I doubt if you can ... I'll make a list of the jobs that need doing, and we'll see what can be done about them. John Oatis said that the agents would pay "any reasonable maintenance expenses". I wonder what they will consider reasonable? Have we got any writing paper, Liz?'

Liz shook her head apologetically.

'A pen? Pencil? Oh, well – that can be the first thing on the list that I can't write without them!'

The dresser was on the right of the range, in the recess between the back wall and the chimney. In the wall beside it, built out behind the back of the cottage, was a big larder, fitted with wide shelves. It took the rest of the morning for the girl to scrub both of these to her satisfaction, before she unpacked the boxes containing their food supplies, crockery and cutlery. Even when the things were all set out, the shelves were pretty bare, but a few bright plates made a cheerful splash of colour on the dresser.

For lunch they had bread and cheese, and an apple each. Tea was made with milk from a tin. Edward tried it and grimaced.

'Tastes like the stuff we used to have in South Africa,' he complained. Liz looked at him apologetically. 'All right, I know you can't help it! But that doesn't mean I have to like it!'

She still would not let him get out of bed; she looked at the wounds several times, and seemed satisfied. After lunch she mimed that it was time he had a sleep.

'Sleep! Heavens, girl – I've done nothing to make me tired!' he said indignantly; but she took away his pillows, so that he was forced to lie flat, and drew the sheet up over him. So far as possible, she intended to keep to the hospital routine. Within ten minutes he had dozed off and begun to snore. Liz changed her light slippers for a pair of sturdy boots, wrapped herself in her warm shawl, and quietly let herself out of the cottage.

The early sunshine had given way to a cloudy afternoon. It was cold and windy, but yesterday's frost had gone. Moving quickly to keep herself warm, Liz scrambled up the rough steps in the cliff, and found the path above. She followed this in the direction Mr Willoughby had indicated the previous day. She lifted her skirts as she crossed the boggy area, but got them stained with yellow clay a little further on where she had to negotiate a muddy bank. Presently she found a stile, on the far side of which a herd of brown cows stared at her curiously.

Living in Barminster Liz had never before come into contact with a herd of cows – or even one cow, come to that. It took a lot of courage to cross that field. But soon she saw the farmhouse in the distance, and hurried on. The grass was very damp, and in places the cows had trodden the ground into a muddy morass. By the time she reached the farmyard she was wet to the knees, and her dress was thick with mud around the hem.

Henry Willoughby came out of a barn and saw her hesitating at the gate.

'Hello there! I wondered if you'd come,' he called. 'Come in – come into the house and meet the wife!' He led the way into the farmhouse. Liz followed, looking nervously at the chickens and ducks they had to bypass. A big collie dog came frisking out of the barn and ran up to her. She held her ground, but the farmer could see that she was terrified.

'Rover won't hurt you, girl – don't you worry about him.' Willoughby opened the back door, and they went into the kitchen, scraping the mud off their boots on a metal grid at the doorstep. Liz was amazed to see two new-born lambs lying in a clothes basket in front of the kitchen range.

Mrs Willoughby was a fat, smiling little woman, her red hair turning grey. She had heard all about the new tenants at the cottage from her husband, and knew that Liz was mute. She welcomed her guest cheerfully and offered her a cup of tea. Liz shook her head, pointed at the clock, and pointed at the door.

'Ah – you're in a hurry – I guess you've come for some milk?' Liz nodded gratefully, and pulled a clean bottle and some coins out of her pocket. She had a little change left from the notes John Oatis had given her yesterday.

'Never mind the money – I'll not miss a little milk,' Henry Willoughby told her as his wife filled the bottle from a huge pitcher in the larder. Liz held out the money again anxiously. 'Well, I'll tell you what – I'll supply you with milk, and you can pay me at the end of the week. Right?' Liz smiled and nodded. His wife came back from the larder with the bottle and a paper bag full of something.

'Henry told me you'd just moved in, and I guessed you'd be pretty busy today, so I made a few extra scones while I was baking this morning. There's a piece of my fresh butter in there too. I hope you and your father enjoy them.' Liz looked startled. Mrs Willoughby looked puzzled. 'He's not your father? Oh – you work for him perhaps – a sort of housekeeper?' Henry had also told her about the narrow bed he had helped Jack set up for the man in the wheelchair.

Now Liz's face was a picture of confusion. She did not know how to explain her situation. It didn't occur to her to pull off the thick woollen mittens she was wearing and show her wedding ring. So when Henry Willoughby, mindful of her plea that she was in a hurry, opened the back door to let her out, she left them to speculate on the strange household at Honey Beck Cottage. A gaunt, morose man of perhaps forty-odd, by his appearance, and a young girl who had recently suffered a beating – what sort of arrangement was that?

Rover accompanied her a little way on her return journey, but turned and ran back home when they came to the first of the three stiles. Edward was still asleep as she quietly let herself into the house. Liz stood for a moment, watching him sleep. His face was gaunt and lined, the skin an unhealthy greyish colour. Could good food and fresh air restore him to normal health? Would she be able to tend those dreadful wounds until they healed? She sighed, and turned away. She put the milk and scones on the table, and crept silently up the ladder to her loft. She took with her one of the wooden crates the kitchen goods had been in. This she set beside her makeshift bed, and put her clothes tidily inside.

She took off the muddy dress and put on one of the new ones, a pretty gingham check in lavender and grey. She combed her long hair and wound it into a tidy chignon, securing it with several large metal hairpins. She crept downstairs again and rinsed the hem of the black dress in the sink under the window. Edward woke up and lay watching her. The walk in the cold wind had brought the bright colour to her cheeks. The dark hair – nearly black, but with a glint of auburn – waved back from her brow. The dress brought out the colour of those enormous eyes.

He watched her from half-closed eyes as she moved about the room. Her movements had a quiet grace about them; she was a pleasure to watch. Indeed, she was almost beautiful.

How had he failed to see it when she had been working about the ward at Barminster Abbey? He recalled the drab, drooping figure of the little ward-maid. Dull, white-faced, the lank, lifeless hair dragged back and tied with a shoe-string. Lack-lustre eyes, and an apathetic, hopeless expression. Could it be the same girl?

On the morning of her wedding day, Liz had been to the public baths and not only bathed her body, but had spent some of her precious wages on a shampoo for her hair. Usually it was washed about once in three months. If you lived in an overcrowded slum, this was a great luxury. Now it was truly a crowning glory, no longer drab and lifeless. And hope for the future had given her expression a new glow, putting an unaccustomed spring in her step. He had given her this new beauty; but Edward did not realize that he was responsible for the blossoming of this gentle flower.

All he knew was that he had trapped this lovely girl into marrying a crippled wreck; and he wondered bitterly how long it would take her to grow to resent the hard work and unpleasant duties this entailed. And how long it would take her to learn to hate him.

Chapter Nine

Henry Willoughby and his wife Ada were good-natured country people, busy with their own hard-working lives, but not above taking an interest in their neighbours; and they spent a considerable time speculating on the relationship of the new tenants at Honey Beck Bay. When another day had passed without sight nor sign of the girl, the farmer decided to drop into the cottage to make sure that all was well with them. Driving the cows out to a field near Honey Beck in the middle of the morning, he took with him a basket containing a large cider-bottle of milk, a dozen fresh eggs, and a cabbage freshly cut from his vegetable patch. He put a couple of recent newspapers on top to cover them.

The weather had improved, and the sun was shining from a cloudless sky when he reached the cottage at about eleven in the morning, and rapped loudly on the door. The door opened a moment later, and the girl stood there, white-faced, looking scared out of her wits.

'Who the devil's that?' Edward Clayton demanded from his bed. He sounded unreasonably irate – as if he had been interrupted whilst at a particularly difficult task. The girl stood back, so that he could see the visitor.

'It's me, Henry Willoughby,' the farmer said loudly, stepping into the cottage; and stopping short. Edward was lying on his bed on the rubber sheet, in his nightshirt, the stump and the wounded ankle exposed. His eyes were bright with fever. Liz had been bathing his wounds with warm disinfectant water when they heard the knock on the door. The farmer was shocked at the sight of the injured limbs. It crossed his mind that if an animal of his, on the farm, had injuries like this, he would have it put down rather than let it suffer unnecessarily. They were, in fact, looking better than they had two days earlier, but they were still a fearsome sight to come upon without warning.

'My God!' Willoughby exclaimed. 'I'm sorry, Mr Clayton – I didn't mean to disturb you – can I do anything to help?'

'Come in, and close the door,' Edward said wearily. 'No, thanks, Liz can manage – she's nearly finished for the moment. Come on, girl, get on with it, and then make our visitor a cup of tea.'

'I brought a few things – I thought you could use some fresh milk and eggs,' the farmer said apologetically, setting down the basket and sitting at the table in one of the two upright, hard wooden chairs. He looked round the room. It was spotlessly clean and tidy; the few bright plates on the dresser added a homely touch to the otherwise spartan surroundings. Liz went back to bathing the wounds, and Edward lay back and relaxed, glad to have someone to talk to. It helped considerably to have something to take his mind off the painful performance. He and the farmer discussed the weather for a few minutes, and when Liz had finished she removed the rubber sheet, pulled a light cover up over Edward's legs, and began to make the tea.

'I brought you a couple of newspapers,' Willoughby said. 'I thought you might like to catch up on some of the news – the local paper's there. A namesake of yours, the Honourable Arthur Clayton, is being put forward for the Barminster Conservative candidate, I see. His father is Sir Rupert, our landlord. No relation, I suppose, Mr Clayton?' There was a moment's silence before Edward answered.

'I suppose if we traced our antecedents back far enough, Mr Willoughby, we'd find that most of us are related to each other somewhere,' he said calmly. 'But I don't think that Sir Rupert or his son would acknowledge any relationship I might claim. I doubt if it would bring my rent down, anyway.'

'No, I don't suppose it would,' Willoughby agreed. 'Anyway, you may like to read the papers – it'll pass the time, at any rate. Now, I'm going to Forestwidden this afternoon. I wondered if there's anything I could bring for you, or for – for the young lady. It's a long way for her to walk, but if she wants she can come in the trap with me and the missis.'

At the range, making the tea, Liz was shaking her head.

'Thank you for the offer,' Edward said, 'but she says she'd rather not, this time. But if you could get one or two things for me, I'd be most obliged.'

'Just give me a list, and I'll see to it,' Willoughby assured him. Edward gave a rueful grin.

'That's where the trouble starts, friend – I've no pen, pencil, or notepaper to make a list!' he admitted.

'Well, here's a pencil,' Willoughby grinned, pulling a stub from his pocket. 'Paper – there's a paper bag in the basket with a few eggs in it.'

Liz brought their tea while they made the list. She ran to the storeroom and brought in a piece of coke, making signs that they needed more. She had been eking out their meagre supply by burning driftwood in the range, gathered from the beach. The farmer said he'd arrange for some to be sent.

'I don't suppose you know of a useful handyman who can do some work for us?' Edward asked.

'Probably,' Willoughby replied. 'What sort of work?'

'Repair the roof, fix the pump, put glass in a broken window, and stop up mouse and rat holes!' Edward said promptly. 'Oh, and before long I want the cottage whitewashed, inside –'

Liz was shaking her head violently, and making signs that she would do that.

'Well, the ceiling, anyway. Liz can do the rest if she wants

96

to. I guess that would be best, anyway – we've no money to spare for luxuries, but we should be able to afford a few pots of whitewash! I wish we could afford to splash out on curtains and a carpet, or at least a few rugs. But even if I had the money, Liz can't get to a town to buy them so I guess we'll have to do without for the moment.' The two men glanced at the bare windows. Liz mimed drawing non-existent curtains, and pulled her shawl closer round her shoulders. 'Yes, it would make it warmer,' Edward said wryly. Liz nodded vigorously.

Willoughby looked thoughtful.

'Next week, on Tuesday, I'm going to a farm sale – you'll find it advertised in that paper. I'm after some troughs for the cattle, but the contents of the house are to be sold as well. I wonder – would the little lady like to come with us and see if there's anything useful there?'

'How about that, Liz?' Edward suggested. Liz looked doubtful. She pointed to him, and then to herself, and then to the door and the clock. 'Hmmmm ... No, you can't leave me for half the day or more,' he agreed.

'I'll talk to the wife and see if she has any suggestions,' the farmer said.

Liz picked up the empty bucket and went out to fetch more water.

'Look, Mr Clayton,' Willoughby said awkwardly, as soon as the girl was out of earshot, 'I saw that leg – d'you want a doctor to take a look at it?'

Edward gave him a sharp look.

'Doctor? No!' he refused explosively. 'Doctors have nearly killed me over the past six months! But I'll tell you what – is there a gypsy camp still over in the valley to the east? There used to be an old woman, Old Meg – but I suppose she'd be dead by now...'

The farmer stared at him, surprised.

'I thought you were a stranger to Forestwidden,' he

remarked. 'The gypsies aren't here yet – they come for the horse-sales in the forest, and they won't be here for another fortnight or so. But I saw Old Meg with them last year. She may still be alive – some of the women live to a ripe old age. We usually know when they arrive – we have to keep everything that isn't nailed down locked up!' But he looked far from happy. 'Look, never mind Old Meg. Let me ask Dr Maine to come and take a look –'

'I'll see no more doctors!' Edward said savagely. Suddenly he was terribly tired. The fever had flared up again this morning, and Liz had had to give him a bed-bath before dealing with the dressings. These were much easier to remove now that the wounds were left open most of the day, but it was still an ordeal for both of them. He had been awake most of the night with the irritation from the rash on his back, which was always worse when his temperature went up. Just before the farmer had arrived he had snarled at Liz because the disinfectant water made his wounds sting, and she had cringed back as if afraid he would strike her. He was ashamed of himself for taking his temper out on the helpless girl, but at times he was unable to control himself. Now all he wanted to do was close his eyes and rest. 'You'll find money for those things in my jacket pocket,' he muttered.

'You can pay me when I bring them,' Willoughby said, getting up. Edward didn't answer. He appeared to be asleep, his face turned to the wall. 'Goodbye, Mr Clayton.' He met Liz just outside the door, struggling with the heavy bucket.

'I think he's asleep,' he told her. She looked at him help-lessly, putting the bucket on the doorstep. 'He – he looks very ill.' Liz nodded; she looked as if she might weep. 'If you need help, girl, come to the farm. My wife, she's pretty good with sick folk. Now show me the broken window, and I'll arrange to get the glass cut.'

Liz showed him the broken window in the storeroom.

He measured it with a piece of string from his pocket. Then he looked round the cottage at the broken slates, counting how many replacements were needed, before going back to the farm for his lunch, where he discussed the sorry situation with his wife.

'The girl looked terrified when she opened the door,' he told her. 'And that poor fellow – God knows what he's been going through! He looks as if he's got a fever, and he's covered in some sort of rash – I took good care not to touch him, I must admit. There's not a comfortable chair in the place, no curtains, bare flagstone floor, and the pump over the sink doesn't work.' He sat down at the kitchen table, and his wife brought him a plate overflowing with good hot stew. 'And to cap it all, there's hardly enough coke left in the store to last the day. I saw that when I measured the window.'

'Well, me dear, it's up to us to lend a hand,' Ada Willoughby told him briskly. 'We'll go into the village and get our shopping this afternoon, and send Job over to see to the pump and the roof – he's not busy this afternoon. He can take a bag of coke from our stock – we'll never miss it. When we get back we'll both go down there and I'll see what I can do to help the girl. Now eat up, Henry, we've got a busy afternoon!'

Edward slept until two, when Liz gave him a meal of hot vegetable soup and freshly made scones; she had no yeast to make bread, although she had sufficient dry stores and vegetables to last them another week. She had brought little meat when they came, expecting to find a shop within walking distance, and having no way of keeping it fresh. They had almost finished the fruit, but there was plenty of bacon, flour, cheese, eggs, and butter.

Edward ate his meal in silence. He had not dressed since he arrived at the cottage. He sat at the table for his meals, in his nightshirt and a thick guernsey, with a rug over his legs. The effort of dressing tired him too much. Liz was clearing the table when they heard a horse on the road, and the crunching of wheels on the gravelly surface. She peered out through the window over the sink. Edward wheeled his chair to the other window, on the far side of the door, and looked out.

Job, the labourer and odd-job man from the farm, had arrived with a cart stacked with ladders, tools, and on top, an old wooden rocking-chair. He was a tall, spare man in his forties, with a scanty black beard. He was in the usual farm-labourer's moleskin trousers and thick jacket, and on his head he had an ancient top hat. He had acquired the hat at a church bazaar some five years ago, and had seldom been seen without it since. The only time he removed it voluntarily was in church. Unmarried, he lived at the farm, sleeping in a loft in the barn, and taking most of his meals in the kitchen with the Willoughbys. Unlike the biblical Job, he was a happy-go-lucky character who never seemed to worry about anything, and could find a joke in almost every situation. Now he knocked loudly on the door, and when Liz opened it, gave her a broad grin and an admiring glance from his deep-set dark eyes. He was clearly related at some distance to the gypsies.

'Mr Willoughby sent me over to fix a few bits and pieces,' he announced cheerfully. 'Shall I begin with the pump? And where shall I put this bag of coke? Oh, and Miz' Willoughby, she said would you be able to find a place for this old rocking-chair – it rightly belongs to Honey Beck Cottage, 'cause she bought it when they sold up the old fisherman's goods, but she don't 'ave nowhere to put it, so she said she'd like to send it back to its rightful 'ome, like.'

Edward stared in astonishment at his grandmother's old rocking-chair, with the familiar flat red cushion still on the seat. Finally he cleared his throat. To his shame, he found that tears were threatening.

'You'd better bring it in,' he said gruffly. 'I'll talk to Mrs Willoughby about it later.'

'She be comin' over when she gets back from the village,' Job remarked. 'Now where's that ole pump? Ah – 'er's valve's rotted, I'll be bound. But I got a new one 'ere – found it in the barn, bin there ten year or more, lookin' for a broke pump.' He got to work without further ado, whistling through his teeth as he took the rusty old pump apart and sorted it out. Half an hour later he had water gushing vigorously into the sink and was setting the ladder up to deal with the slates. When the farmer and his wife arrived at half past four the cottage roof was rainproof again, and Job was just finishing nailing a temporary tarpaulin cover over the roof of the privvy.

'Goin' to rain tonight, me dear, and you don't want that seat wet as well as broke,' he declared, winking at Liz, who blushed and ran back to the cottage.

Having been warned that Mr and Mrs Willoughby were coming, Liz had changed into her lavender gingham dress, tidied her hair, and prepared the tea with fresh scones and a sponge cake made to her mother's recipe. Unfortunately the only cups she had were the thick white ones, she had only three small plates, none of which matched each other or anything else, and nothing in the way of a tablecloth; but she laid the table out as best she could and awaited her guests.

Presently they heard the horse trotting down the lane, and the trap appeared round the corner, coming down and stopping beside the cart. The two horses knew one another, of course, and both neighed amiably at meeting unexpectedly on the beach. Henry Willoughby helped his stout wife down from the trap, as if she had been Queen Victoria herself, and led her to the door of the cottage, which Liz had opened as soon as she saw them arrive. Smiling, she stepped back, beckoning them in. Edward had run his hands through his sparse, short grey hair, tidying it somewhat, and was sitting back in his chair, away from the light, near the back of the room.

'Come in, come in,' he greeted them. Henry Willoughby entered, beaming, his hands full of parcels, followed by his wife laden with a basket.

'Ah, here we are at last, Mr Clayton,' he declared. 'Allow me to present my good lady wife – Mrs Willoughby, Mr Clayton. And of course,' he smiled, turning to Liz, 'you've met – er – this young lady.'

'You've met Liz?' Edward queried sharply. Mrs Willoughby smiled at him, a plump, motherly smile that ignored the irascible tone of his voice.

'Yes, indeed,' she said amiably. 'Miss Liz called on us at the farm for milk a couple of days ago. I'm pleased to meet you, Mr Clayton – my husband has told me about you, and I decided to accompany him to deliver your bits and pieces this afternoon.'

'Then I must introduce you properly to my wife,' Edward said stiffly, and Mrs Willoughby gaped at him in surprise. 'Mrs Willoughby – Mrs Clayton. But I'm sure she'd prefer you to call her Liz. Liz, come and shake hands.'

Liz came forward shyly, wiping her hands on her clean calico apron. Mrs Willoughby overcame her surprise, and they shook hands. Now that she looked at him more closely, the farmer's wife realized that the man in the wheelchair was not as old as he at first appeared; in fact, despite the sparse grey hair and the lines of pain on his emaciated face, he was probably no more than thirty.

Henry Willoughby gave Edward the goods he had purchased on his behalf with an itemized account, which Edward paid in cash. Mrs Willoughby, meantime, took Liz into the far corner of the room and gave her a few things she had put together that she thought the girl might make good use of, including several strong white flour-sacks with small holes in them.

'You might find them useful for cleaning rags,' she said apologetically. 'No housewife ever has enough cleaning rags, my dear. I use them for making aprons and tea-towels, too. And if you make a long sausage from the stuff, and fill it with sand, it's very good to keep the draught from the bottom of the door. Now Henry tells me you might be interested in some of the things at the farm sale on Tuesday. Well, suppose you come with me, on Monday afternoon, to look at the goods, and tell me what you could use, and then I'll bid for them for you on Tuesday – I love going to sales, and I'll enjoy doing it. Makes a day out for me.'

Her face shining with delight, Liz nodded, and so it was arranged. Job would come over on Monday afternoon to finish one or two small tasks and keep Edward company, and Liz and Ada Willoughby would go to inspect the farm sale goods. Henry and Edward came to an agreement over how much could reasonably be spent; they would settle up the account later. Job could not be spared from the farm while Mr Willoughby was at the sale, so it would not be possible for Liz to go with them on Tuesday – besides, the sale itself would be an all-day outing.

Job drank his tea hurriedly now, and went back to the farm to get on with the evening milking, while Henry and Ada spent an hour with Edward and Liz. When they finally left, Ada turned to her husband as soon as they were out of earshot, and commented that those two were the oddest married couple she had ever seen.

'The girl doesn't look old enough to be married at all; and he looks as if he's not fit to be a husband to anyone! They can't have been married long; yet he's just out of hospital, and he was in South Africa for some years, by all accounts, before he was wounded and dragged back home

103

more dead than alive; so she must be a new bride, poor child.'

'Strangest setup I've ever come across,' Henry agreed. 'But none of our business, Ada, me dear. No reason to believe they're not married; odd, but quite respectable. What I can't understand is the sleeping arrangements. I know they only brought the one bed on that cart; and that's hardly big enough for him, certainly not big enough for both of them! There definitely was no bed in the old cottage before – not that that slip of a girl could have dragged it up those stairs on her own, anyway, and it's not in the storeroom – I looked! That's just got a load of rubbish in it. And there was nothing in the loft except half a bag of corn and a bit of straw I left there last year when that heifer and her calf got stranded on the beach in the storm and I had to bed her down in the cottage for a couple of days. No need to mention that to the Claytons, Ada – they might not appreciate knowing that the last occupant of Honey Beck Cottage was a Jersey cow! I forgot about the stuff in the loft.'

'Well, Henry, from the sound of things, I think that straw in the loft must be Mistress Liz's bed! I took her a few strong flour-bags – made out they were worn out. She can at least stuff the straw into a couple of those and make herself a decent mattress.'

In which surmise Ada Willoughby was quite correct. At that very moment Liz was busy stuffing two of the bags with straw, and sewing them together to make a fine palliasse; which made her the most comfortable bed she had ever slept in.

Chapter Ten

The days passed quietly for the couple at the cottage on Honey Beck Bay. The spell of dry weather had broken, and the rain Job had forecast began to fall, steady, soaking rain, making it difficult to get out without becoming wet and muddy to the knees. Liz thanked God that the roof had been repaired, and the pump mended; and what she would have done without that bag of coke Job had brought she did not know. She kept the range stoked up, and it warmed the cottage right through, despite the draughts from the uncurtained windows.

Liz found her time full. When she had finished the daily household chores, and the nursing duties, she tackled the job of cleaning up the storeroom. She threw out the rubbish littering the floor, and swept and scrubbed it until it was reasonably clean. Job had replaced the broken pane in the window; he had found a large piece of broken glass (or so he said) on the farm and cut a suitable piece from it. On a shelf at the back of the room Liz found a rusty biscuit tin; when she picked it up to throw out with the other rubbish it was heavy, so she opened it, and found a thick old black-bound Bible. She carried it out to Edward, who took it wonderingly, and smoothed the dust off the black leather with a careful hand.

'This is my grandfather's old Bible,' he marvelled. 'Where did you find it? Look – it's got all the family births and deaths for a hundred years written into it! Here – look – that's my mother's birthday, and wedding date, and the day I was born!'

Liz peered over his shoulder at the spidery, faded squiggles on the paper, but they meant nothing to her. She smiled at him apologetically, and shook her head. Edward frowned.

'I'll have to teach you to read and write, Liz. But first, I'm going to record your name in the book, and our wedding date. And my grandparents' deaths. Get the pen and ink for me, there's a good girl.'

Liz brought him the pen and ink, and went back to the task of cleaning out the lean-to. Apparently everything from the cottage had been sold when the old fisherman and his wife died – only two days apart – about eighteen years ago, with the exception of a big old chest of drawers, which was too large to get through the door, and had been abandoned at the back of the room, covered in old sacks. It was empty, but she set to and cleaned it up and stored their scanty stock of linen and Edward's clothes in it.

On Sunday morning she was up early to stoke up the fire, and from the coke-bin at the side of the cottage she stared out to sea. A young man was pulling a boat up on to the beach. He looked up and saw her; he waved his hand. Nervously, she waved back, and then ran inside. She shook Edward awake, risking his anger at being disturbed; she pointed to the door, and tried to mime a man waving, but he couldn't understand what she was about. While she persevered, there was a knock on the door.

'What the devil –!' Edward exclaimed, looking at the clock. 'It's not seven o'clock yet – who can that be? Well, open the door, girl!'

Liz ran and opened the door. A young man, dark and wiry-looking, stood there in black oilskins, high fisherman's boots on his feet.

'Good morning, ma'am,' he began; Liz stood aside so that Edward could see him, and gestured to him to come in. She had put a clean sack on the floor by the door for a

Henry dropped in for a few minutes during the afternoon, and was intrigued to find Edward on his bed reading the Bible. Liz, sitting by the fire in the rocking-chair with some mending, had dozed off. She got up hastily and made the tea. Edward told the farmer that she had found the Bible in the storeroom; but he did not mention that it contained a record of his own birth. For the moment he did not want even this good man to know of his early years at the cottage on the bay.

On Monday morning the rain had ceased, and Liz was up early, getting the washing on the line before breakfast. She finished her household and nursing chores early, gave Edward his lunch of scones and cheese, and made her way to the farmhouse, eating her own lunch on the way. She was wearing her blue serge dress with the smart little jacket and matching bonnet. She took great care not to get it muddy as she crossed the fields.

It was a lovely warm, bright day; April at its best. Liz had seldom been so happy; now and then she broke into a skip out of sheer high spirits.

Mrs Willoughby had the trap ready, and they were soon on their way through the lanes to the farm where the sale was to be held the following day. All the livestock had already been sold at the market the week before. The farm machinery and equipment was all laid out on the grass in front of the house; the household items were in the house itself, marked with lot numbers.

Liz looked longingly at the old, sturdy furniture. Chests, chairs, wardrobes, beds; old but good, most of them, but she knew that for the moment things like that were out of their financial range, and went on to view the more prosaic items.

A laundry basket full of oddments of china and glassware, and kitchen crocks, took her eye. Mrs Willoughby listed the lot number. A tin bath-tub big enough for a man to take a proper bath, with several pairs of curtains folded into it was the next item she remarked, and then a wooden box full of miscellaneous books and old magazines. She reluctantly bypassed a fatly upholstered sofa with broad red stripes, long enough for a man to lie on, piled with odd cushions, and a threadbare but brightly coloured carpet, but pounced on a collection of mats and hearth-rugs. The final item to take her eye was a wheelbarrow packed with gardening tools and earthenware flowerpots.

'Well, my dear, I'll see what we can pick up from that lot tomorrow without putting you into the poorhouse,' Mrs Willoughby promised as they made their way back to the lane where the fat pony waited patiently in the shafts of the trap.

Two middle-aged ladies were coming through the gate; the farmer's wife stopped to chat to them, then called Liz back to be introduced. It was the wife and the sister of the vicar of Forestwidden. They were greatly interested to meet the new tenant of the cottage at Honey Beck Bay; they had already heard about the couple on the village grapevine. Apparently Jack the carter had told his cousin in the village about them, and his cousin had passed the news on to the rest of the inhabitants. Liz was cordially invited to call at the vicarage when she came into the village, and Mrs Hatfield, the vicar's wife, assured her that her husband would call on Mr Clayton as soon as his sciatica improved. Liz smiled and nodded nervously, and was glad to get back into the trap and head for home. She was not at all sure that Edward would make the vicar welcome; she suspected that he might not want to become a member of the good man's flock. She could imagine his comments if the vicar attempted to pray over him; his language, at times, was worthy of the trooper he had lately been.

They got back to the cottage at about four-thirty, Mrs

Willoughby driving the trap right down into the bay so that Liz would not have to walk across the fields again in her good dress. They went into the cottage and found Job, as always wearing the rusty black top hat, busy whitewashing the storeroom, assisted by Edward, who was slowly and laboriously doing that part of the walls he could reach from the wheelchair. When the two women came in he thankfully relinquished the brush to his fellow-painter and went into the sitting-room where Mrs Willoughby gave him a detailed description of the goods his wife had chosen, and discussed the sum she was to bid.

'I'm really looking forward to this,' she said with a smile. 'I love sales, but our house is full, and I daren't buy anything else for myself or Henry says he'll have to move out into the barn!'

Meanwhile Liz made the tea. When Mrs Willoughby left half an hour later, taking Job with her in the trap, the storeroom was finished and would be ready for use as soon as the whitewash was dry.

The sale next day was quite a social occasion, besides being a good way for the local farmers to stock up on various oddments of equipment at a reasonable price. The Willoughbys were there early, as the bidding was advertised to start at ten, and the troughs Henry was after were among the early lots. He bought what he wanted at a reasonable price, and then joined the men round the beer-barrel for an hour while his wife gossiped with the other women until the household goods came up.

Most of the locals knew that Mrs Willoughby was buying for the new tenant at the cottage, a brave soldier who had returned crippled from the war, and consequently as soon as she showed interest in any item, there were no competing bids; everything Liz had listed was knocked down to her at a give-away price – including the fat sofa and the brightly coloured carpet. The Willoughbys drove home triumphant,

111

and sent Job back with the cart to collect their purchases before nightfall. It was too late to drive down the steep, mud-rutted lane, being well after dark when the cart got back to the farm; but they were left safely under cover in the barn for the night and Job and Henry delivered them the next morning, arriving at eleven-thirty, by which time they knew Liz would have finished Edward's dressings, and be ready to receive them.

The girl's beaming face when they hauled the fat sofa, with its stack of brightly patterned cushions, into the cottage, was thanks enough for the trouble they had taken. And when this was followed by the carpet, Liz's delight was unbounded. Edward's bed was taken apart and reassembled in the storeroom, which now became his bedroom; the carpet was laid over the flagstones in the living-room, and the sofa placed against the wall where the bed had been. The box of books, the tub, and the laundry basket of china and kitchenware, were all placed inside the door for Liz to sort out at her leisure, and the men went home for their mid-day meal leaving the cottage overflowing with the girl's gratitude and happiness. Edward had settled the account; he was amazed at the bargains they had achieved.

Liz spent the afternoon happily sorting out her purchases. The books were placed on the shelves in Edward's bedroom; he was delighted to find a good selection of classics among them, and amused to discover a Latin Primer and copy of the *Aeneid*, as well as several history and geography textbooks; apparently the collection had belonged to a student at some time. At the bottom of the box he discovered a chess and draughts set, complete with board. At least, he thought, his boredom problem was solved. He could not only sharpen up his wits by swotting up his half-remembered Latin, he could, perhaps, teach Liz to play chess with him. Draughts, anyway; he doubted if she would take to chess . . .

There were enough faded chintz curtains in the tub to fit out at least two cottages of this size. Liz soon had those she would use in a tub of hot soapsuds, rinsed, and on the clothesline. The others she folded carefully and put away to wash at a more convenient time. The basket full of crockery, glassware, and kitchen oddments was unpacked, the items washed, dried, and set out on the dresser or in the larder. At the bottom of the basket she found an odd collection of cutlery, no two items matching, but a welcome addition to the few pieces with which she had been making do.

The laundry basket she put on the floor in the larder; the wooden box she took up to her loft to store her own personal treasures (particularly the blue hat) out of harm's way; but she was at a loss to know where to put the tub. It was about four and a half feet long, two feet wide, and about two feet deep. Edward finally came up with an answer to the problem. There was a recess on the left of the chimney, similar to the one on the right where the dresser was located. The sink under the window had a long wooden draining-board that ran into the recess, leaving a space underneath. Liz put the tub under this, and stacked the cleaning materials and buckets inside it. At least it was out of the way; she planned to hang one of the surplus curtains across the front, and then it would be hidden, but handy to get out when required.

That evening she sat contentedly in the rocking-chair, sewing the curtains, which had to be altered to fit, while Edward read aloud to her from an anthology of verse. She did not really appreciate the poetry – most of it made little sense to her. But she enjoyed hearing him read, his rich, deep voice rising and falling with the cadence of the verse. She had never been so happy in her life. If only they could get those dreadful wounds to heal, clear up the irritating rash, and get rid of the intermittent fever, she thought, she would never ask God for another thing. As her needle slipped back and forth through the fabric, Liz's thoughts wandered. She wondered what her mother would think if she could see her now. Thank God she would never have to go back to the misery of that house in the slums! She glanced at Edward as she snipped the thread at the end of a seam. She fancied she could see a little colour in his hollow cheeks.

At nine Liz helped Edward to bed in his new room, changed the dressings on his legs (to be sure that they did not stick fast again), gave him a final cup of tea, and left him reading to himself by the light of the lamp.

Then – she dragged out the tub, filled it with warm water, and took a luxurious bath in front of the range. When she finally climbed the steep ladder up to her loft, she felt like a queen: clean from head to foot, and at peace with the world.

Chapter Eleven

Keenlach Lodge stood in the Great Forest; not a big house compared with the others owned by the Clayton family, but comfortable and quite large enough for its purpose. It was in the heart of the hunting country, and each year it was the custom of the men of the family to spend a few weeks here following the Hunt. They usually remained until after the forest pony and horse sales, and the Horse Fair that took place early in April.

Unlike the other Clayton residences, it did not boast a large and well-kept garden. Here the wide lawn almost merged into the surrounding forest. There were a few flowering shrubs, and a group of pines; near the stone porch, which was large and high enough for a man to mount his horse under cover, bloomed a clump of daffodils; that was the total extent of the horticultural effort. The house itself was built of red brick, mellowed by the years. The ground floor comprised several large rooms, low-ceilinged, with oak floors and huge fireplaces, small windows, and comfortable oak and leather furnishings. Above, six bedrooms, each with a large fireplace and small windows, contained massive four-poster beds. It was, in fact, a house built and furnished for winter and spring use, seldom occupied in the summer months. The women of the family hardly ever used it, although at the moment both Lady Imogen and Harriet Grant were staying here with the menfolk.

A short distance from the house, reached by a covered way, stood the most important feature of the property: the stables. Here no expense had been spared. Solidly constructed of brick, like the house itself, they were a veritable palace for the equine occupants. Ranged round a yard wide enough for a coach to drive in and turn, the stable block was considerably more comfortable and better maintained than the accommodation provided for the household servants.

On this dull, overcast morning Sir Rupert had come down to breakfast at eight-thirty, as usual, expecting to find his son, the Honourable Arthur, and his two grandsons, Gervaise and Cecil, already at the table. It had been decided the evening before that they would ride to Barminster Abbey today to confer with the builders who were to refurbish the mansion now that the hospital had been dismantled. However, the only member of the family at the table was Harriet Grant; and though Sir Rupert was glad to see her, he was annoyed that his son and grandsons were apparently still lying in their beds.

'Good morning, Uncle Rupert,' Harriet greeted him, her ready smile brightening the rather gloomy aspect of the dim room. Sir Rupert grunted a reply, and sat at the head of the table. His niece – or niece-by-marriage, for she was no blood relation – obligingly served his breakfast from the heated dishes on the sideboard, and poured his coffee. When the first pangs of hunger had been satisfied, and his irascible morning temper steadied, the old man looked round and remarked testily on the absence of his son.

'I thought he was anxious to get off early,' he grumbled. 'I suppose he'll come down half-way through the day and expect me to race across country to meet the damn builders. Not that I care what he does with the old place; I've no intention of living there myself. If he wants to get into Parliament as the Barminster candidate, it's his worry, not mine. All I have to do, I expect, is pay the bills. Why he can't confine his interests to the family estate, instead of setting up in politics, I don't know.' Sir Rupert chewed

116

noisily for a moment on a piece of kidney. 'And those two boys – men – my grandsons. Useless couple of nitwits. Think they know everything about horseflesh, but when they set eyes on a five-barred gate they turn pale and send a man to open it! Never saw such a pair of ninnies as they made at the Hunt last week. Came down here to hunt, and most of the time they're missing. More interested in the girls in the gypsy camp over by Forestwidden than in the Hunt.'

Harriet sensed that this was not the best time to tackle the subject on her mind, but it was the first opportunity she had had for days to discuss her future with him. The old man was fond of her, she knew; but his temper had been very unpredictable lately. However, she was determined to get her future settled. She took a deep breath and plunged into speech before her courage deserted her.

'Uncle Rupert, when I go to Edinburgh –'

'Where's my morning paper?' Sir Rupert barked at the butler, who had just entered with his hot toast.

'I'm sorry, Sir Rupert, but it has not arrived yet,' Beale said evenly, putting the silver toast-rack by his plate.

'Send someone to hurry my son and those two young layabouts down to their breakfast,' the old man ordered as the butler turned to leave the room.

'Mr Arthur and his sons have already breakfasted and gone to the stables, sir,' Beale answered calmly. After more than thirty years in Sir Rupert's employ he was accustomed to his manner. The old man grunted, and returned his attention to his plate.

'Uncle Rupert, I wanted to ask you about the arrangements for my lodgings when I go up to start my training in Edinburgh –' Harriet persisted, but was interrupted by her uncle.

'Lodgings – Edinburgh – what are you babbling about?' He lost interest in the kidneys and glared at her.

Harriet took a deep breath, and calmed herself before speaking again.

'I'm going to Edinburgh to study medicine, Uncle Rupert, and I'd like to know –'

'You can forget that, Harriet! I've had enough of that nonsense – you'll stay at home, like other girls, and find yourself a suitable husband. Or help Lady Imogen run the house. I don't want to hear another word on the subject.'

'But Uncle Rupert, you promised! If I did a year working in the hospital, and still wanted to become a doctor, you promised to make the arrangements and increase my allowance to cover the expenses! I did my part – and now I expect you to do yours!'

'Hold your tongue, girl! I told you, forget it! I'll have no female member of my family earning her living in the slums of Edinburgh! You were raised to be a lady, not a doctor. I'll hear no more of it.'

Harriet's voice shook as she persisted.

'I'm not asking you to provide for me, Uncle Rupert. The money is my own. For the moment you're my trustee, and you can decide how and when I get it; but it isn't fair –'

'That's enough!' The old man slammed his fist down on the table, making the china jump and the coffee spill. 'I can, as you say, decide how and when you get the money – and I've decided that you'll get a dress allowance as long as you behave as a young woman should, and nothing more! When you reach the age of thirty you can do as you damn well please with your money. Until then, you needn't think you can make a laughing stock of the family who have fed and raised you by going off like one of those disgusting females who haven't the sense to remember they're women, not men! Now forget all this nonsense and look about you for a decent husband. That's the end of the matter!' He drained his coffee cup, and stood up.

'I'm going to the stables. I expect we'll be back late this

afternoon. I suggest you go and do some sketching or embroidery, or something on those lines, instead of making yourself a laughing stock grizzling about becoming a doctor. You'll be joining those bloody suffragettes next!' He stumped from the room, leaving Harriet white-faced and furious.

An hour later Lady Imogen, Arthur Clayton's wife, came down the stairs to find Harriet in the drawing-room writing a letter, dressed warmly in a dark skirt and a fur jacket.

'Harriet, my dear – you're going out?' she exclaimed in surprise. There wasn't much to do at Keenlach Lodge except ride or walk in the forest, so she assumed that Harriet was going into Barminster to do some shopping, or perhaps meet some of the friends she had made while playing at being a nurse at the Returned Soldiers' Hospital; a most unsuitable occupation for a young lady, but at least it kept her occupied and stilled her constant nagging about a career. Besides, when the nation was going through a patriotic fever about the Boer War it was good for the family reputation to have the only girl in the household engaged in nursing; just as it was good for them to have donated the use of Barminster Abbey, whilst they did not require it themselves, for a temporary military hospital; and Lady Imogen was confident that her husband's ambition to become the Member for the constituency would be furthered by these patriotic activities, and remembered by the grateful voting population.

Lady Imogen was the only daughter of Lord Farlington, and had brought an additional fortune into the family, a fact which she made sure the Claytons did not forget. She considered that she had married beneath her, for the Claytons, although wealthy and powerful, were not, after all, an aristocratic family; but as she had not been endowed with a beautiful face, attractive figure, or a graceful manner, she was fortunate to have attracted the attentions of the

119

Honourable Arthur Clayton, who had been a good catch on the marriage market, if rather too fat to appeal to the taste of most debutantes, and too arrogant to consider a wife from among the lower classes.

Now she looked down her aristocratic nose at her husband's young cousin, and noted the traces of tears on the girl's face. She sat on a chair near Harriet's, carefully smoothing her dove-grey skirt, and waited for an explanation.

'I tried to ask Uncle Rupert about my allowance, and – and –'

'Your allowance, my dear? But I thought you had a very generous allowance,' Lady Imogen said indulgently. 'After all, you have few expenses, and Sir Rupert pays all your accounts for you, does he not?'

'Oh, yes – that's not what I mean, Lady Imogen. I mean the allowance he promised while I was in Edinburgh training at the medical college.'

Lady Imogen's indulgent expression changed to one of refined disapproval.

'Oh, my dear, you're not still hankering after that?' she protested. 'We discussed it – your uncle, Arthur, and I – and we all agreed that it would be most inappropriate for a young woman in your position to enter medical school, particularly so now, with all this shocking business about the female suffrage movement. No, my dear Harriet, you owe it to your family – and to yourself – to forget all about that, and behave in a way more likely to find you a good husband. Just think: what young man would want to marry a woman who – well, never mind; we won't go into the details. Just forget the matter. Now how about helping me make out the guest list for the dinner party we're having at Eaton Square next month –'

'Damn the dinner party!' Harriet exclaimed. 'We had an agreement, Uncle Rupert and I, that if I worked for a year in the Returned Soldiers' Hospital, I could go on to medical school if I still wanted to. Well, for a year I emptied bedpans, gave bed-baths, dressed amputated limbs, and even laid out corpses. And now he's gone back on his word and refused to let me take the training. It's not fair – and it's not right!'

'If you're going to take that attitude, Harriet, I think I'll go back to my room and do my guest list up there,' Lady Imogen said coldly, rising to her feet. 'I warned your uncle that you were becoming a very self-willed young woman; not, I must say, what I expected from a girl of your upbringing. I'll leave you to calm down. Just remember, my dear, that no man is likely to look twice at a girl who flies into a temper if she doesn't get her own way all the time, even if she has a fortune coming to her on her wedding day. As for your allowance, I understand that it will cease entirely if you insist on pursuing this unsuitable course.' She got up and left the room, her straight back expressing her displeasure. Harriet watched her go with a bitter expression.

Now she knew why her uncle had gone back on his word! It was Lady Imogen's influence. Not that the old man was incapable of breaking his word if he felt so inclined. But it would not be convenient for him to be on bad terms with his daughter-in-law, despite his dislike of her; for Lady Imogen saw to the staffing and general upkeep of the family houses, and life would be far less comfortable for him if he were not surrounded by reliable and deferential servants. And also, without her dominating influence, his two grandsons were likely to get themselves into all sorts of trouble. Both weak-willed, interested in little except gambling and horses, they were easily led into the many pitfalls awaiting wealthy and foolish young men. Already their father had been called on to extricate them from several unsavoury scrapes; they had the reckless irresponsibility of their disgraced uncle, Captain Robert Clayton, without the saving grace of his charm and good nature. Harriet had resisted the family's efforts to push her and Cecil into marriage. He had been willing to marry her but she had detested him from the day she met him, and was determined not to marry purely for the sake of gaining her independence.

Now she finished the letter she had been writing, addressed it to Sir Rupert, and left it on the mantelpiece where it would be found and given to him when he came in. She picked up the small case she had hidden behind her chair; it contained her overnight necessities. The maid who waited on herself and Lady Imogen was upstairs at this moment packing the rest of her things into her trunk, to be sent on later. Harriet went to the front door; the carriage she and Lady Imogen used was waiting in the drive.

'Take me to the railway station in Barminster, James,' she told the young coachman; and so she departed from Sir Rupert's household.

Mr George Steadman, Sir Rupert's solicitor, was surprised, several mornings later, to be informed that Miss Harriet Grant had called and wished to see him immediately. He was the second trustee in charge of her fortune; but it was his usual habit to defer to Sir Rupert's instructions in all his dealings with Miss Grant, or any other members of the family, come to that. Now he wondered uneasily what the girl wanted. He had agreed with Sir Rupert, some time ago, that if she were to complete a full year of nursing at the military hospital she would be financed from her own funds to take a medical training. He knew the year was now up; and he knew that Sir Rupert, confident that she would leave the hospital as soon as the work became tiring or unpleasant, had never expected to be called on to keep his side of the bargain. Now the solicitor wondered unhappily if he was to be put in a position of conflict with his client.

His clerk ushered the young woman into his office. He

offered her a chair, and instructed the clerk to bring coffee. He remembered the girl, the last time he had seen her, as being a charming, but shy and reserved young woman, with a rather childish manner, beautifully dressed in a highly fashionable pale beige costume that showed up the green eyes and tawny hair to advantage. Now she came in, still beautifully dressed, but with an air of assured independence that was quite new. Instead of casting her eyes demurely down, she met his gaze directly; and it was his own eyes that wavered when he realized that she was here on business, and confidently intended to get her own way.

'Good morning, Mr Steadman,' she began briskly, seating herself in the chair he indicated. 'I've come to discuss my financial arrangements for the medical college.'

'Ah . . . Yes, of course.' The solicitor returned to his seat behind the imposing desk. He felt more able to impress her with the expanse of expensive leather-topped walnut between them. 'I've not yet had instructions from your uncle, my dear, and until I have his approval, I think we should – er –'

'Mr Steadman, you know what the arrangement was; you were present when we discussed it in my uncle's study in Eaton Square. I've completed my part of the bargain; now it is time for my trustees to do theirs.'

'Well, yes, Miss Grant, but it was, as you know, merely an informal, verbal arrangement. I must have your uncle's agreement before I can do anything more.'

'And if he's changed his mind?'

'Then I'm afraid I'm not able to do anything about it, my dear. As I said, it was a verbal agreement –'

'Supposing I could produce a letter, setting out the terms of our "verbal agreement", signed by my uncle?'

'Well, then,' George Steadman nodded, confident that she could do nothing of the sort, 'that would alter the case, of course.'

123

Harriet opened her handbag, and drew out an envelope. It was addressed to herself, at the Eaton Square house.

'I think you had better read that, Mr Steadman. You may remember, Uncle Rupert went to Yorkshire the day after we made that "verbal agreement". I wrote and asked him if he'd spoken to Dr Mansfield at the military hospital before he left, and this was his reply.'

The letter, in Sir Rupert's own hand, confirmed that he had arranged for Harriet to work for a year, if she had not changed her mind, at the Returned Soldiers' Hospital at Barminster Abbey, in preparation for a medical training. He emphasized that if she found the work uncongenial, she was at liberty to cancel their agreement, but in that case he would not agree to her taking up a medical career, and would not feel himself bound to authorize the necessary financial arrangements for her training.

It was not, by any means, an official document, but merely a hasty note sent by an uncle to his niece; but it did confirm the agreement to which they had come.

Mr Steadman was shaken. He had had no idea that his client had put anything about the matter in writing; but he also knew that if Miss Grant were to go to court to demand that the income on her considerable capital be released for this purpose, and she produced this letter, she would most likely get the court's support. Also, he and Sir Rupert would get a great deal of unwelcome publicity, and probably be made to look fools in the eyes of their friends and the world in general.

'I'll have to discuss the matter with your uncle, Miss Grant,' he said hastily. 'If you leave this with me –'

'I'll keep it, if you don't mind,' Harriet said coolly, leaning across the desk and neatly retrieving it from his hand. 'I believe my aunt left me some money – is that also tied up so that I can't touch it?'

'I'm afraid so, Miss Grant. Unless you marry first, it will

124

not be available until you reach the age of thirty.'

'In other words, I can't have it, but if I marry some utter scoundrel who is interested in nothing but my money, he can have it tomorrow?'

'Er – well – that's not quite how I'd put it –'

'Yes or no?'

'Miss Grant –'

'Yes or no?'

'Yes,' Mr Steadman said weakly. Harriet looked at him steadily; again he found it difficult to meet her eyes.

'And did you advise my aunt to make that condition?'

'Well, yes, I must admit that I did – but for your own protection, Miss Grant. It is the usual arrangement, you know. If a young lady comes into possession of a large sum at an early age, she can very easily become the victim of an unscrupulous man –'

'So it's preferable that she hands it over to a young man of her family's choice, and he can spend it how he wishes whether she likes it or not, I suppose?'

Mr Steadman was relieved of the necessity of a reply to this comment by the entry of his clerk with the coffee. By the time the clerk had left the room, having poured the coffee from a very handsome silver pot, and fussed about like an old hen over the cream and sugar, he had regained his composure and was ready to continue the interview.

'I understand that my aunt also left a small legacy to my cousin Edward Clayton,' Harriet remarked. 'Did she, under your guidance, arrange for the same condition to be attached to his inheritance?'

'No, Miss Grant,' the solicitor replied, a slight smile touching his features. 'He was to have the interest on his capital immediately, without any restrictions, and come into possession of the full capital at the age of thirty-five; so you see, she demonstrated more confidence in your good sense than she did in his!'

'I suppose that, considering his father's record, that was not to be wondered at,' Harriet commented, returning his smile. At least, he thought, she doesn't hold a personal grudge against me. Not that he would blame her, under the circumstances. He privately agreed that she had been unfairly treated. 'However, I believe that Edward didn't return from the war, so he never did get his legacy. What will become of it now, Mr Steadman?'

'Well, Miss Grant, we have recently had some good news regarding that young man,' Mr Steadman told her, glad of a change of subject. 'He was, I'm afraid, a rather unsteady character; he worked in these offices, you know. A likeable young fellow, but more interested in the delights of the city than in his work, I'm sorry to say. More than once I considered asking him to leave but kept him on because I had, after all, known his father in his early days. Despite his somewhat irresponsible attitude, he did well and qualified a couple of years before he left us. We were informed that he was missing, believed killed, shortly before the end of the hostilities. However, less than a month ago, he was discovered in this country suffering from a temporary loss of memory. He has now been discharged, and I have no doubt that the legacy his grandmother left him will be a welcome addition to his pension.'

'Oh – I'm so glad he's alive!' Harriet exclaimed. 'I know his father was a bad lot – I'm not sure just what he did, but it must have been something awful! But I've always thought that the family were rather hard on him.' Her green eyes met the solicitor's; he found himself suddenly wishing that he was thirty years younger. 'Mr Steadman, I'm a big girl now. Will you tell me what Captain Robert Clayton did that was so very wicked?'

Steadman cleared his throat, fussed with his papers, and generally looked most uncomfortable.

'Well – actually, he married a poor fisherman's daughter, a nobody, without a word to the family or the girl he was engaged to at the time. Oh, a great scandal, I'm afraid. His father cut him off. He found himself unable to pay his mess-bills, and would have been cashiered if Sir Rupert had not come to the rescue, I believe. I don't know all the details. After that no-one knew what had become of him until his son turned up, with the news that his father had been killed in an accident – he tried to stop a team of runaway horses, and was trampled.'

'Oh dear, poor man! It sounds as if his worst crime was falling in love with the wrong girl,' Harriet said sadly. 'If he hadn't been cut off, he wouldn't have got into financial trouble. I suppose if you're used to a large allowance it would be difficult to keep your expenses down. Now if he had married a rich aristocratic bitch like his brother did, all would have been well!'

'Miss Grant!' Mr Steadman exclaimed, scandalized; but having several times been snubbed and severely put down by Lady Imogen himself, he was not able to deny the truth of her comment. As Harriet saw the vacillation in his expression she threw back her head and laughed; and shame-facedly Mr Steadman joined her.

But she had not come here to gossip about her relations. She finished her coffee and got back to business.

'Mr Steadman, I've written out my address – I'm staying with a friend until I start medical training; and this card will also give you the directions of the bank I intend to use in Edinburgh. I've left my uncle's household, and I don't intend to return. I'm told that my dress allowance will cease forthwith. Can I depend on you to – er – refrain from passing this information on to Uncle Rupert? Yes – good. Now, please tell him that if an adequate sum is not paid into that bank account within a month I'll be taking the matter to court.'

'I'll tell him, Miss Grant, but I warn you, he's not going to like it!'

'I don't expect him to like it, Mr Steadman – I just expect him to do his duty as my trustee. I'll have no compunction in going to court, and don't forget I have the letter.'

'Miss Grant, you realize that I cannot act for you in this matter? You will have to retain another lawyer –'

Harriet smiled, and stood up.

'I've already done that, Mr Steadman. But if I can prevent it, I don't want the matter to go any further. That's why I came to you first. To give my uncle a chance to keep his word without a third party being drawn into the matter. Now I'll be going, and I hope to hear that the matter has been sorted out amicably. Goodbye, Mr Steadman.'

The solicitor jumped up to escort her out. He had a feeling that Sir Rupert had met his match here. Had the girl learned the art of attack from the old man himself?

'Oh, I wonder if you would give me Edward Clayton's address?' Harriet asked, pausing at the door. 'I'd like to write to him.'

'I'm sorry, Miss Grant, but I don't have it. Our contact is made through his solicitor – he particularly stipulated, apparently, that his whereabouts were to be kept from the family. I could, however, give you the name and address of the solicitor. Perhaps he would forward a letter on to your cousin.'

'Oh, thank you – let me have it, and I may get round to writing if I'm not too busy. It might be amusing for the two black sheep of the family to exchange greetings!'

The clerk wrote out the information, and Harriet slipped the paper into her bag without looking at it. Later, in her lodgings, she found it and almost threw it away unread, as she had so many other things on her mind at the time. But she glanced at the name and address casually, and then read it again, with a frown on her face.

John Oatis, Solicitor, of 97 The High Street, Barminster. An odd coincidence, she thought. Barminster. Why had Edward engaged a solicitor in that town, of all places? She slipped the paper into her address book and forgot about it.

Chapter Twelve

The good spell of weather continued, and the days sped past with incredible speed for Liz, as she worked about Honey Beck Cottage. Edward, too, was content, reading his books, and watching Liz as she swept and polished, cooked and sewed. Every day he made her spend an hour at her reading and writing lessons. Now she did not resent the waste of daylight hours so much; she had begun to enjoy the intimacy they shared as they sat together over the alphabet, and even the laborious exercise of copying out the letters. She had learned most of the capital letters, and was now pairing them up with their lower-case counterparts.

Two or three times a week she walked over to the farm and collected fresh milk. The weather was still cold enough to keep milk fresh for two days if she left it out on the stone windowsill. Mrs Willoughby also supplied her with fresh meat about twice a week when she had been to the butcher in the village. Liz never went to Forestwidden herself. With the speech handicap she was shy of strangers, and preferred to let Mrs Willoughby do her shopping. In return she did the sewing and mending that the farmer's wife never had time nor inclination to tackle; and as Mrs Willoughby liked going to the shops, and hated working with a needle, the arrangement suited them both.

The days were never long enough for Liz to complete all the tasks she set herself. When she was living in the slums of Barminster and working long hours at the hospital, she had woken each morning with reluctance, facing a day in which she could find little pleasure, and an evening when her most fervent hope was to keep out of her step-father's sight. Now it was a pleasure to waken each morning, and although she was working quite as hard as she had done formerly, each task was a pleasure, with the exception of dressing Edward's injuries; and even that she would not have relinquished to other hands.

Four weeks had passed since the Claytons had come to the cottage. Edward was beginning to put on weight, and was much more cheerful but, to his disappointment and Liz's distress, his wounds still stubbornly refused to heal. He had occasional bouts of depression when he would sit morose and dejected, snapping at Liz if she disturbed him, but those times were now the exception rather than the rule. When he left the hospital he had taken no interest in anything except his own misery; now he began to take notice of every thing about him. In the first place he had looked on Liz merely as a means of escaping from the institution. He still treated her very much as he would have done a housekeeper or cook, there to serve his needs; but he was beginning to appreciate her as a person in her own right. His intentions in teaching her to read and write were far from altruistic; he needed to find a way in which she could communicate with him. Now he found that he enjoyed the lessons and the companionship she gave him.

One bright afternoon he was sitting in the doorway of the cottage watching Liz working on the patch of land she was optimistically hoping to turn into a vegetable garden, when a dog ambled out on to the beach from the trees at the far side of the bay. The dog was large and black, a mongrel mixture of many breeds, but with obvious Alsatian antecedents. It came scampering over to take a closer look at them.

Liz threw down her hoe in alarm, and ran back to the cottage, dragging the wheelchair inside and slamming the door as the dog approached.

'Steady, Liz – there's no need for panic!' Edward protested furiously. She had bundled him into the cottage as if he was an endangered toddler! 'The dog only wanted to make friends with us – couldn't you see his tail wagging like a flag of truce? And anyway, he's only a puppy. Open the door and let's make friends.'

But nothing would persuade the girl to open the door. As she kept her back to it, and he couldn't open it himself, Edward went to the window and looked out, half-amused at her protective attitude, but also considerably annoyed that she could lock him into the cottage like this against his wishes. Dammit, she was his nurse and housekeeper, not his nanny!

He saw a slim, dark youth walking across the sands, his rough clothing and swarthy appearance bespeaking his gypsy origins. Edward opened the window and called him.

'Hey – you! Come here, I want to talk to you.' But the boy took one startled look at the man at the window and retreated back into the trees, calling the dog after him.

'Damn!' Edward swore, his face darkening. 'That was one of the gypsies, and I want to see Old Meg.' He sat thinking for a moment, and then looked across at Liz. 'Well, you'll just have to go to the camp and find her for me.'

Liz gaped at him in horror. The gypsy camp was in the forest, she knew that – and she had never ventured that far. How would she find the camp? And how would she contact Meg?

'Well, don't just stand there staring like an idiot – get your shawl, and go and find her!' Edward snapped, exasperated. 'I'll give you a note for her. You can get there and back before dark – it's not far. Look, you go up the lane to the first gate, along the path by the woods, over the hill, and you'll see the gypsy camp in the valley.'

He got out the writing materials, and began a note. Liz went to the ladder and put her foot on the bottom step.

132

'No, you don't have to change your dress!' he said impatiently. 'It's a gypsy camp, not a vicarage tea-party! Go as you are, and hurry!' Liz looked down at the black calico dress; she never went out in it now, reserving it for scrubbing the floor or working in the garden. Her coarse black shawl was on a hook at the back of the door; she put it round her shoulders, and reluctantly took the note.

'If you can't find Meg, give this to one of the others, and they'll find her for you. I've written her name on it. Now – go!'

Unwillingly the girl opened the door and went out. She hurried up the lane, according to his directions. She found the gate. It was years since Edward had been to the gypsy camp, and the path he had told her to take was almost overgrown. However, she obediently followed it to the top of the hill; in the valley below she finally caught sight of the gypsies' caravans, about seven of them, with a crowd of children and dogs running about among them. In the corner of the clearing she could see some horses grazing, each one tethered to a peg in the ground.

Her pace slowing as she approached the camp, Liz followed the path downhill. Presently she lost sight of the caravans as she entered the trees, for this was the edge of the Great Forest; but she was able to follow the sound of the children's voices, and the dogs' barking, and eventually she came to the clearing. The children fell silent as they saw her emerge from the trees, but the dogs immediately set up a concerted barking and yapping cacophony that terrified her. She almost turned and ran, but she knew Edward would be furious if she returned without the gypsy woman. She was even more afraid of his anger than she was of the noisy dogs.

A thin, wizened woman with untidy grey hair streaming down her back was stirring something in a large metal pot hung over a fire. She turned and stared at the girl. Her hostile gaze sent shivers down Liz's spine. She forced herself to step forward.

The woman shouted at the dogs, who immediately cowered back and allowed Liz to approach. The woman addressed her in a language she couldn't understand. She shook her head hopelessly, and held out the note Edward had given her. The woman grunted, took it, and turned it over a couple of times in her hand, leaving greasy thumbprints on the paper.

It was clear to Liz that the gypsy woman didn't understand the writing any more than she herself did! The woman spoke to her again, but she didn't understand a word. One of the children, a boy about ten years old, ran up and pulled at her sleeve.

'Gran don't read, Miss – and she don't speak English, neither,' he said, laughing. He reminded Liz of Job, with his dark flashing eyes and his tousled black hair. 'Don't you speak English, Miss?'

Liz, despairing, pointed to her mouth, and shook her head. She held out her hands and crossed them quickly one over the other, fingers outspread, in the gesture that is almost universally understood as a negative, and the bright boy got her meaning without hesitation.

'You can't talk? You'd better see Old Meg – she's our Gran's mum – I 'spec's she's the one you wants, Miss,' he said, and ran off towards a brightly painted caravan standing a little apart from the others. He stopped by the steps, and shouted. A head, with thick white hair tied back like a horse's tail, appeared at the back of the caravan, which had a stable-fashion door, the top half of which was open, and the bottom closed. A rapid conversation followed, none of which Liz could understand, the boy's shrill voice and the old woman's harsh tones equally unintelligible to her ears.

She walked cautiously up to the caravan. She could feel the first woman's hostile glare on her back, and the children's curious eyes all round her. The dogs, she was relieved to see, were all sitting or lying down now, watching her, but with no particular interest. Warily, Old Meg watched her approach, and then spoke, her voice rasping, but her English clear and surprisingly grammatical, considering that her daughter did not appear to understand the language at all.

'You have a letter for me, missy?' she asked. Her black eyes seemed to see right through the girl. 'I can't read – none of us Romanies can read, except my grandson Samson, and he's away with the horses. And you can't speak, young Jimmy says. What d'you want?'

Liz suddenly no longer felt afraid. She raised her eyes to the old woman's face, and met her gaze; she felt that the gypsy could read her thoughts, almost as if they could communicate without the need of words.

'You want me to come with you? Where?'

Liz pointed back in the direction from which she had come.

'Now?' Old Meg leaned against the doorway, hand on her hip, staring down at the girl. Her eyes were almost black, set in a network of wrinkles. 'Why, girl? Why should I come?'

Liz put her hands together in a supplicating gesture, and then beckoned, meeting the old crone's eyes with a pleading gaze. The woman shrugged, dragged her tattered woollen shawl round her shoulders, and finally opened the lower half of the door.

'All right, missy, I'll come – but you'll have to wait while I fill the lantern. It'll be dark when I get back. Jimmy, you'll come with me.'

The cheeky-faced boy nodded, and a moment later the aged crone, stooped, skinny as a rake, her white hair falling almost to her waist in wild tangles, came down the steps and handed the lantern to the boy. She was dressed in a

135

black garment brilliantly embroidered with bright colours, reds, purples, blues and oranges all mixed together in fantastic patterns and borders; her face was brown, and as wrinkled and lined as a walnut; but the sharp black eyes were as bright and youthful as the boy's. Her feet – incredibly dirty feet! – were in leather sandals that looked as if they had been made by the Romanies. She set off at a rapid pace, followed by the boy, and then by Liz. Her feet never faltered nor stumbled on the rough, overgrown path. Liz had difficulty in keeping up with her. She seemed to know where to go; although it was well over two miles to the bay, she did not stop once or ask Liz if they were on the right track until they reached the door to the cottage. Then she stopped and waited for Liz to open the door.

It was not magic that had told the old woman where to come, although Liz was already convinced that she had secret powers; another of her grandsons had come to the wagon half an hour earlier and told her that the cottage at Honey Beck Bay was occupied again, and had described the girl he had seen at the door, and the man in the wheelchair who had been whisked inside as soon·as the girl saw his dog.

'Stay here, Jimmy, and mind what you get up to!' Meg told the boy, and followed Liz into the cottage.

Edward was lying on the bed in the lean-to room. As usual after a spat of temper, he was feverish; the rash on his neck and face had flared up red and angry.

The old crone walked straight into the room and stood looking down at the man on the bed. After a moment a crooked smile twisted her thin lips.

'Well, then, Neddy,' she said softly. 'You haven't been taking good care of yourself since I last saw you.'

'Hello, Meg,' Edward returned with a wry grin, surprised that she recognized in him the small boy who had always tried to hide when she appeared, convinced that she was a witch; a belief that the old woman had never discouraged. 'You're right – I'm in a mess! The doctors don't seem to do me much good. I think your Romany medicine might succeed where they've failed – I want you to tell me what to do.'

The old woman stared down at him, and gave a snort of laughter.

'Romany medicine? What Romany medicine? I'm not a doctor! I'm just an old woman with a little knowledge of herbs and spices. If I'm caught treating you I'm likely to finish up in one of those prisons your people like to lock us Romanies in . . . Your grandfather used to call me a white witch, but I'm not even that. I just know the healing properties of a few of the old forgotten herbs.'

Edward raised his hands, and let them fall in a gesture of hopelessness. His voice took on a pleading note.

'Look, Meg, the doctors have been dragging me about and I'm no better than when they started – if not worse! Unless these wounds heal soon, they'll get infected and that'll be the end of me. See what you can do – I promise I'll pay you well – because you're my last hope. I've got faith in you, Meg – and none in those damn doctors! Liz, take these dressings off and show Meg the mess I'm in.'

Liz gently peeled off the dressings and revealed the raw, angry flesh of the stump and the ankle. In some places the flesh round the the wounds was yellow and dead-looking; in other places patches of purple and crimson flared. The old gypsy stared at the repulsive sight for a moment, then leaned down and put her cheek close to them, checking for heat; she smelled the wounds, closing her eyes to concentrate all her faculties on the olfactory senses. She stood up again, and gruffly told Edward to show her his back. He turned over with difficulty, and Liz pulled up the nightshirt to reveal the worst of the rash. It was dry and scabby now; at least the moist, weeping patches that had appeared when

137

he wore the woollen undershirt had dried up, leaving scaly, rough areas where the skin had cracked and bled. The old gypsy leaned down and scratched at the scabby scales with a yellowed fingernail. Then she allowed Edward to turn on to his back again.

'Where did you get this fever, and how long have you had it?' she demanded. He told her as much as he knew: he had drunk contaminated water in South Africa, and the fever began shortly afterwards; it was better than it had been, but kept recurring, particularly if anything upset him.

'Bowels?' she asked, her black eyes on his face.

'Now look here, Meg – every doctor and nurse in the country has poured castor oil or extract of figs down my throat –' he began uneasily. The old woman cackled with laughter.

'That probably did their consciences more good than it did your ailments!' she croaked. 'But tell me the truth, man – there's no need to be modest with Old Meg! Are you in trouble with your bowels?'

'Yes – some,' he admitted grudgingly. Meg glanced interrogatively at Liz, who nodded vigorously. Edward had steadfastly refused to take any of the purgatives with which the chemist had supplied her.

'That's because of the fever,' Meg muttered, 'and the rash is due to the fever too. The wounds won't heal because your blood is sour. I'll give you some herbs and a dressing to be left for five days. You'll eat four fresh oranges each day, and bathe in water from the sea.'

'Four fresh oranges? And how can I bathe in water from the sea?' Edward exclaimed testily. 'I can't lower myself into a bath on one leg without risking a broken neck!'

Meg turned to Liz.

'Have a bath ready in the morning, half full of warm seawater. I'll come with two of my grandsons at seven o'clock. Be ready for us. And give him nothing to eat or drink after midnight.' She went to the door. 'And Neddy – keep yourself calm and rest quietly. If I'm to cure you, you've got to do your part – and peace within the soul does as much for a broken body as the lotions and potions applied to the flesh.'

'Neddy!' Edward muttered as she left the room. 'I've not been Neddy since the day my father took me from this cottage over twenty years ago.' It could have been the fever, but his eyes were glittering suspiciously brightly as he watched the old crone go out with the slight figure of Liz by her side.

Meg and Liz went to the outer door. Meg looked at the anxious girl.

'And you'll have learn to talk to him if you're to be a proper wife,' she said sharply. Liz shook her head, and pointed to the tiny scar where the doctors had performed the life-saving tracheotomy five years ago when she had had diphtheria; Meg peered at it closely, and then shook her head.

'That's healed, and can't affect your voice. You'll find your voice again one of these days,' she prophesied. 'I'll come tomorrow – have the bath prepared.'

It was nearly dusk. As she and the boy went back across the bay the lamp winked and gleamed, marking their progress. Liz watched until they disappeared into the trees. She was not afraid of the gypsy woman, and she no longer suspected that the old crone was a witch; she was convinced that she was!

Liz went back into the cottage and dragged the bath out. She collected her two large buckets, and went down to the shore. The sea was icy cold, and she had to wade in a few yards to fill the buckets. She made four trips to the water before she was satisfied that she had enough for the bath. She set the large wash-tub on the back of the range and filled it; the remainder of the water she poured into the bath. By the time she was finished, her skirts were wet through, and her feet icy, but she was perspiring from exertion. Edward watched her from the sofa, where he spent most of the day now.

'I reckon you're wishing you were back in Barminster working at the hospital,' he remarked as she straightened her back after tipping the last bucketful of water into the bath. She looked a bit like a gypsy herself, he thought, with her long dark hair escaping from the pins holding it into a heavy knot, and her black skirts tucked up so that she could wade into the sea without getting too wet. She smiled, and shook her head. Here, despite the hard work, she was happy, and she did not have to worry that her step-father would set about her when he came in drunk.

Edward read a few pages of David Copperfield to her after supper; but after ten minutes, sitting in the rocking-chair by the fireside, Liz fell asleep. He put the book down and gazed at her. Poor child – she was exhausted. She never gave any sign that she grudged the hard work she did on his account. One day he'd make it up to her. She had kept her side of the bargain; he would keep his.

The old woman appeared early the next morning, accompanied by two stalwart young men, two of her many grandsons. Liz was watching for them, and opened the door before they reached it. When Meg crossed the beach the tide was out; she searched along the water line for a particular species of seaweed, which she stowed in an oilskin bag, putting it in the basket on her arm. The younger of the men was thin and wiry, but the other was tall and well-muscled, a fine figure; both were clean-shaven, with thick black hair curling over their collars. Despite the chilly morning breeze, neither wore coats. They sported brightly coloured shirts under leather waistcoats; their skin was dark, with ruddy cheeks and black, merry eyes. Both treated their venerable grandmother with great respect.

The bath of warm seawater was waiting in front of the fire. Liz had been careful not to wake Edward while she prepared it, and the first thing he knew of the new day was finding Meg standing by his bed with a thick mug of a brew she had made from aromatic herbs. He hesitated to drink it, but found it tasted deliciously fresh and spicy. Meg made him finish this before she began her ministrations. Five minutes later he was dozy, and only half aware of what was going on around him.

Meg told Liz to go for a walk and come back in two hours' time. The girl looked at Edward, worried about leaving him in the care of the old woman and the two swarthy young men.

'Off you go, Liz,' Edward muttered thickly. 'I don't think she'll do me any harm ... Go to the farm and fetch some milk ...' His eyes were unfocused, and his words were slurred. Frightened, Liz wrapped her shawl round her, picked up the basket of mending she had finished for Mrs Willoughby, and set off for the steps in the cliff, looking back over her shoulder now and then as she went.

Meg stripped the patient, and washed him from head to foot with fresh water. One of the young men took a pair of scissors and cut his hair very close to the scalp, revealing the matting of scaly tissue where the rash was thick on his head. Meg mixed a handful of white clay with a brew she had made with the seaweed, and laid the mixture thickly over the rash, on Edward's head, trunk, back and legs. She made him lie still until this had almost dried; then she scraped it off with a wooden blade, which removed most of the scabs. She had put two thick pads of the same seaweed on the wounds on his legs. Now she removed them also, and her grandsons picked the semi-conscious man up and carefully lowered him into the bath of seawater, to which she had added some liquid from a bottle in the basket, giving the water a reddish tint.

Edward was left in the seawater for half an hour, the grandsons constantly laving the warm water over his head and the wounds on his legs, while the old woman mixed more strange, aromatic lotions from the contents of her basket. When he was lifted from the water she gave him another drink of the herbal potion; within minutes he was asleep. She took a sharp razor from the basket and began paring carefully at the flesh round the wounds.

Meantime, Liz had walked across the fields to the farm. A heavy mist had rolled in from the sea, and when she looked back from the top of the cliff, all she could see of the cottage was the vague outline of the roof. She had learned that a sea-mist like this in the morning usually meant a bright, dry day would follow. It would probably blow away on the gentle sea-breeze by mid-morning, and she would be able to work in the garden in the afternoon sunshine.

The morning milking was finished, and Job, an incongruous figure in his shirtsleeves and inevitable top hat, was loading the milk-churns into the cart to be taken into Forestwidden. Liz was struck by his likeness to Meg's grandsons. He called a greeting as she crossed the yard.

'Meg at the cottage?' he asked, effortlessly heaving a heavy churn on to the cart. Liz nodded. 'Go on into the kitchen, Miz' Clayton – I told Miz' Willoughby you'd probably be here early.' Presumably he had been talking to some of the gypsies at the camp, Liz thought. She pushed open the door and went into the farmhouse.

''Morning, Liz,' Mrs Willoughby smiled, getting up and fetching another cup from the dresser. 'Have you had breakfast, or will you let me give you some of this bacon?' The bacon smelled delicious, and soon Liz was tucking into a plate piled high with not only bacon, but eggs, sausage, and fried bread. Henry ploughed through another of the same. Job had told him that Meg was at the cottage with Edward. The farmer was far from happy about this, but said nothing to add to Liz's anxieties. He watched her quietly as she ate, realizing how worried she was.

Mrs Willoughby chatted cheerfully over the meal, and then she and Liz washed up together. As usual, there were a couple of weakly lambs in the kitchen, in a basket beside the fire. Breakfast over, she gave Liz a bottle of milk equipped with a teat, and showed her how to feed the lambs, while she finished kneading the bread dough, which had been left to prove overnight, and put four cottage loaves into the oven to bake. The girl forgot her worries for an hour while she helped with the morning chores, taking corn to the chickens, and collecting the eggs. Then she turned the butter-churn for twenty minutes, and was delighted when the thick golden chunks of butter were turned out.

'I'm going into the village this morning,' Mrs Willoughby remarked. 'Can I get anything from the shops for you?'

Liz nodded, but then frowned. How was she to ask for oranges? She drew two round orbs on the table with her finger.

'Eggs? But we've got eggs –' Mrs Willoughby began, but Liz shook her head. Not eggs. 'Apples? Potatoes?'

Liz looked round the kitchen, then jumped up and pointed to some embroidered marigolds on a cushion cover. Mrs Willoughby looked perplexed.

'Flowers? No . . . Yellow – oranges!' She laughed out loud at the delight on the girl's face. 'Yes, I'll get some oranges for you, my dear! How many? Ten – two – twelve? Right – twelve oranges. An expensive luxury, but I suppose you know what you want. Are you planning to make marmalade, my dear?'

Liz shook her head, and mimed eating the oranges. Ada Willoughby looked surprised, then smiled.

'If you eat all those oranges, Liz, you'll have a case of the back-door trots!' She took the four round loaves out of the oven; the freshly baked bread smelled delicious. She slid a tray of scones into the oven, and got out a bowl of eggs to beat the batter for a couple of sponge cakes. When the scones were done she would leave the oven door open for two minutes, then it would be at the right temperature for the cakes. 'What else do you need from the shops? Soap . . . tea . . .'

Liz went back with fresh bread and milk in the basket, hurrying across the wet fields, holding her skirts up to keep them dry. Now she hardly gave the cows a second glance as she passed, and they took little notice of her. Rover, as usual, followed her as far as the first stile, and then went running back to the farmyard to escort the milking herd out to pasture.

Meg was finishing her ministrations when Liz let herself back into the cottage. The two grandsons had emptied the bath, and were sitting on the beach in the mist, waiting for Meg. Edward was on the sofa with a blanket over him. His eyes were closed and he looked white and exhausted. Liz gasped when she saw him; his hair had been cropped so short he almost looked bald. She ran over and took his hand; he didn't stir, and when she dropped it and turned back to Meg it fell limply to his side. Her huge violet-blue eyes questioned the gypsy woman anxiously.

'Never fear, girl, he's not dead yet,' the old crone said tartly. 'He'll sleep for an hour or more. Give him some broth at mid-day, and some of that fresh bread I can smell. Keep him quiet. There's some herbal tea in that jar – give that to him after supper, and he'll get a good night's rest. Tomorrow I'll come again, so have the bath ready.' She packed the remainder of her belongings back into her basket. 'I've put a dressing on his wounds that must not be touched for five days – not for anything, or anyone. D'you understand?'

Liz nodded. The old woman picked up the basket and went to the door. She shouted at the men, and they went off together, walking up the steep road. The two men were talking and laughing in their own language, but their grandmother, striding a few paces ahead of them, was silent, saving her breath for the steep walk. Just before they disappeared out of sight, the older of the men, the one Meg called Samson, looked back and waved. He was a fine looking man; when he smiled his teeth gleamed white against his dark skin. Liz returned the wave and turned back into the cottage. She had work to do; nearly every towel and sheet they possessed had been used and was soiled and damp. Edward slept soundly as she washed and rinsed, waking finally when she returned to the room after hanging the wet things out on the line. The mist had dispersed, and the sun was shining brightly.

For the next five days the same routine was followed; Meg and the two grandsons arrived early in the morning, and Liz went to the farm, returning after two hours, when Meg would be finished and ready to leave. Most of the time Edward dozed, on the sofa or in his chair in the sun when the day was warm enough. He had an orange with every meal, and one before he went to bed. The weather remained fair and bright. Edward's rash was almost gone, and for two days he had shown no sign of the fever. Liz was beginning to believe that the Romany medicine was working; that, or the old woman had wrought some sort of magic. On the fifth day she got back to find the gypsies hurrying to leave; the horse-sales and the Fair began today. Samson had a horse he wanted to sell, and he was anxious to get away.

'I'll come again in two days' time,' Meg told her. 'He

145

won't need the herbal tea, but I've left a tisane on the table. Give him two spoonsful before his meals, three times a day. Remember, two spoonsful. And make sure he continues with the oranges.'

Liz nodded; then looked questioningly at the old woman. Was she to do the dressings tomorrow? She saw the pile of used dressings on the flagstones near the bath, and pointed, then pointed at Edward, peacefully asleep on the sofa, asking the question with her eyes. Meg smiled.

'No, dearie – leave the dressings. Just give him the tisane.' She picked up her basket and left. As usual, Liz watched them out of sight, waving as they reached the bend in the road, and then walked slowly back into the cottage.

They had been in a hurry today, and left the room in even more of a mess than usual. Liz first put the washing to soak in the tub on the top of the range, and then fetched the coke to stoke up the fire. Before putting in the coke, she picked up the used dressings, to drop them into the red embers. For the past five days there had been no dressings; now she had a great handful of them. As she picked them up from the floor a large folded-over piece of linen fell out, unrolling as it hit the flagstones, and spilling the contents across the floor.

From the soiled, discoloured linen fell a mass of fat, white, writhing maggots.

Liz leaped back, and screamed.

Edward stirred, muttered a few unintelligible words, and went back to sleep. Liz stared in shock at the repulsive mass of maggots before realizing that the scream she had heard had come from her own throat. She dropped the dressings still in her hand, and sank into the rocking-chair.

Tentatively, she tried again to use her voice, but no sound came forth. She tried to repeat the scream, but without success. She could still hear the echo of the shriek in her head; she knew it had been her own voice for her throat hurt as if it had been scraped with a knife; but she could not, now, utter a sound.

Shuddering, she got up and swept the disgusting nest of maggots into the coal shovel and threw them into the fire. She dropped the remainder of the dressings in on top, and filled the stove up with coke. She took a bucket of warm water and scrubbed the flagstones where the dressings had fallen with a stiff brush until her hands were almost raw; then she put the kettle on and sat down to wait for it to boil.

Where had the nauseating maggots come from? She was afraid to give herself an answer to the question that would not leave her mind. They were in the dressings; did that mean that Edward's wounds had festered and rotted while those gypsy dressings were left on for five days? What state were they in now?

'Leave the dressings,' Meg had said. She would be back in two days. Did that mean that for two days the wounds were to be left to fester under the dressings she had put on this morning? And what dressings had she used? Liz could see that the supply of clean lint and bandages she had left out on the table had not been touched.

Unable to bear the anxiety any longer, Liz knelt by the sofa, gently removed the blanket over Edward's legs, and folded back the nightshirt to look at his ankle.

Astounded, she sank back on to her heels, and stared. She couldn't believe her eyes. There was no dressing on the wound at all; nor was there any discolouration. A tender new pink skin covered the ankle, as fragile and delicate as gossamer; it was completely healed over. With shaking hands, she raised the hem of the nightshirt until the stump of the amputated leg was revealed, and here she found the same miracle had been wrought. Not a trace of raw flesh, nor a sign of discolouration remained; just a fine new skin, pink, clean and healthy.

147

She put her hands over her face, and sobbed with relief.

Edward stirred, sighed, and opened his eyes. He saw Liz weeping, kneeling by the bed; he put out his hands and took hers, holding them fast.

'Now, then, girl, it can't be as bad as that,' he said gruffly. The last thing he remembered was being lifted from his bed by the two young gypsies; and here was his brave, tireless Liz crying over him.

She lifted her face, and smiled at him, gesturing towards his legs. He struggled into a sitting position, and forced himself to look at the nauseating wounds. When he saw the healthy, clear skin he gave a shout of jubilation. He was as amazed as she was.

'By God, Liz, she's done it,' he breathed. 'I knew she could do it – I just knew it! I'm a new man, Liz – thanks to that old gypsy woman. Now, if only she would pass on her knowledge to the doctors, just think how they could use it! There must be thousands of men in the hospitals who could be cured . . .'

Remembering the seething mass she had found in the dressings, Liz doubted if the doctors would be eager to try the old gypsy woman's methods; but being unable to tell Edward what had brought about the cure, she was also unable to disagree with him. She smiled and nodded; and then went to fill the kettle to make tea.

When Meg paid Edward her last visit, he asked how much he should pay her. She shrugged, and named a paltry sum that would hardly buy her weekly supply of tobacco.

'No, I must pay you a fair rate,' Edward insisted. 'I might have been lying there for another six months without your help – or more like, I'd have died of septic poisoning. So name a decent sum, Meg, and it's yours.'

'My herbs and potions are gathered from the free earth, Neddy, and cost nothing, and the knowledge that puts them to use is not for sale. Pay me enough to buy a warm cloak for the winter and I'll be satisfied. But if you're short of money, pay me nothing. The gypsies look after their own, and don't expect reward.'

'Their own? Do you count me as one of your tribe, Meg?' The old woman looked down at him with a grin.

'Why, Neddy – don't you know your old grandmother was my own sister? And that was the reason your grandfather refused to accept your father's marriage? A Clayton married to a gypsy's brat – that was more than the man could stomach! He might have acknowledged a fisherman's daughter – he wouldn't like it, but he may have accepted it. But a gypsy – that was more than his pride could bear!'

Edward took from his wallet all the money he had. Keeping just enough to meet the food bills for the rest of the week, he gave the old woman the remainder; and that was the last he saw of her.

Chapter Thirteen

Spring turned to summer, and the forest was clothed in green. Primroses were followed by bright clumps of daffodils, which in turn gave way to the wild flowers of the forest. The gypsy camp was long gone. After the Fair the caravans had moved on to the next fairground, taking their horses with them.

At Honey Beck Bay, some of the vegetation proved to have survived the neglect of three years, and shrubs and fruit trees were festooned with blossom. Liz worked hard to restore the garden and soon had a patch of vegetables thriving. She had never had access to a garden before, and every germinating seed was a small miracle to her delighted eyes.

With the help of Job and Henry, she finished white-washing the inside of the cottage. The faded chintz curtains looked cheerful and homelike against the white walls. She took pride in keeping the cottage spotless, and never had an idle moment. As soon as one project was completed she started work on another; she was content, and completely satisfied with life.

Following Meg's instructions, Edward spent many hours in the sun, and soon he was growing fit and strong again. Old Meg's treatment had successfully cured him of the fever and the rash. He learned to get about on his crutches, and occasionally went for a short 'walk' up the lane towards the forest. But the crutches sank into the ground when he attempted to leave the road, and he tired too soon to go far, so he never got more than a couple of hundred yards from the cottage. He spent hours sitting on a log near the high-water line in the sunshine, reading, or just watching the restless ebb and flow of the tide. The constant murmur of the waves on the sand soothed his spirit, releasing the tension in his heart. He felt that his life was akin to the tides, sometimes rising to a high point, sometimes at a low ebb. For years now his luck had been out; but at last he felt that his tide had turned, and was beginning to rise again.

He was, as yet, unable to negotiate the steps in the cliff at the back of the cottage, to reach the little paddock crossed by the stream. But he was able to stump round to the privvy behind the trees; this was a great boost to his morale!

As his health improved, he gained weight. His face filled out, and he looked years younger. Most people would have agreed that he was reasonably good-looking in his own way; to Liz he was a splendidly handsome man. In her eyes he had no failings; he was her ideal. Everything she thought or did was for his benefit; nothing was too difficult or too exhausting if it might add to his comfort. The quick flash of a smile in thanks for a meal or a small favour was enough to keep her happy.

But with improved health, Edward was becoming restless. Sometimes he watched Liz working on her garden and cursed himself for his helplessness; he could not even help her to turn the heavy soil to make a seedbed. Then he became morose and quiet, hardly speaking a word for days on end. His small income was enough for them to live on, but there was nothing to spare. He despaired of finding a way to augment the pension and the interest from the bonds his grandmother had left him and became convinced that he would spend the rest of his life in poverty, dependent on Liz for his day-to-day requirements and unable to repay her devotion in any way. He tried to shake off the depression and keep cheerful, but in his heart he felt that perhaps it might have been better for everyone if he had been killed with the other men when that Boer farmhouse had been attacked.

As soon as it was warm enough he took to bathing in the sea, an activity that so intrigued Liz that eventually, one morning before he was up, she tried it herself – and enjoyed it so much that it became part of her daily routine. Several times she was almost caught in her shift by the young fisherman, who continued to leave them a couple of fish from his catch twice a week.

At Edward's insistence, Liz resumed the habit of spending an hour of an evening practising her letters. She was not very enthusiastic as she saw no practical use for the skill – why would she want to read books? She persevered to please him, and presently her painfully slow letters began to take more shape, and she could put them together to make simple words. One evening she was sitting at the table gripping the pencil in a tight fist, copying out a simple sentence he had set for her, when Edward noticed that as she formed the characters her lips moved, and she was silently mouthing the letters. He watched idly for a moment, wondering if there was some way this development could be exploited. He pushed his wheelchair nearer, and watched more closely.

There was no doubt about it; as Liz made the characters, she was silently mouthing their sounds. He took the pencil from her hand and drew a large S on the notepaper, that being, he thought, the most distinctive and easiest sound. He watched her closely. As he wrote the letter, her lips moved silently and unconsciously.

'Liz, try and make that sound,' he said quietly. Her eyes flew to his face; a flicker of fear moved in their depths. Her mind went back to her step-father shouting 'Speak, damn you, girl, speak', as he slapped her round the face. She flinched away from Edward, and covered her face with her hands.

He stared at her in dismay. It was weeks since she had showed these signs of fear, although when they first came to the cottage she had cringed every time he raised his voice; and when he had been ill and in fear of his legs rotting away he had often snapped and snarled at her, letting her take the brunt of his despair. But those bad times were over. Now he treated her with the consideration he would have given his mother, or a younger sister.

'Don't be frightened, Liz,' he said gently, taking her hand. 'Just try! Put your tongue behind your teeth, and blow.' She shook her head. She couldn't do it, not even for him. He put the pencil into her hand.

'Write an "S", Liz.' Obediently, she drew the letter on the paper; as she did so, she mouthed the sound silently. 'Now write it again, and this time blow out gently as you write.' She hesitated, then did as he asked; and a gentle hissing sound emerged.

She looked up, startled. Edward laughed, and put his arm round her thin shoulders.

'There you are, my girl! You can do it, you see. Now let's try a "P". Close your mouth, pucker up as if you are about to kiss someone, and blow!'

Liz closed her mouth, puckered up, and looked at him submissively.

'Blow, girl – pretend you're blowing out a candle!'

Liz blew; and a small explosive 'P' sounded. There was no voice behind the sound, it was less than a whisper, but it was there. Edward laughed at her surprised look, and gave her a casual hug.

'Now, let's put the two sounds together, and say "Puss".' He wrote P U S S and looked at her expectantly. She looked down at the paper, her lips moving silently; then she put her breath behind the movement, and whispered 'Puss' softly, but quite clearly.

Edward laughed again, and impulsively leaned forward

and kissed her surprised face – a light, brotherly kiss on the cheek. It was the first time he had ever done such a thing, and had he stopped to think he would not have done it now, but the delight on her face, and his pleasure in her progress, had made him act without thinking.

He felt her slight figure stiffen, and her eyes flew back to the paper, avoiding contact with his. He dropped his arm from her shoulders, and moved his chair back to its usual place, several feet from hers; he assumed her reaction was an instinctive repulse to his touch. Obviously she was repelled by contact with him ... Well, what healthy young girl in her right mind would want to be touched by a cripple, a grey-haired man years older than herself – even that grey hair looked repulsive, cut so short, like a convict's ...

Edward picked up his book, and pretended to be immersed in it, wondering why he was so dismayed by her rejection. After all, she had more than kept her side of their bargain; she could not have worked harder to make him comfortable, to make a home for him ... It was too much to ask her to – to what? To give him affection as well as obedience? To be a wife in every sense of the word? Was that what he wanted?

He tried to concentrate on the book, but although his eyes travelled along the lines, their sense eluded him completely. He was unable to concentrate for two minutes. He glanced across at her furtively; she was copying out the sentence he had set for her, her colour heightened, her eyes sparkling almost as if with tears.

Hell! The last thing he wanted to do was make her cry! He turned back to the book and stared unseeingly at the page.

Liz was doggedly copying out the words, letter by letter, her lips moving silently, her mind in a whirl of confusion. She had – not spoken, but whispered, at least! And he had been so pleased – he had hugged her! Given her a kiss – a real kiss! Astonishment had made her stiffen, and drop her eyes. No-one had kissed her for years – not even her mother, since she had borne the twins, her half-brothers . . .

But now he had lost interest again. He had gone back to his book – he was bored with a girl who was so stupid that she couldn't even talk to him . . .

Tears pricked her eyes. She must not let him see her crying! She got up and put the kettle on, then went back and did another five minutes' practice while the water came to the boil. She copied a 'T'. Tea. Tea! She put the leaves in the pot and poured on the boiling water. She cut a piece of cake, and put it, with the steaming cup, on the table by his side. She clinked the spoon against the side of the cup. Edward looked up. She met his eyes, concentrated for a moment, and mouthed 'Tea'.

Edward was delighted. He felt that finally they were making real progress. He wanted to kiss her again, but he knew that would only lead to another rejection; he just smiled at her and patted her hand. Her heart turned over. So he was not angry with her, he was just bored. How tedious it must be for him to waste his time trying to teach such a slow, dull pupil!

'Thank you, Liz,' Edward said quietly. 'Thank you for the "tea".'

Arthur Clayton and Lady Imogen were breakfasting in the house in Eaton Square. Keenlach Lodge had been closed down for the summer, and only an old caretaker and his wife remained; the furniture had been swathed in dust-sheets and the horses sent to their summer grazing meadows.

Lady Imogen was not looking at her best; in fact, she looked distinctly haggard this bright morning. A very late night and rather too much alcohol recently had done nothing to improve her temper nor her complexion, which was far from beautiful at the best of times. She was wearing a soft grey wrap trimmed with yards of fine Brussels lace; even at this time in the day she was dressed in the latest fashion. Arthur's stout figure was garbed in the usual formal morning suit; he was expecting George Steadman, the solicitor, to call for a business conference shortly.

Sir Rupert no longer joined them at meals. After Harriet's departure a mild stroke had left the old man severely depressed. He had always disliked his daughter-in-law, and the dislike now reached the proportions of an obsession. He took to remaining in his own rooms rather than constantly coming face to face with her about the house. Gradually he sank into a lethargic state, apparently waiting to die. The Honourable Arthur took over the management of the estate. He was determined to improve the income from the various properties and enterprises. He raised the rents on some of the farms, and if a tenant-farmer fell behind with his rent he was not allowed time to pay, as before, when Sir Rupert had held the reins.

'Letter from your father, I see,' Arthur said as he spread marmalade thickly on his toast. His father-in-law was far from his favourite relation; the old man had never made any secret of the fact that he considered his daughter to have married beneath her, an opinion shared by the daughter herself. 'I presume he's in his usual good health?'

'Yes, but here's a piece of news,' Lady Imogen said thoughtfully, passing the letter across the table to her husband. He waved it away peevishly; Lord Farlington's handwriting was difficult to decipher at the best of times, and a headache, induced by too much brandy the night before, did not incline him to concern himself with his father-in-law's fault-finding and bemoaning. 'It seems that cousin who was to inherit has died – you remember he went to Australia some years ago? Well, he fell from his horse somewhere out in the wilds and was found a week later by a wandering

156

tribe of aborigines. Father got the news a few days ago.'

Arthur's attention was captured by this report; not that he had ever met the cousin, or cared a fig for his well-being or otherwise, but it altered the line of succession to the earldom. Lady Imogen was the only child of Lord Farlington; if there were no male heir, the title and estate would pass to her son. That meant that Gervaise became the future earl. Even Arthur Clayton, in his present state of alcoholic depression, could not fail to realize the implication of this information. Apart from anything else, it meant that while he was trying to persuade the constituents to vote him into the House of Commons, his idle son would inherit a place in the House of Lords without lifting a finger.

'Well – hmph! Ah, well, I can hardly say that's good news, my dear, as your cousin's death is – er – an unfortunate loss to the family –'

'Don't be such a hypocrite, Arthur,' his wife snapped. 'None of us had seen him for twenty years or more, or wanted to! A wastrel and a fool, as I remember. Thank God he won't have the opportunity of squandering what remains of the family fortune on horses and gambling!'

'No – we can anticipate that Gervaise will do that now,' Arthur said sourly. 'This cousin – he never married?'

'His taste did not run to women,' Lady Imogen said acidly. 'That was the reason, I believe, that he left this country in a hurry some years ago. A fine thing it would be to have a man like that appear and claim relationship! We presumed that he would remain in the Dominions, probably sell Farlington Towers, and leave his estate to a sailor – or a cowboy. Now, however, the case is changed. Gervaise will inherit the title, the Towers, and the estate. Not for a long time yet, I hope,' she added hastily. Her father was a healthy man of seventy-five, and showed every indication of becoming a healthy man of eighty- or even ninety-five.

'And where is the future Lord Farlington now?' Arthur

Clayton asked sarcastically. His wife frowned.

'How should I know? He went off a couple of days ago, without letting me know where, and I suppose he'll return when he feels like it.'

Arthur collected his letters and his newspaper and stood up, grimacing. When the next election took place, he hoped to be the choice of the voting public in Barminster. He had instructed his sons to curtail their extravagant behaviour; any scandal on their part could ruin his reputation. He dreaded a repetition of his brother Robert's infamous conduct.

'I'm going to the study. Tell Beale to send Steadman in when he arrives. And you'd better let my father know Steadman's here – not that he'll want to see him. He leaves all the decisions to me now, he's not even interested any longer. I asked him last night if he wanted to get in touch with young Edward – Robert's son. Apparently he's reappeared somewhere. He was injured in the war, lost his memory or something. But Father wasn't interested – I'm not sure he knew who I was talking about!'

'Hmmm . . . ? What?' His wife was scanning a bill from the dressmaker; she wasn't interested in Edward Clayton either. 'This damn fool has overcharged me again! This bill is ridiculous!'

'I'll tell Steadman to do nothing about Edward. Let sleeping dogs lie. With luck we'll not hear anything more about him.'

Lady Imogen looked up from her letters.

'What are you going to do about that girl Harriet? Will you tell Steadman to let her have the allowance she's demanding?'

'Might as well,' Arthur said indifferently. 'There's a good income in her trust – quite enough to put half-a-dozen young women through medical school. And I certainly don't want her back here, carping about her independence. It's

158

not as if she's my reponsibility, and if Father wrote the letter Steadman reported I'm not going to let her take us to court and make us appear ridiculous! Father's given me a Power of Attorney in her trust. I'll tell Steadman to advance the money, and let the damn girl do as she wishes. No point in mentioning it to the old man, though – let him forget her, it only makes him depressed to remind him that she's deserted him.'

'Just so long as I'm not expected to do anything for the ungrateful girl,' his wife said, rising from the table. 'I'd better write to Father, I suppose, and express my distress at my cousin's demise. Silly fool – should never have gone riding alone. He never was much of a horseman.'

For some time Harriet had been living with a friend in London, one of the girls with whom she had been nursing. She had been in touch with several hospitals where medical training was obtainable, and had decided that Edinburgh was the most suitable for her needs. She did not want to remain in London; she wanted to get as far away from the Clayton family as possible.

Before she could be considered as a student by the authorities she had to provide several references. The matron of the military hospital, Miss Walters, had accepted a post as matron of a small nursing home in Kent. At her age she could not secure another post as matron of a busy hospital, and did not relish having to accept a place in the nursing profession where she would be taking orders from a younger woman.

Wearing a plain dark dress and jacket, with a simple felt hat hiding her tawny hair, Harriet went to visit Miss Walters and was amused to find the nursing home was run on military lines; Miss Walters found the habit of a lifetime hard to break.

She was taken to the matron's sitting-room, where she

sat in a high-backed chair and waited for her hostess. Presently Miss Walters sailed in, wearing a plain grey dress and without the elaborate starched cap Harriet was used to seeing her in; without her uniform she looked a much more approachable character. However, her brisk manner had not abated, and her eyes were as sharp as ever.

'Nurse Grant – how nice to see you,' she exclaimed, shaking Harriet's hand. 'I suppose you are ready to go off and train for a doctor now – or have you been dissuaded from that course?'

'Indeed I have not,' Harriet informed her, smiling. 'That's why I'm here, in fact. Before I can apply for a place I need references, and I hoped you would be one of my referees.'

'I would have thought your uncle could have arranged all that for you,' Matron remarked. A maid came in with the tea-tray, and she sat by the table and began to pour. 'Surely he could ask for references from more influential parties than myself?'

'My uncle has gone back on his word, and refuses to help me. He also refuses to advance me the money I need to live on while I'm studying,' Harriet told her bitterly.

'But I thought that was all agreed,' Miss Walters exclaimed.

'So it was, but you know Uncle Rupert – he hoped I would have second thoughts, and now he insists I should return home and stay there – he suggested I take up embroidery instead! However, I still have my allowance – it hasn't been cut off yet! I've saved most of that during the past year, so I think I can just about manage provided I don't squander any of it on unnecessary things like food and clothes! I haven't seen him since I left home, and I still hope that Mr Steadman, the second trustee, will persuade him to continue, or even increase, the allowance. However, that's all hypothetical until I manage to secure a place at the medical college in Edinburgh. Can you help me?'

'My dear, I can, and I will! I know one of the leading surgeons there, and I'll write and ask him to use his influence in your favour. I believe he's one of the governors of the medical college. Meanwhile, I'll send you a reference to enclose with your application. Who else are you asking for a reference?'

'I hoped to ask Dr Mansfield, but I find he's retired and I can't trace his address.'

'Ah, I can help you there, too! He's living with his widowed sister in Norfolk. I'll give you his address. I'll also drop him a few lines and ask him to make his reference as enthusiastic as possible. I'm all for having more women doctors in the hospitals, Nurse Grant. I know it's difficult for a woman to find a place in the profession, but there are many instances where a woman would be more appropriate than a male doctor. Here, for instance; a woman would be more reassuring to the old folk and the children who are admitted for convalescence. It's about time the men of this country abandoned the idea that a woman cannot follow a career. I look forward to the day when women doctors, barristers, and even politicians have the same opportunities as their fathers and brothers. Just think, one day we may even have a female Prime Minister!'

'Oh, Miss Walters, I think that is flying into the realms of fantasy!' Harriet smiled.

'Of course, we must first have the vote . . .'

For nearly half an hour Harriet was treated to a lecture on the Suffragette Movement, and left the nursing home with the knowledge that she had a strong ally in the matron. Returning to London by train she wondered why Miss Walters had not undertaken a physician's training herself, but realized that when she was a girl it was even more difficult for a woman to enter the profession. She had done the next best thing and become one of Miss Nightingale's nurses. Had she ever been young and attractive? Perhaps

161

even pretty? Or had she been born in a well-starched apron and with that flinty look in her eye?

Harriet wrote to Dr Mansfield, and received a reference by return of post that was positively glowing. She acquired another from the headmistress of her old school. These she enclosed, together with the one from Miss Walters, with her application for a place at the medical college in Edinburgh, and was shortly requested to travel up to Scotland for an interview with the governors of the college. There were a very limited number of places allocated to female students, and without the championship of the matron's old friend she would not have had a chance. However, a few days after her return to London she had a letter from the governors advising her that her application had been successful, and she was instructed to present herself at the Ladies' Hostel early in September. A formidable list of rules and regulations regarding the hostel was enclosed.

'It looks as if a convent would be positively hilarious compared with this,' Harriet said ruefully to the friend with whom she was staying. 'I'll have to look for lodgings outside the hospital if I want so much as to speak to a man!'

'Can you do that?'

'Apparently you can live outside the hostel after the first three months, if the governors agree and you can afford it,' Harriet said, scanning the sheet. 'At the moment, I'll have difficulty affording the hostel! The fees alone will clean out my bank balance. I'll have to go and see old Steadman and hope Uncle Rupert has changed his mind.'

Her visit to George Steadman's office was short, but successful. Mr Steadman informed her that her allowance had been increased to a sum Arthur Clayton considered sufficient to pay her fees and keep her in a respectable manner. When she asked after her uncle's health she was told that he had had a mild stroke, but was recovering.

'Oh – I must go and see him at once!' she exclaimed.

George Steadman looked embarrassed.

'Mr Arthur Clayton also asked me to inform you that you will not be admitted to the house,' he said reluctantly. 'He thinks your presence would be detrimental to your uncle's health, unless you are ready to return home and give up all thoughts of a medical career.'

'Oh!' Harriet was taken aback. 'Was that his personal opinion, that of his doctors, or his wife's?'

Mr Steadman's eyes dropped under the straight gaze of Harriet's.

'I am sure that Lady Imogen has her father-in-law's good at heart,' he said unhappily.

'Ah! Lady high-and-mighty Imogen gives the orders these days, I gather,' Harriet said bitterly. 'Well, we'll see. I'm sure that Beale will not turn me away from the door,' she added confidently.

However, when she presented herself at the house in Eaton Square the door was opened not by Beale, but by a younger, more formidable butler. Beale had become Sir Rupert's personal servant, taking care of him in the suite of rooms on the first floor that he seldom left nowadays. The new butler had his orders. When Harriet announced herself and asked to see Sir Rupert he replied in an icy tone.

'Sir Rupert is not at home to visitors, ma'am.'

'Then I'll see Mr Arthur Clayton, or Lady Imogen,' Harriet persisted.

'Mr Clayton and Lady Imogen are not available.'

'Dammit, man – I'm Sir Rupert's niece!' Harriet exclaimed.

'Yes, ma'am, I am aware of that,' the butler said imperturbably, and closed the door in her face.

Harriet raised the knocker and beat it savagely on the door, but there was no response. After a moment she stamped her foot in rage, turned, and stalked down the road with her cheeks flaming. That was the last time she would call at Clayton House!

Sir Rupert was not informed that his niece had called and been refused admittance. He had withdrawn from the world, and spent his time hunched over the fire in his own room, brooding over the past.

His grandsons, Gervaise and Cecil Clayton, had gone north to attend a horse race. They had bought a filly a few months earlier, and had her trained in Yorkshire by a renowned trainer, who had entered her for her first race at one of the provincial tracks. She was not expected to win, but he thought that she would be placed, and the experience would be useful. The brothers had high hopes of success; the trainer told them that she was coming on very well.

They had expected to find accommodation in York. But when they got there they found that all the reputable hotels were full, and were forced to put up at a small, noisy tavern in a part of the town that they would not normally have deigned to visit.

'You should have made reservations before we came,' Cecil grumbled as he followed his brother up the narrow stairs to their rooms. Although he and Gervaise frequently undertook joint engagements, they spent more time arguing than enjoying each other's company.

'How was I to know that the town would be full?' Gervaise retorted angrily. 'I've never had trouble finding rooms before. No-one told me that there was some religious celebration on at the cathedral, and every bishop in the country would be booked into the city hotels.'

'Well, I don't think there's much likelihood of running into any bishops in this locality,' Cecil remarked, looking round the shabby, cramped room he had been allocated. From the street below a continuous noise of traffic arose, punctuated by shouts from the street urchins, and the clanging of a hammer on metal from a nearby blacksmith's forge.

'Don't be so damned fastidious,' Gervaise said brusquely. 'It's too late in the day to start looking elsewhere, and it's only for two nights. We were lucky to get this; I've had to send Bugle out to look for a room in a lodging house.'

'I doubt if Bugle would have settled for this,' Cecil said resentfully. 'For a servant he has very elevated ideas of his own importance. I don't know why the devil you brought him – we could just as well have managed our own luggage and railway bookings.'

'And I suppose you would have been up at the crack of dawn to arrange to hire a horse and trap to take us to the races tomorrow, and look after them when we got there –'

'Oh, shut up, Gervaise; the train's given me a headache, and I'm just about fed up. I don't feel at all the thing. Let's hope that filly makes the trip worth while tomorrow. Where are we going to eat tonight?' Cecil was fond of his food.

'Here, I think. It's already late, and I don't feel like fighting the bishops for a table. I'll see you downstairs in half an hour.'

They were pleasantly surprised by the meal served at the tavern: excellent roast beef, and plenty of it, followed by a fruit pudding. They went for a walk through the old part of the town before turning in, and later found that the beds were as good as the meal, despite the cramped rooms. They both slept well, and were out early and on their way to the races, optimistic for their filly's success. Bugle drove, and looked after the horse while they made their way to the marquee where refreshments were served.

Their filly was in the second race, and took second place, bringing them a good return on their wagers. The trainer was pleased. For a first-time runner, she had done them proud. Gervaise and Cecil did well on the later races, too, placing several lucky bets; and when they returned to the tavern in the evening they were feeling very pleased with themselves.

Again they dined in, this evening on oysters, roast pork, and a suet pudding. It was so good that Cecil had several helpings of the pork, washing them down with ale. Gervaise partook more sparingly; he was beginning to put on weight and was anxious not to become stout like his father. But during the night he awoke with slight stomach cramps, and wondered if the pork had been as well cooked as it should have been. While he was lying awake, his door opened, and Cecil appeared with a candle, his face as white as his nightshirt.

'Gervaise – God, man, I'm as sick as a dog!' he gasped, on the verge of collapse. Gervaise assisted him back to his bed, and summoned the landlord, who sent a boy running to fetch a doctor.

Less than twelve hours later Cecil died. Whether it was a bad oyster, the pork, or something he had picked up before they came to York was never determined. Gervaise was also slightly indisposed, but recovered within a few hours.

The Honourable Arthur and Lady Imogen mourned their youngest son with the reserve and restraint of their class. Lady Imogen ordered a complete new wardrobe in black, and for several months her social activities were curtailed; Cecil had been her favourite child, and she was very distressed by his death. She soon found consolation in the brandy bottle, however.

The people most severely affected by the young man's death were his bookmaker, his tailor, and a buxom young dancer appearing twice nightly at a night-club called The Hatbox.

Chapter Fourteen

As the summer wore on, Liz and Edward spent more and more time in the garden of the cottage and on the sea-shore. Liz loved the rustic life they had adopted. When Henry Willoughby was haymaking she spent several afternoons working in the fields with Mrs Willoughby, Henry, and some itinerant labourers, bringing in the hay before the weather broke; but as the fine weather went on day after day the urgency proved to be unnecessary. Late in June they had a summer storm, followed by heavy rain, but then the fine weather returned and Liz and Edward were able to spend most of their time outdoors again.

Late one morning when the tide was almost out, Liz was sitting on the sand when she heard a horse coming down the road, and wheels crunching on the gravelly surface. She turned to see who it could be. The only visitor who usually came in a trap was Mrs Willoughby, when she brought more than the daily necessities from the shop. But this was a man. For a moment Liz could not see who it was, then she recognized John Oatis, the solicitor.

Edward was in the sea, enjoying his daily dip. It was his custom to make his way into the water on his crutches; then Liz would wade in, holding her skirts high, take the crutches from him, and he would lower himself into the water and strike out. It was a great moment for him when he discovered that he could swim strongly despite the loss of one leg, as it was the only form of vigorous exercise he was able to take.

It was a few minutes before Edward noticed the man

talking with Liz. Then he made his way towards the shore and called her to bring his crutches. He was self-conscious about being caught wearing only his short undergarments, but he wrapped himself in the towel she brought and hopped up to greet their visitor. As he crossed the beach the crutches sank into the sand, but when he reached the firm ground he was able to move quite nimbly. He seldom used the wheelchair now.

John Oatis watched him with a broad grin. He had heard nothing of their progress since he waved farewell to them four months before in Barminster, when he had, in his heart, feared that Edward Clayton was not likely to live more than a short time. He had been sending Edward's money care of the farm, by post, but had decided it was time to pay the couple a visit. He was delighted to find Edward so well, and amazed at the change in Liz, who was now pounds heavier, and looking fit, well, and happy. Her eyes and her hair shone with health, and she had become a beauty. John found it hard to believe that the poor drudge from the hospital had blossomed into such a lovely woman in so short a time.

They went into the cottage. Liz put the vegetables on to cook, and set the table for the mid-day meal while Edward dried himself and dressed. John watched her quietly, admiring the deft way in which she worked. Could this young woman really be the sad little waif he had met only a few months ago? At the time he had suspected that Edward might shortly regret his hasty marriage, but now he was not so sure. He had brought a bottle of wine with him, a huge wedge of cheese, and a freshly baked loaf of bread. He had not known what he would find here; and he didn't want to find himself in the embarrassing position of a visitor at mealtime if they had nothing to offer him. But Liz brought a savoury-smelling steak pie out of the oven where it had been baking while Edward swam, and put the dish of hot vegetables out for them to help themselves.

'Well, Edward, you seem to be managing very well,' John said heartily as Edward emerged from his bedroom fully dressed. 'And I don't have to ask how you are – I can see that the sun and the sea air have wrought a cure.'

'The cure is mainly due to Old Meg, the gypsy, and splendid nursing from my wife,' Edward told him. 'I think the sun and the sea air helped – not to mention the seawater – but Old Meg and her herbs and incantations should really take the credit.'

'Witchcraft, perhaps?' John Oatis laughed and, although Edward joined in the laughter, he was not sure that witchcraft was too wide of the mark. He remembered little of the treatment he had received; most of the time he had been under the influence of Meg's herbal concoctions, and as far as he knew she could very well have employed spells and magic.

After the meal the men sat on a log out by the sea-shore, and finished the remainder of the wine with a couple of cigars John produced. He didn't want to talk too freely in front of Liz, not knowing to what extent she was aware of her husband's financial affairs. He suspected that she was still a wife in name only; certainly Edward had not been in a condition to consummate the union at the time he was married, and his attitude to Liz now was considerate and affectionate, but hardly husbandly. Liz, on the other hand, treated Edward with the deference and respect that a girl might give a father, or elder brother. She obviously idolized him; but nothing in her manner suggested that she was truly his wife.

John drew two letters out of his pocket.

'These arrived for you a few days ago, and as I'm not very busy at the moment I decided to deliver them in person,' he said, handing them to Edward. 'I also wanted to have a chat with you about your financial position.'

Edward opened the letters and read them. One was from

George Steadman, the solicitor, informing him that his cousin Cecil had died recently. He also mentioned that Arthur Clayton was now managing the family affairs. He hoped that Edward was recovered from his injuries, and he would be pleased to hear from him if he wished to be in touch. It was a routine letter from the solicitor to a beneficiary of a trust in his care.

The other letter was from Miss Harriet Grant, his distant cousin. Edward vaguely remembered meeting the girl many years ago, but had no reason to connect her with the nurse he had known in the hospital. He was surprised to hear from her. She mentioned that she was about to commence medical training; she had heard that he had been injured and hoped that he was now recovered; and as they were both, now, cut off from the Clayton family, she thought it a pity they were not in touch. She gave him an address in Edinburgh, adding that she would be pleased to hear from him if he felt inclined to renew their acquaintance.

'I wonder why she bothered to write,' Edward said thoughtfully, putting the letter back in its envelope. 'Oh, that was just a note from a distant cousin. Apparently she's also fallen out of favour with the Claytons! Do you know anything about Cecil Clayton's death?'

'Very little. I believe he was in York and got food poisoning of some sort. He died within a few hours. There was mention of it in the Barminster Herald, as his father is the proposed candidate for the constituency, and of course Sir Rupert is well known in the town.'

'Cecil was my cousin, but I barely knew him,' Edward commented. 'I met him when we were boys, but we didn't get on. Now, about my financial affairs – am I still solvent? Or have you come to tell me I'm about to be thrown into the debtor's prison?'

'No – not quite that!' John assured him. 'But I think I ought to warn you that there's little prospect of increasing your income, and you've gone through a lot of the reserve. The money from Steadman is paid twice yearly, and is due next month, and your pension is all quite straightforward; but as you know, there's nothing else coming in. I wondered how you are managing. Have you enough to live on here?'

'Just about,' Edward said wryly. 'But at the end of the month there's not two pennies in my pocket to rub together! Liz manages well, and never asks for a thing for herself, but we'll be hard put to it when the winter comes and we need more heat, and the garden won't supply our vegetables. However, we'll face that when we come to it!'

John Oatis left shortly afterwards as he had a long drive home. He went off wondering what would become of these two people. It was quite obvious that for the moment, at any rate, Edward was not able to earn a living for himself. Perhaps in time he would be able to return to practising as a solicitor; but that would be in the future.

Edward was very thoughtful that evening. He, too, wondered how long it would be before he was well enough to work again. He was not keen to return to his original profession; the idea of spending his days in an office was anathema to him. But he would have to consider doing something to increase his income. He hated the idea of leaving the quiet bay, and he knew that Liz was happier here than she would be in a town environment.

He had read most of the books Liz had bought at the sale. That evening he looked through the shelf for something to read and finally took down Virgil's *Aeneid*.

'Liz, you'll have to go to another sale and get me some more books,' he remarked. 'I'm down to reading one of the Latin books I had to study at school! I wonder if I can remember enough to make sense of it?' Liz looked up from her sewing with a smile; she obviously thought that quite a joke. She could read now, slowly, but none of the books

171

they possessed interested her, except the Dickens, and she found them difficult reading. Anyway, Edward read them aloud to her, which was better, she thought, than reading for herself.

Edward sat down and was soon absorbed in the *Aeneid*. Strangely, he found it more interesting now than he had at school. He had to keep referring to the primer, and the dictionary, but he enjoyed the mental exercise.

Perhaps it was time he began to use his brains again, instead of coasting along without thinking deeply about anything.

The next morning Liz went up to the farm early, taking with her the mending she had completed the evening before. She had taken to spending two mornings each week with Mrs Willoughby, helping with the baking, churning the butter, and doing odd jobs about the house. In return, she had her fresh milk, fresh eggs, and her shopping attended to. But this morning Mrs Willoughby had another idea in her head; she was taking Liz into Forestwidden with her, and they were going to do the shopping together. She had not warned her young friend that they were going into the village, because she knew Liz would have refused; but she made the excuse that she had hurt her arm, and needed someone to carry the basket. Liz found herself in the trap, bowling along to the village, before she had time to think about it. Fortunately she had worn one of her pretty gingham dresses, as it was a lovely bright morning. If she had been in the old black calico she would not have felt fit to appear in the village as Mrs Clayton, the wife of the returned soldier.

One of the left-handed blessings of Liz's mute state, Mrs Willoughby reflected, was the fact that her voice could not betray the humble origins from which the farmer's wife suspected she had sprung. Had she spoken with the accent from the slums of Barminster she could never have been presented as a middle-class young lady. As it was, no-one could tell where she came from, and she could mix with all and sundry without being embarrassed by any social prejudice. Although Edward Clayton spoke with the accent of an educated man, Mrs Willoughby had deduced from her inability to read or write that Liz came from a very different background. However, she had copied Edward's manners, was neatly and conservatively dressed, and could hold up her head to anyone in the village.

Mrs Willoughby had no children of her own, and she had become very fond of Liz, who could now communicate with her by writing simple notes. The more she saw of the girl the more she came to like and rely on her.

Liz carried the basket as they went from shop to shop. She kept her eyes cast down most of the time, but when they met several ladies of Mrs Willoughby's acquaintance, she shook hands with them prettily, and smiled and nodded demurely. They met Mrs Hatfield, the vicar's wife, whom they had run into the day of the farm sale, and a couple of farmer's wives, and the school mistress, who was taking advantage of a school holiday to do her shopping.

In the newsagent's shop Liz bought Edward a newspaper and two magazines, remembering his lack of reading matter, and saw a ladies' magazine that took her eye – the *Lady's Home Weekly* – which she bought too, feeling very extravagant. But when she got home and gave the magazines to Edward his pleased expression was more than sufficient reward for the ordeal of facing all those strangers, although they had all been particularly friendly and kind to her. She was very thoughtful all afternoon. That evening Edward read his magazines, and she sat and puzzled over hers. She found it fascinating. It not only set out a whole new world of recipes, but contained notes on the latest ladies' fashions and home-making ideas. Her sewing was not touched that

173

evening. She began to see advantages in her recently learned skill of reading.

The visit to the village, however, had an unexpected sequel. The vicar's wife had been very taken with the modest, demure little Mrs Clayton, and told her husband about her. She reminded him that he had not yet called on the tenant of the cottage in Honey Beck Bay; so the following morning after an early service he harnessed up his trap and made his way out to see the returned soldier about whom the village was so curious, but on whom no-one could find an adequate excuse to call, in such an out-of-the-way location. It took a little time to drive out to Honey Beck Bay and he had another service later, so he did not waste time changing from his cassock.

Liz was sitting on the beach as usual at this time of day, watching Edward in the water in his drawers, the towel and crutches on the sand beside her. The tide was low, and he was quite a distance out. As she had been working in the garden, she was wearing the black calico dress, and was barefoot, ready to wade into the water with the crutches. She heard the vehicle coming down the rough, dusty road, and turned to wave, thinking it was Mrs Willoughby; and stared, embarrassed, as the black-cassocked, white-collared figure climbed out.

The vicar, on the other hand, was enchanted to find Mrs Clayton looking more like a surprised schoolgirl than a married woman, sitting on the beach in a childish pose.

'Don't get up, Mrs Clayton,' he called as he strolled across the sand to join her. Mr Hatfield was a plump-faced, good-natured man in his fifties, his thinning hair standing out wildly on a pink scalp, giving him the look of a slightly demented cherub. He was popular with his flock for the simple reason that he seldom preached to them, and always waited to be asked for his advice before giving it. He was

174

pleasantly surprised when the recipients occasionally acted on it. He now sat down on the sand beside Liz – not without difficulty, for nature had not endowed him with the figure for sitting on beaches – and beamed at her.

'I've come to visit your husband, my dear – is that him in the water? Is it quite safe? Yes – well, perhaps it's not a very good time, but as it's such a long way out here – do you think he'll mind if I wait for him to come out of the sea?' Liz shook her head, which made the vicar remember that he had been told she was mute.

'I'm so sorry my dear – I forgot you can't talk,' he said apologetically. 'Do you mean "No, he won't mind", or "No, don't wait because he will mind"?' He watched anxiously as she alternately nodded and shook her head; he was no further towards knowing which she meant. Liz gave an odd, silent giggle. He looked so amusing, sitting there with a frown on his funny face, trying hard to understand what she meant. She drew in the sand:

HE WONT MIND. DO YOO LIK TEA?

'Oh, indeed I do like tea – yes, my dear. And there's nothing I'd like more right now than a nice cup of tea!'

Liz handed him the crutches and the towel, jumped up and ran to the cottage. She put the kettle on, and scampered up the steps to her loft, where she quickly changed from the calico dress into her pretty pink-and-white gingham; she also remembered to put on her shoes. She slipped downstairs again, made the tea, using three mis-matched but pretty cups from the farm sale, and buttered some scones she had baked earlier that morning. She tidied the room up quickly, putting Edward's books and magazines under a cushion on the fat sofa.

Meanwhile, Edward had swum back towards the shore, and waved to the black-clad figure on the sand. He had salt water in his eyes, and could only see a vague blur and so it was not until the vicar, carrying the crutches, had absent-mindedly waded fully shod almost up to his knees, and was only a few yards away from Edward, that he realized that this was a damp vicar, not his wife. The introduction was so droll and unexpected that Edward burst into laughter. From that moment on he and Mr Hatfield were the firmest of friends. Before Edward joined the colours he had been an outward-going, rollicking character, but so many months of illness and solitude had left him taciturn and introspective, and had the vicar knocked at the cottage door and introduced himself in the usual way, Edward might very well have sent him about his business, determined not to be pitied. Under these circumstances he met the vicar cheerfully and was glad to see him.

The two men came into the cottage laughing, and Edward went to his room to dress while Liz put the vicar's wet shoes and socks to dry. Mr Hatfield sat at the table and watched her pouring the tea, thinking how lucky the crippled man was to have such a capable little wife.

Edward came out and they all took their places at the table. Liz offered the scones round. Edward was always hungry when he came out of the sea, and it would not be time for the mid-day meal for another hour or more.

'I hope you don't find it too lonely here?' Mr Hatfield asked.

'Not at all,' Edward assured him. 'Henry Willoughby and his wife call fairly regularly, and we occasionally see the young fellow who keeps his boat at the other end of the bay – I think his name is Allen something-or-other – but we don't mind the solitude.'

'You find enough to keep you occupied?'

'Oh, I read, and so on. My wife sees quite a lot of the people from the farm, especially Mrs Willoughby – we're quite content.'

'You should try fishing, Mr Clayton – there's good fish in this bay, you know. You could cast your line from those rocks on the headland. There used to be an old fisherman and his wife in this cottage years ago – he made quite a good living, selling his catch in the village.'

Edward was silent for a moment.

'I'm not sure how I'd manage my crutches on the rocks,' he said thoughtfully. 'I'll have to find some way of augmenting my income soon, but I don't think that is the answer. Liz got me some magazines yesterday, and I read a couple of the short stories about action in South Africa; I think I may try my hand at writing. I'm sure I could write as well as that, anyway, and I *could* get the facts right – the men who wrote those stories obviously haven't been anywhere near South Africa! Where are those magazines, Liz?'

Liz got up to fetch the magazines and books she had stuffed under the cushion, glad the vicar had his back to her and couldn't see how she had swiftly tidied the room. Edward put the books on one side and began to leaf through a magazine, looking for the page he wanted.

Mr Hatfield glanced at the books, and then at Edward.

'Latin?' he exclaimed. 'Do you read Latin, Mr Clayton?'

'Oh, a little,' Edward admitted. 'I'd run out of reading matter, and those were to hand –'

'Mr Clayton, I wonder if you could help me with a problem? We have a Brigadier Richardson living near the village – he's retired, a good friend of mine. His two young grandsons are spending the remainder of the school holidays with him, and their tutor has had an accident and had to leave them. Silly fellow fell off his horse and broke his leg. The trouble is, the boys are seriously behind with their schooling – just been sent home from India, where they had a governess – and the Brigadier wants to find someone who can help them catch up before they start at their new school in about a month's time. He asked my assistance, but unfortunately I haven't been able to find anyone up to now. Would

177

you consider giving the boys some coaching if their grand-father sent them out here?'

Edward looked rather disconcerted. He had never had anything to do with boys, and he'd never done any teaching. He very much doubted that he'd be capable of tutoring anyone, apart from Liz. However, just as he was about to made his apologies and refuse, he caught sight of Liz stand-ing behind the vicar, and the look on her face made him think again. It was the first time she had ever expressed an opinion, or asked him for anything; but as he hesitated she pointed to her shoes, and, turning, showed him the sole of one of them. There was a large hole in it, with a piece of cardboard stuffed inside to patch it.

'Well, I don't see myself as much of a teacher, but I'll give it a try if your friend is that desperate,' Edward agreed.

Mr Hatfield left ten minutes later, having arranged that the Brigadier would call at the cottage. Edward watched him go up the road, and then came back into the cottage where Liz was preparing the meal.

'I hope I haven't let myself in for trouble,' he said ruefully. 'I didn't realize that you needed new shoes, and I guess, now that I come to think of it, there are a few other things we could do with. I don't expect this will pay much, but every little helps, as the Bish – er, yes; every little helps.'

Brigadier Richardson called on them next morning, driving himself in a smart turnout with a spirited little bay pony. He was about sixty-five, a very military-looking man with a bristling moustache, thick, greying hair, and a slim figure of which a man twenty years younger might have been proud. He had his high-spirited nine-year-old grandsons, Brian and Stewart, with him.

Edward met him at the door, and they shook hands, each looking the other over warily. The boys were sent to play on the beach while the men talked. Liz was introduced; she shook hands with the Brigadier, and then went out to keep an eye on the boys.

'Well, sir, I'm told you might be willing to take my two imps on for a spot of coaching,' the Brigadier began. 'Where'd you lose that leg?'

'South Africa,' Edward replied, slightly taken aback by the abrupt question. 'Come in, sir, and sit down.'

'Ladysmith?'

'No – but I was there while the siege was on – and I was damn glad to see the relief, I can tell you!' They sat at the table, and for the next half-hour the talk was of military matters. The Brigadier had been in Africa for a short time, but was sent home with stomach trouble. He was very interested to hear about Edward's experiences, and had a few uncomplimentary remarks to pass about the politicians who had got them into the pointless conflict. He asked no questions about Edward's qualifications, but seemed quite happy to employ him as the boys' temporary tutor.

'I'll send them over for a couple of hours each morning,' he said finally. 'At least it will keep them out of trouble, even if they don't learn much. They're a bit of a handful for my wife and me, I'll admit – they're so full of energy we can't keep up with them!'

'Look, sir, I swim for half an hour of a morning,' Edward said thoughtfully. 'If you send towels and things with them, they can come in with me, while the weather holds – and perhaps we can have a picnic lunch on the beach. That will help to expend some of their surplus energy! Then they can read with me for an hour afterwards, and you can pick them up about three. That will keep them occupied for a few hours each day, and give me enough time to really din a bit of knowledge into them. How would that suit you?'

The Brigadier beamed.

'Splendid idea, my boy! And I'll have a hamper made up each day, no need for your little wife to worry about feeding

179

them – I'll get Cook to put in enough for four. Now about your fee . . .'

For a couple of minutes it looked as if the proposition might founder, for the Brigadier insisted on paying what Edward considered an unreasonable amount, and Edward, chary of charity, asked what the Brigadier considered a pittance; but eventually they agreed a compromise, shook hands, and went out to collect the boys, both thoroughly satisfied with the arrangement.

The new regime started the next morning. Liz went to the farm as soon as she had finished washing up the breakfast things. The boys arrived, driven by their grandfather's groom, half an hour later, and when she got back at eleven-thirty she found Edward and the twins engrossed in their books. At twelve they went out to the beach, and while she sat on the sand, ready to slip out of her dress and dash into the water in her chemise, if necessary, Edward swam, and Brian and Stewart played happily in the water at the shoreline. At one o'clock they opened the hamper, and found an excellent meal packed inside, complete with a bottle of ale for the tutor; this was followed by a rest in the shade of the trees, with the boys reading their comic papers and Edward sleeping for half an hour, before another hour's coaching. There was time for the boys to have a final romp on the beach before being taken home; and not only did Brian and Stewart work hard at their lessons, but the day was thoroughly enjoyed by all four of them.

When Liz had something she wanted to tell Edward now, she was able to mouth the words, and he understood, almost like lip-reading, although she was too self-conscious to do this with anyone except him. Even with Mrs Willoughby she now wrote anything she wanted to say. But after a few days the twins saw her 'talking' silently to Edward, and began asking her questions requiring more than a shake or nod of the head, and soon she was 'talking' to them too. They were quite unconcerned about her lack of voice, accepting it as naturally as they did their grandmother's slight deafness and Edward's lack of one leg. Consequently Liz became less self-conscious about it, chatting to them in a voiceless whisper, and laughing her odd, silent chuckle. However, as soon as anyone else came about, she became tongue-tied, and as mute as before. Edward suspected that her inability to speak was more mental than physical, but he did nothing to try to make her speak, as any coaxing immediately made her apprehensive and frightened again. The shadow of her step-father's ill-treatment was still with her.

The first day Brian asked Edward what had happened to his leg, and when he told the two boys he lost it fighting the Boers, nothing more was said on the subject. The boys seemed to forget that he was not as agile as they were themselves. One day they kicked a football in his direction, and he thoughtlessly tried to kick it back, landing in a heap on the sand, which had them all, including himself, in convulsions of mirth.

As August wore on into September, the fine weather held out, and Henry Willoughby took in a bumper harvest. On several afternoons Liz again helped in the fields, tying and stacking the corn into stooks, ready to take into the barns for threshing. She became almost as brown as a gypsy, getting home late in the evening, tired but happy.

It was with real regret that Edward and Liz saw the end of the boys' visits when the time came for them to go to boarding-school. The boys promised to write; they left Liz in tears on the final afternoon; and Edward mooned about the cottage like a lost dog for a couple of days.

'I miss those young devils,' he remarked. 'The cottage seems empty without them.'

181

One wet morning in mid-September Liz was tidying up the living-room when she came across some comic magazines the twins had left behind. She was about to put them in the box of paper used for lighting the fire when Edward picked them up and began to leaf through them.

'These stories are rubbish,' he remarked in disgust, after a few minutes. 'Badly constructed, badly written, and the plots are completely incredible! I could do better myself.'

Liz answered by handing him his pen and a pad of paper. She was getting worried about seeing him continuously idle. It was too wet to go out and a cold wind had sprung up; there was little for him to do except read all day, and now he was so well he was irritated by the inactivity. His moods of depression had vanished when he was busy each day with the boys but now they returned, leaving him more depressed than ever.

Edward sat down at the table and thought. Soon he began to write. He wrote a tale based on some on his own experiences, and once started, kept going with a compulsion that surprised him. He hardly put the pen down to eat or sleep for several days and at the end of that time he came back to earth with a bump, like a man who has been in a trance. It took a few more days for him to copy the story out to his satisfaction, correcting almost every sentence; but at last it was done, and he put it in an envelope with a covering letter and Liz arranged to have it posted.

Then they both forgot about it, for something else had arisen to occupy their minds.

Chapter Fifteen

The weather had really broken, and autumn arrived with blustering winds whipping the sea up into a rage. While the trees around the bay had their leaves torn off and tossed to the four winds the waves broke furiously on the shore day after day. Intermittent rain fell, sometimes lightly, the showers lasting only minutes, and sometimes with a driving intensity for hours upon hours. For several days Liz was unable to walk to the farm. The path ran alongside the clifftop for some distance, and the strong winds threatened to sweep her into the sea below. Much as she loved their cosy home, she missed the fresh air and the freedom of the shoreline. Her daily walks along the beach, looking for shells or interesting flotsam thrown up by the sea, had become an intrinsic part of her life. Edward, also, was restless when the weather kept them indoors. He began to get depressed again, and snapped at her when she interrupted his reading or his writing.

Then came a morning when the world was at peace again. Overnight the gales had ceased, and a bright autumn sun shone from a blue sky lightly feathered with a few white clouds. There was a slight chill to the air, but not enough to prevent Liz running across the sands of the bay for the sheer pleasure of getting out into the fresh air again after being cooped up in the cottage. It was still very early. She had woken with the feeling that it was good to be alive. After making up the fire and putting the kettle on, she ran down to the shore in her shift, and into the sparkling, clean water. Gasping from the chill, she stayed in for only a few minutes before racing back to the cottage.

Edward had heard her stoking up the range in the big room. When he heard the door being opened so early he was curious, and got out of bed to peer through the window. The tide was high, and she was less than a hundred yards from the cottage; he could see her clearly, frolicking in the water. He had never seen her in the sea before; she ran and splashed about like a young water nymph. He stood at the window watching her until she came running back to the cottage, wrapped in a big towel, and scampered straight up to the loft.

How young she looked, and carefree! And how beautiful, with the wet shift clinging to her body. Her figure had filled out, and the fresh air had brought the roses to her cheeks and a sparkle to her eyes. To him, now, she was the very picture of loveliness. He had never seen her without her dress before, and he was quite enchanted with the picture she presented.

Once Bella Pollard had been his ideal woman, but she couldn't hold a candle to this girl who was his wife. His wife? His housekeeper, his drudge, his obedient slave; but hardly his wife!

As Edward went back to his bed, he wondered unhappily how long it would be before the girl got tired of living here with only himself for company. He had promised, when he asked her to marry him, that when she had nursed him back to health, she would be free to leave him if she wished.

How long would it be before she sought her freedom?

Brigadier Richardson was a wealthy man, and resided in Falldon Hall, the house his father and grandfather had lived in before him. He and his wife were intensely proud of their home, and conscientiously maintained the house, its contents, and the parklands around it, to pass on to their son, who would pass it on in turn to his son. Over the past eighty years or so, the family had acquired a large library, which had never been properly organized and catalogued. Now the Brigadier decided it was time that should be done.

He had no inclination to do the cataloguing himself. In fact, he had very little interest in books at all, having hardly opened one since he left Oxford some forty-odd years ago, and after a certain amount of thought he decided to ask Edward Clayton if he would take on the task. He had a very high opinion of that young man, and suspected that he could do with the remuneration. If he was to have a stranger about the house it might as well be someone he liked, and with whom he could have an occasional chat about his past military life.

Accordingly, when the weather improved towards the end of September, he drove down to Honey Beck Bay, and knocked at the cottage door. Edward opened the door. Liz had taken advantage of the fine morning to go to the farm for fresh supplies. They had been using tinned milk for the past few days.

'Good morning, Brigadier!' Edward beamed, stepping back and gesturing to his visitor to come inside. 'Such a fine morning after the gales! It's a pleasure to see you. How are your two young imps enjoying school?'

'Quite well, I believe, from their letters – but complaining of the food, of course! Their headmaster wrote and told me they were quite up to standard in most subjects, and well above in Latin, so there's no reason why they shouldn't do well there.' He brought out his pipe, and offered Edward a fill from his pouch, for which Edward thanked him, but refused. He had given up smoking when he was ill, and had not gone back to it, apart from the occasional cigar. He had no money to squander on tobacco. 'Now I've got a proposition for you, young man; you might like it, or you might not. All you've got to do is say yes or no. I want the

185

books in my library sorted and catalogued; will you take on the job?'

Edward sat down thoughtfully. He did not think the task would be beyond him academically, but could he, physically, do it? To begin with, he would have to get to Falldon Hall, and he had no means of transport. Then he realized that cataloguing a library would almost surely entail climbing steps to the upper shelves, lifting down books, and carrying volumes from one place to another. How could he manage that when he could only move about on crutches?

'I'm sorry, Brigadier – I don't think I could do it,' he said honestly. The Brigadier was busily puffing at his pipe. He looked at Edward over the lighted match and his eyes twinkled.

'I think you could do it with the help of your wife,' he suggested. 'I can arrange for you and Mrs Clayton to be collected from here three mornings a week, and brought back in the afternoon. I don't care how long it takes you to complete it; spend six months over it – or a year! – if you like. She can bring you the books, dust 'em, and put 'em back in the right order, while you sort them out, and do the listing. You can set aside anything you think should be examined by someone more knowledgeable than yourself, and I'll have a man down from London to value them when you've finished. Think about it before you turn it down, Clayton.'

Edward hesitated. It would solve the problem of their finances for the moment. It would give him something practical and congenial to do while he completed his convalescence. And perhaps Liz would enjoy it as well.

'I'll have to talk it over with my wife,' he said finally. 'Can I let you know in a day or two?'

'Splendid. But don't be too long, old man – if I have to look for someone else, I'll have to get on with it.' The Brigadier had another go at lighting his pipe, successfully this time, and clouds of smoke billowed out into the room. 'I expect your track (I hesitate to call it a road) gets pretty bad at times. While it's passable my groom can bring you back and forth each day. When it's not negotiable you can take a holiday.'

When Liz returned the Brigadier had left, but she had seen him on the road and was very curious to hear what he had come about. When Edward told her about the proposition he had put forward, she became very quiet, and went about the business of getting the mid-day meal without giving him any inkling of her opinion.

She hardly knew what to think; she had very little idea of what would be involved. She could see that Edward was quite keen, and knew he could not do it without her help, but she dreaded the thought of going into a strange house She would have to meet the Brigadier's wife; what would she think of her? And the servants – would they laugh at her, and make fun of her handicap? She hated meeting strangers, and she was frightened of going to Falldon Hall. But most of all, she was afraid of failing Edward, either by not assisting him adequately, or by letting him down through her ignorance.

'What do you think?' she whispered finally, as they sat down to the stew that had been simmering on the back of the range all morning.

'I think we ought to do it,' Edward said firmly. Liz's eyes widened. She wondered if he knew what he was asking of her? But if it would please him she would do her best. She nodded, and smiled as he took her hand and pressed it. 'Good girl!' he exclaimed. 'And I promise I won't let the butler eat you, or Mrs Richardson, either. You'll see – you'll enjoy it!'

Liz doubted that she would, but if it was what Edward wanted, she would try. Putting her doubts behind her, she began to plan what she would wear.

*

The following Tuesday they were ready when the trap came down the lane to collect them. Edward had sent the Brigadier a note of acceptance, and arranged to be picked up with his wheelchair. Liz was waiting nervously, in her best blue serge dress, when they heard the pony's hooves clip-clopping down the track.

It was the first time Edward had left the cottage since they had come here six months earlier. When he tried to get into the trap he nearly gave up, for at first he could see no way of actually hoisting himself up into the vehicle. But Liz held the crutches, the groom gave him a hand, and he managed to drag himself on to the seat. The groom tied the chair on to the small carrying-platform behind, and they were soon on their way, the vehicle lurching dangerously as it negotiated the ruts and potholes in the track. Liz held on tight and hoped that she would not be thrown out. When they reached the road she was able to relax.

At Falldon Hall Brigadier Richardson was waiting to show them into the library. There were thousands of books, and few of them were in any sort of order. Edward suddenly realized the extent of the task, and was tempted to give up before he began. Mrs Richardson came in to meet them, a plump, fussy little woman with a humorous twinkle in her eye. She was so kind and thoughtful towards them both that Edward took courage and set his hand to the task. He began by spending most of the morning just looking at the books, to get an idea of where to start. Liz fetched and carried; he kept her so busy that she forgot to be nervous of the big house and the luxurious fittings and soon found that she was enjoying herself. It was wonderful to see Edward so engrossed in the work. He was a different man, and her admiration for his knowledge went up by leaps and bounds.

The butler brought their lunch at mid-day, and they ate it at a small table in the window. Afterwards, Brigadier

Richardson came in and chatted for half an hour, quite oblivious to the fact that they could not get on with any work while he talked, but as he was quite happy about it, it was hardly up to Edward to complain. However, by the time they were ready to leave at four o'clock they had made a start on the job, and looked forward to returning the next day.

From then on, they went to Falldon Hall on Tuesdays, Wednesdays, and Fridays. Liz enjoyed every minute of it. Soon there were books stacked all over the floor, on the tables, and on the chairs. Gradually they began to bring order to the chaos they had found, and the detailed lists of books grew while the shelves emptied. Both became completely absorbed in the work, and often when they were called at four o'clock they were amazed that the day had passed so quickly.

Sometimes Mrs Richardson would come in and chat to Liz, while her husband discussed their progress with Edward; and sometimes she would call the girl to see something in the house, or to ask her opinion of a dress or blouse. Liz would nod or shake her head in answer to Mrs Richardson's questions, embarrassed to whisper. But as Mrs Richardson prattled on quite happily, talking quite enough for both of them, this was no impediment to their relationship. Soon she discovered that Liz was an accomplished needlewoman, after which she found constant excuses to have her at her side. Edward did not mind when Liz disappeared for half an hour at a time, since she was so obviously enjoying herself, and had become such a favourite with the Richardsons. He was delighted with her success.

With the new interests she was discovering, and the friendly way she was accepted into the household, Liz was finding a new confidence in herself. A year ago her horizon had been bounded by working up to fourteen hours a day for a pittance; in the evenings she had hidden herself away in the tiny bedroom she'd shared with her half-brothers, sewing for the family, and doing the mending her mother brought home from her laundrywork. Now that her life was so changed, and she was not constantly tired and apprehensive, she began to use the innate intelligence that previously she had never exercised, and she consciously set out to learn all she could in order to be worthy of Edward. She watched Mrs Richardson about the house, and soon began to understand why there was such a gulf between that lady's demeanour and her own mother's.

Occasionally Mrs Richardson had other ladies to tea at Falldon Hall, and invited Liz to join what she called 'her hen-parties'. Liz watched, listened, and learned.

One Friday morning in early December, Mrs Richardson asked Liz to help her sort out her wardrobe, as she had put on a few pounds, and many of her dresses had become too small. She and the girl were about the same height, but the older lady was decidedly plump, whereas Liz was very slender. Liz offered to let out several of the dresses, and Mrs Richardson gave her several others that had already been let out to the limit of their seams.

'I really should give up eating puddings, but Cook would be mortally offended if I did,' she sighed. Liz spent the weekend sewing; with a few clever alterations she now had a new wardrobe.

A week before Christmas, Edward and Liz tidied up the library on the Friday afternoon, as they would not be coming back to the Hall until after the New Year. The two boys were expected home from school the next day, as their parents were still in India. Edward and Liz said farewell to the Richardsons, wished them a merry Christmas, and went out to the trap to be driven back to the cottage. Edward had become adept now at hoisting himself into the trap, but the ground was slightly frosty, and as he tried to jump up on to the step he slipped, and fell heavily to the ground.

Liz, standing behind him holding the crutches, screamed; a shrill, piercing scream that brought the Brigadier and Mrs Richardson running out from the entrance hall where they had just wished them farewell. Edward was now sitting up on the drive, rubbing his knee. The groom was staring at Liz, and the Brigadier and Mrs Richardson stopped short, at the front door, gazing at the astonished girl.

The scream had astounded Liz as much as it did everyone else.

'Scream again, Liz,' Edward said. But she couldn't repeat it. She couldn't even produce a whisper.

The groom and the Brigadier hoisted Edward upright, but he couldn't take his weight on his one leg. He had twisted his knee, and although, had he had two good legs, he would have been able to limp, with only one he was helpless.

'Well, Clayton, there's only one thing for it. You'll have to stay a night or two until you can get about on those crutches again,' the Brigadier said without hesitation. Mrs Richardson calmly told the butler and the groom to carry Mr Clayton into the house, and he was put into his wheel-chair in front of the fire in the drawing-room, while the bed was made up in one of the spare bedrooms. The house-keeper was sent to fetch liniment and a crepe bandage to bind up the strained knee.

Liz's cheeks were flaming and she was feeling almost faint with embarrassment. Edward realized how disturbed she was, and turned to Mrs Richardson, who was, of course, quite unaware of the fact that her unexpected guests did not usually share a bedroom.

'Mrs Richardson, I'll be quite all right, I'm sure, as soon as Liz has put some liniment and a bandage on my knee,' he said hopefully. But Mrs Richardson patted his hand in a motherly way, and assured him that it would be no trouble to give them a bed until he was fit to travel, pointing out how thrilled the twins would be when they got home tomorrow to find their dear Mr and Mrs Clayton in the house.

'Besides,' she added, 'it will give my husband a chance to tell you again, after dinner, how he fought the battles of the Crimea. Surely you won't deprive him of that pleasure?'

As it became clear, after Liz had bandaged the knee, that Edward was quite incapable of standing on it, there was no point in further argument. Mrs Richardson loaned Liz a nightgown and wrapper, and the Brigadier found a nightshirt for Edward. After a very good dinner, the butler and the groom between them assisted Edward up the stairs, practically carrying him, to a spare bedroom, where Liz helped him into bed as she had done so many times earlier in the year. But then she stood there nervously, fidgeting with the row of tiny buttons on the front of her dress.

'Liz, I'm not going to jump out of this bed and bite you,' Edward said finally. 'Get that dress off, put on your nightgown, and get into bed. Heaven knows, it's big enough for both of us – we can leave a good two feet between us, and still have enough room to turn over!'

Liz turned her back, and began to undo the row of buttons. Edward sighed, and turned his face to the opposite wall.

'All right, girl – I promise not to look! Now hurry up – I'm tired, and I want to put the lamp out.' Hurriedly, Liz dropped the dress to the floor, and pulled the nightgown over her head. She took the pins out of her hair, and let the cloud of dark hair fall; it reached to her waist. As she began to brush it with the borrowed brush, Edward turned back and watched her. The lamplight brought out the red tints in her dark hair, and he thought she looked perfectly lovely as the brush rose and fell. At last she was ready, and walked slowly over to the bed. She slipped between the covers, and lay stiffly on the edge of the bed.

Edward turned out the lamp. They both lay unnaturally still for some minutes, each supremely aware of the other lying so close.

'Liz, my knee hurts, and I'm cold,' Edward said after a few minutes. Liz turned over to look at him; the movement brought them closer. He could smell the slight perfume of the soap she used, and feel the warmth of her body. He put his arm round her, and drew her to him.

'Goodnight, my dear.'

'Goodnight, Edward,' she whispered. It was the first time she had used his name. She lay rigid; her mother had told her that she would be expected to sleep in the same bed as her husband, and men did things that a wife had to suffer without complaint. That was part of married life. It was best to let it happen without attempting to defend her privacy, and then she was less likely to be hurt. Deprived of their marital rights, Agnes told her, men became beasts, sometimes vicious and sadistic. It was the price women paid for the doubtful protection and security of marriage.

Up to now Edward had shown no signs of demanding his marital rights. While he had been so ill, of course, he was in no condition to do so, but now he was so much better, would the situation change? Or would things be different in their case? After all, he had married her for a nurse and housekeeper, nothing more. There was a bargain between them; this was purely a marriage of convenience. And he was so much older and wiser than herself; he would not be interested in an ignorant girl. She was foolish to even imagine that he looked upon her as a desirable woman. Soon she relaxed in his arms, and her regular breathing told him she was asleep.

Edward lay quiet, the pain in his knee catching him each time he moved. A shaft of moonlight fell over the bed. Liz looked so childlike and sweet in her sleep she made his heart ache. Why should such a lovely, innocent young girl be condemned to stay with a helpless, grey-haired, crippled man? He fought down the flame of desire he suddenly felt rising. Her unspoken trust in him was a torment, but he could no more have violated that trust than he could have whipped her. She was his wife – and thus denied the joy of finding love and fulfilment with a complete man of her own age. What a terrible wrong he had done her!

He lay wakeful for some time, and it was not only the pain in his knee that kept sleep at bay.

Chapter Sixteen

Liz woke early and was up and dressed before Edward was awake. She took advantage of the rare opportunity to have a hot bath with running water. Such a luxury was not to be lightly disregarded! But when Edward pulled back the bedclothes and exposed his knee they looked at each other in dismay.

'Well, Liz, here's a pretty kettle of fish!' Edward said ruefully. The joint was swollen to double its normal size, and when he attempted to stand he found it far too painful to use. Liz bathed it with hot water, and then with cold, but the swelling remained, and it was clear that Edward was not going to be able to hop about on his crutches that day.

Liz went downstairs and found her hostess. Very self-consciously she whispered to her that Mr Clayton was unable to get up. Mrs Richardson was torn between distress that he was no better, and delight at finding Liz could communicate in her strange whisper. She sent the Brigadier's valet to attend to Edward's toilet, and had his breakfast sent up to him. She took Liz to breakfast in the morning-room with herself and the Brigadier.

Brigadier Richardson wanted to call in the doctor. After breakfast he took the newspapers up to Edward, and insisted on seeing the knee for himself. However, as Edward pointed out, it was obvious that the injury would recover with rest, and the doctor could do nothing more than look at it and prescribe a stay in bed, so it would a waste of that gentleman's time to bring him out.

'I suppose you're right,' the Brigadier conceded reluctantly. 'Best stay where you are for the moment, my boy, and we'll see how it goes. I remember when I was in the Crimea one of my officers came off his horse and sustained a similar injury. His groom slapped on a dollop of horse liniment – he was up and fit for battle in two days, and never a doctor in sight! I'll send up the newspaper for you when it arrives, Clayton, and perhaps later we'll have a game of chess.'

Mrs Clayton was going to Barminster, which was only a matter of ten miles from Falldon Hall, to fetch the boys, who were due to arrive on the two-thirty train. She wanted to take the opportunity to do some Christmas shopping at the same time, so she invited Liz to go with her. They would have lunch at the Golden Eagle before meeting the train. She suggested this to Liz when she went up to see the invalid, and Edward had a suggestion of his own to make.

'Perhaps, while you do your shopping, Liz can visit her mother,' he said. 'She hasn't seen her for some time, and this could be a good opportunity.'

'Of course – what a good idea!' Mrs Richardson exclaimed. 'I'd love to meet your wife's mother –'

'Perhaps it would be better to do that another time,' Edward said hastily, seeing the dismayed look on Liz's face. 'If you set Liz down in the town – I think she would like to buy herself a pair of shoes – she can do her shopping and then walk round to Mrs – to her mother's house, and meet you afterwards.'

Mrs Richardson looked from Edward to Liz, and nodded. If the girl wanted to talk privately with her mother she was quite agreeable, and it would give her more time for her Christmas shopping.

'Splendid, my dear. Now get your coat – the carriage will be at the door in five minutes, and we must be away.' She hurried out to get her own coat, and Liz and Edward had time for a few words to themselves.

'I don't like to leave you,' Liz whispered. 'Are you sure –'

'I'll be all right,' Edward assured her. 'If you look in my coat you'll find some money. Get yourself a pair of shoes, and anything else you fancy. And give my compliments to your mother – but keep away from your step-father. I don't want you coming back with a black eye. If you have time you could look into John Oatis's office – perhaps he'll walk round to your mother's house with you.'

'Oh, no, that won't be necessary,' Liz assured him. 'That man only hit me when he was drunk, and he'll be at work this morning. Do you want me to get anything for you?'

'Yes – a new knee! Or two new knees, come to that.' Liz giggled, her odd voiceless chuckle, and Edward smiled. It was good to see her happy. Until recently he had never heard that chuckle; that was another blessing the twins had brought with them.

The drive into Barminster was very comfortable in the well-sprung coach. Not by any means new, it was nevertheless a very luxurious vehicle, by far the most opulent Liz had ever travelled in. She watched the countryside pass with interest. She loved the Great Forest, even in winter when the trees were bare.

They alighted in the town square, and Mrs Richardson gave the groom instructions to meet them at the railway station at half past two. She and Liz parted, arranging to meet at the Golden Eagle at one o'clock.

Liz first went and bought her shoes, a neat black pair with high heels and tiny gleaming silver buckles. They were the most expensive shoes she had ever owned, and she felt like a queen as she walked down the narrow terraced street to her mother's overcrowded, dingy rented house. She saw several people she had known when she lived here, only eight months ago, but it seemed like a lifetime. They turned

197

to stare after the well-dressed young woman, but none of them recognized in her the dumb skivvy who used to work at the hospital.

The door of the house opened to her touch; it was seldom locked. The first thing she noticed was the smell – she had forgotten how the house always smelled of damp laundry and boiled cabbage. She walked into the kitchen. Her mother was at the sink, rinsing sheets the youngest boy had wet during the night. She heard Liz's footstep on the stone floor, and turned.

For a moment she stared blankly at the girl, and then threw herself into her arms with a cry of welcome.

'Liz! My dear – oh Liz!' she exclaimed. 'What a lovely surprise – how well you look!' She stood back and gazed at her. 'And how pretty – oh, dear, whoever would have thought you could look so nice, Liz!' She touched the blue serge. 'Your dress looks as fine as it did when you were married. How is – how is your husband?'

The question was put warily. Like John Oatis, Mrs Spragg had thought Edward Clayton was more likely to die than recover when he left the hospital. Now she was suddenly afraid her daughter was a widow, come back to beg a place in the overcrowded house. Things were bad enough here, with Joe drinking more heavily than ever, and the boys getting out of hand. She could not turn her girl out into the street, but the thought of having her back, and the trouble it would cause with Joe, made her fearful to hear Liz answer.

To her surprise, Liz answered in her whisper. At first Agnes couldn't catch her words, but then she watched her daughter's mouth moving, and understood what she was saying.

'Edward is fine, Mam – he's in bed with a sprained knee, but he's fine,' Liz whispered. 'The wounds have healed, and his rash is better, and the fever's gone. Mrs Richardson – a friend – was coming into Barminster so I came with her – in a carriage, Mam, with two horses!'

'A carriage!' Agnes Spragg exclaimed. 'How do you come to know someone with a carriage?'

'Edward works for her husband,' Liz explained.

'I never thought to see the day when he'd be well enough to work again, nor to see you so fine, and riding in a carriage!' Agnes marvelled.

'Edward hasn't got much money, Mam, or I would have asked him for –' Liz began uncomfortably.

'Never mind that, Liz, dear – I don't expect you to cadge off your husband for my benefit,' Agnes said quickly. She put the kettle on, and turned back to the sink. 'You'll have a cup of tea? The boys are out now, playing somewhere, and I don't expect them back for a while. Real little devils, they are. I never know what they'll be up to next. Now tell me about your cottage.'

The next half hour passed quickly. Liz had so much to tell her – about Meg the gypsy, about the farm and the Willoughbys, the harvest, and coaching the twins.

'So he's out and about, is he?'

'Well, just to Falldon Hall –'

'Then watch out, Liz; he'll soon be hankering after his own sort of people. I doubt if he'll be satisfied for long with a wife who can't read and write.'

'But I'm learning to read and write, Mam – I'm learning fast, while we work in the library.'

'Hmmm … Well, Liz, you know him better than I do, but remember my words. Birds of a feather flock together – watch out, my girl, and try to keep him happy. Men like Edward Clayton don't often settle down to marriage with the likes of us – women from places like this! Keep an eye on him. If he's feeling better, he'll soon be wanting to stretch his wings.'

'But he's not like that, Mam –'

'All men are like that, Liz. You mark my words!'

Then it was time to go, and Liz hurried away, anxious to leave before the boys came home. She was quite fond of her young half-brothers, but she did not want to risk being here when they came in. She didn't want Joe Spragg to know she had called, and the boys could not be relied on to keep a secret. A shiver ran down her spine at the thought of Joe finding his way to Honey Beck Bay.

She called at John Oatis's office on the way back through the Square, but found the door locked. This gave her the opportunity of spending half an hour doing a little Christmas shopping. Edward had given her enough money to buy a few Christmas cards, and one or two little gifts. She lingered wistfully in front of the jeweller's shop, where she could see a watch in the window that she would love to have bought for Edward, but it was far above her means. A gentleman like Edward Clayton ought to have a watch.

Lunch at the Golden Eagle was another treat. The dining-room was busy, so close to Christmas, but Mrs Richardson had sent them a postcard earlier in the week reserving a table for herself, and they set a second place for Liz. The meal over, they walked round to the railway station in plenty of time to meet the train, and found the groom waiting with the carriage.

The twins leapt out of the train, delighted to find that Mrs Clayton was with their grandmother, and kissed and hugged both of them indiscriminately. A porter was found to drag their trunks out of the guard's van, and haul them out to the carriage where they were swiftly stowed in the boot, and soon they were on their way back to Falldon Hall.

'Hello, Mr Clayton – are you staying until after Christmas?' the twins greeted Edward, stampeding into his room the moment they got into the house.

'No, I'm not,' Edward said. 'I think your grandmother will have quite enough to do with you two on her hands without having me in the spare bedroom! Now tell me all about school. Did you find yourselves in trouble with your Latin?'

'Oh, no, sir,' Stewart assured him. 'We're both all right with Latin – better than most of the boys. But they do awfully hard sums, and I don't even know what the questions are about, most of the time, let alone the answers!'

'Well, in that case,' Edward said seriously, 'we'd better do a bit of coaching in arithmetic –'

'Oh, gosh, sir – it's holidays!' Brian protested indignantly.

'But if I'm stuck here in bed,' Edward pointed out, 'I've got to have something to occupy my time, and it might as well be teaching you two young rascals how to add up and subtract.'

'We can do adding up and taking away,' Brian said quickly. 'It's algebra and geometry that gets us black marks. In India they didn't have algebra and geometry, but at school they seem to think it's even more important than breakfast and dinner.'

'Nothing is more important than breakfast and dinner,' Stewart said soberly, 'except supper.'

The next morning Edward's leg was considerably less swollen, although he still could not stand on it comfortably, but the valet assisted him to get up and dress. Brigadier and Mrs Richardson, and the two boys, had gone to church in the carriage, and when they returned the valet and the groom helped Edward out to the carriage, hauled him up into it, and accompanied them to Honey Beck Bay. They then helped him into the cottage, deposited him in the wheelchair, and left him and Liz alone in their peaceful home.

The cottage was cold and damp. The fire had been out for nearly two days, and the temperature was just above freezing. Liz brought the blanket from her bed and wrapped it round Edward while she hurried about, lighting the fire, getting the kettle on, and preparing lunch. She was warm enough, on the move all the time, but Edward's teeth were almost chattering. But by the time she had the onion and potato soup made, and the scones baked, the cottage was warm and comfortable again, and they ate their late meal in comfort. Liz had enjoyed the luxury of staying at Falldon Hall, despite her anxiety about Edward, and the constant fear of doing something wrong. She had nearly overcome her awe of the butler and the unapproachable housekeeper, but she was relieved to be back in her own home.

Liz spent the evening laboriously writing a short message in each of the Christmas cards she had bought. Edward addressed them, and the next day they were posted in Forestwidden. It was the first time Liz had ever sent out Christmas cards, as she had only recently learned to write, and Edward had never bothered before. The despatching of those cards was for Liz one of the proudest moments of her life; and in the years to come writing Christmas cards was one of her greatest pleasures, for it always brought back memories of the cottage, with the fire in the old range warming them, and Edward lying on the fat sofa, his leg propped up on a cushion, laughing at the childish way she stuck the tip of her tongue out as she wrote.

When she ran up to the farm next morning Liz found that the postman had left several letters for the cottage. She brought them back with the eggs and milk, giving them to Edward to open. Although some of them were addressed to 'Mr and Mrs E. Clayton' it did not occur to her to open them herself.

There were cards from the Reverend and Mrs Hatfield, John Oatis, the Willoughbys (unstamped), and the solicitor, Mr Steadman. There was a short letter with a card from Harriet Grant. Liz was glad she had remembered to send her one, with a few words from Edward scribbled on the back. And there was one letter with a printed heading for Edward. He read it with amazement; it contained a cheque for three pounds.

Dear Mr Clayton,

We are very pleased to tell you that we will be using the short story you sent us recently in *The Boy's Universal Weekly Adventure Magazine*, and enclose a cheque herewith.

If you are interested, we will be delighted to receive any further stories you produce on the same lines. Would you consider writing a series using the same characters? Perhaps it would not be possible for you to produce one each week, but fortnightly, or perhaps longer stories to be published in serial form.

We look forward to your comments on our proposition, and hope to hear from you in the near future.

Yours sincerely,
David Wilson,
Editor.

'Well, I'm blessed – look at this!' Edward said, handing the letter to Liz. She glanced at it, and handed it back impatiently. It would take her too long to spell it out, she wanted him to read it to her. He did so, and she stared at him, astonished and delighted. She had quite forgotten the story he had written and sent off weeks ago.

'So now you're a writer!' she whispered.

'It looks like it,' Edward chuckled. 'Three pounds – not much, but a good beginning. Anyway, it'll pay for the shoes! All I have to do now is think up another story every fortnight. Liz, we'll be rich soon at this rate – with the money we get from Brigadier Richardson for the work in the library, and this, we won't have to worry too much about the cost of coke for the range!'

Liz smiled doubtfully. She had never been in a position where she did not have to worry about money. She mistrusted his optimism. Until the money was actually in his hands, she did not quite believe in it. As for the cheque – she did not see how a piece of paper that had to be sent to the bank in Barminster would pay for mutton and cabbages. However, if Edward was happy and satisfied, she was content.

Their Christmas dinner was a good fat bird from Mrs Willoughby's chicken run. They had a bottle of wine, and one of whisky. Liz gave Edward a pullover she had knitted for him in the evenings after he had gone to bed, and he gave her a shawl he had conspired with Mrs Willoughby to buy when she went to Barminster with Henry on market day. In Barminster Liz had bought Mrs Willoughby a box of the chocolates she was so fond of, and fudge for Stewart and Brian. To Mrs Richardson she gave a fine Swiss lawn handkerchief. In return she received a tiny bottle of perfume, a pair of warm gloves, and a box of chocolates from the twins.

The gifts were few and simple, but they were given and received with affection and respect. Had they been gold, frankincense and myrrh, they could not have been more appreciated.

On the morning of Boxing Day Edward sat down and started to work on another story. Having completed one, he was able to get on much more quickly. The first one had taken six days in all; the second was finished in three. On New Year's Day he sent off two episodes in what was to become a series of adventures, written about two soldiers, thinly disguised, that he had served with in Africa. He was reluctant to use his own name, in case his old mates recognized themselves, so adopted the pseudonym Edmond Carlton.

After the New Year, Edward and Liz resumed their work on the library at Falldon Hall. The twins were still at home for the first two weeks, and their enthusiastic assistance did not delay the work unduly. Edward even managed to teach them the rudiments of algebra and geometry.

February brought a week of heavy snow, keeping them at home, and preventing Liz from making her usual calls at the farm. Henry battled through the snow to deliver their milk and see how they were faring. Liz kept the fire banked up, and the cottage was warm and comfortable. Edward spent the enforced holiday writing

As the war was still very fresh in everyone's mind, the adventure stories were read avidly by the schoolboys whose fathers and uncles had been in khaki only a short time ago. Consequently they were very popular and became a regular feature of the magazine. The sales figures went up, and Edward began to receive letters from boys who had read and enjoyed his stories. Before long the editor accordingly raised his remuneration.

In mid-April the work on the library at Falldon Hall was complete. The Brigadier and Mrs Richardson were more than satisfied with the results, and gave the Claytons a celebratory dinner on the last day they spent at the Hall. Mrs Richardson was very sorry to see them go. She had enjoyed Liz's company, as her husband had enjoyed the hours he had spent talking with Edward. After the meal she took Liz to the drawing-room for coffee while the men smoked a cigar and drank their port.

'Can't understand why you didn't apply for a commission, Clayton,' Brigadier Richardson said over the port. 'Man like you – educated, intelligent – would have made a fine officer. Too many damn fools at Headquarters, I found.'

'I nearly did, at one point,' Edward admitted. 'When I joined up with a crowd of other young fellows in London, we all went into the ranks. I was at Headquarters for a few weeks, and applied for a commission. Unfortunately, one afternoon, I failed to see one of the brigade officers come into the stores, and he thought I had deliberately neglected to salute him. Not only did I not salute the man, but as the temperature was in the eighties in that tin-roofed stores, I'd taken my shirt off, and he took strong exception to my bare chest! Instead of forwarding my papers with a recommendation, he returned me to the lines, minus the promotion to corporal I'd recently achieved, and I found myself out on night patrol again. Captain Harringay, I think he was; none of the chaps had much time for him. Too fond of spit and polish, and rather heavy on the bottle at lunchtime, too, I suspect.'

'Harringay? Never came across him – probably after I was sent home with stomach trouble. One thing I noticed – chaps that drank a lot didn't seem to go down with dysentery. D'you think whisky's a good disinfectant, Clayton?'

'Probably comes under the heading of "preventative medicine", sir,' Edward grinned.

'It certainly prevented a lot of officers I knew from rising any higher than captain,' the Brigadier remarked. 'Nothing like a heavy mess-bill for sorting out the wheat from the chaff, especially when the going got tough . . . You know, at one time, I knew a young fellow with the name of Clayton, a captain in the regiment – came from round this way, I believe. No relation, I suppose?'

'Captain Robert Clayton?' The Brigadier nodded. 'Yes, sir – that was my father.'

'Indeed? Nice chap. We got on well. Fell out with his family, I believe, and then ran into financial trouble.'

'Yes, so I understand,' Edward said evenly. The Brigadier refilled his glass.

'Well, young man, don't feel too badly about it. In those days you needed a private income to afford to stay in the Regiment – and if you were used to living comfortably, and that income was suddenly withdrawn, it was pretty hard going. Robert Clayton was a fine young fellow, and I liked him. If things had been different – or if he had been on active service at the time, instead of living the expensive social life that most of us got caught up in – he would have been a colonel or even a general now. You know, luck plays a great part in most of our lives. If I hadn't married Mary, I may have wound up with someone who wouldn't have put up with an absent husband half the time; and then I would have left the army and spent my life here, no training for anything but command, and nothing to be in command of. Miserable, that would have been. If you hadn't married that splendid little girl, where would you be now?'

'Dead, I suspect,' Edward admitted. 'And if she hadn't been so unhappy at home, I don't expect she would have considered marrying a one-legged, half-dead cripple; I just hope she never regrets it.'

'My dear chap, the girl idolizes you! I said to the wife only the other day, Clayton's a lucky fellow; not many wives as devoted as that little lady! Now tell me, what are you going to do with yourself now your job here's finished? Can't sit back and go rusty, you know. Anything in view?'

'Well, sir, I've been doing a bit of writing.' Edward flushed; so far he had not told anyone else about his scribbling, and he felt very self-conscious about it. 'Not anything very ambitious – boy's adventure stories, as it happens. I may be able to earn a living at that.'

The Brigadier looked at him dubiously.

'Hmmm ... Well, don't think I doubt your capabilities, but it's pretty hard to get started at that sort of thing. You wouldn't think of going back into the Law?'

'I don't think so,' Edward said. 'I never did enjoy it much, and I'm sure my old firm wouldn't have me back now! Not after walking out on them without notice when I joined up! And a one-legged, out-of-touch solicitor without much experience, no references, and no money would have a pretty thin time of it, I suspect, even if I could afford to buy into a partnership. Besides, I think Liz would be happier to stay at the cottage than return to town life.'

'Well, if you change your mind, let me know. I might be able to put in a good word for you somewhere. Good luck with the writing. You never know, you might make a name for yourself like that fellow Edmond Carlton the twins have been raving about recently. There's the devil to pay if I forget to get that magazine and send it to them every week – and I'll admit that I enjoy reading his yarns myself before I despatch them! Now, shall we join the ladies?'

Chapter Seventeen

With the spring came the annual horse-sale, and the Fair. Gervaise Clayton returned to Keenlach Lodge. The house was not opened up or staffed; he stayed there alone, waited on by the elderly caretaker and his wife. He went out a couple of times with the Hunt, but without the company of Cecil and his father he did not enjoy it as he had done in the past. He fell in with a Major Harringay who was also staying in the district, with his wife's family, for a few weeks. They had little in common, except that both were alone, but struck up a lukewarm acquaintanceship.

The gypsies had returned to their usual camp in the forest near Forestwidden, but Old Meg had died during the winter. Her daughter, a bad-tempered, suspicious crone, had taken her place as matriarch of the tribe. The men, as usual, brought several horses for sale, and worked in the sales-ring and at the Fair.

On the first day of the Fair Gervaise rode the five miles through the Great Forest to the horse-sale. He spent an hour there wandering about alone. He saw no horses that interested him, and without the company of his brother, although they had argued much of the time, he was soon bored. He ran into Major Harringay and they went to the King's Arms, where they spent some time talking and drinking. Gervaise went back to his friend's house for dinner and a game of cards, but did not meet the Major's family as they had dined earlier. Lady Fortune did not smile on him over the card table, and when he left the house his pocket was considerably lighter. It was well after two o'clock when he finally returned to Keenlach Lodge, where he was surprised to see lights in several of the windows. He had told the caretaker not to wait up for him. The front door was thrown open before he reached it.

'Thank God you're back, sir,' the old man cried, holding a lamp up to light the steps to the door. 'A telegram from your father – it arrived soon after you left, sir.'

'A telegram?' Gervaise exclaimed. 'But Father didn't know I was coming here.'

'No, sir – it was addressed to me,' the caretaker said. 'Asking if you were here – reply paid, sir.'

Gervaise's face darkened in anger.

'And I suppose you let him know I was staying at the lodge,' he snarled. 'I'm a grown man, Jenkins. It's a fine thing if I have to report my whereabouts to my father every move I make!'

Jenkins put the lamp on the table, and took his coat and hat. The old man was clearly afraid of the younger one, for if he lost this job he and his wife would be without work and homeless.

'Yes, Mr Gervaise, I did,' he said shakily. 'The matter seemed urgent – and I *am* employed by Mr Clayton, sir.'

'Damn you, man, bring me a brandy!' Gervaise strode to the fireplace where the embers cast a glow over the brass fire irons. He stretched his hands out to the warmth. 'I'm frozen to the marrow – that wind is enough to freeze your very bones!' The old man hurried off to do his bidding. Gervaise stood warming his coat-tails, wondering what had prompted his father to send the telegram.

A second telegram arrived early next morning, requesting him to return to London immediately. He lived in a serviced flat in Knightsbridge, but he went straight to Eaton Square. His father was in the study. Despite the early hour, there was a brandy glass by his hand.

'I've been waiting for word from you for days – if you

leave the city, Gervaise, at least have the courtesy to let us know where to find you! Your mother has been at her wit's end. I've sent telegrams to every place I could think of before I finally ran you to earth!'

'It's good to know you're so concerned about me –' Gervaise began sarcastically, but his father cut him short.

'Your grandfather – Lord Farlington, not my father – is down with pneumonia and not expected to last the week. Your mother is already on her way to Yorkshire, and we're to follow as soon as possible. As you're his heir the least you can do is try to get there before he goes to meet his maker. How many times have you visited him in the last five years? Twice? And then only when you're driven to it! Well, get yourself about, my boy There's a train in an hour's time, and I told your man to have your things ready.'

They caught the train with minutes to spare, but they reached Farlington Towers too late to take their leave of the old man, who died an hour before they arrived. Lady Imogen was in the drawing-room with the family solicitor and the estate manager. She was consoling herself with brandy, and her son and husband joined her.

The new Lord Farlington returned to London with Arthur Clayton and Lady Imogen the day after the funeral.

'I suppose you'll be giving up your flat and moving into Farlington House now,' Lady Imogen remarked as they got into the cab outside the station. She had not yet come out of mourning for her son, and now she was in black for her father. The weeds did not suit her; she dressed well, but nothing was shown at its best on her bony frame, and her prominent nose and scanty hair were not improved by the black crepe. Her husband, on the other hand, looked very distinguished in his black suit, as did her son.

'Tomorrow I'll go and have a look at Farlington House,' Gervaise said thoughtfully, 'but I doubt if I'll live there.

The house hasn't been done up for donkey's years – it's like a museum. I could have it refurbished, but I don't think I want to live in a place like that alone. Perhaps I should let it. The Farlington estate is not exactly prosperous.'

'He seems to have let things go these last few years,' his mother agreed. 'I don't think much of that bailiff who has been in charge of things in Yorkshire. I believe the housekeeper's his wife, and she seems quite competent, but I wouldn't trust Bodger very far without having his work superintended.'

'Well, my boy,' Arthur said brusquely, making his son wince (he was getting on for thirty, and did not appreciate being called 'my boy'), 'now you'll have to think about getting married, and think seriously! There must be some young woman you'd like to see as Lady Farlington. A pity that cousin of yours – Harriet – wasn't more amenable. A good-looking girl like that, with a fortune of her own – she'd make you a good wife if she dropped this damn career nonsense!'

'Spare me that, Father,' Gervaise said disagreeably. 'The last thing I want is an independent, wilful wife who fancies herself as a – what do they call them? Suffragette! As for her fortune, I've no need to marry for money. No, thanks, I'll choose myself a wife when I'm ready.'

'Better make it soon, Gervaise,' his mother advised. 'You have to think of the future now. You must have an heir.'

'I'm not thinking of passing on for a year or two, Mother,' Gervaise said impatiently.

'Perhaps not,' Arthur Clayton said sardonically, 'but if you do, Edward will be the next one in line. So get yourself a son – a legal son – as soon as you can.'

'My God!' Lady Imogen gasped. 'Edward – that dreadful fellow – he can't –'

'Oh, yes, my dear, he can,' Arthur said drily. 'If Gervaise doesn't produce a direct heir, Edward Clayton will be the next Lord Farlington, as well as coming into the Clayton estate. So the sooner your dear son gets down to raising a family the better!'

In Edinburgh Harriet was studying assiduously, and although much of the time she could not honestly say that she enjoyed it, she found it satisfying and rewarding. She did enjoy the company of the other students, particularly that of another young woman of her own age, Miss Ann Cowper. They had met at the beginning of their training, and each found in the other many qualities to admire. Both had become addicted to the sport of bicycling. Harriet was invited to Ann's home in Yorkshire for Christmas, and they spent several days cycling in the Dales, although the truth was they walked nearly as far as they cycled, for every time they free-wheeled joyously down a hill, they had to toil up the next on foot. But the two girls enjoyed each other's company, and the excercise and fresh air, after weeks spent in the hospital, were a welcome change. When they returned to Edinburgh they found themselves a flat near the hospital, received permission from the college governors, and moved in together.

Harriet read in *The Times* that her cousin had become Lord Farlington. Out of courtesy she wrote her condolences to Lady Imogen, and received a polite acknowledgement on a black-bordered card; but that was the end of the correspondence, by mutual agreement. Ann Cowper was intrigued to find that her friend was related to Lord Farlington, as Farlington Towers was near her father's home, but none of the family had met the heir. As Lady Imogen was not acquainted with many of the Towers' neighbours, this was not surprising, but Ann's three younger sisters and two brothers were hoping to meet the young peer some time in the not-too-distant future. It did not occur to them that he would have no interest in a family of country neighbours of no particular fame or fortune. Young Lord Farlington had no inclination to spend his time rusticating in Yorkshire.

As spring turned to summer Harriet and Ann planned to take a holiday when the medical college closed, and after much thought they decided to take their bicycles down to the south coast by train, and explore the countryside. The obvious centre to make their base was Barminster. Harriet accordingly wrote to the Golden Eagle and booked two rooms for a fortnight. Mr and Mrs Cowper were not sure they approved Ann's staying at a hotel but as they had met Harriet and found her a most respectable companion for their elder daughter (who usually did as she wished with or without their permission), they eventually gave the undertaking their blessing, and the two girls embarked on their holiday in high spirits.

The first day they pedalled out to Barminster Abbey where Harriet had worked in the Soldiers' Hospital, and found the gates locked, and the mansion deserted. The workmen were finished, but Lady Imogen did not feel inclined to engage staff and move in while she was in mourning, so for the moment only a caretaker was living in the newly-decorated mansion. It was planned to open it up the following Easter, when Arthur would invite all the local gentry and important county dignitaries to visit, in preparation for his venture into politics. Lady Imogen hoped that a General Election would not be called before then. Besides, she was enjoying being in London this year, which, after the long awaited coronation, was full of gaiety, much of which she was able to enjoy despite her state of mourning.

The following day the girls took a train to Bournemouth, where they went swimming in the sea, a novel experience for both of them. Unfortunately, on the way back Ann developed a tickle in the throat, and the next day was down with a heavy summer cold. It was not serious, but they decided that it would be advisable for her to spend the day indoors, rather than risk going out and making it worse.

Leaving her friend in the hotel lounge reading a book, Harriet went for a walk in the town. She had received a Christmas card from her cousin Edward and his wife, but he had not given her an address. However, she remembered that the solicitor who looked after his affairs was in Barminster. As she walked through the Square she found his offices, and impulsively went in.

The middle-aged lady at the reception desk regretted that she was unable to supply the young lady with Mr Clayton's address, but offered to forward a note. At this point John Oatis came in, and was introduced to Harriet.

'I'm sorry, Miss Grant, I'm not at liberty to give you my client's address,' John said regretfully, admiring this forthright young woman, and wondering how she came to know Edward. 'But I can give him a message from you, if you wish.'

'Oh, it doesn't matter,' Harriet said hastily. 'He's my cousin, you see, and I wondered how he was faring – I know he was wounded. I suppose he's quite recovered now?'

'Yes, indeed,' John said uncomfortably. He knew Edward did not want any of his family to know of his disability; did this apply to this handsome young woman? Her tawny hair and green eyes were very attractive – she was a most engaging and charming girl. He asked her if she would care to join him for a cup of tea, as he had no appointments for the next half hour. Harriet smiled, and said reluctantly that she had promised to return to the Golden Eagle for coffee with the friend with whom she was on holiday.

'You're on holiday in Barminster?' John enquired. 'In that case, I wonder if you and your friend would do me the honour of allowing me to show you something of the countryside – not tomorrow, I'm fully engaged at the office, but the next day. Let me take you to see the famous gardens at Solney; it's only half-an-hour's drive, and perhaps we could have a picnic.'

'Delightful!' Harriet exclaimed. 'We came here to bicycle, you know, but Ann – Miss Cowper – has a cold, and I'm afraid she won't be fit for bicycling for a few days. But a drive, and a picnic, would be splendid. I know she would enjoy that, if the weather holds.'

'Excellent. I'll pick you up at the Golden Eagle at eleven, then, and I'll supply the picnic. Until then, my dear Miss Grant, goodbye,' John beamed. Harriet went back to the hotel feeling that things were looking up. She was very taken with the young solicitor.

At the Golden Eagle she found Ann Cowper had returned to her bedroom, with her eyes streaming, and her throat sore, wanting only to sleep. Harriet sent to the kitchen for a lemon and honey drink, and went to her own room to write some postcards to their fellow students in Edinburgh. In her writing case she found the card she had received from Edward and his wife at Christmas, and the postmark was quite clear.

Forestwidden. She remembered seeing that name on the map. After luncheon she put on her calf-length, divided cycling skirt and jacket, and went down to get out her bicycle. Several people in the vestibule stared; in this country town the fashionable cycling skirt that revealed the lower part of the calf was as yet seldom seen. The ladies glared at her reproachfully, while the men noted her neat ankles and slender calves and allowed themselves an appreciative smirk before their wives drew their attention elsewhere.

Harriet spoke to the porter, who retrieved her bicycle from the luggage store, and wheeled it out to the road. She mounted, and rode out of the town, following the main road through the forest to Forestwidden. It was not difficult, as the signposts were quite clear, and she enjoyed the ride, but it took her over two hours. The afternoon was sunny, and she soon had to take off her jacket and stow it in the carrier. When she reached the village she was parched.

She found the village shop and post office, and went inside. She bought a bottle of lemonade. The man behind the counter, a red-cheeked countryman with extraordinary large red ears, could scarcely drag his eyes away from the revealing skirt. He looked surprised when she asked him if he knew a Mr Edward Clayton.

'Know 'im, as you might say, miss – no, I don't; but know of 'im – yes, I does that, I does. No-one don't know 'im, like, except vicar. And the Brigadier, I b'lieve. Aaaarr.'

'Oh.' That sounded a little odd. Perhaps her cousin was a solitary man, after the dreadful ordeal he had experienced in the war. She remembered him as being a bashful and gauche schoolboy, but ready to speak up for himself none-theless. 'Well, perhaps you could tell me how to find him,' she said hopefully.

'Aaaahhh . . . Well, you sees that lane? If you goes down there until you passes the farm – 'Enry Willoughby's farm, that be, miss – then the lane turns into a track. You follows it until it reaches the sea. And that be 'Oney Beck Bay. Edward Clayton and 'is missis lives there, y'see. In a li'l ol' tumbledown cottage, miss. It be about four mile.'

Four miles! Oh dear! Well, she'd come so far, she wasn't going to turn back now.

'Can I send a telegram from here?' she enquired.

'Yes, miss – 'ere's the form.' Hastily Harriet wrote a message for Ann, warning her that she might stay the night in Forestwidden. Then she re-mounted her cycle, and went down the lane. It doubled back on the way she had come, the lane running south-east; Forestwidden was south-west of Barminster. Had she come by the other road, south through the Great Forest, she would have saved herself a

217

good six miles of hard pedalling. She found a grassy bank under a tree and drank the lemonade from the bottle before continuing on her way.

Having passed the farm, she reached the steep, rutted track. Mindful of the bicycle's tyres, she got off and walked the rest of the way. It was nearly five o'clock when she finally reached the bay, and thought that of all the places she had seen on this coast, this was surely the most delightful and secluded spot she had come across. In front of her, at the end of the track, she could see the cottage, now bright with fresh paint, the windows winking in the sunshine, roses and honeysuckle blooming with that brilliance that the salt air imparts. At the side of the cottage a vegetable patch was thriving. The tide was out and the sand was clean and golden. At the eastern end of the bay she could see a girl in a gingham dress walking slowly along the waterline, apparently engrossed in beachcombing.

Harriet was about to walk to the cottage door when she heard a voice hailing her from the trees that separated the track from the bay. She looked back and saw a man sitting on a fallen log. Edward Clayton? She slipped off her shoes, left them with her bicycle near the cottage, and walked in her stockinged feet across the sand towards the man.

As she got closer, she saw that he was a cripple, with only one leg. Two crutches lay by the log. His hair, now rather long but not unkempt, was prematurely grey, but his face was young, his eyes bright, and his skin tanned by the sun: a good-looking man, if not conventionally handsome. It was not until she was almost within reach of him that Harriet realized she had seen him before.

'O'Malley!' she exclaimed, her eyes lighting up with delight at seeing him looking so well.

'Nurse Grant,' he said, smiling, and attempting to get up, but she waved him back, and took a seat beside him on the log.

'What on earth are you doing here?' she asked, pulling off her tammy, revealing the tawny hair.

'I could ask you the same thing,' Edward said.

'Oh, I came looking for a cousin of mine – a fellow called Edward Clayton,' she replied; and then stared. O'Malley – Edward . . . ? 'Good Lord, are you Edward Clayton?' she exclaimed.

'Yes, I am, and you must be the Harriet Grant who wrote to me last year!' Edward chuckled. 'I'll be damned – I never connected the little girl I met all those years back with Nurse Grant! Had I known you were my cousin I may have been able to save myself a great deal of trouble! I had to produce a wife to get me out of that place, as I had no relative I could call on.' He was quiet for a moment; had he known Nurse Grant was his cousin, he would have asked her help to get him out of the hospital, and then he would not have married Liz . . . The tides of fortune had been working for him even then, had he but known it.

Harriet was staring at him curiously.

'How did you find yourself a wife so suddenly, in that godforsaken place?' she marvelled. 'Oh – I suppose you were married all along, and had – had forgotten . . . ?'

'No. A good angel took pity on me, and took me under her wing with a couple of days' notice,' he told her. 'Here she is now. Liz! Look who's come to visit us!'

Liz had wandered up from the beach, curious about the woman Edward was talking to so animatedly. She was wearing her pink-and-white gingham dress – now a little faded from much washing, but still particularly pretty and fresh-looking, flattering her faint tan and her violet-blue eyes. Her dark hair was a little untidy, soft tendrils curling about her brow and ears; her small, shapely feet were bare. She looked curiously at the handsome young woman in the short cycling skirt. She had seen illustrations of such garments in the fashion magazines, and marvelled that any young woman could wear them so unselfconsciously, heedless of showing her legs. She recognized Nurse Grant immediately, and wondered what she could be doing here in their secluded bay. Edward was smiling broadly; obviously he was delighted to see his erstwhile nurse. A sudden stab of dismay ran through Liz as she recalled her mother's words of warning. Nurse Grant, with her glorious tawny hair and her superb figure, her air of confidence that proclaimed her the equal of any man; how could Edward fail to admire her? In the past Liz had idolized the kind nurse who had always treated her gently, often protecting her from Sister's sharp tongue; but suddenly she saw her as a threat to her happiness. But then Edward smiled at Liz, and took her hand. Her misgivings faded.

'Harriet, this is Mrs Clayton. You've met before, of course. Liz, Nurse Grant is my cousin! You remember, she wrote to me a few months back.'

Harriet stared at Liz for a moment without recognition; then she had the second surprise of the afternoon.

'Liz! The skivvy!' she gasped – and clapped her hand to her mouth, deeply ashamed of her involuntary exclamation. But Liz laughed, an odd, silent chuckle, and the sudden frown cleared from Edward's face as he saw that his wife was not offended. 'I'm sorry, my dear, I didn't intend to be rude,' Harriet said apologetically, standing up and taking Liz's hand. 'I'm just so surprised – and so pleased! You both look so well and happy. I came here to introduce myself to a cousin I hadn't seen for ten years, and find two people I know – oh, I really can't believe it! Now, Edward, tell me all about it. What happened?'

While Edward related to his cousin the peculiar story of his marriage, and his recovery, and she told him of her break with the Clayton family and her studies in Edinburgh, Liz went to the cottage and prepared the tea. She was genuinely pleased to see Harriet, but a seed of uncertainty remained.

Edward's eyes had told her that he was delighted to meet his cousin again; he obviously admired her, and they were out there now, chatting comfortably together. Harriet's reaction had reminded her that she was the ward-maid, the skivvy. Harriet's amazement at finding Liz married to her cousin was not to be wondered at; he was an educated, cultured man, and Liz was a child of the slums. How could he fail to compare her with his beautiful, charming cousin?

She set the table with a cloth she had embroidered, with the new teaset and silverware Edward had recently bought in Barminster. Now they were comfortably off, he was gradually buying the things she had longed for. She had fresh bread, farm butter and cheese, and a fine sponge cake she had baked that morning, spread with raspberry jam she and Mrs Willoughby had made between them. She wondered wistfully if Harriet had to make her own jam? She cut a few slices from the cold bacon joint she had cooked the day before. When Edward and Harriet came into the cottage she had set a table fit for a queen.

But as Liz saw them standing at the doorway together, that sudden chill returned, for despite his crutches, he was a fine-looking man, laughing with this well-spoken, handsome girl. They made an outstanding couple, both radiating the confidence bestowed by good health, a good education, and independence. Liz suddenly realized how much he had given up when he married the skivvy.

Harriet came in and stood looking at the table.

'Liz, what a splendid spread! How lucky you are, Edward, to have won a good cook as well as a lovely wife!'

The chill vanished, and Liz was happy again, but still a tiny cloud remained to spoil her peace of mind.

While they were eating, the bright afternoon sky clouded over and a storm began to brew. The air became thick and heavy, and lightning flashed on the far horizon out at sea.

Liz ran to fetch in the washing she had left on the line, and Harriet's bicycle was hastily stowed in the new garden shed with the wheelbarrow and hoes.

'I hope this doesn't last too long – I've got to ride back to the village and look for a room in the tavern,' Harriet remarked, staring through the window at the sea, which had suddenly become leaden, with deep swells replacing the light, playful waves of an hour before.

'You certainly can't bicycle back to the village in this,' Edward said firmly. 'And I'm not sure the village tavern lets rooms – do you know, Liz?'

'No, they don't,' she whispered. 'Miss Grant will have to stay the night. She can sleep on the sofa.'

'I'm sure we can do better than that,' Edward frowned. 'Liz, let Harriet have your bed –'

'No – the sofa!' Liz whispered hurriedly. Edward looked at her in surprise; this was the first time she had refused any suggestion he made.

'The sofa will do fine,' Harriet assured him. 'And if Liz will lend me a nightgown, I'll be as comfortable as a bug in a rug!'

For the next hour the storm raged, and thunder and lightning roared and flashed across the English Channel. Then the rain came, a steady, soaking rain, which threatened to wash the vegetables out of the soil, and produced a hundred miniature waterfalls flowing over the cliff-face from the fields above. Suddenly it was all over; the sun shone again, low on the horizon, producing a theatrical show of gold and red and amber in the west. Only the steady pounding of the waves on the shore remained to remind them that they had had a grand storm little more than an hour ago.

Liz finished washing up – she refused to let Harriet help her – and went out into the garden.

'She's gone to check on her vegetables,' Edward told Harriet. 'She fusses over them as if they were her children!'

222

'You haven't any children?' Harriet asked. Edward turned away, staring out at the gathering dusk.

'No,' he said shortly; his tone did not invite any further discussion. He paused for a moment, then turned back to her, and sighed. 'I doubt if there ever will be any children, Harriet – I'm not much of a prize for a lovely young girl, am I?'

'Don't be a fool, Edward,' Harriet said awkwardly; then her eyes narrowed. 'Do you mean – you haven't –'

'No, I haven't, and I don't suppose I ever will,' Edward admitted bitterly. 'At first, of course, I was too busy being ill to care, and now – well, I don't think she wants me. I think she sees me as an old man, a father, perhaps. Certainly not a lover or a husband.'

'You damn fool, Edward,' Harriet said slowly. 'I knew something didn't feel quite right . . . So that's it! Poor Liz! She adores you, and you haven't made a wife of her yet! I don't suppose she's going to make the running, Edward, so it's up to you to do something about it! I gather you don't share a bedroom?'

'No, Liz sleeps up there,' he said, gesturing towards the loft. 'My bed is in that room – it's little more than a lean-to, actually, but big enough for a narrow bed, and I can't get up those damn steps!'

'Then I suggest you have a decent staircase put in, and learn to get up it!' Harriet said briskly. 'Or you could have that ramshackle little room demolished, and another built, twice as big. To take a double bed!' She looked at him. 'And another thing – it's about time you did something about an artificial leg, Edward Clayton! Hasn't your doctor ever suggested it?'

'I haven't seen a doctor since I left Barminster,' Edward admitted.

'Well, there are some marvellous artificial limbs available now,' Harriet told him, 'and you ought to think about

223

getting one fitted. You can have a simple peg-leg, or you can have a leg with a joint and a shoe although I must admit, I've not seen anyone use one successfully yet, I'm told they're inclined to fold up at the wrong moment! But you should find out about them. Can you afford to spend a few pounds on it, Edward?'

'Oh, yes – I'm doing very well, Harriet. I'm earning more than we need with my writing, though of course, I don't know how long that will continue. We're far from rich, but I've put a certain amount in the bank. How would I go about finding out about these artificial legs?'

Harriet hesitated.

'I don't really know – but I'll make enquiries and let you know by letter,' she promised. Edward glanced up at the loft.

'It's getting dark. I'll light the lamps. Will you go up and fetch the one Liz uses up there? She must have forgotten to bring it down this morning.'

'Of course,' Harriet said, standing up and climbing the steep steps. When she came down again she had a puzzled expression on her face.

'Edward, you've never been up there, have you?'

'Not since we came to live here,' he admitted. 'I told you, I can't get up the steps! I went up there often enough when I was a child. Nothing wrong with my legs then! Why?'

'Where do you think Liz sleeps?'

'In a bed, of course; where else?' he said, carefully trimming the wick of the lamp. He looked up, and saw a furious gleam in Harriet's eyes.

'Men!' she exclaimed. 'What bed? Edward, have you ever wondered what sort of bed she's got? Where did your bed come from? Did you buy it – or did she?'

'I don't know what you're talking about!' Edward said in bewilderment. 'Liz bought the beds – I never saw either of them until they were put up in the cottage. Wait a minute.

224

Come to think of it, I never did see hers. I don't remember seeing it brought into the cottage, and I don't remember seeing anyone carry it up those infernal steps!'

'That's because she hasn't got a bloody bed – she sleeps on a straw palliasse!' Harriet snapped.

Edward gaped at her incredulously.

'Good Lord! I never gave it a thought! That poor girl – I'm sleeping down here on a feather mattress and she's up there on a straw palliasse! My God, Harriet, what a selfish, unthinking brute I am!'

'Well, don't embarrass her now by letting her know I've told you, but do something about it, Edward! Now, let's play a hand of cards before we go to bed – here's Liz. Can you play cards, Liz?'

The game of cards began quietly, but became more hilarious as the evening wore on. At ten Liz made tea, and produced a fruit cake, of which nothing remained but crumbs when they went to bed shortly afterwards.

Next morning Harriet was up early, and they all had breakfast together. Edward asked her to deliver a note to John Oatis for him, and was amused to see the colour rise in her cheeks. Despite her claim to be an independent, modern young woman, she obviously felt the same emotions as a simple milkmaid! She was soon away on her bicycle, or at least, she was last seen by the couple at the cottage pushing the bicycle up the rough track. Liz would not admit it even to herself, but she felt a certain amount of relief as Harriet's figure disappeared from sight. She watched Edward as he turned back to the cottage door. He did not seem unduly concerned to see his cousin go. Liz went back into the cottage and began to clear up the breakfast dishes. Soon the calm of the bay soothed her disturbed emotions, and she settled back to her contented, peaceful routine.

*

When she reached the road, Harriet mounted up, and cycled steadily through the forest, taking a shorter route back to Barminster. There she found Ann looking much better, and delighted with the idea of a picnic the next day.

'And Ann, I tracked down my cousin Edward at Forestwidden, and guess what – he's the fellow O'Malley I told you about! The one who had lost his memory. He's married, and I know his wife. She was working at the hospital in Barminster too.'

Harriet did not tell her friend that he had married the ward-maid, or that the girl had been sleeping for the past twelve months on a straw palliasse in the loft. She realized that it was due to thoughtlessness, not indifference, on Edward's part, but her independent friend might think otherwise.

Chapter Eighteen

Late in the afternoon Henry Willoughby and his wife called at the cottage. His usually jovial face was sober, and Mrs Willoughby looked far from her normal happy self. They had been inspecting the storm damage. Most of the vital barley crop, almost ready for harvesting, had been laid flat.

'I intended to start cutting tomorrow,' Henry told them, dropping heavily into a chair. 'I reckon it'll be about three days before it's dry enough to cut and half will be black with mildew. If only we had a good stiff breeze! While the corn's flat and damp this humid weather will ruin the crop.'

'I had four pans of cream ready to make butter, and that's all curdled, too,' Mrs Willoughby lamented. 'At least it will make cheese, but there'll be no butter this week.'

'A pity we can't make cheese from mouldy barley,' her husband said despondently. 'The annual rent's due shortly. I was depending on a good price for the grain. It promised to be such a fine crop, too! Now it looks as if I'll have to sell old Daisy and her foal, and as most of the other farmers will be in the same boat, selling off spare animals, I'll be lucky to get half her value.'

'How much will you be short?' Edward asked quietly.

'More than you can spare from your pension, my friend,' Henry said glumly. He named a figure, and Edward looked startled. 'To tell the truth, things haven't been too good this year,' Henry admitted. 'Perhaps I'm getting too old for this game – farming's a job for the young and active. We lost five calves in the spring, and the lambing was poor – that cold snap came at the wrong time. On top of that the

227

rent's gone up and now I'm in a financial mess. I had a good crop last year and, like a fool, I invested the money in a few industrial shares; now the company I invested in has gone bust, so I've lost that too! I should have known better, but it looked as if that company would pay a far better dividend than the bank interest. Three generations of Willoughbys have farmed this land, but it looks as if we've come to the end of the road. Not that I've got anyone to hand it on to. Under these circumstances, perhaps it's as well we have no children to worry about.'

'But surely the landlord will give you a chance to make it up next year?' Edward suggested. Willoughby laughed bitterly.

'Not likely! Old Sir Rupert might have given me a bit of leeway but Arthur Clayton's a different matter! He'll grab every penny, and more if he can get it. No, things are pretty black right now. I was depending on this crop.'

Liz put the tea and biscuits on the table, and Henry cheered up a little when he had slaked his thirst. He remembered why he had called, and handed Edward a couple of letters.

'These came this morning, Edward. Nearly forgot them! They're addressed to E. Carlton but I thought they might be for you. The writer's got the name wrong. If the weather holds we'll be cutting in two days – like to come and lend a hand, Liz?' Liz nodded. 'I'm getting some men from the village to help. There's plenty of labour about this year. Joe Ball, the builder, has lost a big job he was counting on, and all his men are at a standstill. Trouble is, they'll all have to be paid.' He and his wife went off despondently, climbing the steps in the cliff-face and crossing the paddock to the road.

Edward opened his letters. One was from the magazine he wrote for; they had received an offer from an American publication for a second printing of all the series to date, and were offering a generous royalty. The copyright was jointly owned by Edward and the magazine.

'I'll settle for half the royalties,' Edward told Liz. 'I reckon that's fair.'

The second letter was from a publisher. Edward had written a short book, an account of his time in the cavalry, but presented in an amusing vein, with no mention of his injuries or his months in hospital. Liz had read it before it was sent off and found it hilarious. It appeared that the publisher also found it entertaining, for he wrote that he would be delighted to accept it. He already knew the name Edmond Carlton from the boys' magazine, and was sure the book would sell well. He enclosed a cheque as an advance payment, and a contract for Edward to sign.

'I'll have to get John Oatis to study that,' Edward said, after glancing through the document. 'I think this fellow's trying to push a hard bargain. If I accept the cheque, I've virtually agreed to the contract. I'll see what John thinks of it.'

John Oatis called on them a couple of days later. A new branch railway line had been opened with a halt just outside Forestwidden, and now it took only an hour to get to and from Barminster. John was able to hire a trap from the blacksmith to drive out to the cottage.

'Harriet remembered to give you my note, then,' Edward said with a grin as John alighted from the trap. When the pony had been watered and left in the shade of a tree they went into the cottage. Liz was out. She had gone for the day, to help with the harvest.

'I don't know how Miss Grant found you,' John said apologetically. 'I wouldn't give her your address –'

'Oh, we'd sent her a Christmas card, she still had it, and the postmark gave us away! Apparently she enquired for us in the village, and someone told her how to find the cottage.

It doesn't matter, anyway – she's all right. It's the rest of the family I'm not keen on!'

'Well, now I'm here, what can I do for you?' John asked, making himself comfortable on the fat sofa.

'I want you to make enquiries about buying the cottage,' Edward told him. 'But without revealing who the would-be purchaser is, mind you! I'll have to borrow from the bank against the capital old Steadman holds for me. I want to add another room to the cottage, but on a monthly lease it isn't worth the outlay. Since I wrote, another matter has come up, a couple of contracts I need your advice on, and I want to lend Henry Willoughby some cash without his knowing where it came from.'

'You seem to be very affluent all of a sudden,' John remarked with a grin. 'Been gambling with your pension?'

Edward told him about his venture into the writing profession.

'And very well it's going, too,' he added. 'I expect interest will die off as memories of the Boer War fade, but for the moment I'm doing far better than I expected – certainly a lot better than I would do in the legal profession!'

'You'll soon find something new to write about,' John said. For an hour they discussed business, and then John reluctantly departed. The air was heavy and sultry, and only here in the bay was there the slightest breath of a breeze. Edward tried to tempt him into the sea for a swim, but he had several appointments during the afternoon, and resisted the temptation.

'It's all very well for you to hop around in your underwear, Edward,' he grinned, 'but supposing Mrs Clayton came back and found me practically naked? She'd likely send for the constable!'

He did not confess his other reason for hurrying back to Barminster. That evening he was taking Harriet and Miss Cowper to the Variety Theatre. They had enjoyed the day

230

out at Solney Gardens, with a delightful picnic, and he was looking forward to another meeting. John had persuaded his younger brother James to accompany them, to partner Miss Cowper; that would give him the opportunity to get to know Harriet Grant better.

Liz came home in the late evening very weary. Edward had the supper ready, and she was touched by his thoughtfulness. She knew he was feeling left out, unable to help get the corn in when everyone else was working so hard. As more storms threatened, the workers would go on as long as they had the strength to stand, until the harvest was safe. The crop was not as badly affected as Henry had feared, but it was far from good. A lot of the ears had shed, leaving almost as much barley on the fields for the birds as in the barn. The gleaners would do well this year.

'Remember Meg's grandson Samson?' Liz whispered. 'He was there, and he can carry more barley in one sack than most of the other men can carry in two trips!'

'He lifted me into the bath as if I was a babe in arms,' Edward recalled.

'He's Job's cousin,' Liz told him. That means Job's my distant cousin, too, Edward thought. 'When we were nearly finished I saw a man on horseback looking over the fence – a toff, he was. I wonder what he was doing there?'

'Watching the harvest being brought in, I suppose,' Edward said absently. 'He probably thought you were a gypsy, too, in those clothes! Now off you go to bed, Liz; because not only do you look like a gypsy, you look tired out! I'll wash up, and then do a little more writing before I go to bed. I didn't get much done today.'

The next day Liz left early again, and Edward tidied the cottage, washed up, and then went out and stood staring at the steps in the cliff-face. He had not previously attempted to ascend them, but now he got down on his hands and one knee, and toiled his way painfully to the top, dragging his crutches after him.

He sat for ten minutes on the cliff edge, looking about him. What a marvellous view! The little paddock was green and lush after the rain, and the brook ran through with a burbling song, just as he remembered it as a boy. He turned to the west, and followed the path towards the farm. Negotiating the stile was difficult, but he managed it, and soon was in sight of the field where the straw was being tied and stooked so that it would dry, ready for the stack.

Liz waved and ran to greet him when he reached the field. The look of joy on her face, at his venturing so far, was enough reward for the effort. The men waved but did not pause in their work; time was precious in this weather. Henry was working alongside the men. Job made light work of the stooking, his top hat bobbing up and down. Edward had been thinking of Liz's remark about the horseman watching them and a nagging anxiety remained with him.

Henry looked up from his back-breaking task.

'D'you think you could drive the cart, Edward? I was going back to the farmhouse to fetch the missis with the morning tea, but could you do it for me?'

'Surely,' Edward said eagerly. At last there was something he could do to help! He swung his way across the field, the crutches catching in the stubble, threatening to toss him to the ground, but he reached the cart without mishap and scrambled awkwardly on to the bench at the front.

It felt good to have the reins in his hands again! As he set old Daisy towards the farmhouse, he remembered that the last time he had held the leather of reins in his hands had been that day on the veldt when he and his mates had been ambushed at the deserted farmhouse . . .

Mrs Willoughby had a small milk-churn full of steaming tea ready, a couple of loaves of bread cut into cheese sandwiches, and a large, freshly baked cake. At least the workers were not in danger of starvation, Edward thought, as they loaded the refreshments on to the cart, and headed back to the field. Mrs Willoughby was as surprised to see him as her husband had been. Today, with plenty to do feeding the workers, and the harvest going on apace, she looked a lot happier.

The workers relaxed under a tree and drank the strong, dark tea, tucking into the sandwiches and cake as if they hadn't eaten for a week. Edward accepted a thick mug of tea, and drank it sitting on the driver's bench at the front of the cart. From there he had a good view of the country-side. He let his eyes wander across the vista of fields and woods, the epitome of English rural domesticity. A black-bird was singing his heart out in the oak tree the harvesters sat under. Surely this was the most beautiful, satisfying land-scape in the world . . . Liz scrambled up and they sat com-panionably side by side. She smiled happily as their eyes met over the steaming mugs.

Suddenly Liz stiffened, and nudged him, nodding towards the lane, within their view over the hedge. The harvesters, sitting on the grass, could not see the horseman who had just come into their sight.

'The toff,' she whispered. The man, about the same age as Edward, was riding a handsome grey horse. He trotted in a leisurely way up the lane, glancing over the hedge at the field as he passed. Hearing the iron-shod hooves, Henry stood up to see who was passing. Daisy threw up her head, and snickered, jolting the cart a few inches, making Edward lose his precarious balance on the bench and topple over, landing on his back in the loose straw that littered the cart.

Liz gasped and turned white. Had he injured himself again? But to her relief Edward was all right, merely winded and struggling to get himself upright.

The horseman glanced back. He had reached a gap in

the hedge, and could see the workers under the tree. He halted and stared for a moment, and grinned when he saw the grey-haired man who had been sitting on the cart now lying on his back with one leg in the air. That girl with the dark hair was bending over him anxiously, fussing like a hen with one chick. Pity she couldn't find a younger man to practise her charms on – Gervaise wouldn't mind a bit of that fussing himself . . . He drove his booted heels into the horse's flanks and cantered away.

Henry ran to assist Edward back on to the seat.

'Did you see who that was?' he said grimly, when Edward was restored to his seat and a fresh mug of tea had been passed up to him. 'Young Gervaise Clayton – Lord Farlington now. Come to check on the progress of the harvest, I'll be bound! Can't think of any other reason he'd be here at this time of the year. Are you all right, Edward? You look a bit shaken. Shall I drive you home?'

'No – no thanks, I'm fine,' Edward assured him. 'I'll be off now, Henry, and leave you good people to your work. Don't want to hold up the harvest. I only wish I could help!'

'If you're up to it you can help in a couple of days' time, driving the cart when we bring in the corn,' Henry said. 'That'll leave another man free for stacking. But at the moment there's nothing you can do.'

Liz watched him anxiously as he swung himself through the stubble back to the gate. Then she returned to her work, lifting and tying the stooks of corn, stacking them to dry in the breeze.

Edward made his way back to the cottage thoughtfully. What was young Gervaise doing here? It could not be anything to do with him. He was sure his cousin had not recognized him, as it was a good five years since he had seen him. Gervaise had called at the solicitor's offices to sign some papers when Edward was working for Steadman. He had no reason to notice the young man he handed the papers to, and it was doubtful if he had known they were cousins.

Gervaise was in Barminster attending to a few items of business for his father. He had been at a loose end for weeks; he would never have thought he would miss his younger brother so much. When the Honourable Arthur asked him to inspect the building progress at Barminster Abbey, and ride round the estate and the outlying farms to give him a report on the state of the buildings and the roads, Gervaise had made one excuse after another, but finally agreed to devote a few days to the task. He was, at the moment, somewhat involved with a lady several years his senior, and he knew his father would not approve his latest fancy. Mrs Adele Street was divorced, one of the fast set who had appeared in society following the death of the old queen. However, at the moment she was in America visiting a cousin, and he was finding London dull without her lively company.

Barminster Abbey had been restored after its military hospital use. No maintenance had been carried out since it was refurbished at the time of Sir Rupert's marriage, so there was a lot to be done. Among other things the new electrical lighting had been installed; the local people were expecting the whole place to go up in flames the first time it was turned on. Some of the dressing-rooms ajoining the bedrooms had been turned into bathrooms, again to the amazement of the locals. Why did they need five bathrooms in the mansion? Everyone knew that frequent bathing was extremely bad for the health. Too much soap and water could only destroy the natural oils in the skin.

Gervaise had no wish to stay at Keenlach Lodge. Not only was he reluctant to face the reproachful reception he would get from the elderly caretakers, but the house was not intended for summer use, and was too gloomy for his present mood. He booked into the County Club near the theatre, and left his horse at the livery stables nearby.

Gervaise inspected Barminster Abbey, then he rode round the outlying farms that belonged to the Clayton estate. He found the same story everywhere; the crops were being gathered with haste, the harvesting made difficult by the storms which had flattened most of the fields, and much of the grain had been lost. He knew little of farming, but he could see that the harvest was not far from a disaster.

Now his inspection was finished, but he had to wait another day for the completion of a lease on a cottage by the sea. He expected to pick it up late Tuesday afternoon, and the next day he would set out for London early in the morning. He was surprised, at breakfast, to find Major Harringay also staying at the club. He did not particularly like the man but he was someone to chat to over breakfast. The Major welcomed him heartily; he also liked someone to talk to, and if that someone was titled and wealthy so much the better. He hoped for another game of cards, later in the day; in their recent game he had found it child's play to relieve Gervaise of the contents of his wallet.

'Between you and me, old man, when my father-in-law asked me to do a bit of business for him I jumped at the chance of spending a couple of days in civilized society,' he admitted to Gervaise over their breakfast coffee. 'The wife's mother is a bit of a harpy. Got to spend a month down here in the summer, keep the wife happy, you know. Funny creatures, women. They have to return to their mothers every so often or they go into a decline. Anyway, things are very quiet up north at the moment. In a couple of months, when the shooting starts, it will be different.'

'Good shooting at your place?' Gervaise asked idly.

'Excellent! I let the shooting out, actually; hold a couple of weekend parties, you know the sort of thing. Not much money in it, of course, but it helps to cover the cost of keeping the heath stocked. You should come up and join us some time – our charges are very reasonable. Fishing's good, too.'

'I'm not interested in fishing,' Gervaise told him. 'And I prefer a bit of rough shooting to organized parties.'

'Well, that can be arranged,' the Major said heartily. 'Any time, old boy – just send me a telegram to say when you'll arrive, and you'll find the "Welcome" sign on the mat.'

'Very kind of you, Major,' Gervaise said, having no intention whatever of taking him up on the offer. After breakfast they each went their separate ways, but arranged to meet for lunch at the club.

The previous Saturday morning a letter had arrived at the cottage from John Oatis. He had several items to discuss with Edward, but would not be able to spare a day to visit him. Could Edward come to Barminster on Tuesday morning, go over their business, and have lunch with him? Unless he heard to the contrary, he would expect him at eleven-thirty on Tuesday.

As Edward had several reasons for wanting to visit Barminster, he decided to go and take Liz with him. She could visit her mother, and perhaps have lunch with Harriet and her friend, who would be at the Golden Eagle until the end of the week. She might have time to do some shopping in the afternoon. Edward himself wanted to visit the tailor. He had only the clothes that Liz had bought him when he came out of hospital, plus a rather threadbare, ill-fitting suit she had acquired second-hand from a travelling merchant who had called at the farm. Until now, he had not had call for anything better, but if he was to get out and about he wanted to look respectable. He had decided to go to London for a few days to call on the publishers, so he needed to do something urgently about the contents of his wardrobe.

Liz was delighted at the prospect of a day in Barminster.

Mrs Willoughby obligingly offered to drive them to the station before doing her shopping in the village.

It was Liz's first ride in a train, and she was as excited as a schoolgirl. She wore her blue serge dress with a white lace-edged collar – far too warm for such a hot day, but without the coat it was bearable, and she looked very fetching in it. As the train pulled slowly out of the station she sat tensely gripping her bag and umbrella, unconsciously holding her breath; then the train gathered speed, and the contryside flew past at a terrifying pace, and she let out her breath. She relaxed, and sat back in her wooden-slatted seat to enjoy the journey. They reached Barminster at ten, and the first call was at the tailor's. Liz went to do some shopping and visit her mother while Edward called at the bank.

Agnes Spragg was thrilled to see her daughter, but they had only a short time as she had to go to work at noon. She worked in different houses each day, ironing, cleaning, and mending, staying at home on Tuesday mornings to do her own housework. Liz had bought two lengths of material to make herself a couple of dresses for the trip to London, so they discussed styles and patterns, and had a very satisfying hour together before Agnes hurried off to work, and Liz walked back to the Square to meet Harriet and Miss Cowper at the Golden Eagle. Edward had sent them a postcard and they were expecting her.

Liz was very apprehensive. It was one thing meeting Harriet at the cottage, on her own home ground, but quite another to see her in the Golden Eagle with her friend. Still very shy of strangers, Liz would have preferred to spend the time waiting for Edward in a quiet tea-shop. However, he had made the arrangement, and would be annoyed if she ran out on it now, so she gathered up her courage, and entered the Golden Eagle.

'Liz, you look lovely, dear!' Harriet cried when Liz came

diffidently into the hotel lounge. She brushed Liz's cheek with her lips in a token kiss. Liz was slightly surprised to see that Harriet was wearing a touch of make-up. She smelled like a spring flower; perfume, to the unsophisticated girl, was almost as exotic as the touch of rouge Harriet had used on her lips. 'Come and meet my friend Miss Cowper. You must call her Ann, as I do.'

Liz had not yet got round to calling Harriet by her Christian name. Now she carefully avoided calling either of the self-possessed young women anything at all.

'Harriet tells me you can't talk,' Ann Cowper said directly.

'I can't – can't use my voice,' Liz whispered, completely awed by this straight talking.

'Why? No – wait until we're settled, and then tell me about it,' Ann directed. She sent the waiter for three sherries without consulting her companions, and turned to Liz, giving her all her attention. Liz blushed and fell silent; but under Ann's kindly gaze soon told her about the diphtheria, the tracheotomy, which she called a hole-in-the-throat operation, and the resultant mute condition.

'Edward taught me to whisper,' she finished. 'But I still can't use my voice, although, twice, I screamed when I was frightened. When I want to I can't make a sound.'

'It must be a psychic trauma,' Ann decided with the assurance of one year's study at the medical school, and smiled at the alarm that appeared on Liz's face. 'No, that's not a dreadful disease; it means that something happened inside your head to block the nerves that control your voice production.'

'D'you mean that I could talk if I wanted to?' Liz said, nearly in tears. Did this young woman really think she had not tried? That she was shamming her mute condition?

'Well, something like that,' Ann agreed. 'But it's not so simple as that. Something made you disown your voice; if we could discover what it was, perhaps we could help you get it back.'

'My step-father used to say that I could speak if I tried, and when I didn't he hit me,' Liz whispered unhappily.

'That certainly wouldn't help,' Ann said decidedly. The waiter came with the menu.

'Let's forget about Liz's voice for the moment, and decide what we're going to eat,' Harriet said cheerfully. She smiled at the younger girl. 'After all, there are thousands of men would give anything to have a silent wife. Just think how thrilled Edward will be one of these days when you get your voice back and learn to argue with him!'

Edward and John finished their business, and John told him he had ordered lunch at his club.

'We can talk there without being interrupted,' he explained. 'If we have lunch with the girls we'll be too busy being polite to discuss anything that matters!'

'Speak for yourself, old man,' Edward grinned. 'You don't think we'd be better going to the pub? This suit is not exactly the last thing in sartorial elegance!'

'Bedamned to that, Edward,' John exclaimed. 'From what I gather you're probably quite as well off – and a lot better mannered and educated – as most of the fellows at the club! Come on, it's just round the corner, past the theatre.'

Edward halted in front of a poster outside the theatre, and stared at the girl depicted: a plump, voluptuous blonde wearing a silk dress bedecked with lace and flounces that did little to hide her generous curves.

'Bella Pollard!' he exclaimed.

'Yes, she's top of the bill,' John said. 'I took the girls, Harriet and Ann, to see her last week. Lovely voice, and what a figure!'

'I used to know her once,' Edward said, resuming his pace, hop-and-swing, hop-and-swing, past the theatre. 'Knew her quite well, in fact.' They turned the corner, and went down the side road. A door opened a few yards in front of them, and a couple of young women, laughing, came out of the stage door to the theatre. He found himself face to face with the girl who had inspired him to rush off and sign on for a soldier.

Bella stood aside to let him pass, giving the crippled man with the grey hair a compassionate smile, and ran a few paces to catch up with her companion, who had passed them without a second glance.

Edward went on, keeping pace with John, who gave him an amused grin.

'Well, old man, you obviously remembered her better than she remembered you,' John remarked. 'You should have kept in touch – she's certainly a good-looking piece, though I should think the running costs are pretty high!'

Edward thought of the desperate letter he had written to this woman when he was at Ladysmith. He wondered if she had answered it; many letters sent to South Africa had gone astray.

'I think I'm well out of it,' he confessed. 'Anyway, I bet she can't cook like Liz does!'

He didn't want to admit it, but he was beginning to feel tired. It was another hot, sultry day; there would be a storm soon, he thought. His knee was hurting, and it felt as if it had been twisted again. He was glad to get into the cool lounge of the club, where John ordered a couple of beers. The deep leather chairs in the lounge were very comfortable, and he was almost sorry when the waiter came and told them their table was ready.

They were the first into the dining-room. They had a table near the window, set with heavy silver cutlery and a fine damask cloth. Several other diners came in while they were eating. John knew most of them. As they finished their dessert a sharply dressed fellow with a military bearing came in with a younger man.

The Major nodded to John as he passed, glancing at Edward – and then stopped and stared. Edward stared stonily back; he had never expected to set eyes on Captain – now Major – Harringay again.

John looked from one to the other. Harringay's face registered incredulous indignation, Edward's was expressionless.

'Morning, Oatis,' the Major grated. 'Odd company you keep, old man.'

'I beg your pardon?' John said, astounded. 'Er – let me introduce my friend –'

'We've met,' the Major said coldly. 'Last time I saw your friend he was practically naked, sweating like a pig, and filthy to boot. He actually had the audacity to apply for a commission! I sent him back to the horse-lines where he belonged. I'm surprised, Oatis – I thought you knew this club was for officers and gentlemen!'

John jumped to his feet and was about to lay hands on the Major when Edward shook his head.

'Sit down, John; we don't want a brawl,' Edward said quietly.

The Major walked on, followed by his companion, Gervaise Clayton, who gave John and Edward an amused glance. They made their way to a table at the far end of the room, but even from there Edward could hear his cousin telling the Major that he had also seen that fellow only a few days earlier, in a harvest field, lying in the litter of straw in a cart.

'Couldn't keep his balance on the seat. I suppose he'd been drinking. His sort can't hold their liquor.'

'Damn cheek, coming into a decent club!' the Major snorted, making no effort to keep his voice down. Red-faced, John was too embarrassed to speak. Edward gave him a rueful grin.

242

'Don't worry, John. I've got more sense than to take their insults to heart,' he said quietly.

'Edward, I can't apologize enough. I know Major Harringay because he's a client of my father's, but I assure you he's no friend of mine! And I've no idea who that is with him – arrogant young puppy!'

'Well, there I can enlighten you,' Edward remarked. 'That's my cousin Gervaise – Lord Farlington! Now you can see why I'm not keen to be in touch with the Clayton family. Now, shall we go? I'm sorry, but I don't much care for the company in your club. I'd like to find a good, wholesome pub and wash the taste of this place out of my mouth with some decent beer.'

Chapter Nineteen

Edward collected Liz from the hotel in time to catch the four o'clock train back to Forestwidden. He was feeling utterly weary, first from the strain of travelling and having spent much more time than usual on his feet, or rather, foot; and secondly as a reaction to the unaccustomed noise and activity of the city after the peace of Honey Beck Bay. Also, although he would not have admitted it, the encounters with Bella and Major Harringay had shaken him.

The platform from which their train left overlooked the goods yard and they sat for five minutes idly watching a gang of men loading barrels on to a truck. After a while Liz turned and looked the other way; had Edward not been so tired he might have noticed that she had paled, and was keeping her back turned to the workmen. One of the sweating, muscular men was staring curiously in her direction.

Liz prayed that she had been mistaken, but she was afraid that Joe Spragg had seen and recognized her. She felt sick; the mere sight of the man frightened her. She told herself that Joe could never have recognized his wretched step-daughter in the smart young woman on the platform. Perhaps he had seen some likeness, and had been staring through pure curiosity. Could he trace her to Forestwidden? After leaving Barminster, this train meandered through the countryside calling at many small halts before reaching its final destination at Southampton, many miles to the west. He didn't even know she was married, according to her mother. Agnes said that he had never mentioned her since the day she left, not even to remark on her absence. He would never find her once she boarded the train. Why should he bother, anyway? He might hope to cadge some drinking money from Edward, but Liz knew her husband would stand no nonsense from the likes of Joe. If he met the step-father who had mistreated her, Liz was afraid Edward might lash out at Joe, and if it came to a fight she knew that Joe would have no compunction in beating up a one-legged man.

Liz kept her face turned away and presently Joe went back to his work, throwing the occasional glance in her direction. She breathed a sigh of relief, but kept her back turned.

The engine puffed noisily into the station, sending clouds of steam into the dusty afternoon sunshine. It was difficult for Edward to board, and he self-consciously manoeuvred himself on to the step, and then into the carriage, infuriated by the pitying stares he received from some of the other passengers. He slumped wearily into a seat by the window. Liz watched him anxiously as the train wound its unhurried way through the forest, stopping at country halts to let a few passengers on and off. His face was ashen, and he made no attempt to talk, but leaned back in his seat with his eyes closed. She sat erect, wondering anxiously if Joe had noticed that Edward was a cripple. He would be a lot easier to trace than herself.

The storm which had been threatening for days suddenly broke, and they alighted from the train in pouring rain. Liz hoped Henry had finished bringing in his corn.

Passengers far more agile than Edward had already secured the two carriages that had been plying for fares outside the station. They found themselves without transport, a mile from the village, and several miles from home. They took shelter in the waiting room while the worst of the storm expended itself, and then started to walk to

Forestwidden, Liz carrying the parcels they had collected in Barminster. She, at least, had the protection of the umbrella she had had the foresight to bring; Edward could not juggle with an umbrella and his crutches.

They had been walking for no more than ten minutes when a carriage came bowling along the road. As it passed, the horses were checked, and Brigadier Richardson threw open the door.

'Get in, get in before you're soaked,' he cried, and helped Edward into the carriage. He insisted on taking them all the way back to the cottage, although it was several miles out of his way. He watched with concern as Liz hurried to open the door and Edward dragged himself after her. The Brigadier carried the parcels in while the groom turned the carriage, noting with approval the spotless condition of the place.

'You'd better get straight to bed, Edward,' he advised, dumping the parcels on the table. 'You look all in. Mrs Clayton, can I do anything for you before I go?'

'No, thank you, sir,' Liz whispered. 'We'll be all right now. Thank you for bringing us home.'

As soon as the Brigadier had gone, Edward took himself to bed, and slept soundly until the next morning. Liz, however, was far too overwrought to sleep. She lay worrying about Joe. Had he seen her? Recognized her? Would he come looking for her, to turn her changed circumstances to his own account? And what had Miss Cowper meant when she suggested that Liz could speak 'if she wanted to'? She tossed and turned; the birds were beginning to wake and chirp outside her window before she finally fell asleep. She slept later than usual, and got up in a hurry to light the range for Edward's hot water.

He awoke later to hear Liz in the next room, and lay thinking about the previous day's events.

John had not been able to arrange for him to buy the

cottage, but had secured a twenty-year lease at a fixed rental. At the end of that time a further lease could be negotiated, the valuation being decided by a third party, or the property would revert to the landlord. Edward was satisfied with this, and decided to go ahead with the alterations he had planned, but he said nothing to Liz. It was to be a surprise.

As requested, John had also been to London and sorted out the contracts with the magazine and the publisher. Now Edward was considerably in credit at the bank. The remuneration for his writing was better than he had expected, making him a gentleman of independent means, and he was able to make his plans accordingly.

During the next few days he used his leg as little as possible. The active day had left him with a swollen and painful knee. He arranged for Joe Ball, the builder from Forestwidden, to call, telling Liz he was having the roof attended to before the winter.

'Thank goodness for that!' Liz exclaimed. 'There's water coming in over your bed since that storm, and a damp patch on the wall under the window.'

While she was at the farm collecting milk and eggs the builder and Edward took measurements and drew up plans for the alterations. The wooden lean-to room was to be demolished – which would not be difficult, for it was threatening to fall down in the first good blow. A room more than double its size would be built, with a proper bathroom attached at the back. There was to be a staircase to the loft, with firm handrails on each side; a large dormer window would look out over the sea, with a second dormer making more headroom at the top of the stairs. The loft was to become a study. A new kitchen and scullery were to be built at the back of the cottage.

'And I want a glass door from the new bedroom opening on to a conservatory so that we can take advantage of sunny days during the winter,' Edward finished.

Joe scratched his head, and took another look at the rough plans they had drawn up.

'I suppose you know this is going to cost you a fortune?' he said bluntly. 'I understand you're renting the cottage –'

'Let me worry about that,' Edward advised him. 'I'll get the agent's permission in writing, so you'll be in the clear if any question comes up about it. Right?'

'Right, Mr Clayton. I'll let you have an estimate, but sit down when you open it, or you might collapse with shock!'

'One more thing. I'll give you a fortnight's notice of the day you're to start, and I want it finished within a month.'

'A month!'

'That's what I said. So you'll have to have the materials ready, and the men standing by to start work.'

A few days later he received Joe's estimate. He thought it a bit steep, but agreed the sum provided Joe guaranteed to meet his conditions. It would leave him considerably in debt, but he was confident that he would be able to repay the debt within the time specified by Mr Billings, the bank manager.

Henry Willoughby received a note from the bank asking him to call before he went to the agent to pay the annual rent. Knowing that his balance was considerably short he was shown into the manager's office feeling very apprehensive.

''Morning, Henry,' Mr Billings beamed. 'Sit down, man – we've got something to discuss.'

'Yes, I know,' Henry said heavily. 'I'm in trouble –'

'Wait till I tell you what I wanted to see you about,' his old friend advised. 'Someone whose name I'm not at liberty to disclose has opened an account to cover your shortfall on the rent this year. You don't have to use it if you've made other arrangements; but if you do, you can repay it at any time over the next five years.'

248

Henry's mouth fell open and he stared at him in stupefaction.

'You can't be serious!' he gasped.

'Oh, yes, I am – I don't know just what's entailed, but it seems you've done this fellow a favour, and he wants to repay it. I can't discuss him, or the arrangement, with you – as a matter of fact, I don't know his name myself although I have some idea. It was arranged through a third party, but it's all legal and above board. Now all you have to do is sign this paper confirming the arrangement.'

The manager passed the document across the desk. In a daze, Henry signed on the dotted line, and drew the money to pay his rent to the agent and if he guessed the name of his benefactor, he refrained from mentioning it to anyone except his wife. The whole business was past his comprehension, but he and Ada Willoughby were more than grateful to their unknown friend.

In the last week of September Liz and Edward closed up the cottage and set out for London. Liz knew Mr Ball was doing some maintenance on the cottage while they were away, and had cleared the lean-to bedroom and the loft in readiness. She had made herself two new dresses, and packed the best of her wardrobe for the trip. As they went to the station in a hired carriage she was almost too excited to sit still.

At Barminster they collected Edward's new suits from the tailor, one of which he donned on the spot, and took the train to London. They reached the metropolis in the middle of the afternoon, and a hansom cab took them to the modest hotel at which Edward had arranged for them to stay. To Liz the room was the last thing in luxury; even the fact that there was just one huge bed did not dismay her for long. She busied herself unpacking the bags she had borrowed from Mrs Willoughby while Edward had a rest, and then they went down to the lounge for tea, served in a silver pot, with a selection of dainty sandwiches and cakes.

Edward watched his wife happily pouring the tea, and tucking into the repast with a childlike appetite; her capacity for enjoyment was one of the qualities he loved in her. Replete, she sat back and took in the scene, looking slightly enviously at the fashionable gowns the other ladies were wearing.

'Edward, these ladies make me feel shabby,' she whispered.

'Tomorrow morning we'll do something about that,' he announced. 'This evening we're going to the theatre, and we'll have supper at a place I used to go to years ago. Liz, this is the beginning of a new life for both of us, and we're going to enjoy every minute of it!'

The theatre was a music-hall, and Liz was enthralled. She laughed at the comics, she was enchanted with the jugglers, and mystified by the magician; but most of all she was delighted by the singers and dancers.

Edward, on the other hand, was dismayed to find that the old magic he had known in the music-hall was gone. He saw the tawdry costumes, the tatty scenery, and the over-painted showgirls with new eyes, and wondered why he had been so infatuated with it all a few years earlier. Or had it just been Bella he was infatuated with? Now his chief delight was the happiness it was giving Liz. Apart from that, he found it slightly boring.

They went on to the supper house where he had once been a regular customer with Bella and her friends after the theatre. Liz gazed about happily at the noisy throng, ate an enormous meal, and drank more than half the bottle of champagne he ordered. Edward wondered why he had ever thought all this was such fun.

'I must be getting old,' he reflected, pouring the last of the wine into Liz's glass. A girl in a red satin dress sat across the room from them, who kept glancing at him. He recognized her as one of the crowd he used to know, and gave her a nod. She made her way across to their table.

'It is Eddie, isn't it?' she asked uncertainly. He noticed that her dress was not quite clean, her face had too much make-up, and there were mousy roots to the dark tresses.

'Yes – Gloria? Gloria, I'd like you to meet my wife.'

Gloria stared at Liz for a moment, then chuckled.

'Your wife? I thought she was your daughter, you old reprobate! Pleased to meet you, Mrs Clayton – you've got a good man here, and good luck to you! Now excuse me, my friends. See you again some time, Eddie.' She weaved her way back to the man with whom she had been sitting.

Liz was far from inebriated, but her eyes were sparkling, and she was very slightly tipsy by the time they returned to the hotel. In their room he had arranged for a second bottle of champagne, this time a much better vintage. Liz looked at it doubtfully, then giggled.

'Will that cork go pop! like the other one?' she asked, sitting on the bed.

'I expect so,' Edward said. 'Let's drink it in bed. My leg's aching and I'm tired.'

Sitting up in the huge bed with a good two feet of white linen between them, ten minutes later, he eased the cork out of the bottle with the requisite pop! and Liz caught the sparkling wine in the glasses. She giggled as they drank, and whispered happily about the wonderful evening she had enjoyed. He thought she had never looked more beautiful; and she was his wife. His wife?

The bottle was still half full. Edward took her empty glass and put it on the bedside table. He slid down in the bed, and drew her close to him. Would she reject him again? For a moment she stiffened, then relaxed, and giggled.

'Your friend Gloria thought you were my father,' she whispered.

'Silly Gloria,' he murmured, his lips against her hair.

'Silly Gloria,' Liz agreed, snuggling up close to him. He turned towards her, and his lips found hers, and suddenly she found herself being kissed with all the fervour of his long-repressed passion. For a moment she was passive, then she returned his kisses eagerly, her body responding to his caresses. Edward was not an inexperienced lover; he knew how to arouse her, and Liz, dizzy from all that champagne, was only half aware of what was happening. Suddenly she was aflame, as passionate as he was himself, her arms straining about him, her heart beating as if it would burst from her body. At one point a sharp, tearing pain shot through her. She stiffened, shocked; but a moment later she was filled with an ecstasy that almost took her breath away.

'Oh, Edward!' she gasped as they fulfilled the love that had grown up between them over the past eighteen months. Could this joyful experience be the distasteful 'marital rights' of which her mother had warned her?

Later Edward refilled the two glasses. She sat up, and he handed her a glass.

'To my darling wife,' he said softly, clinking the glasses together gently. 'Liz, I love you.'

'And I – love you,' Liz said wonderingly; and they stared at each other in delight. She had spoken! She had used her voice, and it was a moment of joy for them both.

'Say it again,' Edward said, hardly daring to believe his ears.

'I love you,' Liz repeated, and they both laughed from sheer happiness, spilling the wine. 'Oh, don't waste it! Pour some more – is there any more in the bottle?'

'I can always send for some more,' Edward said. 'But you might wake up with a headache in the morning, and we have a busy day tomorrow.'

'Oh no – I want to have a clear head in the morning. I think I'll always be happy now . . .'

'We'll never forget this night.' He took her hand, and gently kissed the palm. 'Darling Liz. Never leave me, my dearest. I couldn't bear it.'

Leave him? Never! Liz laughed at the preposterous idea.

Chapter Twenty

At breakfast the next morning several of the older ladies among the guests nodded knowingly in the direction of Mr and Mrs Clayton.

'Newly-weds,' murmured one stout old lady to her companion. 'She looks young enough to be his daughter. And the man is a cripple. Poor child – he's taken advantage of her kind heart.'

'Honeymooners!' whispered another busybody to her uninterested spouse. 'Well, better an old man's darling than a young man's slave, they say. No doubt he has enough money to sweeten life for her.'

Edward noticed the glances and whispers and was mildly amused. He knew many people would deplore the match between the older man, a cripple at that, and the young girl, but he was quite indifferent to their opinions.

Liz, on the other hand, was utterly oblivious of their stares. She was supremely happy. She smiled at him over the breakfast dishes, and wondered that the whole world seemed to be brighter, more friendly, this morning. Her whole attention was given to this wonderful man who had become a true husband to her at last. How lucky she was to have such a handsome, clever, loving husband! His knee touched hers. Under cover of the damask tablecloth they held hands, to let go only in order to deal with knives and forks. Her love blossomed like a flower in the sunshine.

'Happy, Liz?' Edward murmured as she poured his coffee.

'Oh, yes, dear – very happy!' she smiled.

They were both delighted to find that she was still in

command of her voice this morning. And such a voice! Soft and low, slightly husky – Edward thought it was the loveliest sound he had ever heard. He had been confident that one day she would regain its use, and had been afraid that when she began to speak it would be in the accents of the slums of Barminster, like her mother. However, for the past eighteen months she had been constantly with him, listening to his cultured pronunciation, and now, when she spoke, it was with a similar intonation to his own. Even her grammar, he noticed, was excellent, not knowing that for the past year she had carefully copied, in her mind, his pronunciation and syntax. Now it came to her perfectly naturally. She was sufficiently intelligent to recognize that such things matter, and she was determined that she would not disgrace him.

Harriet had sent Edward the name and address of a consultant who specialized in fitting artificial limbs, and it was to his clinic that they paid their first call this morning. Liz waited anxiously in the elegantly-appointed waiting-room while Edward was ushered into the presence of the doctor.

The room in which Dr Steinberg saw him was more like a Society drawing-room than a doctor's surgery, and the dapper little character waiting for him looked more like the tenor in a comic opera than a distinguished consultant.

'Well, young man, you can begin by telling me about yourself, and then we'll have a physical examination,' he said, gesturing to an armchair opposite his own. 'How did you lose that leg?'

By the time they went through to the adjoining examination room Edward had taken a strong liking to the little man, who gave him a thorough examination. His heart, lungs, and general health were declared in excellent condition, but the doctor tut-tutted fussily over the condition of the troublesome knee.

'Under a severe strain, my boy; not up to carrying your

255

considerable weight all the time. Unfortunately, when you were laid up all those months the muscles and ligaments wasted seriously, and they've not recovered yet. Well, when we get you fixed up with a spare limb much of the strain will be taken off that knee, and it should recover completely before too long.'

'I'm told there are artificial legs that look almost like the real thing,' Edward said, but the doctor shook his head sadly.

'Yes, they look very good, but unfortunately they're so heavy that they're not really practical. You need a wheelbarrow to carry them about in! Also, the false foot is inclined to trip you up. I think that for the moment you'll be better with a straightforward peg-leg. In time, perhaps, they'll develop materials that are strong enough to take the strain, but light enough to be practical, but at the moment we've not reached that stage. Maybe when you've learned to walk again we can try something more sophisticated.

'Now your problem is going to be this: the bone is very close to the surface, and we'll have to fit you with a cup that won't chafe. I'll take the measurements, have it made, and you can come back in seven days and try it. It may take a couple of fittings to get it just right, but don't worry, by this time next month you'll be walking on your own two legs.'

After the consultation was over, they took a cab to Harrods' famous department store, and Liz spent a dizzy hour walking about looking at things before they had lunch. The dazzling array of goods bewildered her, and Edward had been afraid she would go on a spending spree that would clear his bank balance, but there was so much to choose from she could not bring herself to spend a shilling.

'Buy a couple of dresses and a warm coat, Liz,' he coaxed.

'Not yet,' she insisted. 'First I want to look at everything to decide what I like best.'

At four they returned to the hotel for tea, and Edward rested for a while before dressing for dinner. Liz lay beside him on the big bed, with a magazine; and consequently neither of them slept.

'You're supposed to be having a rest!' she pointed out, giggling.

'Then you'd better go and sit in the ladies' lounge, out of my sight,' he murmured. 'But not yet; I can sleep later.'

'Dr Steinberg said –'

'Dr Steinberg would fully approve of what I have in mind; it's my knee I'm resting.'

'Good gracious, Edward – oh!' But she was delighted with the new games they were playing and her protests were soon overridden.

The next afternoon Edward had a meeting with his publisher, and Liz went to the shops alone. She wanted to buy herself some pretty underwear. The salesgirl, a superior young woman with a face like a horse, urged her to spend more than she had intended, but she told herself that it was for Edward, not for her own vanity, and excused her extravagance. Loaded down with parcels, she met Edward at a tea-room in Piccadilly.

'I hope you've got yourself a party dress, Liz,' he said cheerfully as they sat at a table set for two. 'We're invited out tonight. My publisher's having a sherry party to celebrate the new books out this season, and we're invited. My book is going well, and he's very pleased. He wants to meet my wife.'

'Oh, no, Edward – you go, but I don't think –'

'Of course you'll come,' he said firmly. 'Did you buy an evening dress?'

'No, and I don't want to go! I like going out with you, but not with strangers –' Liz looked terrified. She had never been to a sherry party. Her only experience of polite society was with the Richardsons at Falldon Hall, and she was filled with dismay at the prospect of meeting a roomful of strangers.

'But, darling, I'll be there – I'll take care of you,' Edward assured her.

After tea he took her back to the shops and chose a dress, a very elegant dark red gown in the latest fashion, which the dresser altered slightly to perfect the fit while they waited. Edward bought Liz a modest gold locket to wear with it, and a short black velvet cloak. When they went to the party she felt like a princess – but a very shy princess; she was completely subdued, and hardly spoke. She was dreading the ordeal.

The sherry party was held in a private room in a very select hotel in Knightsbridge. The room was crowded when they went in, the buzz of conversation sounding like a hive of bees preparing for the swarm. Mr Antrobus, the publisher, charged through the throng and welcomed Edward in a loud, booming voice that terrified Liz. She shook hands with him nervously, accepted the glass he offered, but was panic-stricken when he took Edward off to talk to a group of men at the far side of the room, leaving her with two sophisticated young women who were intrigued to hear that she was visiting London for the first time.

'How fascinating! You must see the new exhibition at the Acadamy,' one of the ladies said brightly.

'The – the Academy?' Liz said uncertainly.

'The Royal Academy – portraits, of course, mainly in the modern style. You must see them – everyone's talking about them.' The young woman sipped her sherry, her eyes on the girl's face. 'Not quite what we expected, but the critics are frightfully impressed. I went this afternoon. Lavinia, what did you think of the portrait exhibition?'

Lavinia and Dorothy chatted on, occasionally directing a remark to Liz, who hadn't the faintest idea what they were talking about. She smiled uncertainly and nodded, hoping this was the right response. The French school, the Impressionist influence, the Naturalist movement, and more phrases completely new to Liz were dropped negligently into the conversation. She glanced round the room, observing that everyone appeared to be talking at once, each trying to be heard over the other guests. She wished fervently that she was at home in Honey Beck Cottage, with the friendly lamps glowing and Edward reading aloud while she sat in the rocking-chair sewing.

When Edward rejoined her half an hour later she was nearing desperation.

Edward began chatting to the two women about the Academy as if he had known them all his life. He had not seen the paintings, but had read the reviews, and his good education ensured that he could hold his own in any company. Liz listened, bemused, while he talked about the books being published, his own among them. The two ladies were delighted to discover that he was the new author they had read about.

'Of course, Mr Carlton, we know your name from the children's series. My two sons wouldn't miss an edition of that magazine for the world!' Lavinia declared, her bright eyes avidly watching Edward's face.

'My name is Clayton,' he told them. 'Carlton is only a pseudonym.'

'Ah – Clayton? No relation to young Lord Farlington, I suppose?' Dorothy asked archly.

'Lord Farlington? I'm afraid I don't know him,' Edward said evenly. 'Now, if you'll excuse us, ladies, I must introduce my wife to Mrs Henry.' He led her across the room to where a very fat, very vivacious lady of uncertain years sat holding court. She had a mass of white hair, piled on top of her head with the help of several tortoiseshell combs, and her face was unashamedly painted. Her plump fingers were loaded with flashing rings. If they were genuine stones she was a very rich novelist.

'Edward, I want to go home,' Liz whispered unhappily.

'Just say hello to Mrs Henry, and then we'll go,' he promised. Mrs Henry wrote romantic love stories, and was at the moment at the peak of her career, although, had she but known it, in ten years' time she would be quite forgotten. She had met Edward during the afternoon at the publisher's offices.

'Edward! My dear boy!' she gushed, as if she had known him for years. 'You promised to introduce me to your wife – what a beauty! So young and fresh! Just like one of the heroines in my novels...' To Liz's utter confusion she kissed her on the cheek, as she did Edward also. After ten minutes he announced that they must leave – they had an engagement for dinner.

'Dear boy, must you go? I was going to invite you to join our party at the Dorchester –'

'I'm sorry, dear Mrs Henry, perhaps another time – prior engagement – quite impossible to cancel – forgive me,' Edward smiled, and led Liz to say goodbye to their host.

'I didn't know we had an engagement for dinner,' Liz said suspiciously when they were in a cab, heading back to their hotel.

'No, only with each other,' Edward admitted with a sheepish grin. 'But I had to make some excuse. I thought you wanted to leave.'

'I did! I didn't know what anyone was talking about!' Liz confessed. 'Did you know those women – that Lavinia and Dorothy?'

'No, never seen them before in my life,' Edward said cheerfully. 'But I've met dozens like them – Society gossips!'

'Tomorrow, I want to go and see that – that Acadamy,' Liz announced after a few minutes' silence. 'And then I want to see all the other paintings in London.'

'All of them?' Edward exclaimed, startled.

'I'm going to learn about things – all sorts of things – opera, ballet, and those Gilbert and Sullivan plays at the Savoy theatre they were talking about. And Shakespeare – the plays. Oh, there are so many things in London! Then when I go out with you I won't feel such a fool.'

Edward found himself being taken to the Tower of London, the Monument, which Liz climbed while he waited below, and every church and cathedral she could find. She devoured all the leaflets she found about the various places, savouring the history with much the same enjoyment as she gained from the plays and operas. By the time he was fitted with his artificial leg, he had cultural indigestion. But Liz was as full of enthusiasm as when they began.

Edward's first steps with the new 'peg', as he called it, were not very successful: he attempted to stride out, and fell flat on his back. Dr Steinberg had fitted the limb in a special room provided with handrails, and with an attendant standing on each side of him, but Edward had been determined to try it out without assistance. Now that he knew how *not* to do it, he set about learning how to walk again. For the first week he went to the practice room for an hour each morning; then he was allowed to take it with him and practise alone.

'Don't try to overdo it, my boy,' the doctor advised. 'You'll only tire yourself out and chafe the stump. Use the crutches until you're steady enough to do without safely. You'll probably need to use one crutch, anyway. But don't despair; you'll get the hang of it in time.'

They stayed a month at the hotel. Liz's enthusiasm was boundless, and she grew to know the city almost as well as her husband did. Edward never mentioned his years spent working there, so Liz was unaware that he had walked those streets as a young man studying the law. One afternoon they strolled through Eaton Square. Edward looked at the house where he had met his grandfather and grandmother, but did not point it out to Liz. That part of his life was over and best forgotten. When they returned to Honey Beck Bay the summer was over and the trees of the forest were turning russet with the onset of autumn.

Chapter Twenty-one

Gervaise, Lord Farlington, rang the bell at his grandfather's house in Eaton Square and waited impatiently for the door to be opened. He strode in without a word, handing his coat and hat to the butler, and went into the study where his father was reading *The Times*, the usual glass of brandy by his side

"Morning, Father,' he said, rubbing his hands together by the fire; the October air was chilly so early in the day. Arthur Clayton looked at him coldly over the top of his paper. The hair of the dog had allayed his morning headache, but it would take more than a glass of brandy to make him welcome a call from his son at this hour.

"Morning, Gervaise. You're very early. I suppose there's some particular reason for your call? Your mother's not up yet, she's got one of her headaches.'

'Just came to let you know I'll be out of the city for a few days – going up north for a bit of sport. Shooting, you know.'

'Shooting? Ah – going up to inspect the covers on the Farlington estate, I presume? If you'd let me know earlier, I'd have gone with you.' Arthur was prepared to overlook his son's deficiencies for the sake of a few days of good rough shooting.

As Gervaise had no intention of visiting Farlington Towers he let this pass without comment. Mrs Adele Street had returned to London, and a furious row had led to an unpleasant scene in a night-club. For a few days, at least, he had decided that it would be wise to drop out of sight;

263

by that time her temper should have calmed down. She was threatening a breach of promise case. Gervaise was confident that she had no grounds for going to court, and any lawyer would advise her to drop the idea, but meanwhile he did not want to risk running into her or any of her friends. Also, he intended to be well out of reach when his father heard of the incident. He had sent a telegram to Major Harringay suggesting a week's shooting on his estate, the confirmation of which arrangement was in his pocket now.

'I'll be back in about ten days,' he said. 'So there's no need to start scouring the countryside for me. Give Mother my compliments, and tell her I'll be back in time for her birthday.'

His father looked at him thoughtfully.

'I'm thinking of giving her one of those new automobiles for her birthday. Only thing is I'm afraid she might take it into her head to try to drive the damn thing herself!' Gervaise chuckled at this idea. Fancy a woman learning to drive a horseless carriage!

'I think she's got more sense than that,' he commented. 'I was out with my bays the other day, and we met an automobile on the highway. It was all I could do to hold them. Bloody animals tried to climb the hedge!'

'Perhaps it's not such a good idea,' his father agreed. 'I think they'll be banned in the city before long. Dangerous machines. Well, when you get to Farlington Towers, check those cottages on the western drive – I noticed that they were looking pretty dilapidated when we were up there at your grandfather's funeral. That agent, Bodger, isn't much good; I wouldn't be surprised if he's robbing you blind.'

Gervaise departed looking thoughtful. It might, at that, be a good idea to call at the Towers and see what was going on there. He was making the journey by rail, and had not yet informed Major Harringay which train to meet. Perhaps he should visit Farlington Towers first, and then go on to the Harringay estate.

Two days later an early visitor disturbed the Honourable Arthur and Lady Imogen at their breakfast. The butler came in and told them that a Superintendent Watkins from the local constabulary was at the door insisting on seeing Mr Arthur Clayton immediately.

Arthur Clayton lowered his newspaper, and glared at the butler.

'Tell him to state his business, and I'll see him later in the morning.'

'He says it's very important, sir – a personal matter.'

Arthur threw the newspaper on the floor, and got to his feet. He turned to his wife before he left the room.

'I hope Gervaise isn't in some scrape,' he snapped. Yesterday he had heard about the episode in the night-club where his son and Mrs Adele Street had shouted and snarled at each other in a drunken scene of unrivalled vulgarity, and her furious threats to sue Lord Farlington for a breach of promise, but he had kept the news from his wife.

Lady Imogen, unperturbed, looked up from buttering her toast.

'Well, you'll know soon enough,' she said calmly. 'Better go and see what the man wants. It's probably something to do with the servants.'

Arthur stalked through to the study, followed by Superintendent Watkins, a mild-mannered man in his fifties, his nose red from the biting wind. The Superintendent cleared his throat.

'Mr Clayton, I'm sorry to have to tell you that your son Gervaise, Lord Farlington, is dead,' he said quietly.

'What!' Arthur stared at him, incredulous. 'Of course he's not dead. He's in Yorkshire, shooting grouse!'

'I'm sorry, sir, but a message was received at the station

early this morning. Lord Farlington was found in the grounds of Farlington Towers, shot in the head, and the body of his bailiff, a Mr Bodger, was found nearby. The man had been dismissed the previous day for negligence in discharging his duties. When Lord Farlington arrived unexpectedly at the Towers he found Bodger drunk. Apparently Lord Farlington went for a stroll before retiring last night, and Bodger followed him, shot him, and then turned the gun on himself. The man had been drinking in the local inn most of the evening.'

Arthur Clayton sank into one of the big leather chairs.

'I can't believe it!' he muttered. 'He was here two days ago – I told him to check on that bailiff, I didn't trust the man. My God, not long ago I had two sons; now they're both dead. I can't believe it.' He dropped his head on to his hands. 'My wife – this will kill her! And my father! Who identified him? It couldn't have been a mistake –'

'No, sir, there's no possible mistake. His valet identified the body. Lord Farlington is dead.'

Lady Imogen came into the room to see what the Superintendent had called about, assuming that one of the servants was in trouble again. When the story was told she went to her room with the brandy bottle and was not seen for several hours.

Sir Rupert took it with greater equanimity than they had expected.

'I'm not surprised. That boy was a fool,' he muttered, when told that Gervaise had been murdered. The old man had almost recovered from his stroke, but all the fire had gone out of him; he didn't seem to care what happened to him, his grandson, or anyone else.

Gervaise's body was at Farlington Towers. Arthur and Lady Imogen therefore set out for the north by train. They travelled in a private carriage, the blinds drawn and a black ribbon tied to the door to ensure their privacy. Little was said on the journey; both were too shocked to talk. Arthur took the precaution of carrying a bottle of brandy with him. When he and Lady Imogen alighted from the train they were both half-numbed by the effects of the intoxicant. A carriage had been arranged to meet them.

'A terrible day to be making such a journey, sir,' the coachman observed. He received no reply.

They set out for the Towers in the rain, the sombre weather matching their unhappy circumstances. A thick mist had descended on the moors, and visibility was poor. In any other situation the journey would have been delayed until the weather improved. Exposed to the elements, the coachman was soon wet through and his face numb with cold, but the horses knew the road, so he let them have their heads, as they could see their way more clearly than he could. The road had a sheer drop on one side, a rocky cliff on the other. The journey was slow and miserable. Arthur peered out of the window, but could see nothing. He sat back in the leather upholstery, mumbling about the vile weather.

'Stop grumbling, Arthur, things are bad enough without that,' Lady Imogen said irritably.

As they turned a corner one of those noisy, smelly automobiles appeared without warning out of the fog. The horses reared and swerved, and the carriage went hurtling over the steep edge, dragging the screaming horses with it. The coachman, sitting high up in front of the carriage, saw the inevitable fall in time to leap to safety, but Arthur and Lady Imogen, trapped inside the carriage, had no chance. They were both killed before the carriage, crashing from one jagged rockface to the next, finally reached the bottom of the chasm.

Chapter Twenty-two

Liz heard the horse's hooves in the lane before she saw the trap turn the sharp bend into the final steep incline leading down to the beach. It was a calm Monday morning in October. She was working in the garden, tidying up the remains of the vegetables, a chirpy little robin at her feet waiting for any worms that might be turned up by the busy hoe. Over the past few months it had become so tame it almost hopped on to her feet, and she was constantly aware of it, afraid she might step on it. As she worked she occasionally spoke to the robin, who put his head on one side and appeared to listen with interest. He chirped indignantly and flew off as the trap approached.

Liz straightened her back, and stood watching the trap. She could have passed for one of the gypsy tribe. Her hair was tied back in a red kerchief, a few dark tendrils escaping to soften the line of the brow, and she had a bright apron over the old black calico dress, now rusty with age and washing. The black woollen shawl was tied round her shoulders. Her skin was still brown from the summer sun, but the morning's bright sunshine, glinting and sparkling on the sea, had little warmth in it now.

The trap slowed to a stop near the vegetable patch, and John Oatis alighted, carrying a heavy briefcase. Liz watched him anxiously. His usual genial smile was missing, and there was an air of gravity about him. On his rare visits he usually wore a tweed suit of lovat-green check, but this morning he was dressed in dark grey. The last time he had visited them was a couple of days after they got back from London, when he had been delighted to find that Liz had regained her speech, and had admired the alterations to the cottage. Before he spoke she knew that today he had come with grave news.

'Good morning, Mrs Clayton – Liz,' he said awkwardly. 'I've come to see Edward. Is he at home?'

'Of course,' she said, laying aside the hoe, and wiping her hands on her apron. 'He's in his study.' She smiled. 'That's what he calls the old loft, now that it's all done up. Come inside.' She opened the cottage door, and led him into the main living-room. This was little changed, except that the steep ladder had been replaced by a sturdy staircase with firm handrails on each side, and the sink under the window had been replaced with a sideboard. 'Edward! Edward!' she called. 'You have a visitor!'

John heard a chair scrape on the wooden floor above, and Edward's head appeared over the waist-high half-wall.

'John! Good to see you, but what brings you out here so unexpectedly? Come on up – that's quicker than my coming down!'

Carrying the briefcase, John ascended the stairs, and Liz heard Edward greeting him. She went back to the garden, released the horse from the shafts of the hired trap, and hitched him to a post where he could graze on the coarse grass. For more than an hour the two men remained in the study, their voices low and serious. Liz was back indoors and had changed her clothes when they came down. Edward led the way, hopping down with the aid of the firm handrails; a crutch waited by the newel post at the foot of the stairs. The other crutch stayed in the study. He could manage quite safely with one now, and used the 'peg' most of the time.

'Elizabeth, John has brought me some news of my family,' Edward said quietly, as he took his place at the table. Liz had set out a meal of soup, bread and cheese, and apple pie. 'A cousin has died –'

'Oh – not Harriet?' Liz exclaimed.

'No – no, a male cousin.' He and John had decided not to mention the triple tragedy to Liz for the moment. 'It means I'll have to go to London. I'll go to his funeral in Barminster on Wednesday, and I'll go back to London afterwards. I'll be home late on Friday. Will you be all right here on your own, or shall I arrange for someone to stay with you?'

Liz looked at him, her eyes wide and apprehensive.

'Can't I come too? I'll stay in the hotel –'

'Not this time, dear.' Edward's tone was firm. 'This is family business – I don't want you involved.' The girl's eyes fell. She had thought they they had no secrets from each other, but not for a moment did she think of questioning him further. 'I'll tell you all about it when I come home. Look, why don't you go and stay with Mrs Richardson for a few days?'

'No, I'll stay here.' Liz looked as if she was going to cry. 'If you like I'll go to the Willoughbys. Yes, that's what I'll do. Just at night, I might be – be lonely. When do you have to go?'

'As soon as I've packed a bag. John and I will get the train back to Barminster.'

'Oh – you'll need a black suit if it's a cousin,' Liz exclaimed, her mind immediately flying to practical matters, her personal fears forgotten. John cleared his throat.

'I took the liberty of speaking to the tailor before I left Barminster – he has Edward's measurements, and he'll have a mourning suit ready late this afternoon. He keeps a stock for emergencies, just needing final adjustments. So you needn't worry about that.'

'Edward, you'll remember to rest in the afternoons, won't you? And wear your warm underwear – the days are chilly now, and you don't want to catch cold –'

'Don't worry about me, dear; I'll take care,' he assured her, taking her hand.

John was watching them. What a change in their manner! Six months ago there had been a bond of affection between them, nothing more, but now they were clearly deeply in love with each other. He could see that this separation was a wrench for both of them.

'Liz, my dear, I'll be with Edward some of the time, and I'll make sure he takes good care of himself,' he assured her. She gave him a startled glance; it must be a very serious matter if he was going to London too! Edward had never discussed his family with her. She had been unaware that he had any, apart from Harriet. This cousin must have been a black sheep; she hoped he had not left Edward a lot of debts to clear . . .

She went into the bedroom and put Edward's clothes in his bag while he changed into his dark suit. Half an hour later he and John had gone, leaving her alone in the cottage. Desolate, she packed her own nightclothes into a basket, and, locking up the cottage, climbed the steps in the cliff and walked to the farmhouse. She was already missing her husband. Her last glimpse of him had been a smile and wave as the trap rounded the bend in the track. She had a panicky feeling that it would be a long time before she saw him again. Why had he not told her about this cousin? In fact, he had told her he had no family! Perhaps he was ashamed of them – or was he ashamed of her, Liz? He should have married someone like Harriet, someone he could be proud to have by his side. For the past few months they had been so happy together she had forgotten that to the outside world, beyond this haven in Honey Beck Bay, he was an educated man and she was nothing more than a skivvy from the slums of the city. Now the world had intruded into their private Eden. The serpent had invaded their garden.

Tears blurred her eyes as she followed the path to the farm.

*

Edward and John reached Barminster at three, to find George Steadman waiting for them in John's office. He looked tired and strained; the last two days had been a considerable ordeal for a man who usually lived a very quiet, uneventful life.

He had received the news of Lord Farlington's death on Saturday morning, soon after Arthur Clayton and Lady Imogen were informed, and he heard of their fatal accident late that evening. It was his unhappy duty to go to Eaton Square and see Sir Rupert, whom he found in his room, as always, sitting hunched by the fire, a shawl over his knees. He looked as if he was close to death himself; there was no light in his eyes, and he appeared to be barely aware of his visitor.

The old man listened to his news and his condolences without a word. They had taken the precaution of calling his doctor to the house before telling him; but the physician was not needed. Sir Rupert sat silent in his chair for a full fifteen minutes, without expressing any emotion whatsoever. Steadman was not sure he had understood what he had told him. Suddenly Sir Rupert burst into laughter, his shoulders shaking with mirth, finally coughing and spluttering to regain his breath.

'Robert's done it again! He's done it again!' he gasped. George Steadman watched him with alarm; was the old man demented with shock?

'Robert?' he echoed, frowning. He could think of no Robert – the police had not mentioned anyone of that name.

'Robert – my son Robert!' Sir Rupert said impatiently. 'Always did manage to put one over that dull stick Arthur! When they were boys, if Arthur won a prize, Robert immediately won a better one. When Arthur met a pretty girl, Robert would carry her off from under his nose, and then drop her a month later. Until he met that half-gypsy girl, that is; stupid fellow married her. Should have known better! All the young Claytons fooled about with the gypsy girls – almost a tradition. But never married them. My brother Sebastian . . .' He fell silent again.

George Steadman wondered what this had to do with the triple tragedy in the family. He had never heard of Sebastian, and Captain Robert Clayton had been dead for nearly twenty years.

'Sir Rupert, did you understand what I told you?' he asked gently. 'Your son Arthur, his wife, and your grandson –'

'Of course I understand – d'you think I'm senile?' The old man stared into the fire for a few moments. 'It's you, Steadman, who doesn't understand, you fool! Robert let down the family, broke his mother's heart, so I cut him out of everything, disowned him, left him penniless! But now his son – that oafish, lanky, scarecrow of a boy I sent to you to train – will come into everything I've got! Not only that, he's Lord Farlington now – I've to call him my lord! Robert has won yet again. Even from the grave he has bested Arthur!'

'Sir Rupert, Edward Clayton is –'

'Edward Clayton. Lord Farlington! What a joke! Through Gervaise, he's inherited a title he probably has never even heard of! What's he doing now, eh? He left you to join the army, didn't he? We heard he was dead, then he turned up again – the bad penny! Where is he now?'

'I don't know, Sir Rupert,' Steadman admitted. 'I've been in contact with his solicitor, but he wouldn't give me any address, and frankly, I don't know anything about him, except that he's still alive and apparently recovered from his injuries.'

'Then you'd better get hold of that solicitor, and make sure you *do* find out about him!' The old man glared at Steadman as if he held him personally responsible for his grandson's disappearance. 'If he didn't ask you for references you can depend on it he's abandoned the law; he's probably taken up horse-training, like his father. Part gypsy, it's in the blood! Or he's working as a labourer somewhere – he talked about working on the land as a boy. Perhaps he's emigrated. He could be anywhere! God, man, what a joke this is! I wonder if he married a gypsy too?'

'I think he was more inclined towards the ladies of the chorus, if my memory serves me rightly,' George Steadman said cautiously.

'A chorus-girl! Oh, Lady Imogen would love that,' the old man snorted. 'Steadman, help me out of this chair; I'm going downstairs. For more than a year I've been stuck in this room, alone, waiting to die. I'll postpone that for a while. There's life in the old dog yet! Get me downstairs, we've work to do. You'll have to arrange the funerals – three together, at Barminster. Send Harriet a telegram. And on Monday morning you'll be at that solicitor's office when it opens. Find my grandson and bring him home, or you'll be looking for a new client.'

Now George Steadman rose as John and Edward entered John's office. Having not seen Edward for several years, he was not sure he would have recognized him. He was shocked at the change he saw. The black hair was grey, the face was lined, and the limp and crutch told their own story. The man had aged ten years or more.

'Edward – Lord Farlington,' he said, holding out his hand. Edward gave him a rueful smile.

'Not the best circumstances to meet, Mr Steadman, but I'm pleased to see you again,' he said, shaking hands. He sank into a chair, his peg-leg extended before him; it had no joint, and could not bend. George Steadman found his eyes constantly drawn to the weird limb. He, too, was looking older, but the passing time had not ravaged him as it had his one-time pupil. 'Now tell me all you can about this

274

tragic business – but first, how is my grandfather? How did he take the news?'

'He's old, and he's –' Steadman hesitated, searching for the right word.

'Confused? Senile?' Edward prompted him.

'Not exactly . . . No, just shocked, I think. Shows no great sorrow – no grief at all! I think he felt so close to death himself he has no fear of it, and he – well, he seems to think it doesn't matter. His main worry, Edward, is that you might have married a showgirl or a gypsy!'

Edward began to chuckle. Steadman looked at him suspiciously.

'Are you married? *Did* you marry a showgirl?'

'No, not at all! I married a fine young lady, a perfect wife. John can tell you.' He turned to John, who looked highly uncomfortable. Would Sir Rupert prefer a ward-maid – a skivvy! – to a showgirl?

'Mrs Clayton – I mean, Lady Farlington, is a very – er – is a splendid young lady,' John said finally. George Steadman breathed a sigh of relief. 'I understand,' John added cautiously, 'that she is a friend of Miss Harriet.'

'Thank God for that! As you know, Edward – or you might not know – Sir Rupert holds very strong views about young women who insist on earning their own living. Look at all the trouble about Miss Harriet! If he learned that your wife had been keeping herself by appearing on the stage he might have another stroke.'

'No need to worry about that,' Edward said, a wicked twinkle in his eye. 'Liz – Elizabeth never earned her daily bread on the stage.' He wondered how his grandfather would feel about a young woman who had earned her living scrubbing the floors in Barminster Abbey . . . He frowned. 'You said "*another* stroke"?'

'Yes. He had a stroke after Harriet left, about eighteen months ago. Not a serious one, but it's taken him a long time to get over it. I think he just gave up. He's never been the same man since Lady Amelia died, frankly, and then Miss Harriet left . . . However, when I had to give him the news of his son's death, he – er – he rallied, and seems to have – er – ' How could he tell Edward that Sir Rupert had seen the new heir as a challenge, and had come out of his corner prepared to do battle? 'We'd better get down to business,' he said hastily. 'We'll be reading the will at Eaton Square after the funeral. You know about the funeral arrangements. Will you return to London with me to meet your grandfather?'

'Of course.' John Oatis would accompany Edward to London for the reading of the will after the funeral. But Edward had something to attend to before going to London today. He had to call on Liz's mother.

Mrs Spragg had just come in from work when he arrived. The three boys, Liz's half-brothers, were in the kitchen eating bread and dripping. Joe Spragg would not be home for another hour; several hours, if he called at the Red Lion on the way, but as he had been penniless when he left this morning, he was more likely to come straight home. However, if he had received a few tips there was no knowing when he would be back, nor in what condition.

Agnes was taken by surprise when she saw Edward at the door. The last time she'd met him she'd thought he was near death; now he was strong and fit. Shouting to the boys to stay in the kitchen and behave, she took him into the shabby, minute parlour.

'Has something happened to my Liz?' she asked anxiously as she closed the door.

'No, she's fine, and she's got her voice back,' Edward told her. 'I've come about something quite different. A cousin of mine has died, and I've come into – er – into some money. Now the thing is, I'm afraid the press may be interested –

and they just might discover where Liz came from, and come to you for – er – details of our marriage. I'd rather they didn't find them.'

Agnes looked down at her rough, calloused hands.

'You mean, Mr Clayton, you don't want to be embarrassed by Joe Spragg and me as in-laws,' she said matter-of-factly.

'I don't want Liz upset by your husband, Mrs Spragg,' Edward admitted. 'She's still terrified of him. As I'll now be in a position to help you, I'd like to make you an allowance – but I want to be sure Liz can take her place in society without having her step-father badgering her. If he discovered that she had come into money he might come to see her.'

'Her step-father doesn't know she's married,' Agnes said. 'So far as he knows, she just up and left one day, and never came back. I doubt if he'd connect Liz with Mrs Clayton – he always said no man would have her.'

'She's still afraid of him, Mrs Spragg. And now she's not only Mrs Clayton – she's Lady Farlington, though she doesn't know it yet!'

'Lady Farlington! Oh my goodness – my Liz!' For a moment Agnes did not know whether to laugh or cry, then she took a deep breath and pulled herself together.

'Mr Clayton – oh, Gawd – I mean, Lord Farlington! – did you mean that about an allowance?'

'Yes. I thought perhaps five pounds a week?'

'Five pounds! Lord – that's more nor Joe gives me a month, after he's taken his drinking money! Now, if you mean it, I'll pack up and get out of here – it's the only way I'll ever get away from that man, 'cos I could never keep them boys on my own! Then if anyone comes asking questions they'll find no-one to answer them. If someone tries to tell Joe my Liz is Lady Farlington they're more likely to get a smack in the face than a straight answer!'

'Where will you go?'

'I'll go to my sister in Portsmouth until I find a place somewhere. But you'll have to make sure I gets the money regular.'

'Yes, I'll do that, Mrs Spragg,' Edward assured her. He took out his wallet and handed her a generous sum. 'Let me know where you are – write to Mr Oatis, you know his address – and he'll make the arrangements. When will you go?'

'As soon as I've washed those kids' faces, and packed that mantel-clock, the only thing I've got worth keeping. I'll be gone before Joe gets in, and thank God I'll never set eyes on 'im again!'

Edward called on the tailor, where a black suit, coat and hat were waiting for him. Then he and George Steadman walked to the station and boarded the train for London.

Sir Rupert received his grandson in the drawing-room at Eaton Square. He had dressed with particular care, determined to present himself as the alert, vigorous man he had been at their last meeting. The possibility that Edward might find him an object of pity, a decrepit, feeble old invalid in his second childhood, spurred him on to make the effort. He expected to find his grandson a coarse, shambling fellow; the last time he had seen him he was an overgrown schoolboy, bashful and inarticulate, hoping to find work on a farm. He was astonished when the tall, well-dressed man with strong, well-formed features and a head of thick grey hair entered the room.

His intention to dominate the man as he had done the boy vanished as soon as he saw him. Edward resembled his father, apart from the hair; not so handsome as Robert, but with more strength of character in his face. His father had been whimsical and weak-willed, but this man clearly would not be influenced by anyone except, perhaps, a woman. Sir

Rupert was surprised; he had never thought to see that young bumpkin develop into a gentleman! This was a grandson of whom he could be proud!

'Edward! I'm pleased to meet you, my boy,' he said, coming forward to shake his hand. He had to look up to him, whereas he had been able to look down to Arthur and his sons. Edward shook his hand, and took the chair offered. George Steadman sat a little apart from them; he was interested to watch this meeting.

'I kept dinner back, hoping you'd be here,' Sir Rupert remarked. 'Beale! Fetch the decanter – we'll have a whisky before we eat.' The butler departed, wondering if this really was the scruffy boy he had almost turned away all those years ago.

'I don't know that we should stay for a meal – I've reserved a room at the Belmontaine Hotel –'

'Well, you'd better unreserve it, sir!' Sir Rupert said testily. 'While you're in London you'll stay here, of course – that is, until you have your own place done up. Gervaise called it a museum, but you may think *this* a museum, for all I know.' He glared at Edward, daring him to agree. Edward grinned, and the old man suddenly felt that he was looking at the son he had particularly loved, who had betrayed him so callously by marrying a girl he had never had the opportunity to meet.

'It will be a privilege to stay here, sir,' Edward said quietly. He could glimpse the bereft old man behind the facade of autocratic aggression, for his own experiences had given him an insight into his grandfather's helplessness. He had escaped, thanks to Liz; but this old man could not be rescued by a girl driven to desperation by a brutal step-father. From old age there is no escape in this life.

George Steadman departed, leaving Sir Rupert and his grandson to get acquainted with each other. He had been half-expecting fireworks, and thought he might have to stay as peacemaker, but the two Clayton men appeared to have taken to each other.

It was hardly a cheerful meal, but not a mournful one. Sir Rupert wanted to hear how Edward lost his leg, and his experiences in South Africa, and to know why his grandson had chosen to serve with the thousands of uncommissioned troopers, rather than as an officer. He chuckled when he heard the outcome of Edward's application for a commission.

'You're a bloody fool, boy,' he exclaimed. 'If you'd let me know I'd have sent Kitchener or that other fellow – what's his name – Baden-Powell – a word. Yes, I know them both; should have some influence. Now tell me about this wife of yours. No children? Better get on with it, Edward – look at Gervaise. I told him to get married, but he didn't listen ... Odd fellow, Gervaise – never did like him ... Should have married Harriet, but she wouldn't have him, and I couldn't blame her for that! She wants to be a doctor.' He stared at his dessert moodily. 'I miss the girl. Dammit, why couldn't she be content at home with me? She was the only one in the whole bunch I cared for! I've never set eyes on her since she walked out on me. She never even came to see me when I had that stroke.' He was unaware that Harriet had called and was turned away. 'I've sent her a telegram about – about the deaths. She'll be here in the morning in time for the funerals. Now, about your wife – tell me about her.'

Edward finished his dessert and put down his spoon.

'I married a wonderful girl I met at Barminster Military Hospital,' he said quietly. 'I met Harriet there, too, but I didn't know she was my cousin. I only knew her as Nurse Grant.'

Sir Rupert looked up, alert again.

'Your wife was a nurse, was she?' Many aristocratic young women had taken up nursing at that time, inspired by the example of Miss Nightingale in the Crimea, and encouraged by Queen Alexandra, at that time the Princess of Wales. Well, that was one thing off his mind. Edward had not married a gypsy or a chorus-girl!

'Elizabeth was the best nurse any man could wish for,' Edward told him.

'Family?'

'She has a mother and three young half-brothers; her father's dead – I believe he was in the navy.'

'Step-father?'

'A brute of a man. Her mother's left him. I'm going to make her an allowance now that I can afford it –'

'Let them go to one of the houses on the estate – God knows, there are enough of them, and you can't live in all of them yourself.'

'I might do that, Grandfather.'

'I suppose I'll meet your Elizabeth at the funeral?'

'No, she won't be there. She didn't know them – as a matter of fact, I merely told her a cousin had died. She knows no more than that. She doesn't know I have any family apart from Harriet.'

'Ahhh ... So at least you can be sure she didn't marry you for your money, eh?'

Edward smiled bleakly.

'When I asked her to marry me, I hadn't a penny – I wasn't even sure of my pension, then. It was quite possible that *she* might have had to support *me*!' His grandfather looked disconcerted.

'I suppose you think I was very hard on your father, Edward.'

'Well, sir, I don't know any of the details –'

'Then it's about time you did, sir! To begin with, I'd better explain that the men of this family have always been a bit wild. Always sown their wild oats, as you might say, before settling down to marry sensible women of their own class; and most of those alliances have been happy although perhaps they started out as marriages of convenience. My wife, Lady Amelia, was a very young girl just out of the schoolroom when we went to the altar, but she brought me more happiness than I could ever have hoped for with any of the flighty young women I imagined myself in love with. She also, as you know, gave me two sons.

'Arthur, the first, was a dull dog from the start. He never did anything to cause us a moment's uneasiness, and he never did anything to make us laugh or cry. He did well at school and university; at the age of twenty-five he married a sensible, wealthy young woman with an impeccable pedigree and a face like a horse, and that was that. I don't think he ever loved, or was loved by, anyone in his life.

'Robert, however, two years younger, was trouble and strife from the word go. As a baby he was delicate and consequently spoiled, and he was such a handsome little fellow no-one could deny him a thing. He was a born clown, making everyone laugh. At school he was so bright he never had to exert himself, everything came too easily. He went to Sandhurst, and emerged with a splendid record. Arthur was jealous, as well he might be; he never did anything remarkable, and Robert did remarkably well in everything. Or remarkably badly. But he was never mediocre.

'Each year the men of the family spent some time at Keenlach Lodge in the Great Forest, hunting, going to the horse-sales and the Fair. And, of course, we frequently amused ourselves with the gypsy girls. Harmless fun. Mostly it was just a frolic at the fair, dancing with the gypsy girls, and crossing their palms with silver, but unfortunately my brother Sebastian was foolish enough to get one of the girls into the family way. A boy from the village – a fisherman – was in love with her and married her nonetheless. My father gave him a cottage on the shoreside for his lifetime, which came back into the family estate after his death.

282

Sebastian died in battle, unmarried, and only my father and I knew about the child born to the gypsy girl. Incidentally, she was the sister of Meg, the matriarch of the tribe. I heard that she died only recently.'

'Meg! Good heavens – so it was true! She cured my injuries, you know,' Edward told him.

'Bit of a witch, Meg was. Damn pretty girl when she was young, too!' Sir Rupert glared defiantly at his grandson. Edward wondered if he, too, had sown his wild oats in that direction. 'Anyway, young Robert stayed at Keenlach Lodge and met the girl at the fair. Of course, he didn't know she was his cousin. They fell in love, and in the heat of the moment he married her without a word to me or his mother. We knew nothing of it until one of his brother officers came here looking for him when he was on leave. Then the whole business came out.'

'Even so, Grandfather, he had not really done anything dishonourable –'

'He had been engaged to a very well-connected young woman, a Miss Delafield, before he met this girl, and we were left in a very embarrassing position. Arthur's wife was furious. Miss Delafield was a close friend of hers, and Robert had humiliated her unforgivably. I had to go to the girl's father, and make abject apologies for my son.' The old man looked very weary, reliving the past.

'When Robert came here there was an almighty row. We both said terrible things in our anger, and he left the house, never to return. I cut off his allowance, thinking he would be forced to come back and apologize for his conduct, and we could make our peace. But he was too proud to apologize and I never saw him again.' He finished the last of his wine.

'You must have been very distressed,' Edward said quietly.

'We loved that boy! He was our golden son, our darling. His mother was brokenhearted. Had we known he wanted to marry the girl we might have found a way of putting a good face on it. Anyway, he was sent to Ireland on active service, and then to the Continent. After some years we heard that the girl had died, and I tried to contact Robert but found he had resigned his commission and vanished leaving considerable debts. I cleared them up to save further scandal, but unfortunately someone talked, and the whole business was brought to life again. At the time Arthur was going into politics; he couldn't face the gossip, and dropped his political ambitions for nearly twenty years.

'The next thing we knew was that you arrived on our doorstep, with hardly a rag to your back, and talking like a stable-boy. I arranged for you to be educated, and then articled to Steadman where I could keep an eye on you, but you didn't seem to want anything to do with us. You went off to the war without seeing us, just sending a short, impersonal note. Lady Amelia and I felt that you didn't want to know us. We left it at that.'

'I thought *you* didn't want anything to do with *me*!' Edward exclaimed. 'I was surprised when I found my grandmother had left me a legacy.'

'She did that without telling me!' Sir Rupert admitted with a wry grin. 'Well, my boy, now you know all about it. If Robert and I had not both been so darned pig-headed things would have been different. If either of us had stopped to think – but it's over and done with now. It's time to change the subject. Ring for Beale, Edward. We'll have a glass of port – or would you prefer brandy?'

'Whatever you prefer, Grandfather. I don't drink much these days. And if you don't mind, I'll retire soon – my leg's aching, and I'm rather weary.'

The old man glared at him.

'I suppose you're saying that because you think I'm tired! Well, I'm not too old to stay up after supper, young man.'

'Not at all, sir, but my knee aches after I've been standing on one leg all day.'

'Standing on one leg – makes you sound like a bloody stork,' the old man snorted. 'Ah, Beale, bring the port. And make sure Lord Farlington's room is ready. He keeps nursery hours.'

'Very well, sir.'

Beale left them as silently as he had appeared.

'Grandfather, I'd like to say how sorry I am about –'

'Don't be a hypocrite, Edward. You didn't like Gervaise or Cecil any more than I did, and if you'd known Arthur and that inebriated clothes-horse, his wife, you wouldn't have liked them either! She wasn't too bad while she had Cecil to dote on, but after he died she transferred her affections to the bottle, and I found it easier to remain upstairs in my room than to watch her mooning around the house. My God, that woman was ugly! Don't waste your time telling me you're sorry.'

'Grandfather, I *am* sorry about their deaths. And I'm sorry I've slipped sideways, as it were, into an estate and title I don't believe should belong to me!'

'Well, like it or not, they're yours! So say no more about it, boy. It's neither your fault nor mine that we're the only ones left. Here's the port. Let's drink a nightcap and then retire. Tomorrow will be a trying day for both of us.'

Chapter Twenty-three

Joe Spragg called at the public house after work on Tuesday. He had been loading timber most of the day and was hot and thirsty. He had the price of only two pints on him, a tip from the timber-merchant, so he did not stay long. When he found the door of his home locked he gave it a couple of kicks, and shouted for his wife to open up, but it remained locked. For a moment he stood fuming on the cobblestones, then he walked further up the road, through a narrow alley, and back to the rear entrance.

This was also locked; but the latch on the kitchen window was broken, and he soon had that open and scrambled inside.

He stood in the kitchen, scratching his head. Neither his wife nor his sons were at home. His youngest son was now ten, the twins eighteen months older. There had been two girls, pretty little things, younger than the boys, but both had died of diphtheria. He had never been able to forgive his step-daughter for surviving when his own girls had both gone to their graves. But now Agnes, unaccountably, appeared to be missing, and the boys too. The house was unnaturally tidy and silent. His eye fell on the kitchen table. There was a jug of milk, and a large pasty – from the baker, not home-made – on a plate, with a scrawled note beside it.

> Dear Joe, I am leeving you and going where you
> will not find me. The boys is going with me.
> There is a pasty for your supper. The rent is

paid up to Friday, the tallyman is paid off, and
I sent a note to school that the boys will not be
going there no more in case they send the troont
inspecter. I shall take the mantel clock becos it
is mine. Agnes.

It took Joe several minutes to puzzle out the note, and then
he gave out a great roar and crashed his calloused fist down
on the table, sending the jug to the floor. He sat watching
the milk spreading across the tiles as if mesmerized. His
mental processes were as slow as his body was powerful and
aggressive.

Agnes had never been the same since that dummy left.
She had become almost as silent as the girl had been, but
had not appeared depressed – it almost seemed as if she'd
had a secret, something that gave her quiet satisfaction.
Sometimes he wondered if she was laughing at him behind
his back. When he came home drunk she fed him, as always,
but even when he beat her she refused to answer him
back. He had wondered if she had another man; but one
look at her lined face, and her back bowed from years of
scrubbing, reassured him that no man would give her a
second look.

When Liz disappeared, Joe had never asked where the
girl had gone. He was glad to be rid of her, and did not
care if she was alive or dead. Some time ago he had been
trundling barrels into a goods truck at the station and
thought he saw a young woman who reminded him vaguely
of his step-daughter, but he had only glimpsed her face
before she turned away. She was well-dressed, sitting with
an older man, a cripple with grey hair. Joe would know that
man if he ever set eyes on him, but he never saw either of
them again. He had assumed the young woman to be the
cripple's wife, or perhaps his daughter. Could it have been
Liz? Had she found herself a 'protector'? But that was

impossible – no man would look twice at the miserable, downtrodden dummy.

Joe looked again at the note. The rent and the tallyman paid up, and a shop-made pasty for his supper – where had Agnes got the money? Had she pawned something? There was nothing in the house worth pawning, except that clock given to her by her first husband, or it would have gone long ago! He had tried pawning the clock once, and had soon regretted it; Agnes had attacked him with the poker.

Could her disappearance have anything to do with Liz? If that woman at the station *had* been Liz, she looked as if she had a bob or two. Had that crippled toff taken her for his mistress, and now she had given her mother some of her rewards?

Joe made himself a mug of tea, and drank it black; there was no milk in the house apart from the puddle on the kitchen floor. He ate the pasty and went to bed, puzzled and disgruntled.

The next day he was loading sacks of flour for Jack Johnson, the carter, at the granary near the church, when the Clayton funeral cortege went by, two wreath-laden hearses pulled by black horses with black plumes waving. He and Jack stood with their heads bowed respectfully, their flour-dusted caps in their hands, as the gloomy procession passed slowly down the street towards the church. Joe did not often work with Jack, who, as a self-employed carter, considered himself a cut above the common labourer, and hardly knew the man. This was a casual job he had picked up. As the mourners following the hearses walked by, Jack nudged him.

'See that fellow – the one with the crutch? That's the new Lord Farlington. 'E lost 'is leg in the Boer war, and were in the Military 'Ospital for months, terrible bad, 'e was.'

Joe looked up, and stared. The crippled man walking

beside old Sir Rupert was the man he had seen with the young woman who had reminded him of Liz.

'Lord Farlington? How d'you know? Seen 'im before, have you?'

'Yes. Must be a couple of years, now. Took 'im and a girl out to a cottage at Forestwidden, with a load of second'and furniture. I was told she were 'is wife, but she didn't look like a wife to me. More like a servant. Half-starved, like, she was. She couldn't talk – a dummy. And he was terrible ill, 'ad to travel on a mattress on top of the furniture. I thought 'e'd be dead before we reached the cottage.'

Joe gaped at him. A dummy – it could only have been Liz! He stared after the procession.

'Where was the cottage?' he managed to ask after a moment.

'Out beyond Willoughby's Farm, on the sea-shore. Come on, Joe, let's get the rest of these sacks loaded. They've got to be delivered before nightfall.'

Joe finished the loading, collected his money, and amazed Jack by refusing a drink, although loading flour was hot and dusty work. Joe dusted himself off with his cap, the flour flying into the clear autumn morning air in white clouds. Then he hurried after the cortege to the church.

The service was over, and the mourners were gathered about the open graves when he reached the churchyard. There were two graves; the Honourable Arthur and Lady Imogen were to lie together, with Gervaise on their left. Cecil's marble tombstone stood on their right.

Joe kept back in the shadows of a yew, as he did not want to be seen. The man with the crutch stood on one side of Sir Rupert, and a tall young woman in black stood on the other. She was lightly veiled, but Joe could see that she was remarkably handsome, with a coil of dark chestnut hair under her hat. As the mourners started to leave she was weeping, and the grey-haired man limped over to put a comforting arm round her for a moment. They appeared to be very close. Was this his wife? There was no sign of Liz in the crowd.

The young woman appeared to pull herself together with an effort. She took Sir Rupert's arm; and with Edward limping on his other side, they left the churchyard and walked out to the carriage waiting at the gate. Joe had heard in the town that Sir Rupert was failing fast after his stroke, and practically bedridden, but the old man walked erect and proud between his two young companions, and shook hands with several of the many who had attended the funeral, before getting into the carriage with the two young folk.

Joe remained hidden under the yew until the mourners were out of sight and two workmen had come to fill in the graves. He walked back into the town and found work at the railway station for the afternoon. He needed money; he worked later than usual, and when he was paid he returned home without calling in for a drink with his cronies. He had stale bread and a crust of cheese for his supper, and set the alarm clock before going to bed. He had an early start tomorrow morning.

The first train on the branch line that served Forestwidden went out just before five. It carried mail, the early newspapers, a few paying passengers, and Joe Spragg. In the darkness he slipped unseen into the guard's van just before it left the station. At the halt near Forestwidden he alighted unobtrusively as the mail was put off, climbed the fence at the far end of the short platform to avoid showing a ticket, and cadged a lift into the village from the driver collecting the newspapers. It was full daylight now, but still too early for many people to be about.

'D'you know Willoughby's Farm?' he asked the driver.

'Willoughby's Farm? A'course I do – everyone knows Willoughby's Farm,' he was told. 'Down that lane by the green – it's about four mile or so. Willoughby's Farm is at the end of the lane, which turns into a cart track and runs down to 'Oney Beck Bay.'

"Oney Beck Bay?"

'Ain't nothing there, mate, 'cept an old cottage where a crippled trooper lives, though I think I heard tell that 'e's done the old place up and made it decent, like. You looking for Henry Willoughby, then?'

'Aye.'

'You'll likely find him in the village during the morning, he usually comes in Thursdays.'

'I'll walk out to the farm and find him. Thanks for the ride.'

'D'you want a newspaper? This'n's torn, you can have it for free.'

Joe stopped in the village long enough to buy himself a loaf of bread from the baker, the only shop open at this early hour, and then trudged down the lane to Willoughby's Farm. It was a fine autumn morning, a light mist on the sea promising a sunny day later.

He followed the track down to the bay, and found the cottage securely locked, and peering in through the windows could see no sign of life. He walked along the shoreline, and sat down on a grassy bank above the sand near the headland. Behind him loomed the trees growing on the slope; beyond lay the woods and farmland bordering the Great Forest. From here he could keep the cottage under observation, whilst keeping out of sight himself. He dug the loaf out of his pocket, and satisfied the hunger he had worked up with the long walk. Then he opened the torn newspaper to fill in the time while he waited. He was a slow reader, but he persevered, and read about the deaths in the Clayton family, and the romantic story of the returned trooper who had become the heir to the family estate, despite his father's having been disowned by the family thirty years ago. Recently married to a nurse from the Soldiers' Hospital, the newspaper reported; presumably the red-haired woman Joe had noticed at the funeral yesterday.

It was two hours before his patience was rewarded. He saw a figure in a fresh flower-sprigged dress carefully descending the rough steps from the meadow above the cliff behind the cottage. He folded the newspaper, stuffed it into his pocket, and watched closely; was this Liz? The young woman had a basket on her arm, and a light woollen shawl round her shoulders. She was plumper than Liz had been, and there was a spring in her step that had never been evident when she trudged the cobblestones of the slums in Barminster. Her dark hair, tied back with a black ribbon, curled almost to her waist, the soft tresses blown by the mild morning breeze.

If this was Liz, she had changed considerably since she left Barminster!

She went straight to the cottage, took a key from her pocket, and unlocked the door.

Joe got up, stretched his limbs, and walked across the sand, keeping close to the trees. As he stealthily approached the cottage, keeping out of view from the windows, he caught the sound of singing, a country ballad. He stopped and listened.

He had wasted his time. The girl could not be his step-daughter. Liz could not talk, let alone sing! He crept up to the cottage, going round the back so as not to be seen from that glassed conservatory extending at the front, to the window at the left of the front door. Furtively, he peered into the main room of the cottage, and saw the girl go through the door on the right, into the room behind the glass conservatory. He only had a glimpse of the girl's face; but that was enough. He recognized his step-daughter.

Liz had found her voice. He had known she was only keeping silent to aggravate him! Now he had caught the sly

292

little bitch. Quietly, he opened the door and went into the cottage. There was a rocking-chair in a corner, away from the bright sunlight streaming in through the window. He crept across the floor and sat down.

Liz had come down to the cottage early this bright morning, intending to do some work in the garden. She had brought a basket of eggs and fresh vegetables from the farm, ready for Edward's return tomorrow. She felt happier this morning – who could be otherwise on such a lovely day? Since Edward left on Monday she had been depressed and miserable, despite Ada and Henry Willoughby's efforts to distract her. Scarcely an hour went by in which she did not think of him, and worry about him. What was he doing? Was he with Harriet? And had that unknown cousin who had died left him a stack of debts that would have to be paid off somehow? Was he resting enough – she knew that if he stood for too long, or walked too far, his knee became painful, and only a couple of weeks ago he had rubbed a blister on the stump of his leg where the peg chafed. Was he taking proper care of himself? And would he have enough clean shirts and underwear with him?

The walk from the farm in the fresh morning breeze had cheered her, and tomorrow Edward would be home. As she set the eggs and the vegetables in the larder she sang a country ballad she had picked up from Henry in the milking shed; he always sang at the top of his tuneful voice as he milked the cows, and they seemed to appreciate his song.

She placed the empty basket on the table in the living-room, and went into the bedroom to change. When she was gardening she always slipped into the old black calico dress, now much darned and patched. She put the sharp little pruning knife, which she had carelessly left on the dressing-table on Monday, in the pocket, to cut back the overgrown bushes. She opened up the windows of the bedroom and the conservatory to let in the fresh morning air, and then went back into the living-room to put the kettle on before she started weeding. Now she had a small single-burner oil stove to boil the kettle, so she did not have to use the range during the hot weather.

As she stepped into the big room she saw a figure in the rocking-chair. Edward? Had he returned early? No – this burly figure was not her husband. Her heart lurched; she let out a shriek of fright.

Joe grinned at her from the shadows. Liz's hand went to her mouth, and her throat tightened. How had he found her? What was he doing here? *Oh, Edward – Edward, come quickly, I need you so!* But Edward was far away, and could not help her.

'So this is where you've been hiding with your fancy man,' Joe sneered. 'Not that you'll see much more of him, I reckon. Now that he's a lord and back into the bosom of his exalted family, I doubt if he'll want to see you again, miss! How long is it? Eighteen months? I'm told he was ill when he latched on to the skivvy; now he's healthy again he'll go back to his own kind. He'll have no time for his doxy now he's got a handsome wife to warm his bed!'

Liz shrank back. She didn't know what he was talking about, but cowering here, face to face with the brute she had been terrified of most of her life, she couldn't speak. Her voice was gone; she couldn't even scream. She wanted to shout at him, tell him that Edward was her husband, that he loved her and would never leave her, but she could not utter a sound. She stared at Joe in horror.

He dug into his pocket and pulled out the newspaper.

'Edward Clayton – Lord Farlington – heir to Sir Rupert, the owner of Barminster Abbey and half the farmland between the city and the sea – your lover!' He flourished the grubby newspaper under her nose. 'I saw him myself, yesterday, at the funeral, and mighty proud he looked, with

Sir Rupert and that red-haired woman – his wife, is she? Oh, I'm sure they would be very happy to hear about you, Liz, tucked up here, out of their sight, the skivvy from the hospital! The newspaper says he married a nurse – I wonder if she knows you? Very loving, they were, over the grave.'

Liz sank into the depths of the fat sofa, her face covered by her hands, utterly terrified. She was far too frightened to take in what Joe was saying. He could have been talking in a foreign language. But he wasn't finished with her yet.

'The paper says that Robert Clayton, your Edward's father, was disowned by the family when he married beneath him. Oh, no, that family don't want no poor, shiftless hangers-on – if the girl weren't born with a silver spoon in her mouth, she's ain't good enough for them! So what's the old bugger going to say when I tell 'im that 'is newly discovered grandson's been living with a slut from the slums of Barminster? Eh? Speak up, damn you – I know you can speak – I heard you singing!'

Her step-father stood over her, his face working with rage, determined to force her to speak. Liz cowered back, not understanding a word above the tumultuous beating of her own heart. She tried to lose herself in the depths of the sofa, but Joe wasted no compassion on the girl. He brought his hand across her face, nearly jolting her head from her shoulders. Still she made no sound.

'So you're dumb again, my girl?' he snarled. He looked round the room, and licked his dry lips. He had not had a drink for nearly two days. 'Got any drink here?'

Liz shook her head, but another blow to the face forced her to get up and bring the bottle of whisky from the larder. She offered him a glass. He grinned, and put the bottle to his lips.

'I'm not so fastidious as your precious fancy man,' he sneered, sitting down at the table. 'Food – got any food? I'm fair famished – I 'aven't 'ad a decent meal since your mother left me two days ago.' His eyes narrowed. 'Is she 'ere? Or 'iding out somewhere in the village?'

Liz shook her head again. Now that she had gathered her wits she understood some of what he was saying, and was relieved to know that her mother was out of his reach. She went to the larder and brought him a large piece of fruit cake – the only thing she could think of that wouldn't need cooking. He began to stuff it into his mouth, washing it down with more whisky. She edged towards the door, but Joe Spragg noticed the movement and raised his fist.

'Oh, no, you don't – another step towards that door and I'll knock every tooth out of your 'ead! Where d'you keep your money?'

Liz stared at him fearfully. Was he going to steal Edward's money? For the first time she remembered that her husband had left some money in the chest in case of emergencies. Could she buy Joe off with that?

'Money, girl – you must 'ave some money somewhere!' Joe insisted. 'Get it, or I'll go straight to the old man and tell 'im 'is precious grandson's been living with a gutter-brat for the last two years! That'll give 'im something to think about; he disowned 'is son for marrying against his wishes, so what will he think of 'is grandson then?'

Liz was bewildered, with no idea what Joe was talking about. She closed her eyes and prayed that Edward was safe. Joe had apparently found something about the dead cousin in the paper – something that had led him to Honey Beck Bay.

Joe's huge fist crashed down on the table. He glared at her, his bloodshot eyes slightly out of focus. Nearly half the bottle of whisky had gone, and he was unaccustomed to spirits.

'Money, girl! I told you, gimme the money!'

Doggedly, Liz shook her head. Joe lurched to his feet, and caught her by the hair, his muscular arm forcing her face within inches of his. His unwashed body stank and his breath was sour. Liz felt sick. Suddenly she remembered the sharp little pruning knife in her pocket.

Dragging cruelly on her hair, Joe snapped her head back, and slapped her across the face again.

'Fetch that money, or your fancy man won't recognize you when – or if – 'e comes back,' he snarled, letting go of her hair and throwing her to the floor. Before she could dodge he kicked her on the hip. As she slowly got to her feet she fumbled in her pocket for the knife, hiding it in her hand as she stumbled into the bedroom, closely followed by Joe. Now her face was swelling from the blows; one eye was almost closed. Barely aware of what she was doing, she went across to the chest of drawers, and fumbled among Edward's winter underwear for the money. Her hands closed on a wallet, and she turned to face her step-father, holding it out. As Joe lurched forward to grab it, she brought her other hand, with the knife extended, up with all her might, and buried the blade of the knife between his ribs.

As he fell, utter amazement on his face, he grabbed at the bedclothes. He sank to the floor, and the patchwork quilt Liz had lovingly made for Edward's bed fell over him. Liz stared in shock at the crumpled heap of colourful patchwork, but then her knees buckled, and she passed into merciful oblivion.

Chapter Twenty-four

Liz struggled up from the swirling mists that enveloped her. For a moment she lay on the floor where she had fallen as memory reluctantly returned. Horror-stricken, she gazed at the quilt lying on the floor beside the bed. A calloused, dirt-encrusted hand protruded from the heap of crumpled fabric.

She could not bring herself to look under the quilt.

She had murdered her step-father. She had brought shame and disgrace down on her beloved Edward. Whatever happened now, there was no way of undoing this terrible deed.

Murder. She would be hanged. And Edward would be branded the husband of a murderess. She dropped her head into her hands and broke into uncontrollable sobbing. This would be the end of their Garden of Eden in Honey Beck Bay. Her tears mingled with the blood on her grazed cheeks. A cut under her eye stung with the salty tears. There was nothing left for her to live for. If she lost Edward, she had nothing; and how could an honourable man like her husband fail to be repelled by a woman who had killed another human being? For even Joe was human, she thought in despair. She had broken the Sixth Commandment. The ultimate sin.

If only she could turn the clock back a few hours! If only she had stayed up at the farm and helped Mrs Willoughby with the baking this morning! If only, if only . . .

Perhaps she could hide the body, and disappear from the cottage . . . But she could not bring herself to touch the thing under the quilt. She could still smell his foul body odour. And blood – she could smell blood.

She ran to the bathroom and retched, vomiting again and again until her stomach was empty.

Suddenly she knew that the only thing to do was to run, to go as far away as she could, to a place where no-one would know her, where she would never be found, brought to trial, and have to pay the penalty for her crime. Edward would be free to return to his own kind. Perhaps her mother had been right, and he was already regretting his hasty marriage. Perhaps he would eventually marry Harriet, for he had obviously admired her, not only for her beauty but for her intelligence and independence. Harriet had all the virtues and talents that she, Liz, lacked. What had Joe said? Something about Edward's father being disowned by the family when he married beneath him. Only a girl born with a silver spoon in her mouth was good enough for a Clayton.

When Joe Spragg's body was found he might be taken for a common burglar who had drunk the whisky, stolen the wallet, which was still clamped in his hand under the quilt, and fallen on the knife when he was overcome by drink.

Liz knew that she could not face up to questioning by the police. If she were found here, the constable would soon have the whole story out of her. The very thought of it turned her cold. And what about Edward? When his family found out that Edward had married a skivvy from the slums, and a murderess at that, they would never accept him back. He would be doubly disgraced. In her despair, Liz was unable to think coherently; every instinct told her to run.

If only she knew where to find her mother! But one of the few facts that had penetrated her mind from Joe's diatribe was that her mother had left him, and he had come here in search of her.

'Oh, Mother, what am I to do?' she whispered. She

299

fancied that she could hear her mother reply with a saying that was frequently on her lips.

'God helps those who help themselves.'

Now she knew what she had to do. Again she was like the leaf tossed hither and thither in the wind. She had no control over her destiny. She had to leave her beloved cottage in Honey Beck Bay, and go as far away as she could, where the authorities – and Edward – would never find her.

Where would the wayward wind send her this time?

Shaking from head to foot, she dragged herself to her feet, and began to pack her small dressing-case with the things she would need for a few days: clean underwear, a couple of dresses, and a warm shawl. Nightwear. Washing necessities. She remembered that the wallet Joe had snatched had been very slim; she looked further into Edward's drawer, and found the roll of money he had left for her. In his haste he had neglected to put it in the wallet. So Joe Spragg had, in fact, died for a few paltry pounds, not the fortune he had expected. She took a few notes off the roll, put them into her purse, and stuffed the remainder into a stocking in the dressing-case. After a moment's thought, she added the envelope containing her birth certificate and marriage licence.

She went into the bathroom and looked into the mirror. Her face was swollen, and one eye was now completely closed, with blood oozing from a graze under it. She bathed the swellings with cold water; that brought some relief from the pain if it did nothing else.

Finally she changed from the black calico dress into the sprigged cotton she had worn this morning, but she was too disturbed to put the black calico back into the closet, and left it lying on the floor by the bed. Beside Joe Spragg. She pulled a straw hat with a wide brim and a veil on to her head, hoping to hide some of the bruises, and picked up the light shawl she had worn earlier. She hurried out of the cottage, carefully locking the door after her, leaving the key in the shed, under a flowerpot in the wheelbarrow. Then she set off up the track, carrying her dressing-case, with tears on her bruised cheeks. From the bend in the track she looked back at Honey Beck Cottage. Would she ever see it again?

She struggled up the lane until she reached the path to the gypsies' camp, then she headed into the Great Forest.

Later in the morning Mrs Willoughby walked down to the cottage with a loaf fresh from the oven, and some cheese to give Liz for her lunch. The girl had been depressed while Edward had been away, and the kindly farmer's wife was afraid she might forget to eat at mid-day. She had been out in the dairy when Liz left that morning, and although Liz had called farewell, she had not actually seen her go.

She found the cottage deserted. The sun had moved round now, and the interior was in shadow. She hurried back to the farm to tell Henry Liz was missing. An hour later he came down himself, and searched round. He found nothing to indicate that Liz had been to the cottage that morning, and returned to the farm very puzzled. But after some thought he concluded that Liz must have gone into Barminster on the train to see John Oatis; after all, she was a free woman. There was no reason why she should confide in them if she wanted to consult the solicitor. He went on with his daily work, not happy, but not unduly disturbed. He felt slightly offended that they were not taken into her confidence.

There were no caravans in the clearing now; the gypsies had left some months ago. Not knowing or caring much where she went, anxious only to put distance between herself and the cottage, Liz followed the path through the forest for several miles. At one point she stopped to bathe her aching feet in a stream, but although she was thirsty she resisted the temptation to drink. The water looked brackish. Leaving the forest, she turned south. Eventually, in the early afternoon, she reached a small hamlet on the coast where she had never been before, where no-one could recognize her.

She was hungry and thirsty. She went into the one shop and bought a couple of buns, the only thing she could see to point to; she tried to speak, but her voice was gone completely. The plump woman behind the counter stared at her curiously as she handed her the buns in a bag. Liz paid her and went out into the bright autumn sunshine again. Now where was she to to go? She would be too conspicuous sitting on the green to eat her buns, and the last thing she wanted to do was draw attention to herself. The best course would be to follow the road – wherever it went.

A young man in working clothes was standing by the forge, holding the bridle while the blacksmith finished shoeing a horse. Short and stocky, he had powerful shoulders and muscular arms, and a friendly, freckled face. He watched the girl in the wide, shady hat carrying her case down the street. As she came nearer he saw that she had bruises on her face under the veil. She looked very tired. The blacksmith finished his job, and went back into the forge.

"Afternoon, miss,' the young man said cheerfully. Liz started, looked at him nervously, and nodded uncertainly. The young man wondered who she was, and who had inflicted those blows on her face; the brute should be horsewhipped! She was a stranger to the village, and looked as if she was running away from someone, with that case in her hand. 'Going far?' he asked casually. Liz stared at him nervously. 'Mebbe I can give you a lift,' he suggested. 'I'm going to Portsmouth as soon as I've got Buttercup here back between the shafts.' He indicated a light trap that stood nearby.

Liz hesitated. He looked respectable enough, despite the rough working clothes, and he spoke kindly. But – Portsmouth? She had been born in Portsmouth, her mother had told her, but had not been there since she was a baby. She thought her mother had a sister who lived there, or had lived there, many years ago, before Agnes met Joe Spragg. Portsmouth was a big enough city to hide herself, and perhaps she could get work of some sort before her money ran out. Finally she nodded, and gave the young man a tremulous smile.

'Right, miss, just sit there, on the bench, while I pay the blacksmith and hitch Buttercup to the cart.'

Liz obediently sat herself on the rough bench and ate her buns while she waited for him. The sun was very bright, and it was surprisingly warm for late October. She was very tired after the long walk, and thirsty; but the only drink available was the water in the horses' trough, and she was not desperate enough to drink that. Presently the young man came out of the forge with a mug of water.

'Thought you might be thirsty,' he said cheerfully, handing it to her.

'Th – thank you,' she whispered.

'Lost your voice, miss?' Liz nodded. 'Then there's no fear of you talking my ears off before we reach Portsmouth!' he joked. He soon had the horse between the shafts and helped her into the trap, and two minutes later they were bowling along the Portsmouth road.

The young man told her his name was Jim Peters, and he worked for a local farmer.

'He and his wife adopted me out of the orphanage. Just like me own mum and dad, they are. I live in the farmhouse with the family. I'm going in to Portsmouth to collect Mrs

Jones – that's the missis; she's been visiting her daughter. Miss Julia – Mrs Williams, she is now – is married to a Naval officer. Four kids, she's got, and she's not twenty-five yet. Every time the ship comes in she's in the family way again. Her mum's been with her for a month after the last one was born.' He grinned. 'I guess she'll be glad to get back to the farm and have a rest! Mr Jones is getting fed up with my cooking and we ain't got a clean shirt between the pair of us!'

The road led them through the countryside, now and then passing a village. The afternoon was cooling now. Presently Jim reined in Buttercup so that she could take a drink from a roadside trough, then walked her on slowly for a few minutes to let her cool down.

'I'll drop you at the Cathedral – that do?'

Liz nodded. It did not matter where he dropped her, the city was new territory to her.

'Thank you, Jim. You're very kind.'

'How did you come by those bruises on your face? Did someone beat you, miss – er – missis? I don't know your name, either.'

Liz hesitated. How far could she trust him? She daren't give her true name, or the law would be sure to trace her. She decided to revert to her maiden name.

'I'm Mrs Elizabeth Fuller,' she whispered, flushing. 'And I – I hit my face on a – a wall. I wasn't looking where I was going.'

Jim looked at her sceptically. The right side of her face was grazed and swollen, the bruises coming out in an angry purple, and the left side clearly showed the imprint of a man's hand. But that was her own business.

Poor little woman – presumably it was her husband who had beaten her. What sort of brute had she married? No wonder she wanted to get away.

Liz lapsed back into silence, not noticing the pleasant

countryside passing. She wondered how long it would be before someone discovered the body of Joe Spragg.

Portsmouth was a busy and bewildering city, full of people, many of the men in Royal Naval uniforms. Jim seemed to know his way without hesitation, and set Liz down at the Cathedral. Liz found an unoccupied seat in the grounds and sat down to think out what she should do next. It was getting colder now. She wished she had put on the warm shawl that was in her bag instead of this light one. For over two hours she had been jolted unceasingly on the seat of the trap, and her head was aching abominably; her face was sore and throbbing. Her hip, where Joe had kicked her, was hurting. She closed her eyes for a moment to ease the eye that was now badly swollen. Where could she go? She had a little money – she was not sure how much, but it was surely enough to keep her for a week or two until she found work. But first she had to find somewhere to stay the night.

A slight sound alerted her. She opened her eyes in time to see a grubby fist closing round the handle of her case. A shifty-looking youth of about fifteen years old was about to make off with it. Without a second thought she lashed out with her stout walking shoe and caught him on the shinbone, making him yelp and take to his heels, disappearing into the gathering dusk. Liz looked after him, and then glanced at her sturdy shoe, surprised at her instictive reaction. She had never kicked anyone before in her life!

Perhaps it was time she learned. From now on she would have to look after herself. It was no good waiting for someone to solve her problems for her; she was on her own.

Wearily she got to her feet, picked up the case, and left the Cathedral grounds. The sooner she found a lodging the better. It was not safe to be wandering about the city with all her money and possessions in that case.

Besides which, by now the police might be looking for

her. Walking about the streets with that suitcase, she felt as if every eye was on her. She could not go to a hotel; that would be asking for discovery. She walked aimlessly, finding herself in ever narrower and meaner streets. Finally, in a tall, shabby house opening directly on to the street, not far from the Naval dockyards, she saw a hand-written notice in a window: *Vacancies. Bed and Breakfast. No sailors. No Forriners. Cash in advance.*

Well, she was not a sailor, and she was not a foreigner. The house did not look very inviting, but it was better than walking the streets all night.

Liz walked up the three steps and rapped on the door.

Liz had thrust the knife into Joe Spragg's ribcage with all her strength, but Joe was a big man, and was wearing a heavy waistcoat over his thick shirt. Although she was sure she had buried the stubby blade of the knife in his body, in fact she had not penetrated deeply into his flesh before the knife was deflected by a rib, and very little damage was done. He passed into unconsciousness as much through shock as through his injury; the spirits he had consumed also had considerable effect on him. As he lay under the quilt, unconscious, he bled copiously from the wound, but a man of his size could afford to lose a lot of blood before his condition became serious. When he regained consciousness several hours later he was weakened by the loss of blood, but was a long way from dead. Joe tried to get up; the pain in his chest soon led him to find the knife. He wrenched it out, with an oath, and dropped it on the quilt. Memory began to return to his befuddled brain, and he searched about under the quilt until he found the wallet he had snatched from Liz.

He swore again when he discovered that the wallet he had expected to be crammed with banknotes contained only a few pounds. He pulled up his blood-soaked shirt and examined the wound, then grinned to himself; it was no worse than he had sustained several times in the past in a drunken brawl after a night out with his mates.

Dragging himself to his feet, Joe went back into the big room and took several swigs of whisky while he searched for food. He found a few biscuits in the bottom of a tin, which went down well with the liquor. When the bottle was empty he dropped it on the floor and it rolled under the table.

His wound was bleeding again. In the cupboard in the bathroom he found some dressings and plaster that had been put away unused after Edward's wounds healed, and clumsily dressed his own wound, after which he felt weak and hazy, so he lay on the bed and slept for several hours.

It was dark when Joe awoke again. He was hungry once more. He had not had a good filling meal all day, and a man used to heavy work and starchy food cannot be satisfied with bread, cheese, and biscuits for long. He got up, and stretched, wincing as he felt the pain in his chest. His shirt and waistcoat were sticky and cold where the blood had soaked through earlier. He peeled them off, threw them on the floor, and helped himself to some of Edward's clothes from the chest and the closet by the light of a candle he found on the bedside table. In a final effort to find food, he discovered a bottle, one third full, of brandy, which he slipped into his pocket, and went to the door.

It was locked. Not a flimsy door, it was constructed of stout timber to withstand the winter gales, and set in a solid stone frame, so he could not force it open. He went through to the newly built kitchen, at the back of the cottage, and climbed out through the window, leaving it open, and leaving the prints of his clumsy hob-nailed boots on the windowsill. The moon had risen now, on the wane, but sufficient to light his way. Stumbling occasionally in the deep ruts, he set out for Forestwidden, following the track that led past Willoughby's Farm.

It took him nearly two hours to reach the village. Lights beamed from the cottages round the green, the public house was open, and voices and laughter floated out from the bar. He pushed his way in and ordered a beer.

'Got anything to eat?' he asked the landlord.

'Pork pies or mutton pasties,' he was told. He ordered one of each, and settled into a corner seat to drink his pint. The local men looked at him askance; he reeked of whisky and sweat. He finished his beer, and ordered another to drink with the food. He asked the landlord to direct him to the station, and was told that the last train left within the quarter hour. He drained his glass and lurched out into the moonlight. The locals were glad to see him go.

By the time he was half-way to the station the loss of blood and the alcohol Joe had imbibed began to take its toll. His legs felt weak and his head ached. He took a swig of the brandy to sustain him, and finally reached the station as a train pulled in. He had enough wits about him to slip on to the platform without troubling the ticket collector, and dragged himself into an empty carriage, slumped into the corner seat, and fell asleep, under the impression that he was on the way to Barminster.

The train pulled out of the station and continued on its journey to Southampton. It was nearly midnight when Joe staggered out of the station, having again eluded the ticket collector by joining a noisy crowd of merchant seamen and slipping though the barrier under cover of their noisy company. Mistaking him for one of themselves, a couple of men realized that he was considerably the worse for drink, and good-naturedly assisted him, one on each side, to their destination: a rusty old cargo boat, loaded with machine parts and bathtubs for a newly industrialized city in South

America, sailing on the morning tide. At which time Joe Spragg found himself reluctantly enrolled as a stoker in the Merchant Navy.

Six weeks later he jumped ship and went to work for a sugar company in the West Indies. With a good supply of cheap rum, and a plump local woman to keep his palm-thatched hut tidy and his bed warm, he became an overseer in the sugar fields. The hot climate suited him, and with his immense strength he worked hard and did well. If he drank too much his woman good-naturedly threw him out of the house to sleep on the ground under a palm tree. Not for her the miserable life Agnes had put up with for so many years! If he missed his daily dip in the sea she refused to feed him, so he soon learned to keep himself clean, and took a belated pride in his personal appearance. Joe was thoroughly under her thumb, and achieved a respectability he had never aspired to in the slums of Barminster.

Chapter Twenty-five

Having paid her two weeks' rent in advance, Liz moved into a room on the second floor of the shabby house in Wellington Road. At first the landlady had looked at her askance, and her whispered enquiries about the room had been answered abruptly, almost rudely. Then the woman had realized that the young girl with the bruised, swollen face was a runaway wife, not a street-walker who had taken a beating from a dissatisfied customer, and had agreed to let her have the room. Mrs Smith had high principles; she accepted no sailors and no prostitutes in her boarding house.

Liz looked round the dingy room. It contained a narrow bed, a chair with a sagging seat and a cushion flattened by much use, a chest of drawers with one handle missing, and a wardrobe. An oil-lamp provided light. The fireplace looked as if it had not seen a burning ember in a decade, but there was a bucket of coal on the hearth; she would have to pay extra for more coal when it was required. There was a bracket on the grate with a kettle, so at least, if she lighted the fire, she would be able to make herself a cup of tea – if she had had a teapot, a cup, tealeaves, and milk.

Liz put her bag on the bed, got out her soap and towel, and walked down the corridor to the bathroom. As she returned, feeling much better for having washed and attended to her toilet, the door of one of the other bedrooms flew open and a fat woman with brassy yellow hair came out and barred her way.

'Aha! You'll be the new one in number four!' she said,

looking at Liz closely in the dim light. 'What happened to your face? Boyfriend catch you with another man?'

'No! I'm a married woman –' Liz whispered.

'Husband beat you up?'

'No – please – let me pass –'

'Had your supper?'

'No –'

'Then you better come with me, I'm just going down to the café. Get your coat, it's cold out.'

Liz suddenly realized that she was really very hungry. This woman was not the companion she would have chosen, but she was good-natured and friendly. It was hard to judge her age, but she was older than Liz, though not above forty, and was dressed in brightly coloured, shabby clothes, with a lot of bright, brassy jewellery hung from her ears, and round her neck and wrists. Her plump cheeks were highly coloured, and even Liz, with her unsophisticated eyes, could see that the colour was painted on. However, to Liz, the friendly twinkle in her eye was like a lamp on a dark night.

'Just a minute,' she whispered and hurried into her room. She rummaged in her bag for the wad of notes, and slipped them into her bodice. She was not going to risk losing them, and there was no lock on the door. She had a small sum in her pocket – enough, she thought, for supper. Throwing her warm shawl round her shoulders, she rejoined the fat woman on the landing.

'Me name's Jane Pottle, but everyone calls me Pots,' she was informed cheerfully as they went down the stairs.

'I'm Liz – Elizabeth Fuller,' Liz returned.

'Why are you whispering, Liz? Lost your voice?'

'Yes.'

'Hmm . . . Well, I talk enough for two, so that's no problem,' Pots laughed. 'Come on, this way.'

The café was crowded, but they found two seats with a

number of young women who knew Pots, and welcomed Liz to their group, looking curiously at her swollen, bruised face, but making no comment. Soon Liz was tucking into a heaped plate of stewed lamb with dumplings, potatoes, and cabbage. The conversation flowed cheerfully around her, most of it about their friends and their work. She gathered that they all worked together in a laundry somewhere nearby. She sat quietly, half-listening to their voices, but her mind constantly flying back to her own problems.

Would Henry Willoughby have missed her by now and gone down to the cottage to investigate? Would he go in and find the body of Joe Spragg? Edward was not due home until tomorrow. Would Henry send him a telegram and call him back? *Oh, Edward – when will I see you again?* If only it were possible to turn the clock back, if only she had stayed at the farm this morning to help Mrs Willoughby instead of going to the cottage . . .

Suddenly Liz was aware that someone had spoken to her and was awaiting a reply. They were all looking at her expectantly. She felt her colour rise as their eyes all remained on her bruised face.

'I'm sorry – I didn't hear what you said,' she whispered.

'I wondered if you were looking for a job,' a woman they called Joan asked.

'Yes, I am.'

'Well, we'll be a girl short on the line tomorrow – Mary's gone off to London with her feller – so if you come in with Pots in the morning, happen you'll get her place.'

'Oh – thanks, I'll do that.' Liz wondered if she would be well enough tomorrow to try for the job. The kick Joe had landed on her hip was very painful, and her bruised limbs were getting stiff and sore. 'Thanks for telling me.'

When the meal was over the others went off to a public house, but Liz walked back to the boarding house in Wellington Road. She let herself in with the key Mrs Smith had given her. She opened her bag to find her nightgown, and stared at the contents in dismay.

Someone had been in and searched her bag. Looking at the bed she realized that someone had also searched under the pillows and the mattress. There was nothing missing, for there had been nothing worth stealing, as she had taken her money with her. The envelope containing her birth certificate and marriage licence was still there, although she was certain that it had been opened and examined – the flap was loose, and she had left it tucked in.

Was that why Pots had invited her out to supper – so that the way would be clear for someone to come in and rob her? Or had it been the landlady? Surely she could trust Mrs Smith?

No, she could not trust anyone. And now someone knew her real name and identity. If the murder was in the newspapers tomorrow the thief could go to the police and probably claim a reward. On the other hand, the name on the marriage licence would not mean anything to him – or her, and might be forgotten in the failure to discover ready cash.

Liz went to bed, but it was some hours before she slept. Her face hurt; her bruised hip ached; and her heart was broken. She wept into the pillow but found no solace there. All she wanted was the haven of Edward's arms, but that consolation was forfeit. He did not deserve a murderess for a wife.

She was awakened abruptly before daylight by a sharp rap on the door.

'Hey, Liz! If you want that job, you'd better get a move on!' Pots shouted. 'Breakfast in ten minutes!'

Liz crawled out of bed, every movement hurting. A glance in the mirror revealed that her face looked as if she had fought several rounds in the boxing ring. She made a hasty toilet, pulled on her clothes, again concealing her money in her bodice, and hurried downstairs for her breakfast.

Pots had saved her a place at the table, where eight other lodgers were already eating their breakfast. It was half past six.

Mrs Smith placed a large plateful of porridge in front of her.

'Help yourself to milk and sugar, duckie,' she said. The porridge was hot and lumpy, but what it lacked in quality it made up in quantity.

'That bloke sure made a mess of your face,' Pots remarked, handing her the sugar. 'But don't worry, if he comes here looking for you he'll get a flea in his ear.'

Liz looked shyly round at the other lodgers, mainly working-class men, middle-aged, busy with their food. There was one young man, and a woman of about fifty with grey hair and an air of defeat. Had one of these people been through her dressing case – searched her dresses, handled her underclothes?

Breakfast over, she put her shawl round her shoulders, wishing she had brought a warm coat, and followed Pots out into the street. Five minutes' brisk walking brought them to the Portsmouth Sunshine Laundry premises. There was nothing very sunny about the place; inside the door the steamy heat, and the soapsuds smell, hit them like a hot, damp blanket. Pots took her to the dingy office and introduced her to the foreman, a short, bald man of about forty, who looked at Liz critically.

'You don't look strong enough to do a day's bloody work, and what the hell happened to your bloody face?' he demanded.

'Oh – I –' Liz began self-consciously in a whisper, but Pots came to her rescue.

'Never mind her face, Albert – some man beat her up, but that's no business of yourn! And she ain't got no voice. Give the girl a chance. You can always turn her off if she can't do the job.'

314

'All right, Pots – when she's signed on, you can show her the bloody ropes. But you'll have to keep up with the bloody line, miss, or you'll be out as bloody fast as you're bloody in!'

The preliminaries sorted out, Liz found herself part of a long line of girls folding and sorting linen for the ironing-presses. At first she had difficulty keeping pace with the other girls, because her arms and shoulders were stiff from yesterday's beating, but soon she got into the swing of it, the stiffness wore off, and she found that it was not by any means as hard as her work in the hospital had been. At twelve the bell rang, everyone stopped work and went out to a stall at the end of the road where a woman was selling hot, greasy pies. Pots bought three and ate them noisily; Liz bought one, and had trouble getting it down. Hot sweet tea in thick mugs completed the meal, then it was back to the factory and back to work. There was a ten-minute break for more tea at three-thirty, and the bell finally rang for the end of the working day at six. By that time Liz was exhausted.

As she wearily trailed back to the lodgings they passed a newspaper-boy at the crossroads, crying the headlines at the top of his voice. She bought a paper.

'Never read papers, meself,' Pots remarked 'Magazines, sometimes, but I'm not interested in politics and all that.'

'I wanted the paper to line the drawers in my room,' Liz lied. When she got back to her room she searched the paper, but there was no mention of the murder in Honey Beck Bay.

On Friday Edward left London on an early train and arrived in Barminster before nine o'clock. John Oatis had returned on Wednesday evening, immediately after the reading of the wills. Gervaise, Lord Farlington, had refused to make one, declaring that the matter could wait until he was married and had a family. His parents had left their entire

315

fortunes to him, but as he had predeceased them their estate went to their nephew Edward Clayton. Being Gervaise's only cousin and consequently his next-of-kin, Edward also inherited his estate as well as his title; the outcome of all this was sufficient work to keep the solicitors occupied for some time.

Edward was now a very wealthy man, and the heir to the Clayton estate. His circumstances had changed dramatically since the day he had left Barminster Military Hospital in a second-hand wheelchair.

Harriet also left London on an early train, but she went north, to resume her studies in Edinburgh. She asked Edward to give her love to Liz, and let her know if there was anything she could do for either of them.

'I expect to be in Barminster some time during the Christmas break, and I'll see her then, if not before,' she said.

'Oh?' Edward was surprised. 'I rather think Sir Rupert will be spending Christmas at the house in Eaton Square. I've not made any plans yet, but we may be there too.'

Harriet turned her face away and needlessly checked the catch on her small overnight suitcase. Edward was amused to see that the colour had risen in her cheeks.

'Yes, I'll be with him for Christmas Day, of course, but I – er – I have someone else to see in Barminster.'

'Ah! Then I'll make sure John is not too heavily occupied with my affairs over the break!'

John Oatis was waiting for Edward at the Barminster station. He carried the luggage as Edward swung himself along on his crutch to the platform for the branch line to Southampton, which stopped at Forestwidden Halt.

'A bit different to the first journey you made in this direction, Edward! I mean, Lord Farlington –'

'For heaven's sake, John – I've been Edward to you for over eighteen months, there's no need to stand on ceremony now!' Edward said irritably as they took their places in the well-upholstered seats of a first-class carriage. 'Oh, sorry, John – I'm out of sorts this morning, with the early start, and one thing and another! It's damn good of you to come with me, I couldn't have managed my luggage and these boxes of documents I have to study without your help.'

'Don't worry about me, old man,' John said cheerfully. 'We've still got a lot of bits and pieces to discuss, and we might as well do it at the cottage as at my office. Though I can't think what you're worrying about, with the Clayton estate behind you, and a fine new handle to your name!'

Edward grimaced wryly.

'Well, to start with, I've been on my feet most of the time for the last couple of days, walked miles, and my peg-leg is chafing abominably! It'll be a relief to get it off and have Liz dress the blisters. Then there's that Clayton estate – I know nothing about managing an estate, and I find the prospect daunting, to say the least. My uncle, I gather, has been looking after it for the last few years, with the help of George Steadman. Now I've got to get in and learn all about the management side of it. But first I've got to break the news to Liz. The whole business is going to be a terrible shock to her, and I'm afraid she may take fright at the prospect of meeting Sir Rupert. She's still very shy of meeting strangers – she has no self-confidence at all. Heavens knows how she would cope if I wasn't around to look after her. I just hope that she hasn't seen the newspapers before I get home.'

'Is it likely?'

'I don't think so. Not unless Henry Willoughby's been into the village and brought them home. But I daren't delay my return any longer.'

At Forestwidden Halt there was a horse and trap waiting hopefully for custom. Edward and John got in and instructed the driver to take them to Honey Beck Bay. He was reluctant to take his vehicle down the cart track after the recent rains, until Edward produced a sovereign from his pocket, and then he went willingly enough.

'Wait here, until I find my wife. She may be at the farm, in which case I'll want you to take me back there,' Edward told him when they reached the cottage. He had expected to find Liz waiting eagerly for his return, but there was no sign of her. The door and the windows were all closed. The cottage looked deserted.

He swung himself to the ground and John passed him his crutch, and followed him to the cottage. Edward unlocked the door and went inside; there was an unpleasant smell about the place. The first thing that caught his eye was the empty whisky bottle on the floor under the table. He picked it up, puzzled, and looked round the room.

'Good heavens, what the hell's been going on here?' he exclaimed, the colour draining from his face.

Every drawer was open; every cupboard door was ajar. There was a general untidiness everywhere, which dismayed him; he couldn't imagine Liz leaving her home like this. He went into the kitchen, where the window was open, and a large footprint, like that of a hob-nailed boot, was imprinted on the windowsill.

'Liz! Liz!' he cried urgently. 'Where are you?'

There was no answer.

John had gone into the bedroom; now he called.

'Edward! Come here – what do you make of this?'

The unpleasant smell was stonger in here. It was whisky, and something else – something unclean. Edward stood at the door, staring at the room in horrified silence.

Here, also, the drawers and cupboard doors were all half-open, the contents thrown haphazardly on the floor as if the room had been hastily searched. The brightly coloured patchwork quilt of which Liz had been so proud was lying beside the bed, and her old black dress lay on the floor near the dressing-table, jumbled up with some dirty workman's clothes. But most disturbing of all, the middle of the bed was disfigured with a huge bloodstain about which flies were buzzing in the still air. Edward realized that the unpleasant smell in the cottage came from that blood.

'My God!' he cried. 'She's been murdered!'

The trap-driver was despatched to Forestwidden to fetch the police, but first he called at the farm on the way with a message for Henry Willoughby to go immediately to the cottage. Henry found Edward distraught.

'Someone's broken in and murdered Liz,' Edward told him brokenly as he came into the cottage.

'Wait a minute, Edward,' said John, who had been examining the clothes on the floor in the bedroom. 'There might be another explanation. See this shirt – I don't know who wore it, but he didn't believe in washing – it stinks. It's got a hole here, soaked in blood. And the waistcoat. There's a little blood on the dress, but not much. I think it was someone else who was wounded, not Liz.'

He lifted the patchwork quilt off the floor, underneath which was another bloodstain. As he moved the quilt the knife, which had been hidden in the folds, fell out.

'That's Liz's pruning knife!' Edward exclaimed. 'And look – there's blood on the blade – it's been used for a weapon.'

John had gone into the bathroom.

'Come and look at this. There's blood on the sink, and someone has been to the first-aid box.'

Edward joined him, and stared at the mess.

'Liz would never have left the place in a state like this,' he said finally. 'Whoever used those bandages, it was not my wife!'

'And whoever it was,' John pointed out, 'he managed to take himself off, despite the loss of blood.'

'You'd better not touch anything else until that constable

arrives,' Henry advised. 'I collected a newspaper from the village yesterday, Edward; it gave details of the Clayton tragedy. I gather that you're now Lord Farlington. I don't know if I should offer you congratulations or commiserations.'

'Goddamnit, I don't want to hear one word about that until this mystery's cleared up and I've found Liz!' Edward exploded. 'I should never have left her here alone – oh, God! Where is she? Is she injured – surely no one man could have lost all that blood and walked out of here unaided?'

'It's not your fault – it's mine,' Henry said heavily, sitting down at the table. 'When she went off yesterday, I thought she'd gone to Barminster to see Mr Oatis, then when she didn't return I assumed she waited to meet you. I should have known she wouldn't disappear without a word, and raised the alarm then.'

'Look here, it's no good your sitting around brooding,' John told them sharply. 'Have you looked about outside? There might be something out there to tell us what happened. Edward, she couldn't be in the shed, could she?'

They all went out to look.

'She's not here,' Edward said, and then he noticed the upturned flowerpot in the wheelbarrow. Liz was always very particular about the pots; they were kept on a shelf by the window. He looked under the pot, and found her key.

'She locked the house when she left it,' he said, 'so she – wait a minute.' He went back to the bedroom. Her dressing-case was missing, and some of her clothes.

'It looks as if she's run away,' he said bleakly. 'Oh, Liz – where are you? I'll not rest until you're found.'

Two policemen arrived and searched the cottage from end to end. They examined every bloodstained item, paying particular attention to the knife, and they made copious notes,

320

but they were unable to come up with anything more significant than the obvious fact that there had been an unknown man there, he had apparently been stabbed, and he, and Lady Farlington, were both missing.

A gang of volunteers spent several days searching the fields and the forest, but nothing and no-one was found. Edward was terrified that they might find Liz's body somewhere in a ditch, or in a shallow grave under the trees. But still there was no sign of her, and no word. He was almost insane with worry.

Enquiries in the village brought to light the story of the stranger who had arrived at the inn late on Thursday evening. He had apparently missed the Barminster train, because several other passengers were sure they would have seen him; but he could have been among a group of seamen who had been on the Southampton train. They had sailed for the West Indies on the morning tide, and it was possible that he sailed with them . . .

Further enquiries, suggested by Edward, disclosed that Joe Spragg had disappeared from Barminster.

The local newspaper ran a sensational story about the strange happenings at Honey Beck Bay, but with nothing but a few bloodstains and a torn shirt and waistcoat for evidence interest soon died away. The disappearance of Lady Farlington was mentioned in the national press, but she was not a criminal, nor a celebrated figure, and received only one short paragraph. After all, women ran away from their husbands every day; it was hardly news.

Edward cleaned up the cottage with Mrs Willoughby's assistance and returned to Barminster. He could not bear to remain in the cottage without Liz. He would not find her by sitting in the old rocking-chair brooding.

Chapter Twenty-six

Gradually the swelling on Liz's eye and cheek subsided and the bruises faded. The work in the laundry was tiring, and each day she went back to Wellington Road with an aching back and feet swollen from standing for long hours. She bought the newspapers and scanned them for a report of the murder at Honey Beck Bay, but to her surprise and relief she found no mention of it. As a sensational story of this kind usually made banner headlines she was puzzled; it was impossible that Joe's body had not been found. A brief paragraph reporting the disappearance of Lady Farlington held no interest for her, and she did not even bother to read past the headlines. Lady Farlington meant nothing to her.

She worked five and a half days each week, having Saturday afternoon and Sunday to herself. Most evenings she went to the café with Pots and her friends, but sometimes she just had a sandwich and an apple in her room. Mrs Smith allowed them to make tea in the kitchen so long as they left it clean and deposited a few pence in the jam jar on the shelf to cover the cost of the tea and milk. There was always a cheerful fire in the sitting-room the guests shared, and the other lodgers took little notice of her sitting in the corner reading. There was no shortage of reading matter; the bookshelves were crammed with dog-eared books that had been abandoned by past lodgers.

She still did not know who had tried to rob her. As time passed she almost forgot about the incident, but always kept her money safe in her bodice. With the landlady's permission she had a firm lock with a key fitted to her door, but as she had to leave the spare key with Mrs Smith so that she could clean the room occasionally – though not very often – she still felt that her belongings were insecure.

As winter approached, and the sea mist crept over Portsmouth in the mornings, she had to spend some of her precious money on a warm woollen skirt, and a coat. She bought it second-hand, a thick tweed overcoat several sizes too big. Pots laughed when she saw it.

'Heck, Liz – there's room in that coat for you and me both!' she joked.

'It's warm, and it was cheap,' Liz whispered.

'Well, when you've finished with it we can put it up in the yard for a marquee, and hold a party in it!'

One of the girls in the wash-tub area developed a whitlow on her finger, and Albert, the foreman, asked Liz to change places with her until it healed.

'Check these bloody sheets for stains and scrub them with the bloody brush before they go into the bloody tub,' he directed.

Now Liz's hands were in hot soapy water all day, and the washing soda made them red and sore, but the wages were slightly higher, and she saved a little each week. When the girl's whitlow recovered she demanded her job back, and Liz was glad to relinquish it.

Christmas was approaching. When Liz thought back to last Christmas, when she and Edward were so happy together in Honey Beck Cottage, she could have wept. She wondered where he was, and what he was doing. He had a fine family now; that much she had gathered from Joe Spragg's vicious diatribe. Joe had said that his father had been disowned by the family for marrying beneath him; if she was to return, no doubt they would disown Edward too. She wondered if he was with the woman Joe had talked about, or with his cousin Harriet. She missed him every minute of the day and night. But she did not dare to contact him, even had she known where to find him, because she was sure the police would still be searching for her. Where murder was concerned they would not give up so soon.

Edward was spending most of his time in London with his grandfather, who had been outraged when he was told that his granddaughter-in-law had run away, taking it as a personal insult.

'Dammit, man, why would the woman do that?' he snorted when Edward returned to London alone and had to explain her absence. 'Did you beat her or something?'

'Good God, no!' Edward exclaimed. 'I wouldn't hurt her for the world – I love her, Grandfather! I think – well, you might as well know the truth. I think she may have tried to kill her step-father.'

'She what?'

Edward told him what he had found at the cottage. In telling him about Joe Spragg, he had to tell Sir Rupert the whole story, starting with how he had married the mute skivvy in the hospital solely in order to get himself discharged.

'At the time it never occurred to me that I might fall in love with her, but now – well, I can't live without her. I've got to find her!'

His grandfather heard him out without speaking, then rang for Beale and told him to bring in the brandy decanter.

'We both need it, my boy,' he said, pouring the brandy into two crystal glasses. 'Frankly, Edward, it sounds as if she married you for your money, and I can't help thinking that you may be better off without her.'

'My money!' Edward exclaimed. 'I had nothing but my pension. It seemed more likely she would have to support me than t'other way around! I was more dead than alive; it was only her nursing that kept me going until Old Meg turned up and worked her miracle cure.'

'I look forward to meeting this paragon!' Sir Rupert said. 'I don't give a damn who she is or where she came from. This family has suffered far too much already from stiff-necked snobbery.'

'I shan't rest until I find her,' Edward declared. 'I'm going to buy one of those horseless carriages and scour the countryside until I find her. Someone must have seen her. She didn't go to the village or the railway station, that's quite clear from the police enquiries, so she must have gone somewhere on foot.'

'Well, if you get yourself a horseless carriage don't expect me to set foot in it!' Sir Rupert told him. 'Inventions of the devil. They should never have repealed the red-flag law!'

'The time will come when there won't be a horsedrawn carriage in London – everybody will travel in automobiles,' Edward prophesied.

'Balderdash!' Sir Rupert snorted.

Edward bought himself an automobile; it was easier for him to manage than a horse and trap. He spent days driving round the villages and hamlets asking if anyone had seen his wife. He had a photograph of her, taken when they were in London, and he went into every hotel, public house, and village shop, showing it to the staff and asking if they remembered seeing the girl.

In one shop, in a small country village some miles from Forestwidden, the woman behind the counter stared at the photograph, and told him sharply that she had never seen the girl, and had no time to stand looking at photographs.

'I've had hundreds of customers since the beginning of October, sir. I doubt if I would remember if I had seen her. You're wasting your time here.'

When Edward left she stared after him thoughtfully. Jim Peters, the lad who worked at the farm, came in for some candles for Mrs Jones.

'Remember that girl you gave a ride to Portsmouth, Jim?' she remarked.

'The one with the punched-up face? I'm not likely to forget her, poor little beggar,' Jim said.

'Well, a bloke's been in asking about her, saying he's her husband. He looks a lot older than she is, grey hair, got a peg-leg; been in the wars, by the look of it.'

'That's no excuse for beating the poor girl up. Peg-leg or otherwise, I'd like the opportunity to tell him what I think of him! I hope you didn't tell him I took her to Portsmouth?'

'No, I didn't. He must be a brute. I wonder what happened to her?'

'I just hope she found somewhere safe to go. I felt bad about leaving her there alone. But what else could I have done?'

'Nothing, Jim. She's not your responsibility. Now, those candles; how many does Mrs Jones want?'

At the Portsmouth Sunshine Laundry they gave the girls two days off, Christmas and Boxing Day. Unpaid, of course; generosity could only go so far! Liz and Pots went to church on Christmas morning and sang carols with the good citizens of the city. Most of the lodgers at Mrs Smith's boarding house had families to visit for the day, but the remainder clubbed together and bought a goose which Mrs Smith cooked for them and served up with all the trimmings, including a very fine Christmas pudding complete with flaming brandy and a sprig of holly. Pots contributed a bottle of sherry, and they had to put Mrs Wilson, the other female lodger, to bed afterwards; she was unused to wine, and before she fell asleep at the table had sung them all twenty verses of 'On Ilkley Moor B'aht 'At'. Liz and Pots helped Mrs Smith wash up, and then Liz went to her room while Pots went out to meet some of the girls from the laundry to continue the celebrations. She got back very late and very tipsy.

Despite the good food she had eaten, and the glass of sherry, Liz was very depressed. She sat in her room, and cried bitter tears. How she missed Edward! What was he doing now? Who was he with? If only she could see him!

For there was something she wanted to tell him. She was going to need the extra inches in that coat; she was expecting a baby. She had known for several weeks now, and her clothes were getting tight. She would have to keep the secret at the laundry as long as possible, for they would probably give her the sack when they knew; pregnant women were not able to do the heavy work, and there were always plenty of girls ready to fill their places.

Would Mrs Smith let her stay when she knew that Liz was pregnant? And how would she pay the rent for her room? She would need every penny of that precious hoard she kept in her bodice.

Edward was with his grandfather at Eaton Square. Harriet was home for the holiday, too. The cook provided a splendid meal for them on Christmas Day, but the atmosphere in the house was far from cheerful. Edward was still searching for Liz, and despite Harriet's and Sir Rupert's efforts he could not shake off his depression.

In the afternoon he took himself for a walk through the streets of London, thinking of the time he and Liz had stayed here while he had his peg-leg fitted and she tried to educate herself by visiting all the art galleries and museums. He stood outside the National Gallery and remembered the way she had laughed at the pigeons thronging the steps, moving only when they were in danger of being trampled. How happy they had been in their newly discovered love!

He limped down to the Embankment, and sat on a seat overlooking the river. The Thames was grey and sluggish today. A young woman walked past pushing a pram in which sat a red-cheeked child. He watched her out of sight, almost in tears with his longing for his darling, his lost girl.

'If things had been different, one day we might have been pushing a pram down this pavement,' he thought.

A tramp approached, staring at him.

'Spare a coin for an old soldier, squire?' begged the man, putting on a pathetic expression.

Edward felt in his pockets, and pulled out a handful of coins.

'Take these, old fellow, and buy yourself a Christmas dinner,' he said, dropping the coins into the man's hand. The tramp thanked him jubilantly, and went off to the nearest pub, where he drank himself insensible before the night was out.

On Boxing Day Harriet took the train to Barminster, where John Oatis was waiting at the station.

'My dear!' he cried, running to meet her as she came through the barrier. 'I was afraid you might not come! How well you look! Life in Edinburgh must suit you – how are you getting on? And how are Edward and your grandfather? How long can you stay?'

'Oh, John – one question at a time!' Harriet laughed, taking his large square hand in her firm, capable one. 'Edinburgh's fine, I'm getting on splendidly. I can stay for two days, I'm booked into the Golden Eagle. Grandfather is well. And Edward – he's in a terrible state, fading away before our eyes. He's getting so thin, he's nearly as gaunt as he was when he left the hospital. I wish to heaven I could think of a way to help him, but I can't.'

'Oh, Lord – if we could only find poor Liz!' John groaned, running a hand though his rumpled hair. 'But let's forget that for now, and make the most of our two days. I must find a cab – my family are expecting you for luncheon.

Mother has been baking for days, and there's enough food in the house to feed an army. I hope you're hungry!'

They spent two happy days together, but the shadow of the lost girl hung over them, never far from their thoughts. On the second day John took Harriet for a walk through the old town, and showed her a house he was thinking of buying.

'I'm very comfortable at home with my parents, but I think it's time I became independent,' he told her. 'I'm doing well in the practice, too busy if anything! I do all Edward's work in Barminster, and that takes up quite a time nowadays, so I should be able to afford the house. What do you think of it, Harriet?'

Harriet met his eyes squarely. She was as tall as John, and neither had to look up to nor down on the other; but her eyes were troubled as they met his.

'John, it's a very nice house, and I'm sure you would be very comfortable there, but why ask my opinion? It's a matter for you to decide, and you alone.'

John took her hand and held it firmly.

'I hope you will share it with me, Harriet. I want you to be my wife.'

'Oh, John! You don't understand, do you?' Her colour had risen, and her green eyes flashed. She took a deep breath. 'I'm working hard at my studies – I mean to qualify and practise as a doctor! I'm not going to drop everything to stay at home cooking and cleaning. I fought too hard for my independence to give it up so soon. That isn't the life I want!' She turned away from him. 'I thought you, of all people, understood. But you seem to be as blind as the rest of them. I don't want to turn myself into a docile little wife. I want to live my own life without having to answer to anybody!'

John looked hurt and bewildered.

'But I love you! I want you to marry me – not tomorrow,

but when you finish your training, and I want you to do what *you* want – if that's a career as a doctor, go ahead! I love you as you are, darling, the last thing I intend to do is change you into a housemaid!'

'You say that now, but I know what would happen. The moment we're married you'll want me at your beck and call, little more than a housekeeper – no, John, that's not the life for me!'

'You don't love me –'

'I didn't say that! But I'm not going to spend the rest of my life being dictated to – as I find all my married friends are!'

John glared at her; her green eyes flashed as she glared back.

'Then what do you want, Harriet? What am I to you? A friend?'

'You *are* my friend –'

'I damn well am not!' John said savagely. 'I love you, I want to live with you and take you into my bed! If you don't understand that you're not the woman I thought you were! I have no intention of hanging about for the next ten years like an obedient lap-dog waiting for you to work out your independence. I don't give a damn if you have your own career, you can work in the hospital or join a practice in town, or do whatever you want so long as you marry me and live with me! Dammit, woman – I'm not going to give up being a solicitor because I'm taking a wife, so why should you give up doctoring?'

Harriet's anger evaporated, and she smiled.

'I'll marry you as soon as I'm qualified. So long as you understand. Hey – where are you going?' For John had pushed open the gate and was on his way up the path to the front door of the house. He looked back over his shoulder and grinned.

'I promised to let them have my decision today. I'm just

going to give them the cheque – it's in my pocket. Come on, you might as well see over the house you've talked me into buying for you!'

The Portsmouth Sunshine Laundry reopened and the girls were back at work. Most of them were rather subdued after two days of overeating and overdrinking; several girls had not turned up at all, and Albert was ranting and raving about their truancy.

'How the hell am I supposed to make these bloody deliveries if there's no-one to check the bloody laundry books? I told the governor it was a mistake to give them a bloody holiday on bloody Boxing Day! Hey you, Liz Fuller – you look as if you can read and write – come into the bloody packing room and check the bloody books against the linen being returned.'

So Liz was moved again, and this time for the better. She spent the day checking the laundry-marks for Joan to make up the parcels to be returned. It was almost time for the knocking-off whistle to blow when she came to a book that had a familiar name in it.

Mrs Agnes Spragg, 17 Harcourt Avenue, Marchbanks.

Liz stared at the book in astonishment.

Could there be *two* Mrs Agnes Spraggs?

And what could her mother be doing in Marchbanks? She had never been there, but she knew of the area; to the west of the city itself, it was one of the better suburbs. No, it could not possibly be her mother. She looked at the items set out in the week's collection.

Sheets, four; pillowcases, four; towels, tablecloths, lady's underwear, boy's underwear, boy's socks, boy's shirts – this appeared to come from a household where there was one woman and several boys. Her mother and her three young half-brothers? Was it possible?

The following day the missing girl returned to work in the packing room and Liz was relegated to the line again. The weather had turned bitterly cold and miserable, and for two weekends her Sundays off were so wet she hardly left the lodging house. But then there was a bright, fresh Sunday morning when it would be a pleasure to be out of doors. She got up early, and set out for Marchbanks. The first part of the journey was easy; she travelled by tram half the way, then got out and walked.

She was glad of her warm coat, as the wind was fresh, coming in from the sea, and without the thick tweed she would have been very cold. She set her face towards the distant line of low hills and enjoyed the brisk exercise. A wintry sun shone out of a blue sky. There were not very many people about, and as she approached the select residential area the few pedestrians looked curiously at the young woman in the shabby, oversized tweed coat.

Liz had no intention of calling on her mother. She just wanted to see the house, and hoped, perhaps, to catch a glimpse of her through a window, if she lived here, which Liz was still very doubtful about. She was sure that her mother could not afford to rent so much as one room in this area, and she would need several rooms to make a home for four of them. It did not look like the sort of district where there would be rooms to let, anyway. Good solid brick houses, each with its own tidy garden; family homes, not lodging houses.

Liz had nothing else to do today, so she could take her time, and get back to Wellington Road to go out for supper with Pots. The fresh air, after the thick damp atmosphere in the laundry all week, would do her good. In her pocket she had a couple of buns bought yesterday from the baker in Wellington Road; she would find somewhere to sit and eat them. Perhaps there would be a park in Marchbanks? Somewhere she could sit and watch the fashionably dressed residents on their Sunday afternoon walks.

Presently she found a long street of shops, and spent half an hour looking in the windows, dawdling along, wondering how she was to find Harcourt Avenue. She came to an estate agent's office, and in the window was a street map of Marchbanks. After a brief search she identified Harcourt Avenue, just a short distance from where she stood; on the other side of the Municipal Park, in fact.

A policeman strolled past, and she thought he looked at her suspiciously. She stopped dawdling, and walked hurriedly towards the the park, sure he was watching her. The memory of Joe Spragg's body lying under the colourful patchwork quilt leapt into her mind and she almost took to her heels. Had the policeman guessed she was Elizabeth Clayton, the woman who had murdered her step-father with a pruning knife three months ago? He might have recognized her description, which surely must have been circulated to the police stations on the south coast. At the entrace to the park she stopped and glanced back over her shoulder; the policeman was walking away down the road, taking no notice of her or anything else. She breathed a sigh of relief and walked into the park.

Just inside the gates two boys were arguing fiercely over a kite. There seemed to be some debate over whose turn it was to raise it. They were dressed alike in brown tweed knickerbockers and matching jackets, with brown corduroy caps pulled down over their ears to protect them from the biting wind. A third boy, a little younger, stood nearby, looking bored. Liz walked round the children, wondering which of the houses she could see at the other end of the park was Number 17, Harcourt Avenue.

There was a pond in the park, quite a large one, well populated with mallard ducks, who were busily dabbling about among the reeds, looking for food. Liz began to feel a little tired and hungry. She had walked a long way. She

333

sat on a bench near the pond, turned up the collar of her coat against the wind, took the buns out of her pocket and began to eat, idly watching the ducks.

The third boy, the youngest of the three, wandered past, looking at her closely. Now the ducks, wise in the ways of park-walkers, were crowding round Liz hoping for crumbs from the buns, and she watched them, smiling to herself, as they waddled about hopefully within inches of her feet. She did not see the boy suddenly turn and run off; if she had, she would not have taken any notice. Why should she? The world was full of small boys.

Chapter Twenty-seven

Edward and Sir Rupert were both delighted that Harriet had accepted John, and had duly portrayed suitable surprise when she sprang her news on them on her return from Barminster. They had not been surprised that John had put the question to her, but they *had* been surprised that their independent Harriet had accepted him!

'That should put an end to all this doctoring nonsense,' Sir Rupert remarked with satisfaction.

'Indeed it will not!' Harriet told him with spirit. 'We'll be married after I qualify, and I intend to work at the Barminster Hospital, if they'll have me!'

'Good heavens!' Sir Rupert exclaimed in horror. 'If I'm run over in the street I might find you examining me without my trousers!'

'I doubt it. I intend to specialize in pediatric cases,' Harriet informed him loftily, and stalked off to her room. Sir Rupert despatched Beale to fetch the dictionary. He had not come across that word before, but was reassured when he had looked it up; at least it sounded more suitable for a lady of quality, and his niece in particular, than general practice.

When the holidays were over, Edward drove down to Forestwidden and called on Henry and Ada Willoughby. They made him more than welcome, but had to tell him they had heard nothing from Liz. He had been hoping that she might have sent them a Christmas card.

'I light the fire in the cottage every week to keep the

place aired,' Ada told him. 'It's ready for you to come back any time.'

The cart track was too rutted for the car to negotiate after the rain, so Henry harnessed up old Daisy in the trap, and drove Edward down to Honey Beck Cottage. He went in with a heavy heart. Ada had cleaned every corner, there was no trace of the horror that had taken place here; she had even managed to clean and repair the patchwork quilt, but the cottage was full of ghosts for Edward. It was not the same without Liz. He looked round, made sure that all was well and the winter storms had done no damage, and left. Unless he found Liz, he never wanted to see the cottage again.

He was staying overnight at the Golden Eagle, and had time to call into John's office to take him out for a meal. After congratulating him on his engagement, he asked John if he had heard from Agnes Spragg lately. Edward had tried to persuade Mrs Spragg to move into a house on one of the Clayton properties, but she said she would rather rent a house in Portsmouth.

'It's home ground to me, sir; I'd rather stay in Pompey than try to settle somewhere new,' she said. 'Then there's the boys; I'd like them to go to school in Portsmouth.' A house had been found and furnished, and the boys had been enrolled at a good school, where they were doing surprisingly well, considering that in Barminster they constantly played truant.

'I had a card from Mrs Spragg at Christmas, but she didn't say much,' Edward told John now. 'I don't suppose you've heard from her?'

'Just a card, nothing more,' John said. 'She hasn't heard from Liz, I suppose?'

'I'm sure she would have written if she had any news,' Edward said. But later, back in London, he began to wonder; if Liz had been in touch, and asked her mother not to mention it, would Agnes let him know? Of course, he would know immediately if they were face to face; but if it was a matter of not telling him it might be different.

One Sunday morning in mid-January he woke in Eaton Square very early, more depressed than ever. It was three and a half months since Liz had disappeared and he had no more idea now about where she could have gone than he'd had the day she vanished. It would not be daylight for some time yet, but he could not sleep; he would lie here for the next two hours or more, torturing himself about his lost wife. Surely there must be something he could do? Somewhere he had not yet enquired ... Or was she lying out there in the forest, dead under a mantle of leaves ...

With an oath, he leapt out of bed, throwing back the bedclothes as if they burned him. Not sure what he was going to do, he shaved, washed and dressed, fitting his peg-leg with impatient hands. He could not lie there worrying – the uncertainty was driving him mad! There was no-one about downstairs; the servants would not stir for another hour. He left a note on the table in the hall, and crept out of the sleeping house. Ten minutes later he was recklessly accelerating out of the city at a speed of nearly twenty-two miles per hour, ignoring the speed limit as he headed for the south coast. When he left the city streetlamps behind he had to slow down, for his eyes could scarcely pierce the darkness just before the dawn. He was glad of his windproof leather coat; unprotected by a windscreen, the drivers of the sports cars imported from the Continent were at the mercy of the weather. Just where he was going he did not know; he just had to go somewhere.

Daylight brought a fresh, bright morning. Edward called into a country hotel and ordered breakfast. When it was served he hardly touched it, his appetite had vanished. He sat over his coffee, brooding. This was crazy, aimlessly tacking backwards and forwards around the Great Forest and the South Downs. He caught sight of himself in a mirror and stared; he was as thin as a rake and his eyes looked burned out, great dark caverns in that gaunt face. No wonder Harriet and his grandfather worried. He looked like a man with a curse on him.

It was hopeless. He would never find her this way. He paid for his breakfast and went back to his automobile.

He nearly turned the vehicle round to drive back to London, but decided that now he was half-way there he would drive on and visit Agnes Spragg in Portsmouth. After all, it would only be polite to call on his mother-in-law and see that she was settled in the new house. The house was rented on a long lease, but if she was really satisfied he might consider buying it for her.

The three boys were absent when he reached Marchbanks, but their mother was at home, and delighted to see him.

'Edward! Oh, I mean Lord Farlington –'

'Edward, please,' he said with a smile.

'Come in, come in – I was just going to make myself a cup of tea, and there's a fresh sponge cake.' She took his coat, and led the way into the kitchen. He could smell beef roasting in the oven. 'I hope you don't mind the kitchen, just while I make the tea. Now tell me, what brings you to Portsmouth? Have you got any news for us? About my Liz?'

'No – I was hoping you might have some news for me.'

Another disappointment. Mrs Spragg had obviously not heard anything of her daughter. She made the tea and took it into the sitting-room.

The house was well furnished, if not to Edward's taste; his inclinations did not run to aspidistras and plum-coloured velvet. It was spotlessly clean, the furniture gleaming and fragrant with wax polish, although not unduly tidy, there being some signs of the boys' occupation here and there, a half-finished jigsaw, comics on the chairs and a half-eaten apple on a side table. Agnes Spragg obviously did all the housework and cooking herself. After a life of drudgery, keeping this house clean and sparkling would be a labour of love.

'So you're happy and comfortable here?' he asked, but the question was clearly superfluous; she was the epitome of a contented housewife. She looked different. Gone was the careworn drudge in second-hand rags; she was well-dressed, her grey hair neatly confined in a chignon. The stooped back had straightened, and she walked with a confident grace. Her face had filled out, and had almost become pretty. She was not as old as Edward had thought; she looked years younger than the poor down-trodden creature who had come to see him in the military hospital.

'I love the house, and the boys are doing well at their new school,' she told him. 'There's only one thing troubling me, and that's my Liz. What could have become of her? Do you think – oh, Edward, d'you think she's still alive?'

'I don't know. I've tried every avenue I can think of,' Edward said heavily. 'I came to ask if you had thought of anyone she might have gone to, but obviously you haven't. I'm at my wits' end. She seems to have disappeared off the face of the earth.'

They heard the back door close noisily.

'That will be the boys back. I didn't think they would be in yet,' Agnes remarked, glancing at the mantel-clock – the one she had brought from Barminster, now her only link with the dingy house in the slums. 'They've been playing with a kite in the park.'

Thomas, the youngest boy, came running into the room. He was tall for his ten years, and filling out with the good food he was getting now after years of deprivation. He had been running, and was out of breath.

'Mum! Mum! I saw someone in the park –' He caught

339

sight of Edward and stopped abruptly. Thomas had never seen him before, and was taken aback at the sight of his mother entertaining a gentleman. Agnes beckoned him into the room, and he came in eying the visitor curiously.

'Thomas, this is Lord Farlington, Liz's husband. Edward, my son Thomas.'

'Oh! Hello, sir.' Thomas turned back to his mother, bursting with news. 'Mum, in the park, I've just seen someone –'

'Never mind, son, tell me later. Shake hands with Lord Farlington, and then run out and change those boots – they're carrying mud on to my carpet. And where are the twins?'

Thomas shook Edward's hand self-consciously and turned back to his mother again.

'They're still in the park –'

Agnes looked vexed.

'You shouldn't have left them – I told you to stay together –'

'But Mum – I saw someone in the park who looked like our Liz!' Thomas burst out desperately. 'Charlie and Josh are watching her in case she goes away – if she moves they're going to try to keep her talking –'

Edward had risen, grabbed his crutch, and was limping to the door.

'Come on, Thomas, show me the way to the park!' he commanded, and followed the boy through the kitchen, down the back garden, and through a wicket gate into the Municipal Gardens as fast as his crutch and peg-leg would allow him.

'She's over there, sir,' Thomas said, pointing to a figure on a seat near the pond, surrounded by ducks. She had her back to them. He could see the twins keeping out of her sight behind a rhododendron bush a few yards away.

Edward's heart sank. That could not be his Liz. He could

not see the face, but that thick, shabby tweed coat with the collar turned up against the wind – Liz would hardly be wearing that! Then he noticed the small feet and slender ankles, just visible under a thick black skirt ... And the hair; dark hair, unruly tendrils escaping to curl wildly in the fresh January breeze ...

'Take your brothers home, Thomas. I'll go and see if it's Liz,' Edward said, his voice shaking slightly with the sudden hope that gripped him. 'Tell your mother I'll be back shortly.'

Thomas beckoned his brothers frantically. They came running over and retreated to the wicket gate, casting anxious glances over their shoulders as they went. Agnes was at the gate now, staring across the park at the tall man swinging himself across the turf. She gathered the three boys and took them inside the house, knowing that if it was Liz, she would want to see Edward first. But she was sure Thomas was mistaken. He had not seen his sister for some time, and he could have forgotten exactly what she looked like. And what would Liz be doing in the park on a January morning?

Thomas knew his mother was worried about his sister. In his efforts to help he had let his imagination run away with him. What a bitter disappointment it would be for that poor man!

As he approached the girl Edward slowed down and moved quietly. She was sitting at the end of the bench, facing away from him. The ducks scattered, but the girl did not look up; she moved away a little as he sat down at the other end of the bench, leaning his crutch against the side. Still he could not see her face, but he could see her hands now, and those small, capable hands looked familiar. On the fourth finger of the left hand she had a worn wedding ring.

Edward was almost afraid to draw her attention. When

he spoke, would she turn – and would he see the face of a stranger?

Liz had eaten one of her buns, and scattered the second to the hungry ducks; while they scrambled round her feet she felt less alone. She heard someone approach and sit on the other end of the bench, and shrank back into her thick coat, not wanting the company of a stranger. There were plenty of other seats around the pond; why had he chosen to sit on this one?

There was no-one else in the park now. The boys who had been playing with the kite had disappeared. Ten minutes ago several couples had been strolling along the path, but now they were all out of sight. A panicky feeling made her breathless, her heart beat faster, and her hands suddenly went clammy with sweat despite the chill wind that blew across the park. The roll of banknotes tucked into her bodice seemed to burn into her skin; had the stranger sensed that she had money – was he going to rob her? She was about to rise to her feet and take flight when a single syllable set all her senses quivering.

'Liz?'

She sat frozen to the seat. She was afraid to turn her head to face the stranger; she had lost the ability to move.

'Liz – please – look at me!'

She turned her head slowly, unbelievingly, and stared at the gaunt face of the man sitting so close to her.

'Edward!' she gasped. 'Edward! Oh, great heavens, Edward!'

Her voice had returned, but she was too overwhelmed to notice. She was suddenly in his arms, weeping, while he kissed her dear face and hair, holding her close, murmuring her name over and over. The ducks, disappointed that no more buns were forthcoming, made angry little noises as they waddled away and splashed into the water, V-shaped wakes streaming out behind them as they swam away in disgust.

Liz drew back and Edward wiped away her tears.

'My darling, can you tell me what happened at the cottage that day?' he asked quietly. Liz drew a deep breath. Now her voice was stronger, but trembling with emotion.

'Joe came,' she said. 'He – he was dreadful! He hit me, he kept saying terrible things – I didn't understand most of it, I think he was out of his mind. He said you had a wife in Barminster. He said you had a grand family – they disowned your father because he married a poor girl, they would disown you if they knew about me. I was so frightened I lost my voice again, and I couldn't speak until – until you came. Joe demanded money, and when I wouldn't give it to him he hit me again –'

'You should have given him the money!' Edward exclaimed. 'Anything to have got rid of him!'

'But I knew that would not satisfy him for long,' Liz said unhappily. 'He would have been back, and demanded more – and he would have made sure he always found me on my own. I think he really enjoyed hurting me. Here, take the money.' She burrowed into the coat and produced the roll of banknotes from her bodice.

'Keep it, Liz. Why didn't you use it when you got to Portsmouth?'

'I thought I might need it for an emergency . . . I found work in a laundry, and that paid my rent.'

'Oh, my poor darling! What happened then – in the cottage?'

'Joe dragged me across the room by my hair – oh, Edward, that hurt! Then he kicked me. I was so afraid. And if – if you had been there he might have killed you, he was so strong – like a mad bull! My pruning knife was in my pocket and – and I stabbed him. I'm a murderer, Edward; if they find me they'll hang me! I couldn't face the police, and a trial, and – and everything. So I ran away. I hoped you'd never find me, so that you'd not have to see your wife hanged. Oh, Edward – what are we to do now?' She began to sob again.

Edward took her into his arms and held her close.

'Darling, you didn't kill Joe,' he said gently. 'He lost a lot of blood, but he was able to get up, and he ran away too. I've been searching for you for months.'

'You mean – the police are not looking for me?'

'Well – yes, but only to tell you to come back to me! Everyone has been looking for you!'

'Oh . . . Then we can go back to the cottage at Honey Beck Bay?'

'Yes, darling, of course we can, if that's what you want. But there's something else I have to tell you –'

'And I have something to tell you, Edward –'

'Me first, my love! You know my cousin died?'

'Oh! Yes, John Oatis came – he looked so worried! Did he leave you a lot of debts, Edward? It doesn't matter, we'll pay them off somehow – I don't mind if we're poor again, not if we're together – and babies don't have to cost much if you're careful –'

'No, darling! He was rich – he was Lord Farlington, and now I'm Lord Farlington, and you're Lady Farlington . . . Liz, what was that about babies?'

'Lady Farlington? But didn't I read in the paper –'

'Liz! What was that about babies?'

'Edward, if you're Lord Farlington – can we still live in Honey Beck Cottage – Edward, stop shaking me!'

'What was that about babies?'

'Oh! We're going to have one. In about five months' time.'

Edward took her into his arms again.

'My darling – my darling . . .'

*

344

Agnes set two extra places for dinner. The three boys hardly took their eyes off Liz and Edward as they did justice to the meal. Agnes was wreathed in smiles; everything in her world was wonderful now. She thanked the good Lord for his blessings in the only way she knew, by serving enormous platefuls of good food to her family. Liz did not remember her mother having been a particularly good cook – how could she have been when she could afford so little in the way of ingredients? – but she was sure she had never tasted more succulent beef or a more delicious apple pie. No wonder the three boys were growing so sturdy!

'Liz, you can't go back to Sir Rupert's posh house in that awful coat,' Agnes said firmly when the reunited couple were ready to leave her. 'Come upstairs and see if I can find something a bit more respectable, like. I've got some lovely clothes now – your generous husband set me up lovely, he did! There should be something decent in my wardrobe that will fit you.' There was, and Liz thankfully discarded the coat and bedraggled black skirt. She felt much better for having had a hot bath, and borrowed a warm blue woollen dress and a coat trimmed with fox-fur. Agnes was not as slender as her daughter, so the few extra inches around Liz's waistline were adequately catered for.

Before Edward could take Liz away he had to take the three boys for a turn in the automobile. They were thrilled with the ride, and pointed out gleefully that no other boys at their school had been in a horseless carriage! Liz said goodbye to her mother and Edward drove her back to Wellington Road to collect her things and say goodbye to Pots – who was as impressed when she rolled up in the automobile as the boys had been. When she heard Liz speak her chubby face was one great beaming smile of delight.

Liz gave Mrs Smith an extra week's rent and said she would not be wanting the room again, and Mrs Smith looked on disapprovingly from the doorway as Liz and

Edward cleared her belongings. There would be no shenanigans in her boarding house. Mrs Fuller's husband? That well-dressed toff with the posh horseless carriage? She did not believe *that* for one minute!

'Goodbye, Pots,' Liz said, giving her fat friend a quick hug. 'Thanks for being such a good, kind friend, and say goodbye to the girls at the laundry for me. Here –' she pressed a few notes into Pots's pudgy hand '– take them out and treat them all to a slap-up supper.'

'How about Albert?' Pots asked impudently. 'He's going to be furious at losing one of his best workers!'

'Give him my compliments and buy him a couple of bloody pints!' Liz giggled.

'Come on, Liz – we've a long way to go and I want to be back in Eaton Square for dinner,' Edward told her.

Liz followed him out to the autombile, now surrounded by several admiring men and a crowd of excited small boys. Wellington Road did not often see vehicles like this one. But now she was suddenly subdued, already apprehensive about meeting Edward's grandfather. At the military hospital even Matron had been in awe of Sir Rupert.

What would be his reaction when he met his grandson's wife?

Chapter Twenty-eight

Liz settled herself into the seat in the automobile, her shawl over her head, and the rug pulled up to her chin. Edward switched on the ignition, then hopped round to the front of the vehicle and swung the handle; as soon as the motor fired he hopped back swiftly, adjusted the throttle, swung himself into the driver's seat and coaxed the motor into a smooth, even action, let off the brake, blew the horn to disperse the spectators, and proceeded down Wellington Road to the 'Oooh's' and 'Aaah's' of the gathered crowd. The small boys could scarcely keep up with the astounding pace of the automobile. They watched it disappear into the distance with wonder.

It is just over seventy miles from Portsmouth to London. Stopping only for a few minutes on the way to drink a cup of hot tea and warm themselves before the fire of a wayside inn, for driving in a horseless carriage is a very cold occupation, they finally drove into Eaton Square just before half past eight. Edward was very pleased with the performance of his vehicle.

'Not a single puncture!' he said jubilantly. 'There's no doubt about it, darling, this is the only way to travel! Not as fast as the train, I admit, but then the train doesn't carry you from door to door. Don't you think the automobile is a fantastic invention, Liz?'

Liz was not quite so sure. She was feeling rather sick from the jolting, her nose was quite numb with cold, and she was absolutely terrified at the prospect of dining with Sir Rupert. She would not mind if they did not arrive until midnight.

Then the old man might be in bed, and she could postpone the dreaded meeting until tomorrow. If only they could have gone straight back to Honey Beck Bay and settled back into their beloved cottage! But suddenly the memory of Joe Spragg in her bedroom and that awful hand sticking out from under the patchwork quilt returned and she was not sure she wanted to go back to Honey Beck Bay just now, either.

Edward brought the automobile to a stop outside Sir Rupert's imposing house, and pulled on the brake. The gas streetlamps were gleaming in the darkness, casting a yellow glow over the square. He hopped out nimbly, and came round to help her down.

'I'll put the car away after I've taken you into the house,' he said. 'Come on, darling.'

She slipped down, into his arms, wincing as her frozen, numb feet reached the ground.

'My feet are so cold,' she said as he looked at her anxiously. He laughed.

'Only one of mine gets cold,' he joked, knocking his peg-leg against the paving with a wooden thud. Liz tried to smile, but was trembling with nervousness. 'Let's get you into the warm,' Edward said hastily.

Beale answered the door and had difficulty in retaining his usual impassive expression as Edward led Liz into the hall.

'Beale, this is my wife. Is Sir Rupert here?'

'Yes, Lord Farlington. He's in the study. He asked for dinner to be delayed, since he thought you would be home for the meal as you had not been in touch with us on the telephone, sir.'

'Good. Let Lady Farlington warm herself in the drawing-room while I put the car away, and then I'll introduce them.'

'Yes, sir. This way, my lady.' He led her into the sumptuous drawing-room. Liz went in nervously. She sat carefully

348

on the edge of one of the brocade-covered armchairs by the fire. 'Can I bring you something to warm you, my lady – brandy, perhaps? Or a glass of sherry?'

'Oh – yes – thank you.' Liz found Beale quite awe-inspiring. If this was the servant, how could she possibly face the master? She hoped Edward would not be long. 'No – I'll wait for Ed – for my husband. Thank you.' Beale departed. Two minutes later the servants' quarters down-stairs were buzzing with excitement. Beale had to exert his authority; the maidservants were in a fair old tizzy over the new Lady Farlington.

Edward returned by the back entrance within five minutes; he kept the automobile in the coach-house at the rear of the house. Sir Rupert no longer kept his own car-riage, preferring to use hired cabs these days because he went out so seldom. Edward went straight to the study and found his grandfather there, reading the paper. He looked up as Edward entered, his bushy eyebrows drawn together in a frown to hide the anxiety he had felt at Edward's pro-longed absence. He had been worrying about him all day. That damned automobile could run off the road, or blow itself up, and Edward could be dead on the roadside for all he knew!

'Ha! So you've come home at last!' he exclaimed testily. 'Good thing I told Beale to delay dinner – you'd better hurry and change, sir, or the cook will be giving notice!'

'Never mind the cook, grandfather – I'm sure she'll not mind this once. Come into the drawing-room with me.'

'What for? Dammit, man – I'm comfortable here. If you're not going to change, call Beale to bring us some whisky –' But Edward was standing by the open door, wait-ing for his grandfather. He reluctantly heaved himself out of his chair, and followed his grandson into the drawing-room.

A slender figure in a blue dress was sitting in the armchair by the fire. Dark lustrous hair was pulled back into a graceful chignon. Great violet-blue eyes looked up as he entered. Sir Rupert stopped short, and stared at her. A beauty, no less! She rose to her feet and looked at him nervously. Edward, his face a beaming smile, took the girl's arm and brought her over to meet him.

'Grandfather, this is Liz, my wife. Liz, Sir Rupert. My grandfather.'

Sharp blue eyes studied her from below the beetling brows. Liz quailed beneath the piercing gaze. This old man had disowned his own son for marrying beneath him; would he turn on his grandson now?

But the old man was smiling. He put his hands on her shoulders and looked down into her eyes.

'Liz, I'm delighted to meet you. Thank God this grandson of mine has found you – I was afraid he was going to fade away into a shadow. Edward, tell Beale to bring a bottle of champagne – tell the cook to lay another place at the table – tell that housekeeper to make sure the fire's lit in the best guest-room –'

Edward was chuckling.

'No, Grandfather – Liz will be quite comfortable in my room! And I think the servants are already prepared for her, Beale opened the door for us ten minutes ago. I'll wager he already has the champagne organized!'

Dinner was very festive. Liz gradually lost her shyness as Sir Rupert set out to charm her, and when he set his mind to it he could still be a very charming man, despite his age. He, in turn, was quite enchanted with Edward's wife. He scarcely took his eyes off her as the meal proceeded, making Liz anxious again, in case she used the wrong fork or made some other faux pas. After dinner, back in the drawing-room, as she sat on the sofa beside Edward, he coaxed her to talk about herself, and listened with deliberate calm as she related the story of Joe Spragg's intrusion into her home at

Honey Beck Cottage. He realized, as Edward did not, that the only way to expunge the horror from the girl's mind was to let her talk it out. He persuaded her to tell them of her long walk through the forest, her meeting with Jim Peters, and the journey to Portsmouth.

'Edward, we'll have to find that lad and reward him for his kindness to our girl,' Sir Rupert announced. 'I'll give him a horse. Young men always like horses.'

'He might not be able to afford to keep a horse,' Liz pointed out anxiously.

'All right, I'll give him a cow as well. The profit on the milk will pay for the horse's upkeep.' Sir Rupert was not going to be balked of his generous offer. 'And what did you think of your half-brothers now they're older?'

'They seem to be nice boys – not like their father,' Liz told him.

'Perhaps if their father had not had such a hard life he would not have taken to drink, and might have been a different character altogether,' Sir Rupert suggested. 'It sounds to me as if the unfortunate fellow felt that life had dealt him a poor hand and he struck back in the only way he knew. There's one thing for sure; he'll think twice before he attacks a defenceless woman again.' He decided it was time to change the subject.

'Now you two young folk will have to decide where you're going to live. You're welcome to stay here – there's nothing I'd like better! – but there's Farlington Towers, Barminster Abbey, Keenlach Lodge, and that draughty mansion in Kensington that hasn't been used for the last twenty years. There's also a castle in Ireland, if you're interested, but that hasn't been used in sixty years, and I doubt if it has a roof worth speaking of now.' He shot a hopeful glance at Liz. 'Barminster Abbey's a good place for raising a family, you know. Nurseries, and all that. Our boys used to enjoy living there when they were youngsters. I'm not – er – pressing you, but I'd like to see some great-grandchildren before I die, and I'm not getting any younger.'

Edward grinned at Liz, put his arm round her and hugged her. She looked up at Sir Rupert with a twinkle in her eyes.

'If you decide to hang on for about another five months, Sir Rupert, I think we can oblige.'

The old man almost dropped his whisky glass in surprise.

'God bless my soul!' he exclaimed. 'Edward, take that young woman and put her to bed at once; she's had a long day and it's time she rested. And then come back down here and we'll discuss plans for moving to Barminster Abbey – I'll have the west wing, of course, and Harriet –'

'Grandfather,' Edward said gently, 'I've had a long day too. We'll make our plans tomorrow. There are other things on my mind just now. Goodnight.'

'Hmph! Yes, indeed,' said Sir Rupert.